SWANSEA GIRLS

In 1950s Swansea, the Pier Ballroom is the place to be on a Saturday night. For Lily, Judy, Katie and Helen it is an evening that fuels jealousies and sows the seeds for friendships and romance. Lily is an evacuee unclaimed by her family at the end of the war; Judy, taught independence by her mother, discovers a painful secret that threatens her peace of mind. Katie believes in independence, until her life is changed by a man who can only offer friendship, whilst spoiled, wilful Helen grabs what she can, chancing her reputation in the process.

SWANSEA GIRLS

SWANSEA GIRLS

by

Catrin Collier

Magna Large Print Books
Long Preston, North Yorkshire,
BD23 4ND, England.

British Library Cataloguing in Publication Data.

Collier, Catrin
    Swansea girls.

    A catalogue record of this book is
    available from the British Library

    ISBN   0-7505-1881-2

First published in Great Britain in 2001 by Orion,
an imprint of the Orion Publishing Group Ltd.

The right of Catrin Collier to be identified as the author of this work
has been asserted in accordance with the Copyright, Designs and
Patents Act, 1988

Published in Large Print 2002 by arrangement with
Orion Publishing Group

Magna Large Print is an imprint of Library Magna Books Ltd.

Printed and bound in Great Britain by
T.J. (International) Ltd., Cornwall, PL28 8RW

For Jill Forwood, journalist, writer, historian, a real Swansea Girl and my most understanding friend.

Acknowledgements

I would like to express my gratitude to all those who helped with the research for *Swansea Girls*. My college tutor, Clive Gammon, whom I haven't seen for over thirty years, for not only instructing me in the finer points of English Literature, but showing me that it was possible for an ordinary person to write. Jill Forwood for her impeccably researched articles on Swansea's past in the *Evening Post* and her unfailing help whenever I asked for it.

My husband John, our children Ralph, Ross, Sophie and Nick, and my parents, Glyn and Gerda Jones, for their love and the time they gave me to write this book.

Margaret Bloomfield for her friendship and help in so many ways.

Everyone at Orion, especially my new editor Yvette Goulden for her tact, generosity, constructive criticism and inspiration.

My agent Ken Griffiths and Marguerite Sloper for always being at the end of the telephone when I need to talk.

In the fifties Swansea was a magical place where my great-uncle Eddie John drove ambulances and my great-aunt Alma laid on sumptuous high teas whenever we visited from Pontypridd. As a college girl in the sixties I saw a different side to the town – as it then was – when I packed my bags and arrived in hall as an excited and naïve student. Since my marriage in 1968 it has been my home and the home of my family.

I can't even begin to thank everyone I have met since then for the friendship, hospitality and kindness I have met in every quarter of the city.

No writer can exist without readers. I am truly privileged to have so many sympathetic and understanding people among mine. Thank you.

Catrin Collier,
September 2000

CHAPTER ONE

'I couldn't.'

'You could. You've been debating whether or not to raid your Post Office account to buy one for weeks. Now's your chance to see if you like the effect enough to get your own.' Helen Griffiths left her bed where she'd been filing her nails and scanning a magazine article on 'How to exercise your legs to Cyd Charisse perfection' and went to her wardrobe. Pulling layer upon layer of pink and white petticoat from the top shelf, she tossed the bundle to Lily. It floated through the air, filling the room with the throat-catching, astringent scent of eau de cologne.

'It looks wonderful on you because you're tall but I'm not so sure it will look good on someone my size.' Lily shook out the froth of lace and net and pulled the elasticised waist over the plain grey skirt that wasn't good enough for work, but was too good to throw out.

'To hear you talk, anyone would think you're a pygmy.'

'These many layers make me feel like a granny spinning-top. I wish I was five foot eight and could wear longer-length skirts without looking as though I was playing dressing up.'

'And I'd give anything to be five foot with long, dark, naturally curly hair. Men love petite, fragile girls. Whenever I stand next to you I feel like one

13

of those clumping great Russian women who drive tractors in Pathe newsreels.' Helen returned to the bed to pedal her legs in the air.

'Why does everyone want what they can't have?' Lily tilted Helen's dressing-table mirror forward to check the length of the petticoat.

'My grandmother would say it's God's way of keeping us in line.'

'My feet no longer belong to me.' Judy Hunt limped into the room and fell alongside Helen on the bed. Kicking off her shoes, she propped her legs high on the wall. 'Since eight o'clock this morning it's been "Judy, do this – Judy, fetch that – Judy, shampoo Mrs So-and-So's hair – Judy, wind curlers into Mrs So-and-So's hair – not those, the smaller ones – Judy, wind them out of Mrs So-and-So's hair. Judy, I'm sure we'd all like a cup of tea. Judy, collect those cups and saucers, take them into the kitchen and wash them, we can't have the salon looking untidy, now can we?" And on top of everything else, "Judy, could you possibly smile? That look on your face would see off a tax inspector let alone a customer." As if anyone could smile after all that. I never should have allowed my mother to talk me into taking an apprenticeship with her. She's an absolute slave-driver.'

'Try café work.' Katie Clay followed Judy into the room. 'I've had a day and a half. Up to my elbows in hot water and soda for six hours, and all complaints and no tips when I did two hours' waitress relief.'

'It will be different after Monday.' As Helen and Judy had commandeered the bed, Lily

14

handed Katie the dressing-table stool.

'You've an interview for that job you applied for last week, Katie?' Judy asked.

'Two thirty Monday afternoon.'

'You sly boots. Not a word...'

'I won't get it.'

'With the best examination marks in your class, you'll walk it,' Helen reassured.

'It was an evening class, not a proper school of commerce like Gregg's.'

'Same exam and your speeds are double mine.'

'Anyone's speeds would be double yours, Helen.' Judy swung her legs down and massaged her feet.

'It's not my fault I can't get enthusiastic about putting words on paper. It makes no difference if it's a shorthand pad or typewriter, there are more interesting things to do in life.'

'If you're Princess Margaret and don't have to earn a living.' Judy closed her eyes as she stretched out on the bed. 'I could sleep for a hundred years.'

'You too tired to go out tonight, then?' Lily swirled in front of the mirror, sending the petticoat flouncing around her legs.

'I won't be in an hour.' Opening her eyes, Judy made a face at Katie. 'I know I promised to do your hair and I will if you sit on the floor beside the bed. You need a wand and a tinsel crown, Lily, if you're thinking of going to the Pier as a fairy.'

'I was wondering how this would look under the blue shirtwaister Auntie Norah made me.'

'Good, I should think. Oh! Oh! Guess what?'

Judy sat up suddenly and poked Helen. 'Mrs Jordan came into the salon this morning.'

'And,' Helen prompted warily.

'She said Adam's finished his National Service. He came home yesterday and' – Judy's eyes rounded mischievously – 'he's going to the Pier ballroom tonight.'

'You asked Mrs Jordan where he was going tonight!'

'Of course. I said my friend Helen Griffiths has the most incredible crush on your son Adam, Mrs Jordan. She moons over him all the time and dreams of him constantly, so could you please tell me where he'll be tonight so she can chase him.'

'You beast!'

'Got you going, didn't I? She was complaining about the rough lot who go to the Pier. "Nothing but Teddy boys and coarse common girls like that Helen Griffiths."'

'She didn't say that.'

'She did, Scout's honour.'

'You were never a Scout.'

'I wish I had been. It would have been more fun than the Girl Guides. Just think of all those boys...'

'Here's my brush and hairclips.' Katie shook her hair out of the bun she wore for work and slithered down on to the floor next to where Judy was lying.

'Your hair looks good, Lily.' Judy cast a professional eye over the neat French pleat.

'I've been practising. One of the typists in work is leaving to get married and I'm hoping I'm in with a chance of her job.'

'You've only been in the bank five minutes.' Bored with mid-air cycling, Helen turned over and flicked her magazine to the problem page.

'And I'm getting desperate. I didn't study in tech for two years so I could run errands, file papers and make tea and coffee. I don't know why they insist on office juniors having good shorthand and typing speeds. If my experience is anything to go by, they never use them.'

'In that case I might survive more than a day.'

'You got a job with the marks you got in your exams, Helen?' Judy asked incredulously.

'I've an interview but it's only a formality. I start a week Monday. And, for your information, I passed my resits – some of them.'

'Half of them and only just.'

'Don't forget, they were Gregg resits. It's the *polish* private school *gives* a girl.' Helen mimicked one of her mother's favourite quotes in a manner that would have infuriated Esme Griffiths if she'd been around to hear it.

'I thought you were going to work in your father's warehouse.'

'So did my mother but, would you believe, Dad wouldn't hear of it, so he fixed me up with a junior's job in his solicitor's office. Can you imagine? Not only will I have to do all the menial chores like you, Lily, but I'll also have to watch myself in case the solicitor carries tales to my father.'

'Knowing you, he'll have plenty to carry.' Judy finally set to work on Katie's hair.

'My mother created the most almighty fuss but for once she couldn't shift Dad. I think he

17

thought I'd cramp his style if I went into the warehouse. Tell Mum about his long lunch hours and boozing sessions with the reps.'

'I'm not at all sure about this petticoat.' Lily frowned at Judy. 'Does it make me look like a Munchkin?'

'Most definitely, but as all Munchkins are loveable you should have the boys flocking round.'

'Be serious.'

'A petticoat like that makes everyone's waist look tiny,' Helen broke in authoritatively, 'no matter how short they are. Once you've pulled your waist in with a belt, it will look fine.'

'In that case, if you really don't mind me borrowing it, I'll take it home and try it on under the shirtwaister. I think the skirt is wide enough not to crush the layers – but if I have this, what will you wear, Helen?'

'Don't tell me you've got something new again.' Judy turned her head, accidentally yanking Katie's hair.

'Ow!'

'You have to suffer to be beautiful,' Judy lectured.

'I was helping out in the warehouse today...'

'More like helping your father's stock out of the warehouse and into your wardrobe.'

Ignoring Judy, Helen continued, 'And I thought, why shouldn't I have the odd perk or two.'

'Or two! You've more clothes than the Queen.'

Helen left the bed and opened her wardrobe.

'Your woolly dressing gown,' Judy sniggered as

18

Helen lifted it out. 'Now that really would be the way to get Adam Jordan to notice you.'

'Taaraa...' Helen stripped back the gown.

'My giddy aunt!'

'It's strapless!' Katie gasped.

'It's stunning, a real film star frock.' Lily fingered the bead-encrusted bodice and satin skirt of the midnight blue ballerina-length evening dress. 'You'd certainly be noticed in this.'

'Which is the whole point.'

'And your mother approves?' Lily asked shrewdly.

'Not exactly. In fact, she went berserk when she saw me trying it on behind the shoe racks in the warehouse. Mind you, that could have been because one of the boys from the loading bay was hovering round the display.'

'I'm not surprised. My mother would have forty fits at the thought of me in anything like that.' Judy finished brushing Katie's hair and scraped it into a ponytail.

'You haven't got enough of what counts to wear it.' Helen arched her back, thrusting out her breasts. 'This has 36C cups sewn in and they fit perfectly.'

'I'm amazed your father allowed you to take it out of the shop.' Katie was irritated, more by her own figure that looked as though it was never going to expand from a 32A than by Helen's gloating.

'He didn't. I sneaked it out under some under-clothes and a sweater he said I could have. Fortunately, my mother was too busy arguing with him about the sweater for either of them to notice what I was doing.'

'If your mother wasn't happy with a sweater...'

'You know what she is, Judy. Sometimes I think she forgets I'm eighteen.'

'Just.'

'Whatever,' Helen dismissed carelessly. 'All I know is, if she had her way I'd still be wearing Shirley Temple bows, frills, flounces and ankle socks.'

'Your parents are bound to find out you've taken it.' Thrusting a clip into Katie's hair to secure what she'd done, Judy left the bed and took the hanger from Helen. She held the dress in front of her and stared at her reflection in the mirror.

'I'll sneak it back into the warehouse on Monday.'

'Your father will see it's been worn.'

'I'll be careful.'

'And if there's scent or make-up on it?'

'I'll sponge it off.'

'It might leave a watermark.'

'It's awfully low,' Lily murmured.

'You sound like my grandmother.' Helen tweaked back the top as she retrieved the frock from Judy. 'Look, once I'm zipped into it the boned, sewn-in bra will stop anyone from seeing what they shouldn't. And–' she lifted the satin bell skirt to reveal an embroidered, scalloped, white silk underskirt – 'It's got its own hooped petticoat attached to the waist, so I couldn't wear the frilled one anyway.'

Judy raised her eyebrows. 'Do you intend to wear anything under it?'

'No knickers and my mother's fur coat on top,' Helen joked.

'Have you given any thought as to how you're going to get out of the house?' Judy returned to Katie's hair.

'Dad's got some men's thing on. Old boy school association or something. He's going straight from the warehouse and my mother's going to the theatre with Auntie Dot. It's the last performance of the play she directed, so she's bound to leave before six to make sure the rest of the Swansea amateurs don't "let down the side" as she puts it.'

'I wouldn't have the nerve to wear that frock through town and on to the Mumbles train.'

'It's warm, but not too warm to wear my green coat, so no one will know what I've got on underneath it until I get to the Pier. Do you want to see what it looks like?' Helen stripped off her skirt and blouse before any of them could answer. 'Watch the door in case my mother comes up.' Tossing her slip on to the bed, she adjusted and tightened her corset over her waist, then slipped the dress from the hanger. 'I never know whether it's best to put things like this on from the top down or bottom up.'

'Top down.' Lily took the dress, folded it carefully over her arm and eased it over Helen's head. 'It's even lower than I thought,' she commented as Helen modestly held up the bodice with one hand while unhooking her bra with the other.

'It's not fastened yet.'

'Breathe in.'

'I am!'

'It's tight.'

'It has to be or I'll spill out.'

'I helped my mother choose a ball gown for the Chamber of Commerce Christmas dinner dance and there's only one way to get into them when they're this close-fitting. Stand up straight and lift your arms above your head.'

'The bodice will fall down.'

'Lily will hold it up for you.' Judy took the zip. Tugging hard, she finally slid it home.

'I can't breathe.'

'I'm not surprised.' Judy folded back the edge of the bodice. 'Good job that sewn-in bra is double-stitched linen, if it was embroidered silk like the underskirt, you'd have burst out of it by now.'

'You can't see anything you shouldn't, can you?' Helen was shocked by the expanse of cleavage, shoulders and arms reflected in the mirror. It had seemed a good idea to borrow the frock when she had tried it on over her blouse in the warehouse but with only bare skin underneath, it was *very* revealing. For the first time since taking it she had second thoughts. It was one thing to purloin one of the most expensive frocks from the rails of her father's warehouse, quite another to get the whole town gossiping loud enough for her mother to hear.

'Depends what you mean by "shouldn't"', Judy qualified.

'I want Adam Jordan to notice me, not think I'm a tart.'

'It's beautiful but it might be a bit much for the

Pier Ballroom on a Saturday night,' Lily ventured tactfully.

'Lily's right, it's gorgeous but...'

'Twelve guineas' worth of gorgeous, Katie, and that's wholesale.'

'Helen! Your father will kill you.'

'No he won't.' Helen didn't even convince herself. She'd done a lot of things over the years that had annoyed her parents but none of them had been quite so drastic. And worst of all, after going to the trouble of spiriting the dress out of the warehouse she didn't feel glamorous and grown-up as she'd expected, but exposed, uncomfortable and unaccountably cheap, considering the price of the frock. 'What are you wearing?'

'I told you, my new blue shirtwaister.'

'Auntie Norah made me a green one from the same pattern as Lily's blue. She brought it round to the salon this afternoon. My mother helped me pick out the material; she said the colour's the same shade as my eyes, which has to be better than my hair.' Flicking a lock forward, Judy pulled at it disparagingly as she sank back on the bed. 'I wish Mam would let me dye it blonde.'

'Auburn suits you.'

'Only you could call ginger auburn, Lily.'

'What are you wearing, Katie?'

'She's borrowing my yellow dress,' Judy answered for her.

'I am?'

'I only said I wasn't sure you could because I didn't know if the green would be ready, but new dresses or not, we're going to look like schoolgirls next to you if you go in that, Helen.'

23

'I'm only wearing it tonight in honour of Adam Jordan.'

'He'll think you've escaped from a posh dinner dance in the Mermaid. And if Joe...'

'My brother's going to a party. Have you noticed how university students go to ten times as many as we do?'

'You could have gone to university if you'd wanted to.' Lily finally relinquished the petticoat.

'With my brains?'

'What it must be to have a father who owns a warehouse full of clothes,' Katie murmured enviously as Helen turned her back for Lily to unzip the dress. Her friends fell silent. Fathers were a touchy subject.

An evacuee who hadn't been claimed by her family after the war, Lily couldn't remember her father – or mother. Judy's had been killed in the last week of hostilities and her secure upbringing was down to her mother's business acumen and the success of the hairdressing salon she had opened, rather than any foresight on the part of her father who hadn't taken out a single insurance policy. Katie's father, like Helen's, lived with his family, but you couldn't get two more different men than Ernie Clay and John Griffiths.

Surly, foul-mouthed and bad-tempered, Ernie kept his family short of money, and spent every minute that opening hours and his night watchman's job allowed in the back bar of the nearest pub. And the remainder of his free time bullying his family and beating his wife, if the shouts that resounded from the Clays' basement

24

flat and Annie Clay's perpetual crops of bruises were anything to go by.

Conversely, despite disabilities, which everyone in Carlton Terrace politely and pointedly ignored, John Griffiths was hardworking, industrious and gave his wife a housekeeping allowance that was the envy of every woman in the street. He had expanded the small fancy goods warehouse his grandparents had left him into a Ladies' and Children's wear trade outlet that supplied the best department stores in south and west Wales. And although GRIFFITHS'S WHOLESALE FASHIONS AND HOUSE-HOLD LINENS wasn't quite the establishment Esme Griffiths liked to think it was, it was successful and profitable. So profitable that John had recently opened a Ladies' wear outlet in the seaside village of Mumbles that catered for holidaymakers' needs as well as locals.

'My father's not rich, just a working man the same as everyone else.' Helen repeated her father's maxim a little too dogmatically as Lily eased the dress back over her head. 'I think I'll run a bath. Pass me the Veet hair remover and Golden Dawn bath cubes, Judy. They're in the top drawer of my dressing table. Not those, the yellow ones.'

'You'd better be quick if you're going to wash off the smell of the Veet,' Judy warned. 'It's a quarter past six now. We ought to aim for the eight-o'clock Mumbles train if we're going to get into the Pier before it's too crowded for you to spot Adam Jordan, let alone stun him.'

'Are you really going to wear this?' Lily

carefully draped the tapes that held the satin evening dress back on to the hanger.

'Most definitely,' Helen retorted, refusing to back down in the face of her friends' collective disapproval.

'In that case, do me a favour, pinch Joe's razor to shave under your arms, otherwise you'll be keeping us waiting.' Judy brushed the end of Katie's ponytail into a neat curl. Satisfied with her handiwork, she held up a hand mirror so Katie could see the back.

'Thanks, Judy, that looks great.'

'As the dress is already there, want to get ready in my house?'

'Please.'

'See you at half-seven.' Helen waited until Lily closed her wardrobe before opening her bedroom door.

'Twenty past, or we may not get a seat on the Mumbles train.' Lily hesitated, glancing back at the petticoat on the bed. 'You sure you won't be wearing this, Helen?'

'Absolutely. Now go or we'll all be late.'

'Lily, is that you, love?' Roy Williams called from the back kitchen-cum-living room as he heard the front door close.

'Yes, Uncle Roy.'

'Come and meet someone.'

Lily walked through to see the brother and sister who had taken her in as a three-year-old evacuee and loved and cared for her ever since, sitting with a strange young man.

'Here's our Lily.' Roy's sister Norah beamed

26

proudly at her foster-daughter. 'Lily, this is Brian Powell, our new lodger.'

Brian rose to his feet and held out his hand. 'Pleased to meet you, Lily.'

'Brian starts work at the station on Monday,' Roy explained.

'You're a policeman?' Lily wasn't good at gauging people's height, but Brian seemed even taller than her Uncle Roy, and he was over six feet.

'I've just finished training in Bridgend.'

'Brian's from Pontypridd. Swansea's his first posting.'

'By the look of you the weather must be a lot warmer in Pontypridd than Swansea,' Norah observed. Brian's hair was black, his skin a rich sunburned brown.

'I only left Cyprus two months ago, Mrs Evans. National Service,' he added by way of an explanation.

'It must be lovely to travel,' Lily murmured shyly as she sat on the sofa next to Norah.

'That depends on how you do it. The army doesn't make first-class arrangements but once we were there the beaches were fantastic. White sand, blue sea...'

'And warmer than Langland Bay I should think.' Roy pulled his pipe from his trouser pocket.

'I wouldn't know. I've never been to any of the Gower beaches.'

'Never?' Lily asked incredulously.

'The furthest Pontypridd people go on day trips is Barry Island or Porthcawl.'

'But now you're here, you have to see the Gower.'

'I have a bike; perhaps you could show me.'

'I wouldn't be happy with our Lily riding pillion on a motorbike,' Norah broke in swiftly. 'Aren't you going out with the girls tonight, Lily?'

'Yes, and I have to get ready. Excuse me, Brian.'

'Nice to meet you, Lily.'

As Lily closed the door she heard Norah say, 'Lily is only just eighteen, Brian. My brother and I lead a quiet life. Some would say we've sheltered Lily, wrapped her in cotton wool as it were, but the truth is she's not used to young men, especially in our home. You see, we stopped taking in lodgers when the war ended, but given the present housing shortage, when the sergeant mentioned you were having trouble finding a place we thought it only right to offer you a room here...'

Lily didn't wait to hear any more. Whether it was his height, suntan or air of confident self-sufficiency, Brian seemed a lot older than her. And there was one thing she agreed on with Judy and Helen. Fair boys like Adam Jordan were more attractive than dark ones. Not that she stood a chance of getting Adam to notice her with Helen around, but that didn't stop her from dreaming – just a little.

Brian remained in Norah's living room only as long as it took to finish his tea, home-made cake and make his excuses. He'd heard enough stories about PC Roy Williams in police training school to know that he was a well-respected officer who had gained the trust and admiration of every colleague he had ever worked with, and nothing, but nothing, happened in Swansea that he didn't know about. He'd been looking forward to working with, and learning from him, but Roy's widowed sister was something else. Roy had mentioned that her husband had been killed at Dunkirk but, German guns aside, Brian decided that the late Mr Evans had proved his courage by marrying the formidable Norah.

More spinster than widow, two minutes in her company had been enough to convince him that he had about as much chance of smuggling a woman into his room as he had of sneaking in an elephant. The thought depressed him. The house and his room were neat and clean, the tea Norah served excellent, but there was something off-puttingly respectable and antiseptic about the atmosphere after three months of communal bachelor living in training school.

Dumping his suitcase and bag in the corner of his bedroom, he took the towels Norah had arranged on his washstand and washed and shaved in the bathroom. Returning to his bed-room, he lifted his case on to the bed, unlocked it, and picked out a clean shirt. He changed, checked his hair and face in the mirror and selected a different tie to go with the grey mohair suit he'd splashed out on after demob, then headed downstairs. Swansea might be uncharted territory but the army had taught him to treat every billet as an adventure. And he was hoping to find at least one unattached, pretty girl who'd look on a newcomer in a strange town as sympathetically and compassionately as a few of the locals had in Cyprus.

'You have your key, Brian?' Norah was in the hall, dusting a highly polished chest of drawers. He sensed that she'd been waiting for him.

'Yes, thank you, Mrs Evans.' He patted his pocket.

'Will you be late?'

Swallowing the resentment he felt at being asked the question after two and half years of coming and going as he pleased in his free time, he answered as pleasantly as he could bring himself to, 'I don't expect to be very late, Mrs Evans.'

'Have a good time.'

'I'll try.' He smiled disarmingly. 'Are there any good pubs close by that you can recommend, Mrs Evans?'

'I've never been in a pub in my life, Brian.'

'Of course, I should have thought...'

'But Roy seems to like the White Rose on Walter Road. Pity he's on duty tonight or he would have taken you there himself. He enjoys a pint. Turn left as you leave the house, left at the end of the street, straight on and you'll see it on the main road.'

'Thank you, Mrs Evans.'

'And stay away from the dock area, but then, what am I doing telling a policeman how to look after himself.'

'You know Swansea, I don't, Mrs Evans. My father always told me to take advice in the spirit it's given.' He dared to wink at her as he opened the door, confirming her opinion that she had

30

been right to warn him off her Lily. Innocent young girls were better off with less showy boyfriends than the likes of Brian Powell, with his dangerous good looks, suntan and overly charming ways.

'You look nice, love,' Roy murmured absently, as Lily ran downstairs.

'Thanks, Uncle Roy.' Lily dropped a kiss on to his bald head as she passed his chair.

'New petticoat?' Norah asked.

'Helen lent it to me to see how it would look.'

'You don't have to borrow clothes from Helen. You've enough money in your Post Office account to buy whatever you want.'

'I know, Auntie Norah, but I really wasn't sure whether it would suit me. Besides, Helen borrows from me.'

'Only books that I can see. That petticoat suits you. Get your own on Monday and have a good time.'

'Home on the half-past-ten train,' Roy warned.

'Promise.' Lily gave him another kiss before hugging Norah.

'That's enough now, get on with you,' Norah ordered. 'And remember...'

'No drinking anything stronger than orange juice, no smoking and no leaving the Pier with any strange boys,' Lily chanted. 'Does that mean I can leave with one I do know?'

The house seemed strangely quiet after she'd left.

'She's grown up fast the last couple of months,' Norah commented wistfully as Roy left his chair.

'That she has,' he agreed flatly, buttoning his policeman's tunic.

'That Pier Ballroom...'

'I've told you a hundred times, Norah, the town's no rougher than it was when we were kids. You know what youngsters are when they're out for a good time. A bit loud, a bit boisterous but there's no real harm in them.'

'Those Teddy boys – the papers say they carry flick knives.'

'I've never seen any.'

'They'd hardly show them to a policeman, would they. Roy...'

'Nothing's going to happen to our Lily down the Pier, Norah. She's too sensible to stray from the crowd, and Judy and Katie are nice, level-headed girls.' He deliberately left out all mention of Helen Griffiths knowing Norah didn't need to ask what he thought of that one.

'I've a feeling...'

'You've been down that Spiritualist Church again.'

'Not for three weeks.

'A seance, then.'

'I haven't been to one of those in six months.'

'You and your feelings. You've been wrong...'

'I am never wrong,' Norah contradicted vehemently. 'I just can't put a timescale on things. Mark my words, there's trouble coming our Lily's way.'

'Then if it's coming, it's coming and there's nothing we can do about it until it gets here. Worrying in advance won't help.' He picked up his helmet. 'Forget the sewing, put your feet up for once. Have a few sherries and listen to the radio.'

'With the new lodger to see to?'

'He's a capable young man, Norah. Let him see to himself. After National Service and training school he's used to it.'

'I'm not sure that bed of his has been aired properly. I'll slip a warming pan into it just in case and peel and boil some potatoes so we can have potato pancakes with the breakfast eggs, laver bread and bacon. I bought a nice piece of black pudding, too, from Mrs Williams's stall at the market.'

'The last thing a young copper needs is mollycoddling.'

'Everyone needs a bit of home comfort now and then.'

'After the army, I doubt he'd recognise, let alone appreciate it.' Roy checked his watch. 'But a few of your potato pancakes always go down well after a night shift. Just don't spend all evening cooking.'

'I won't. And...'

'I'll wander down Mumbles around half past ten.'

'You won't let our Lily see you.'

'Do I ever.' He kissed her withered cheek and opened the front door.

CHAPTER TWO

Roy walked along the pavement and turned the corner into Verandah Street, a steep alleyway bordered on both sides by the blank, grey pine ends of houses. Halfway up, narrow entrances opened into a back lane that separated the gardens of Carlton Terrace from the backyards of Mansel Street. Looking over his shoulder to make sure no one was about, he turned into the lane on his right. After another quick check he pressed the latch on a full-sized door set in a high garden wall. Half a dozen paces through a concrete area that held a washing line wilting beneath the weight of a couple of dozen towels, and a short flight of stone steps took him to the back door of a property that fronted Mansel Street.

He checked his watch before opening the door and locking it behind him. If Norah knew he frequently left the house a couple of hours before his shift began she was too tactful to mention it.

'You're early.' Joy Hunt closed the account book she was working on as he strode through the small kitchen into her hairdressing salon. Roy had no worries about being seen from Mansel Street. The moment her last customers and staff left for the day, Joy invariably pulled down the blinds and bolted the front door.

'Couldn't wait to see you, love.'

'The bed's turned down upstairs.'

'And the hot water bottle?'

'You'll never let me forget that, will you?'

'No.' He smiled.

Switching off the light, Joy led the way up to the second floor. There were three rooms: the smallest a storeroom for shampoo, towels and hair products; the second a workroom where she worked on the wigs she fashioned for 'special' customers who had lost their hair, men as well as women. The third – and largest – she kept locked. When Judy had asked why, Joy told her the floorboards were rotten and needed replacing. In fact, it was an extremely comfortable bedroom. A man, who had lived as a recluse until she had made him a wig almost indistinguishable from his real hair, had delivered a cosy double bed, cocktail cabinet and radiogram. Roy had decorated the room in his spare time and she had bought smaller luxuries – paintings, candleholders and silk sheets especially for this haven, the one place in the world where she could be herself with the man she loved.

'Our Lily's excited about going to the Pier.' Roy sank down on the bed, untied his shoelaces and removed his boots. 'I thought the novelty would have worn off by now.'

'It won't wear off until she finds a young man to take her somewhere other than dancing on Saturday nights.' Joy lit the table lamps she'd arranged on the bedside cabinets and dressing table before switching off the main light. Daylight never reached this room. She had left the blackout curtains up after the war and kept them permanently closed to support her story of dereliction. But when the lamps and gas fire were lit, and the cream velvet drapes she'd hung at the back of the blackout curtains closed, the room was warm, welcoming and inviting. 'Judy's just the same. Not that she'll have much energy to dance after the way I worked her today.'

'You sure you're not too hard on that girl, Joy?' Roy suggested mildly.

'Are you criticising the way I'm bringing her up?' she snapped defensively.

'No, but–'

'There are no buts when it comes to youngsters today. They've got it too easy. Full employment, more money in their pockets at the end of the week than we used to see in a year when we were their age. I don't want Judy growing up thinking that she can have whatever she wants without working for it and before you say another word, Norah agrees with me and is bringing up your Lily the same way.'

Knowing better than to push his point to an argument he would inevitably lose, Roy hung his tunic on the back of a chair before unbuttoning his braces. Folding his trousers on the creases, he laid them over his tunic. His shirt, collar and underclothes received the same careful attention before he climbed into bed.

'I'll never understand how you women put up with corsets,' he commented, as she unclipped her stockings from her suspenders and rolled down her girdle.

'Because we'd flop everywhere without one.'

'Men like the bits that flop.'

'That I don't believe.' Turning back the sheet, she climbed in beside him.

'It's true.' He picked up her hand and kissed her fingertips. 'I love every bit of you, especially the floppy bits and I wish I could see more of you.'

'A widow with a young daughter to bring up...'

'Can't be too careful of her reputation,' he finished for her. 'But all I want is...'

'More than I'm prepared to give you at the moment. I've told you a hundred times; I won't turn you into a wicked stepfather or Judy an ungrateful stepdaughter. I love both of you far too much to allow our lives to become a battleground.'

'It wouldn't be like that.'

'Perhaps, perhaps not.' Snuggling down, she rested her head on his shoulder. 'But it's not worth running the risk of spoiling what we have. Is it?' She looked up, before kissing him.

He tried to hold back but it was impossible. He had done – and would continue to do – anything she asked of him. Ten years was a long time to wait for a settled home with the woman he loved but he would carry on waiting. The only alternative was a life without Joy and that was simply unthinkable.

Helen yanked up the bodice of the dress as she stood in front of the mirror. It was no use, no matter how hard she tugged, she couldn't pull the bead-encrusted satin more than an inch above the bra cups and they barely covered her nipples. She was beginning to regret her boast to the girls. Lily was right – the evening gown was too much for the Pier Ballroom on a Saturday night but she could hardly chicken out now. Perhaps she could say a seam had split. It *was* tight...

'Helen.'

'Can't come in, Joe. I'm changing.' Before she'd slipped on the dress, she'd fastened a rug hook she'd purloined from her grandmother into the top of the zip. Stretching behind her back, she breathed in and pulled. After twists, turns and wriggles worthy of a contortionist she'd seen in the Grand Theatre, she finally managed to slide the zip home but, try as she might, she couldn't reach further than the tip of the wooden handle of the hook to unclip it.

'Dad telephoned. He said I could take the car. Do you girls want a lift to Mumbles?'

'We've arranged to go on the train,' she gasped, struggling to bend her arm higher.

'That's silly when I'm going that way anyway.'

'Aren't you picking up the boys?' Giving up on the hook, she lifted her coat from the wardrobe.

'I'm meeting them at the party. That's the door. You expecting anyone?'

'Lily. Let her in.' Helen slipped her arms into the sleeves of her coat. Whatever people thought of the dress, there wasn't time to change now.

Although Joseph Griffiths was four years older than Helen, he couldn't recall a time when his sister's friends hadn't been around. Charging in and out of the house when he least wanted them to, deliberately annoying him and being as

38

irritating as only immature giggling girls could be. Growing up, he had tried to ignore them, adopting the same offhand, superior attitude he used on Helen. If he deigned to notice them at all, it was only to tease. Some time during the last few months he had seen that Judy Hunt was turning into a fairly good-looking girl, but that evening when he opened the front door to Lily, he saw that she too seemed different.

Lily was as dark as his sister was fair – 'Gypsy dark' his mother had pronounced in one of her more critical moods – and so short he had carried on thinking of her as a child, even after he had been forced to acknowledge grudgingly that his sister was on the brink of womanhood. But that evening Lily's black hair was swept up in a new style and she was wearing make-up. Lightly and carefully applied, as opposed to Helen's, who caused enormous arguments with their mother by stubbornly clinging to the belief that the more expensive the cosmetic and the thicker it was slapped on the more effective the result.

Suddenly aware he was staring, he muttered, 'Nice frock.'

Lily eyed him suspiciously. Joe had never said anything complimentary to any of Helen's friends that she'd heard before. 'Hoping I'd say you look good in evening dress?' she asked as he fiddled with his gold cuff links, pulling his shirt cuff the regulation three-quarters of an inch below the sleeve of his dinner jacket.

'I don't need to be told I look good. I know I do and that really is a nice frock.'

'Honestly?' she questioned sceptically. 'Auntie

Norah made it. You don't think the full skirt makes me look like a Munchkin?'

'A what?'

'Munchkin. You know – Judy Garland – *The Wizard of Oz* – little people wearing tents.'

'Not Munchkin at all, more like upside down mushroom.' The flippant remark was out before he registered it sounded insensitive.

'Tell Helen I'll be a few minutes. I'm going home to take this petticoat off.'

'I was joking, you look great.'

'You sure?'

'Unless a man feels he has a good enough memory, he should never venture to lie.'

'Shakespeare?'

'Michel de Montaigne.'

'Your education is showing.' Familiarity with Helen had led to familiarity with Joe and Lily had no compunction about teasing him the way he teased her.

'And that, I take it, isn't a good thing.'

'Only if you want to make people feel inferior.'

'I'm sorry.' Joe's apology was sincere. Set apart from the other boys in Carlton Terrace by his grammar school and university education and the company he kept, but most of all his own sense of intellectual and social superiority, he didn't want Lily to think him a snob too. 'But I am serious about the frock. You look almost good enough for me to ask you to dance.' He had never noticed that her irises were flecked with gold before or her eyelashes so long...

'Almost! Is Helen ready?'

He stepped back. 'Come in, I think she's applying the final coat of lime wash. You going to the Pier?'

'Where else? Helen said you're going to a university party.'

'One of the boys' birthdays. I offered you lot a lift in the car.'

'Your father lets you drive it?'

'When he's in a good mood, doesn't need it and my mother can't think of anywhere she wants to be taken to beyond walking distance, which is about every other blue moon.'

'There won't be room for all of us.' Helen walked down the stairs clutching the edges of her coat together at the hem, in the unlikely event that Joe caught a glimpse of dark-blue satin and recognised it as a new frock.

'Yes there will. One in the front, three in the back.'

'The three in the back will crease their dresses.'

'With the number of layers you lot wear under your skirts, no one will notice if the top one's creased.'

'Are you saying boys look at what a girl's wearing under her skirt?'

'No.'

'Then you're the only one who does?'

'Grow up, Helen.'

'I'm not the one discussing underclothes.'

'Perhaps I should call our mother out of the theatre so she can see how much make-up you're wearing and check what you're hiding under that thick coat in the middle of summer.'

'It's September, that's autumn, not the middle of summer and I'm hiding nothing.'

41

'So nudity's your secret weapon. Thank you for solving the mystery. I've often wondered why boys dance with a girl as ugly as you.'

'You beast! I'd rather walk to the Pier than get in the car with you.'

'You wouldn't get as far as Christina Street in those shoes.'

Helen hesitated. She hated dancing with boys shorter than her and as few were taller when she wore high heels, she normally wore flat pumps to the Pier Ballroom. But Adam Jordan was six foot one, so for once she had thrown caution to the wind and slipped on her white, three-inch stilettos. The winkle-picker points pinched her toes, the narrow heels made her wobble when she walked and they didn't even match the blue satin dress, but her legs looked slimmer in them and as Adam was bound to look at her legs...

'What's it to be?' Joe demanded impatiently.

'As Lily's got the widest skirt, she can sit in the front with you,' Helen capitulated. 'Judy, Katie and I will sit in the back.'

'Keep your head down. I'd hate it if any of the boys who don't know you're my sister saw you and thought me desperate enough to pick up a hideous bird.'

'Why do you think I want to sit in the back?'

'Shouldn't we be going?' Lily suggested, knowing that once Joe and Helen started sniping they could go on for hours.

As Joe turned to the door, Helen whipped back the hem of her coat an inch so Lily could see she was wearing the blue satin.

'I'll get the car out of the garage and meet you

at the end of the street. Don't take all night to collect the others.'

'We'll be five minutes.' Lily stepped in front of Helen so he wouldn't see his sister sticking her tongue out at him.

'I must have left it in my bedroom.' Katie searched fruitlessly through the contents of her brown-paper carrier bag for the tenth time in as many minutes.

'I can lend you money,' Judy offered.

'It's not just the money; I need my bag to put my comb, compact and lipstick in. I'll have to go back.'

'As long as you're quick about it. Helen and Lily will be here any minute.'

Katie raced down the stairs and out through the front door. She looked up and down the street. There was no sign of her father. Crossing her fingers tightly in the hope that he was safely in the pub, she turned the corner and ran down the steps to her family's basement.

'I thought you were going straight to the Pier.' Her mother's voice was soft, low, as she carried dishes from the table to an enamel bowl in the Belfast sink.

Katie's heart leapfrogged to her throat. Her mother's whispering meant her father was in. It was his night off and as he always spent daytime pub opening hours before his free nights in the Tenby and closing hours in bed, she guessed he had overslept after his afternoon session, cutting into his evening's drinking. Something guaranteed to put him into an even worse mood than usual.

'I forgot my bag.'

'Go quietly down the passage.'

Katie didn't need the warning. Opening the only other door in the kitchen as noiselessly as she could, she slipped off her shoes and tiptoed over the worn quarry tiles, past her parents' bedroom door on the left and down the passage. Of the three rooms in the basement, the one at the end would have admitted the most daylight if it hadn't been partitioned into two. The smaller of the two cubicles had an alcove, which her mother had curtained off to hold her clothes, and a single bed, which took up ninety per cent of the remaining space. It was also as black as a coal-hole, because the window was in the cubicle shared by her brothers.

Retrieving the bag from a shelf in her makeshift wardrobe, Katie retraced her steps, but not quickly enough.

Her parents' bedroom door slammed back on its hinges and her father staggered out on bare feet, braces dangling over crumpled, baggy trousers, his flies open below his beer-stained vest. He stood in the doorway of the kitchen, effectively blocking her escape. 'Tea, woman,' he growled.

'It's all ready for you, Ernie, bar the fresh tea and I put the kettle on when I heard you stirring,' Annie muttered nervously.

'Is that the bloody time?'

'It's not half past seven.'

'You know I wanted to be out by opening time.'

'You hadn't had any sleep since yesterday. I thought...'

'You thought – you thought!' He stepped into the kitchen and scowled at the table. 'Is this all the ham there is? You gave the rest to those bloody boys, didn't you?'

'No, Ernie. I didn't. I swear it. They had cheese like they always do.'

'You bloody liar!'

'There's a drop of tea in the pot. It's still warm.' Annie fluttered around him like a sparrow feeding a fat cuckoo that has taken possession of her nest. 'Would you like it to be going on with until the kettle boils?'

'Knowing you, it'll be stewed.'

'Shall I cut more bread and butter?' Annie moved to the breadboard after she poured his tea.

Steeling herself, Katie prayed that for once – just this once – she'd be able to walk through the kitchen and out of the door without her father passing comment or creating a scene. Summoning her courage, she forced herself to put one foot in front of the other.

''Bye, Mam.' She walked behind her father's chair, leaving as wide a berth as the room and furniture would allow. Kissing Annie's reddened cheek she headed for the door.

'And where are you off to, miss, all dolled up like that?' Ernie pushed his chair back from the table.

'The Pier.'

'You can't be paying your mother enough if you can afford to buy a new dress.'

'It's Judy's.' Katie knew she'd made a mistake the second the words were out of her mouth.

'So, you go begging round your rich friends for

cast-offs now.'

'Girls are always borrowing one another's clothes, Ernie.' Annie hurried to the table, picking up the teapot as Katie backed towards the door.

'I'll not allow a daughter of mine to go out in another girl's clothes so everyone in the street can point their finger and say I don't bring in enough to keep my family decent.'

'Please, Ernie, no one points...'

'This is your fault, Annie.'

Katie winced as her father's fist connected with the table sending his cup and saucer rattling. He raised his arm. Annie stepped back, but not far enough. The back of Ernie's hand slammed across her face. Annie dropped the teapot. It shattered in a mass of brown clay shards, damp clumps of tea leaves and sticky brown puddles as she reeled into the Belfast sink.

'Hit her again and I'll knock you into the middle of next week.'

Katie sank down on the step as her brother Martin stepped through the door that connected their basement with the rest of the house.

'You?' Ernie sneered as Martin moved between him and Annie.

'It's my fault...'

'It's not your fault, Mam, it never is. Jack and I could hear him upstairs. So could Mrs Lannon and we were helping her move furniture on the top floor.'

'I pay the rent. I'll make as much noise as I like.'

'You can have a brass band playing down here

for all I care. But you're not hitting Mam again. Not while I'm here to stop it.' Unlike Ernie, Martin was calm, composed and completely in control. Katie had never been so afraid of, or for him. 'I mean it. Touch Mam again and I'll hit you harder than you ever hit any of us.'

'You young...' Ernie drew back his fist. Martin caught it mid-air as their brother Jack walked in behind him. Gripping his father's arm, Martin flung Ernie into the only easy chair in the room. Ernie jerked back. The thin cushion proved no protection against the wooden frame. Katie heard her father's head crack against the top bar. Dazed, he stared up at Martin in disbelief.

Wiping her eyes on the dishcloth, Annie winced gingerly as she moved from the sink towards the chair.

'He's all right, just stunned.' Martin turned away in disgust as his mother hovered over his father.

'Better all round if you'd killed him,' Jack pronounced acidly.

'Now I'm home from National Service and bringing in a wage, Mam, you and the kids can move out of here. I'll look after you.' Martin glared contemptuously at his father. 'And better than he ever has.'

'You don't understand,' Annie broke in fervently, pressing the damp dishcloth to the back of Ernie's head.

'No, I don't. I don't understand why any woman would stay with a man who beats her.' Martin gripped the back of a kitchen chair so tightly that Katie flinched, expecting the bar to snap. 'Mam, take a hard look at yourself and this place.'

'You bastard,' Ernie mumbled drunkenly. 'Home less than a week and you raise your hand to your father. Is that what they taught you in the army? Well I'll not have you back in this house...'

'I only returned to this pigsty to help Mam.'

'I'll...' Ernie left the chair, tried to square up to his son and crumpled in a heap on the floor.

Annie fell to her knees beside him.

'He's piss-drunk, Mam.'

'Less of that language in front of Mam and Katie,' Martin warned his brother.

'All high-class and refined now you've been away, aren't you. Well I'll tell you something for nothing. You haven't a bloody clue what it's been like for us back here with him while you've been off gallivanting, seeing the world.'

'I said no swearing in front of Mam and Katie and I meant it.'

'Or what? You'll thump me like you thumped him? Or do you only pick on drunks?' Elbowing Martin aside, Jack scooped Ernie none too gently from the floor, slung him over his shoulder and carried him into the passage. Opening the door to the bedroom, he tossed him on the bed.

'Martin – what your father said – when he wakes up you'd better say sorry.'

'Not to that animal.'

'You know how he is,' Annie begged. 'There'll be no peace...'

'There's never been any of that in this house, Mam, and there won't be while you stay with him.'

Annie stared at the mess of broken crockery and spilled tea on the floor, and began to cry. Soft, fat, silent tears that tore at Martin's heartstrings.

'This is my fault. I shouldn't have borrowed Judy's dress.' Katie crouched and gathered the larger pieces of teapot, all the while staring at the floor so her mother and brother wouldn't see her own tears.

'There's only one person to blame and it's neither of you.' Martin lifted the dustpan and brush out from under the sink.

'Out the way, both of you. Katie, you'll dirty Judy's dress.'

'I can wash it.'

'If you're going out you'd best be on your way.'

Martin helped his sister to her feet. 'Don't worry, I'll take care of Mam.' He gave her a reassuring hug.

'I don't feel like going out now.

'Best you don't stay here. You've enough money?'

'I kept back five shillings.' As she opened her bag, her face fell.

'I saw Dad in your room earlier.' Putting his hand in his back trouser pocket, he handed her a ten-shilling note. 'Try and forget this happened. Have a good time.'

'Marty...'

'I'll be leaving but I'll not go far without you.' He pulled out his handkerchief and blotted her tears. 'Go on.' He smiled. 'You'll miss the other girls if you hang around.'

'You really going?' Jack shovelled a pile of old comics on to the floor so he could sit on the windowsill.

'Yes.' Martin flicked the catches on his case, opened it flat on the bed they shared and separated his clothes from Jack's on the rail.

'It must be nice to be able to afford to move on when you feel like it.'

'Army pay doesn't allow for much in the way of savings.'

'You've enough set aside to put this bloody mess of a family behind you.'

'Jack...'

'It's all right, I'd probably do the same in your shoes.'

Martin looked at his brother and saw misery and disappointment behind the swagger and bravado. 'I shouldn't have come back, not here. It was hard enough when I was away thinking of Mam and you and Katie getting the rough edge of Dad's hand but my being here only makes things worse for Mam. And I can't stay and watch it, Jack. I'm sorry.' He pleaded for understanding. 'I just can't.'

'I could come with you.'

'You will as soon as I find somewhere big enough for all of us. But I don't know where I'll be sleeping tonight.'

'I've slept rough before. There's still a lot of houses round here with air-raid shelters. Some of them aren't that damp.'

'And Mam and Katie?'

'You heard Mam. She won't leave him and Katie won't leave without her.'

'I know it's a lot to ask, but please stay until I find somewhere decent for all of us. I'll sleep easier knowing you're here if Dad decides to have another go.'

'The last time I got between him and Mam was the week I got out of Borstal. He broke my arm. That's why my call-up's been delayed for a year.'

'You never wrote...'

'It mended,' Jack interrupted, in a tone that warned Martin to drop the subject.

'I'll find someone to put me up for tonight and I'll start looking for rooms first thing tomorrow.' Snapping the locks on the case, Martin lifted it from the bed and walked to the door. He glanced back at the double bed covered with a patchwork of rags that had been worn even before his mother had laboriously stitched them together. 'I know there's a shortage of rooms around here but I'll try to find a place for the four of us. Then there'll be no more broken arms or black eyes and if I have to, I'll carry Mam there and lock her in so she can't come back here.'

'Between us we could...' Jack's voice trailed as he realised the magnitude of what he was about to suggest.

'Tackle him? We'd probably kill him and there are laws against that.'

'You haven't been here.'

'But I'm here now. And like I said to Katie, I'll not go far.'

'But you won't be in this bloody house.'

'Watch over Katie and Mam until I can get the three of you out.'

'We've managed without you for two years.

51

We'll manage again.'

'I promise you won't have to manage much longer, Jack. I'm going to change things, for all of us.'

'Seeing is believing.' Jack turned his back as Martin offered him his hand.

'Is there anything I can say to persuade you to leave with me?' Martin stood in the kitchen, watching his mother fiddle with the food she'd laid out on the table for his father. 'I haven't much money but I have enough for a couple of days' bed and breakfast for the four of us while I look for rooms,' he pressed.

'Rooms round here are like gold dust and your father's always fine after he's slept it off.'

'Fine enough to hit you again.'

'I deserved it. I knew he wanted to go out and I didn't wake him.'

'Mam, sometimes you can be downright stupid. If you won't think of yourself, think of Katie. She's terrified to draw breath in front of him. And Jack – eighteen and already served two years in Borstal. Before I'd been back in Swansea five minutes, I was told he'd become wilder than ever since his release.'

'Jack's just growing up.' She averted her face as he tried to kiss her cheek, so he wouldn't see the reddish-purple portent of fresh bruises.

'If you won't go, I'll still take Katie and Jack.'

'He won't let you, Martin, and they're under age.'

Feeling frustrated, helpless and weary of useless argument, he went to the door. 'I'm going.'

'Marty, try to see things my way. I married your father for better for worse.'

'And got the worse,' he observed bitterly. 'I'll not go far. I'll try to get a room in this street.'

'Is that wise? Your dad...'

'I know the thought of me earning and paying lodge to someone other than him will hurt his pride and his beer money, and they're the only things he cares about, but I'll not move away from Carlton Terrace. Not while you and the kids are here. First thing tomorrow I'll look for a place to rent that's big enough for all of us. Law or no law, Katie and Jack won't take much persuading to join me. And I promise, if you move in you won't have to worry about house-keeping. I'll pay the rent, bills and put food on the table – and more and better than he pays for.'

'You can drop us anywhere here.' Helen looked around uneasily as Joe slowed the car and turned left off the Mumbles Road on to the crowded lane that led down to the Pier.

'I may as well take you down to the bottom.'

'There's no need.' Helen dug her fingers into the back of Joe's seat as she leaned forward and scanned a group of boys.

'Looking for someone you don't want me to see?'

'Leave off, you two.' Judy opened her evening bag and pulled out her compact.

'I said anywhere...'

'And I can't stop the car in the middle of this crowd,' Joe snapped, turning the wheel sharply to the right.

'Thanks a bundle, Joe,' Judy complained. 'I've now got lipstick halfway up my cheek.'

'Here.' Lily handed Judy a handkerchief.

'I said this is fine!'

'I heard you the first time, Helen.' Joe pulled in close to the rock face on their right.

'Thank you for the ride.' Lily smiled, hoping to deflect any more argument.

Turning off the ignition, Joe opened his door as far as it would go without hitting the cliff, stepped out and walked round to the passenger side. Opening Lily's door, he offered her his hand as Helen, Katie and Judy spilled out of the back.

'You're honoured, Lily.' Helen checked the buttons on her coat were fastened as Judy and Katie smoothed down their dresses.

'See you later.' Ignoring the stares and ribald comments directed at his bow tie and dinner jacket, Joe returned to the car.

'I hope not,' Helen countered through the open window.

'You'll be making your way home at half past ten?'

'Too early for you to leave your party.'

'We'll see.' Pressing the ignition, he drove on slowly through the crowds.

'He's never going to drive up that steep hill.'

'He's idiot enough to do anything, Judy,' Helen bit back crossly. 'And if he does come to fetch us it'll be your fault, Lily. He's after you.'

'Joe? Don't be silly.'

'Has he ever offered us a lift on a Saturday night before?'

'I've never known him to have the car on a

Saturday night before.' Judy brushed a minute fleck of face powder from her skirt.

'That's right, take Lily's side.'

'Side. What side?' Judy stared resolutely ahead as a wolf whistle echoed from behind them.

'I wish...'

'You hadn't worn that frock? I saw the blue satin when we sat in the back of the car.'

'Think you know everything, don't you, Judy Hunt.' Helen stalked ahead, tottering on her three-inch heels as two more wolf whistles resounded towards them.

CHAPTER THREE

'Marty, it's nice to see you. Our Adam said you were back and you boys were off out tonight. Come in, I've just wet the tea, have a cup with me while Adam finishes titivating himself.' Doris Jordan flung the door wide, inviting Martin in.

'Thank you, Mrs Jordan.' Martin stepped inside, self-consciously lugging his case.

'Leaving home?'

'I thought it was time.'

'Oh!' Doris turned away to hide her embarrassment as she walked into the back kitchen and lifted a couple of cups and saucers down from the dresser. Ernie was well-known in the street and there wasn't a woman who didn't feel sorry for his wife and children.

'Well, there's a double bed in our Adam's room.

You're welcome to stay until you get sorted.'

'That's very kind but I was hoping you'd have a room that I could rent...'

'You pay us rent? I wouldn't hear of it.'

'I'm really looking for somewhere I can take Jack, Katie and Mam, Mrs Jordan.'

'Your mam wants to leave your dad?' she asked carefully.

'Not exactly,' he hedged, 'but if I had somewhere to take her, I thought she might change her mind about staying with him.'

'If I had room you'd be more than welcome. But Mrs Atkins has lived in our basement for the last fourteen years and isn't looking to move, and the only way they'll be taking Bert Jones out of our top-floor flat is in a box. But I'll keep my ears open and the minute I hear of something I'll let you know.'

'That's very good of you...'

'Not another word. Stay as long as you like. It will be good for our Adam to have company. Now, sit down and tell me all about the foreign parts the army sent you to. Your mam told me you were in Germany and some island with a funny name.'

'Cyprus, Mrs Jordan.'

'That's it.' She put three of her home-made shortbread biscuits into the saucer of his teacup before handing it to him. She wouldn't have dreamed of asking what had gone on between his father and the rest of his family but she wanted him to know that her sympathies lay entirely with him, not his father, and food was the only way she had of expressing her feelings. 'Some people'

– she lowered her voice, as though the room were full of eavesdroppers – 'like Mrs Hoity-Toity Griffiths think conscription is a bad idea. I think it gives boys like you and our Adam a chance to get on. Adam said you've come back to a mechanic's job with the council and you know our Adam has passed as high as he can go.'

'He told me he'd taken his Civil Service entrance.' Martin was too polite to smile. Like most women of her class and generation, Doris Jordan believed education was an excellent and desirable thing but Martin also realised that she no more understood the system of examinations and qualifications than she understood the mystery of electricity.

'He's set for life, now,' Doris continued solemnly. 'My Arnold said he never thought he'd see the day when a son of his went into an office but our Adam's starting on Monday. In the Land Registry,' she added proudly. 'And look at you.'

'I'm only doing what I did before I went away, Mrs Jordan. Apprenticed to the mechanics in the Council Depot.'

'Our Adam said you passed your examinations.'

'Only the army ones, I've one more to go.' Martin looked to the door, wondering what could be taking Adam so long.

'Well, the army ones must have been a help. That Mrs Griffiths, do you know what she said. "When boys get university degrees, they shouldn't be subjected to two years of mindless square bashing with the common herd." As if you or our Adam are "the common herd." Of course, she was talking about her precious Joseph. No

57

one else in the terrace can afford to let their children remain idle until they're twenty-one. And her Joseph wouldn't be either, if his father didn't work all the hours God sends in that warehouse to keep him. That boy could do with a bit of square bashing to knock some sense into him. Between you and me, he's been spoiled.'

'Who's been spoiled, Mam?' Adam walked in, his best white shirt flapping over his suit trousers.

'That Joseph Griffiths, that's who.'

'Joe's all right. Bought me a pint when I came home.'

'Students shouldn't have the money to go to pubs and buy drinks but I hope you bought him one back.'

'Course.' He winked at Martin. 'Can't have the Griffithses thinking we're charity cases, can we?'

'Not now you're in the Civil Service, we can't. Come here.' She took the cuff links he was holding from him. 'Look at you. Two years in the army and you still can't dress yourself.'

'Thanks, Mam.' Adam lifted her off her feet as she straightened his sleeves.

'Put me down. You're not so big you can't feel the back of my hand. Go and clear space in your wardrobe and one of your drawers for Marty.'

'It's all right, Mrs Jordan, really. I'm hoping to sort myself out with something permanent tomorrow.'

'You moving in?' Adam looked at his friend in surprise.

'For now.' Mrs Jordan fought to free herself from her son's grip as he lowered her to the floor. 'Go on, take Marty's case up to your bedroom while he finishes his tea.'

'I warn you, Marty, she's worse than any sergeant. It's nothing but orders from morning till night.'

'I'll give you...'

'What, Mam?' Adam grinned.

Martin sat back in the cosy kitchen that was so much more comfortable than his mother's for all its home-made rag-rugs and patchwork cushions, and listened to the easy banter. He wished it could have been the same in his parents' basement. The atmosphere in the Jordan's kitchen was no different when Adam's father was home. Quiet, easygoing, Mr Jordan's idea of indulging himself was a radio play or sitting down with a newspaper and his pipe. The only time he set foot in a pub was early on a Saturday evening to buy half a pint of mild and the bottle of sherry that he and his wife took on their weekly visit to Adam's grandmother. Martin had never seen him drunk or heard him raise his voice to his wife or sons. If only...

'Another biscuit, Martin?'

'No, thank you, Mrs Jordan.'

'Growing boy like you needs nourishment.'

'You going to Gran's, Mam?' Adam asked as he returned.

'If your father ever gets home with that sherry. I've never known a man take so long to buy a bottle. I think he must have gone to Cardiff to get it.' She watched Adam reach for his jacket. 'Can I ask where you two are going?'

'You can ask.'

'You're not telling?'

'It's Saturday night, Mam.'

'Then you're going drinking.' She crossed her arms.

'We may have one or two.'

'Not in one of those nasty rough pubs down the docks.'

'Mam!'

'We'll probably go to the White Rose, Mrs Jordan.' Martin could understand Adam's reluctance to submit to his mother's interrogation after semi-independent army life but he also liked Mrs Jordan.

'As long as you stop after two. But you'd be much better off going to the Pier and meeting some nice girls like Mrs Hunt's Judy or Lily Sullivan. Boys your age should be courting.'

'No good me looking at Lily, Mam. Marty's had his eye on her since he was six.'

'I have not.'

'No shame if you have, nice girl like that. You know she's a banker now.'

'She's a typist who works in a bank, Mam.'

Doris sailed on, ignoring her son. 'Norah did well by keeping that girl on in school and sending her to technological college. She passed all her exams, you know, as high as she could go.'

'Lily's a bright girl.' Adam opened the door. 'Time we were off.'

'Here, your suit's got white bits all over the shoulders. Whatever have you been leaning against?'

'Nothing I know about,' Adam protested as his mother took a clothes brush, marked *A present from Tenby* from a hook behind the door and gave

60

his jacket a good going over.

'You fit then?'

'As I'll ever be.' Martin rose to his feet as Mrs Jordan replaced the brush on the hook.

Adam kissed the top of his mother's head. 'Don't wait up.'

'You'll be wanting your supper.'

'We'll stop for chips, Mam.'

'I don't know, you boys today, filling yourselves up with stuff and rubbish.'

'Don't you worry, Mrs Jordan, I'll take care of him.'

'See that you do, Marty,' Doris warned, not altogether humorously.

'I don't recognise that car.' Mrs Murton Davies frowned as a Rover edged slowly down her drive towards the gravelled parking area at the side of the substantial three-storied Edwardian villa that dominated the clifftop above Caswell Bay.

Mrs Watkin Morgan followed her line of vision. 'It's the Griffiths boy. That's his father's car; he hasn't one of his own.'

'Do we know him?'

'Larry and Robin do, he's at university with them.'

'There was a time when being at university meant something, unfortunately not any more.' Mrs Murton Davies signalled to a waiter to bring the champagne tray to the bench they were sitting on. 'Is he a scholarship boy?'

'He went to grammar school.'

'I see.' Mrs Murton Davies pursed her lips, tightening the fine lines round her mouth.

'His mother was in school with us. Pretty girl, bright, you must remember her – Esme Harris. She does a lot with the Little Theatre these days.'

'The headmaster's daughter?'

'The teachers thought she'd go far. She proved them wrong.'

'Wasn't there some sort of scandal there? Didn't she have to marry young, a dreadful man who'd been horribly scarred in a fire, lived in town and worked in a clothes shop.'

'Warehouse, actually, Griffiths's Wholesale, he inherited it from his grandfather.' Mrs Watkin Morgan lifted a champagne glass from the waiter's tray. 'He's done rather well for himself. The warehouse is quite popular these days and he's not long opened Elegance, that chic little fashion place on Newton Road. I'm only surprised Esme hasn't insisted they move out to a better area.'

'But the boy can hardly be our sort. I'm surprised Larry invited him.'

'Joe's very good-looking and positively oozes charm, just like his grandfather the headmaster. Angie adores him.'

'You know him socially?'

'As much as anyone ever knows a student socially. He and Robin are close.'

'I've tried to instil a sense of responsibility into Larry when it comes to the friends he brings home. We simply can't be too careful with three girls in the house. They're at that impressionable age. Introduce them to the wrong sort and we could have a disaster on our hands – like Esme Harris,' she added snidely.

'Richard Thomas is the Griffithses' solicitor.'

'I'm surprised they feel the need to have one.'

'He mentioned some time ago that the boy has a substantial trust fund. His grandfather's sister set it up. She had no children and apparently looked on Joseph as her own.'

'How large is substantial?'

'You know Richard, he wouldn't be drawn on figures but he did say that between the income from the trust and the house – you do know that his grandmother is leaving him the house?'

'The ten-bedroomed one above Langland?'

'I believe that is the only one she owns.'

'What about Esme?'

'Mrs Harris never did approve of her marrying that man. She tells everyone who'll listen she cut her daughter out of her will the day she announced her engagement. Richard says young Joseph's going to be a wealthy man one day and whatever Richard says you can take as given.'

'Wealthy and well-educated if he's at university,' Mrs Mutton Davies mused. With three daughters on her hands, there weren't so many independent, eligible young men available that she could afford to ignore one. 'What is he reading?'

'English, he's taken a research job with the BBC for the summer with Robin. Rumour has it, the powers that be are impressed.'

'So he could be heading for a career in broadcasting?'

'He could.' Mrs Watkin Morgan smiled as she read her friend's rather obvious train of thought. 'He's certainly talented. Two of his poems were published in this month's *Gower*.'

'Larry must introduce him to the girls. They're so fond of poetry.' Mrs Murton Davies's frown deepened, as Mrs Watkin Morgan's smile widened. Angela Watkin Morgan was halfway across the lawn. As they watched, the girl stepped on to the gravel, bypassed the fleet of open-topped sports cars and opened the door of Joseph's Rover.

'Darling Joseph, as handsome as ever. You wouldn't believe how much I've missed you.'

Joe brushed his lips across the cheek Angela offered him before locking his father's car. 'No, I wouldn't, not from what Robin's been telling me about your exploits. How were London and France?' He stood back and looked at her. She seemed taller, slimmer, older and more sophisticated than when she had left Swansea in April for what her mother called 'the season'. He'd expected to admire her less and feel more at seeing her for the first time since their separation. But she was still the pretty girl he had lost his heart to last winter. The only thing that surprised him was the realisation that since then he had somehow managed to retrieve it.

'Bor-ing. Full of silly girls chasing chinless boys, but don't tell Mother that.' She took his arm. 'She thinks she's done me a favour by making me a deb.'

'You were looking forward to it before you left,' he murmured absently, mesmerised by the vista that stretched from the front lawn of the house down to Caswell Bay. Gower scenery never failed to take his breath away, making him glad he lived so close to so much unspoilt coastline and envious of those who could afford to live within sight and sound of the sea.

'I was, after listening to Mother's stories. But then, as she said, and often since April, it was all *so* different for debs in her day. They had proper evening frocks, arrived at the Palace in chauffeur-driven cars and were given evening buffet on gold plate. I had a short afternoon frock my mother picked out. It was hideous. The skirt looked like a chiffon lampshade and after we'd made our curtseys all we got was tea and ghastly little cakes. The whole time I was there, I kept wishing I were back here with you.'

'Poor Angie, it really must have been a let-down.'

'I'm serious, Joe. I'm sorry I said those awful things to you before I left.'

'They weren't awful; in fact, with the benefit of hindsight they were sensible, considering we had to spend the summer apart.'

'Sensible! You've found another girl!'

'None who could take your place,' he responded flippantly, amused by her sudden anxiety.

'Why don't I believe you?' She gave two of Larry's sisters a 'keep off my property' warning look as they scrutinised Joe. 'This way.' She steered him towards a bar set up inside the entrance of a marquee that had been erected on the main lawn. 'I've spent all afternoon mixing cocktails for this bash. There's one I've christened "Gower surprise." You simply *have* to taste it.'

'Joe!' Angela's brother Robin waved him over to where he was standing – or rather swaying – next to Larry Murton Davies.

'I'd better pay my respects to the birthday boy first.'

Angela wrinkled her nose. 'I'm not talking to Larry.'

'What's he done now?'

'Got himself stupid drunk.' She hugged his arm tighter. 'It is great to be together again, Joe. We have so much time to make up – and all the time in the world to do it. I'm starting in art college in September.'

'Robin told me.'

'He shouldn't have, that's my news and I wanted it to be a surprise. Robin showed me your poems. They're good.'

'High praise, coming from you.'

'Every writer I know says you have to be an absolute genius to get published these days.'

'Not in the *Gower*. The editor's a friend of our tutor's.'

'He didn't publish Robin's.'

'That doesn't mean mine are better.'

'Yes it does. And don't try to argue. I've read Robin's, they're banal. And Robin's green with envy at the way you've been given all the best jobs this summer. Pops says you're the main topic of conversation in Alexandra Road. Rumour has it BBC Swansea will close down when you go back to university.'

'They don't think more of me than they do of any other student researcher,' Joe interposed swiftly, hoping that news of his confidential interview with the Director of Programmes in Cardiff hadn't leaked out. He'd already accepted the offer of a job when he graduated, although he knew it would annoy his mother. She assumed he would teach, like his grandfather. He hadn't disillusioned her. An argument delayed meant fewer quarrels and a quieter life in Carlton Terrace until graduation.

'Have you come to wish me happy birthday or flirt with Angie?' Larry demanded petulantly as they approached.

'Both,' Joe answered easily. 'Happy birthday.' Extricating himself from Angela, he shook Larry's hand before delving into his pocket for the gold tiepin his mother had insisted he buy in Samuel's rather than his father's warehouse 'for appearances' sake'.

'Thanks, old man.' Larry tossed the parcel on to a side table set up next to the bar without giving it a second glance. 'Drink?'

'Is that one of the Gower cocktails Angie's been telling me about?'

'Is it hell,' Robin dismissed scornfully. 'It's best brandy.'

Larry tottered precariously as he leaned heavily on Joe's shoulder. 'Come and meet the family, then we can get on with the serious business of the evening. Drinking!'

'Joe...'

'Stop chasing Joe, Angie. This is boys' time.' Dismissing his sister with a wave of his hand, Robin pushed Joe and Larry out of the marquee towards the bench set in front of the french windows that opened into the drawing room.

Looking back at Angie, Joe mouthed, 'Keep me a dance.' She smiled and nodded.

Larry straightened up as he stood in front of his mother and by making an effort to speak slowly, managed to conceal just how drunk he was. 'Mums, I'd like to introduce Joseph Griffiths.'

Mrs Murton Davies looked Joe up and down. 'I've just heard you're poor Esme's boy. I am *so* glad you could accept our invitation. You're in university with Larry?'

'Has been for two years, Mums.'

Joe tried to shake Larry's mother's hand as if he hadn't heard the 'poor Esme'. His admittance to Swansea University had also gained him entry to some of the best houses in Swansea, but he found it difficult to take the pity of his friends' parents for what they regarded as his mother's 'unfortunate' marriage and his even more 'unfortunate' home address.

'You're like your grandfather,' Mrs Murton Davies gushed. 'We girls all absolutely adored him when we were young. I think it was the moustache. Have you thought of growing one?'

'I can't say that I have, Mrs Murton Davies.'

'Yes, well, you're young yet. Poor Esme must have some photographs of her father. You should look at them...'

'Cigar, Joe?' Robin thrust one into his mouth before he could answer. 'Don't worry, Mrs MD, we won't smoke anywhere except out here and in the billiard room.'

'I should hope not. Aren't you young people going to dance? We have engaged a very good band.'

'Just going, Mums. Marquee, boys, last one on the floor has to pour the next round.' Larry stumbled over the lawn towards the shrubbery.

'Robin, where have you been hiding? I've been searching for you for years.'

'And now you've found me what do you intend doing with me?' Robin opened his arms as Larry's sister, Emily, bore down on him. 'You have brought your car?' he whispered over his shoulder to Joe, as he embraced her.

'As ordered.'

'You can take us into Mumbles later.'

'On Larry's twenty-first!'

'Exactly, *my* twenty-first,' Larry slurred from somewhere behind them, 'and I want to have fun, which I can't have with my bloody family and all these damned people around.'

The bar of the White Rose in Walter Road was crowded with young men downing as many pints as they could cram in before it was time to head for Mumbles and the Pier. While Adam tried to attract the attention of the besieged barman, Martin looked around, narrowing his eyes as they adjusted to the dark-oak and polished-brass gloom, after the early-evening, late-summer sunlight outside. He tried to put the ugly scene and problems at home from his mind by concentrating on the simple pleasure of being back in civilian clothes in a pub devoid of uniforms, but his mother's face, lined, bruised, old before her time, intruded into his consciousness. And even when he finally succeeded in relegating her to the shadows, she was supplanted by Katie's thin, cowed figure, small, narrow face and enormous, terrified eyes or Jack's outwardly sharp Teddy boy image. But for all his veneer of truculent defiance, Martin knew his brother feared their father every bit as much as did their mother and sister.

'Clay?' A solitary figure, standing, foot on rail at the opposite end of the bar hailed him.

'Powell?' Martin murmured hesitantly.

'Clay and–' Brian glanced across as Adam finally succeeded in collaring the barman. 'Jordan? I had no idea you two lived in Swansea.' Picking up his beer mug, Brian edged his way through the crowd to join them.

'And I thought you were from Ponty.'

'I am but I've moved into lodgings here. Work,' Brian explained succinctly. 'So what are you doing now?'

'Same thing I did before conscription. Apprentice in the council garage.'

'I thought you passed your mechanics exams.'

'The army ones. I'm carrying on in night school. Fancy a top-up?'

'Ever known me to say no?'

'Look what the cat dragged in, Adam. You remember, Powell?'

'I remember you two getting orders for Cyprus, lucky sods. From the uncensored version Marty gave me I gather it was all sunshine, wine and gorgeous girls queuing up to fulfil your every fantasy.'

'After Germany, Adam served out the rest of his time in Yorkshire,' Martin explained as he handed the pint Adam pushed towards him to

Brian and asked the barman to pull another.

'In a miserable, cold, damp barracks,' Adam embellished dolefully.

'Look on the bright side, with your fair skin the sun might not have agreed with you.'

'I would have liked to have had the chance to find out.' Adam raised his glass and the others followed suit. 'Here's to reunions. So, what you doing in this neck of the woods, Powell?'

'Just moved into digs round the corner, Carlton Terrace. Do you know it?'

Adam glanced at Martin and they burst out laughing.

'What's so funny?'

'It's only where we live. Who you lodging with?'

'Mrs Evans.'

'You always did have the luck of the devil.'

'She makes a good cake.'

'Good cake, nothing,' Adam dismissed. 'You're living under the same roof as the gorgeous Lily.'

'We've been introduced. Pretty girl. Here, have this one on me, Jordan. Clay'll only tell you I owe him one if I don't cough first shout.' Brian thrust his hand into his pocket, pulled out his change, picked out four shillings and sixpence and handed it to the barman. 'I can't quite work out where Lily fits in. She looks too young to be Mrs Evans's daughter but she calls Roy Williams uncle.'

'She was an evacuee. No one turned up to claim her after the war so Mrs Evans kept her.'

'She is a pretty girl,' Adam observed darkly, 'but I'd keep my hands off her if I were you. Marty, here, saw her first.'

'That joke's wearing thin, Adam. Besides, Lily's just a kid.'

'Eighteen isn't a kid.'

'If she is the love of your life, Clay, I don't envy you. From what I saw she's kept on a tight leash.'

'Not that tight.' Adam grinned. 'You on for a trip down Mumbles?'

'What's there?'

'The Mumbles mile.' Reading the mystified expression on Brian's face, Adam explained. 'You haven't lived until you've travelled the Mumbles mile. Pubs stacked up end to end. Rumour has it there's a prize waiting for anyone who can down a pint in every one and stand upright afterwards.'

'Take no notice, Powell, Jordan here has yet to discover delights beyond drinking.'

'Poor bloke.'

'The poor bloke was about to tell you that as well as the Mumbles mile, tonight is dance night in the Pier Ballroom and ten to one the gorgeous Lily will be there along with a selection of the other girls Swansea has to offer.'

'Ah, but will there be any like Maria?' Brian teased.

'I hope not,' Martin muttered fervently.

'Willing little piece, was she?' Adam asked.

'She was willing all right, and sixty if she was a day, but that didn't stop her from trying, especially with this one. "Come, my leetle boy, my sweet Clay. Maria is waiting for you..."'

'Lay off.'

'I'm going to like having you around, Powell.' Adam dug his hand into his pocket. 'Another pint?'

72

'How about we make it in Mumbles?'

'Suits me.'

'And me.' Brian finished his drink in a single swallow. 'Lead the way.'

'You can't sit in the cloakroom all night with your coat on.'

'It's my life, I can do what I like.'

'You look ridiculous,' Judy asserted forcefully.

'Not as ridiculous as I'd look with my coat off.'

'You can borrow my stole if you like.' Lily handed Helen the white mohair wrap Roy had bought for her birthday on the assurance of the sales assistant that it was the absolute latest in luxurious ladies' fashion.

'It won't cover enough of me.'

'I thought the whole point of that dress was to uncover as much of you as possible to attract Adam Jordan's attention.'

'Why don't you shout louder, Judy? I think there's a girl in the corner who didn't catch his name.'

'If you're not careful I might do just that.' Losing patience, Judy tugged Helen's hand. Yanking her out of the chair she dragged her through the crowds of girls trying to reach the mirrors, to the furthest – and darkest – corner of the Ladies. 'Right, off with that coat.'

Helen looked around. Most of the girls were wearing collared shirtwaisters like Judy, Lily and Katie that showed an inch or two of skin below their throats at most. Those who could afford them had wide petticoats that frothed out their skirts beneath waist-clinching leather or elastic belts. A minority of the type her mother would have called 'loose' had opted for skin-tight sweaters and hip-hugging, straight skirts that showed the telltale bumps of their suspenders. None was wearing full-blown evening dress.

'No.'

'Where's all the "I couldn't care less what the world thinks of me, I'm going to do what I like" attitude gone?'

'I'd look stupid among this lot.'

'I hate to say I told you so.'

'You just did.'

'So you're going to ruin the evening for all of us?'

'You don't have to sit with me.'

'I won't. You coming, Lily, Katie?'

'We can't just leave you here, Helen,' Lily pleaded. 'It'll spoil the night for all of us.'

'Speak for yourself, Lily,' Judy chipped in irritably, looking sideways at Katie. Never talkative, she'd been more than usually withdrawn since they'd left Carlton Terrace.

'It won't be the same without you, Helen,' Katie added, sensing Judy watching her and feeling she should make a contribution to the argument.

'All right.' Helen finally unbuttoned her coat. As soon as she slipped the last button from its loop, Judy snatched at the collar, tore it from her and ran across to the hatch manned by a middle-aged woman.

'Judy!' Helen shouted furiously, feeling as though every eye in the room was focused on her bosom.

'If you wrap the stole a little higher than usual no one will notice the low neckline,' Lily suggested sympathetically.

'Keep your stole.' Helen tossed it back to Lily, only to regret her action a moment later when she caught sight of herself in the long mirror above the row of sinks. The amount of flesh she was showing bordered on indecent. 'Give me that ticket, Judy.'

'No.' Careful to keep her distance, Judy waved the cloakroom ticket in the air before stuffing it in her handbag. 'Right, shall we find a good table, then wait for the boys to come to us so we can slay them with our charm, wit, beauty and personality – starting with Adam Jordan for Helen?'

CHAPTER FOUR

'The band's playing.'

'And hardly anyone's dancing, Angie.' Joe leaned indolently against the bar.

'Robin and Emily are.'

'That's dancing? I thought Emily was holding Robin upright.'

'He's not as drunk as Larry.'

'Now, it's a competition.'

'Only among you boys. Come on. Joe,' Angela wheedled. 'We could show the rest the way.'

'Not with my two left feet; besides, I'd prefer to talk. You've told me hardly anything about

London – or France.' Joe sipped his glass of champagne slowly. He'd drunk the brandy too quickly and it had gone to his head before he remembered his father's car. The drive was narrow and he'd only have to put a single scratch on the paintwork to forfeit the privilege of borrowing it again.

'I was only in France for three weeks. Barely time to get a suntan.'

'You must have seen something.'

'The French.'

'I should have known better than to ask. Next, I suppose you'll tell me London was full of the English.'

'And Americans, Dutch, French, Scandinavians, even Germans behaving as though they, not we, had won the war. Foreigners seem to like travelling.'

'And you don't?'

'I told you earlier, not as much as being back here with you.'

'I'm flattered.'

'You're real; you talk about things that matter. Life, the future...'

'Poetry.'

'You're laughing at me.'

'Just a bit.'

'I hate it when everyone holds back at a party waiting for someone else to make the first move on to the dance floor.' Angela wriggled her fingers inside his collar.

'That tickles.'

'It's supposed to make you feel amorous. There are six – no seven – eight couples on the floor now. Can we please join them?'

'You won't give me a moment's peace until we do, will you?'

'No.' Taking his champagne, she placed it together with her own on the bar and led him on to the wooden staging that had been erected for dancing. 'What a shame, we've missed the jive but I prefer slow ones, don't you?' Linking her arms around his neck, she moved close to him as the strains of 'Smoke Gets in Your Eyes' echoed around the marquee.

'Angie, people are looking.' Blood coursed hotly through his veins as she rotated her hips over his.

'So? Old people expect the young to be outrageous these days.'

'Not in front of them.'

'When you ask me out again, we can be outrageous behind their backs.'

He looked down at her. She was indisputedly pretty, ash-blonde hair that curled around a charming, elfin face, slim figure, and soft grey eyes that promised kisses and – unlike last spring – maybe more. Then he had believed her to be everything he had ever hoped to find in a woman.

He only had to close his eyes to remember the pain, hot, suffocating and choking, when she had told him she was leaving Swansea for the summer and it would be better if he didn't write, as they should both be free agents in case either of them met anyone else. He had known she was hoping to meet that 'anyone'. A wealthier, well-connected, better-bred man than him with prospects he couldn't aspire to even in his dreams.

That mythical man had cost him sleepless nights, and given rise to the most incisive poetry he had written on the despair of unrequited love and the faithlessness of women. But instead of being flattered by Angela's change of heart, he felt as though she'd kept him as a fallback: 'Good old Joe, couldn't find anything better in the boyfriend department, so he'll have to do.'

He was amazed he hadn't seen through her before. He wasn't even upset. It was almost as though Angela and the pain of her desertion had happened to someone else. Now she was simply what she looked: a pretty girl – any pretty girl. Whatever power she had once wielded over him had gone more completely than he would have believed possible a few hours ago. She left him cold.

Analysing his emotions, he wondered if he had loved *her*, or simply the idea of being in love. In poetic terms his fixation with Angie could be likened to a comet that burned momentarily, brightly, superficially, and just as swiftly turned to ashes.

And Lily. Since he had opened the door earlier that evening to see her standing on the doorstep he hadn't been able to get her out of his mind. In Shakespeare's terms he sensed that Lily could be his *ever-fixed mark,* his soulmate, his muse. He concentrated hard, committing his feelings for Angela and Lily to memory so he could assign them to paper the minute he was alone. Angie's teasing flirt – *time's fool* – compared with Lily, his Madonna, *the star to every wand'ring bark.*

The poetry he had written on the loss of Angela

had made its way into print, but the poetry Lily inspired would make his reputation. He was certain of it.

Lily deliberately held back for a few moments as the other three walked into the ballroom. Standing close to the door, savouring the heady atmosphere of excitement and anticipation mixed together with the vying fragrances of Evening in Paris, Californian Poppy and Old Spice aftershave, she wondered if she'd ever go to enough dances to end up as blasé as Judy and Helen appeared to be. She loved everything about their Saturday nights at the Pier, from the thrill of discussing what might or might not happen beforehand, choosing make-up, scent, clothes and getting ready in her bedroom, to the train journey alongside the beach. Even the mundane parts of the evening like paying admission and cloakroom, and checking her hair and make-up in the Ladies, seemed out of the ordinary when she overheard snatches of the other girls' conversations and shared in their hopes and expectations, if only for a second or two.

The climax of the evening for her was always this – actually entering the ballroom. Most girls made a point of holding their heads high and walking slowly to a chair, while studiously ignoring the horde of well-dressed young men in narrow trousers and slicked-back hair crowding around the long bar. Unlike Judy, she thought the embarrassment of stares from that quarter, interspersed with the occasional wolf whistle, infinitely preferable to indifference, and as she continued to stand in front of the door she was reassured to see she was attracting some attention.

She took a deep breath. Before her lay the magic of the evening and the dance floor with its glittering mirror ball that reflected tiny glimpses of the couples below. And presiding from the stage, the MC and band in starched white shirts, bow ties and full evening dress. She closed her eyes as the romantic strains of 'Only You', played in waltz time, permeated the ballroom and considered the possibility that *this* might be the night that she'd meet *him* and maybe even fall in love. Every Saturday evening since Roy and Norah had first allowed her to go out dancing with the girls, she had imagined both of them getting ready at the same time, he in his house, she in hers and, as yet, neither aware of the other. *His* face was hazy but she knew he'd be fair-haired, blue-eyed and good-looking. His suit would be fashionable, Italian cut, maybe mohair with drainpipe trousers. Close up, he'd smell of aftershave – 'like a ponce,' her Uncle Roy would say disparagingly – but she couldn't help it. It was important to her that boys smelled nice when she danced with them. She even wondered if he thought about not *her* exactly, but a girl like her, as he polished his shoes, tied his tie, slipped cuff links into his shirt...

'Lily?'

Startled, she opened her eyes.

'You were miles away,' Judy admonished. 'If you're not careful we'll lose you. Do you want an orange juice?'

'Later.'

'Let's sit down,' Helen suggested.

'Over here.' Judy walked to a table set opposite the door.

'That one would be better.' Helen indicated an empty table in a dark corner.

'No one would see us there, including Adam Jordan when he comes in.' Judy sat down, precluding any argument. 'Katie, you all right?'

'I've got a bit of a headache,' Katie lied.

'I'll see if the cloakroom lady has an aspirin.'

'It's not that bad, Lily. I'll be all right in a minute.' Katie sat next to Judy. Wishing Martin hadn't insisted she go out, she had a sudden overwhelming longing for solitude and the close, stuffy blackness of her sleeping cubicle at home.

'What are those boys laughing at?' Helen demanded indignantly.

Judy stifled a giggle. 'I think you're supposed to sit inside the hoop, if you don't want anyone to see your suspenders and knickers.'

Helen glanced down at her skirt. Cheeks burning, she jumped up. After readjusting the hoop she perched gingerly back on the edge of her chair. The hoop bulged upwards, lifting the edge of the satin bell skirt above her waist. She pushed it down, first one side then the other, only to have it rise even higher in the middle.

'I suppose you think it's funny.' Helen leapt crossly to her feet again.

'Hold still,' Judy commanded.

'So you can play some stupid trick on me.'

'You've got something caught in your zip.' Lily unclipped the rug hook from the tab. 'Oh, no!'

'Oh, no what?'

'This has pulled threads in the back of the dress.'

'Is it bad?'

'You can only see it close up.'

'I wish I'd never seen this damned dress...'

'Language! Don't look now,' Judy whispered, sitting primly upright and affecting a sudden interest in Lily and Katie, 'but Adam Jordan has just walked in with Martin. And who is that?' She stared at Brian, looking away quickly as he gazed intently back at her.

'He would pick this moment.' Helen stood in front of the others. 'Are they looking this way?'

'Yes,' Judy murmured through clenched teeth as she smiled, lifted her hand and waved.

'What did you do that for?' Helen hissed.

'Adam waved at me. I couldn't ignore him, could I?'

Helen couldn't resist glancing over her shoulder. Adam Jordan was even more handsome than she remembered. Tall, slim, dressed in a silver-grey mohair suit with white shirt and red tie, his blond hair shining in the muted light of the ballroom, she felt instinctively that he was the right one for her. All she had to do was convince him of that fact. As he saw her, he smiled. Regaining her confidence, she managed a brief nod of acknowledgement.

'They're coming this way,' Judy muttered, applauding the band's final bars. The few couples on the floor moved towards the perimeter of the room as Adam and Martin joined them, leaving the stranger at the bar.

'Any chance of a welcome home for a war-weary ex-soldier?' Adam asked, mesmerised by the sight of Helen's bosom.

'That depends on the soldier.' Helen flirted outrageously.

'And how war-weary he really is,' Judy added. 'I heard you spent your National Service chasing sheep in Yorkshire.'

'There goes any hope I had of impressing you with stories of my heroics...' The MC's announcement that the band was about to play, 'Rock Around the Clock' drowned out the rest of his sentence.

'Do you jive?'

'Do you?'

'I'm asking for a dance.'

Helen stared in dismay at Adam Jordan offering Judy his hand. As she took it, he led her into the centre of the room. 'Did you see that?' she whispered indignantly into Lily's ear as a tall, thin spotty boy who worked in the café with Katie persuaded her to join him on the dance floor.

'What was Judy supposed to say?'

'"I don't dance but why don't you try my friend,"' would have been better than a lot of cringe-worthy flirting and nonsense about sheep and Yorkshire. She knows I'm crazy about him.'

'Would you like to dance, Lily?'

Lily liked Martin but at that moment she would have been happy to dance with Frankenstein's monster if he'd been prepared to take her out of earshot of Helen. She gave Martin a smile that sent his pulse racing. 'Thank you for asking, I'd love to.'

'Thanks.' Adam took the pint of beer Brian handed him as he returned to the bar after the jive. Moving away from the queue jostling to get the barman's attention, he looked back at the dance floor. 'What did I tell you? Martin and Lily. He can't leave the girl alone.'

'I'm not surprised.'

'You like her too.'

'Who wouldn't, but I've been warned off her once today; I'm not looking to annoy my landlady by trying my luck there again.' Joining Adam, Brian studied the ballroom. It was no better and no worse than a hundred others where he had bought beer and hunted girls since he had turned sixteen and been able to convince barmen he was old enough to drink.

The same badly constructed, multifaceted, glue-spattered, mirrored ball in the centre of the ceiling to reflect dim lighting that almost, but never quite, succeeded in concealing the dinginess of surroundings overdue for a coat of paint. A dance floor scuffed, marked and pitted by stiletto heels. Rows of rickety Formica-topped tables and vinyl-covered chairs, spattered with cigarette burns, packed too closely around the fringes. A creaking band with a saxophonist who thought he could play better than he did and a singer who squeaked out every high note.

Even the girls looked much of a muchness. The younger ones in wide skirts and ponytailed hair posing awkwardly as they waited for boys to pluck up enough courage to ask them to dance, reminded him of the Louis Tussaud waxwork figures in Porthcawl Fair. And when they weren't posing or eyeing boys coyly from beneath their lashes, they were fiddling with their dresses or hair. The older ones, in short curls and tight skirts appeared only slightly more relaxed. He couldn't see anyone worth facing the strain of a first and unnaturally polite conversation – apart from Lily, who had been claimed by Martin, and the redhead Adam had danced with, who was nowhere to be seen.

He found himself wishing for a familiar face and just as quickly pushed the thought from his mind. In two years abroad he'd never been homesick; now less than fifty miles from Pontypridd he was being positively maudlin.

'Nice to hear yourself think again,' Adam commented as the band crashed out the final chord of the second jive of the evening.

'Next one's bound to be slow.'

'Martin's hanging on to Lily but there's two stunning girls sitting over there.'

Brian followed Adam's line of vision. 'I trust you're suggesting I take the one in the red dress, her friend looks like a sheep.'

'If you don't fancy either of those, there's Martin's sister over there.'

'She looks about twelve.'

'She's eighteen and a really nice kid.' Adam's tone revealed more than he'd intended.

'Then why don't you ask her to dance?' Brian suggested.

'Friends' sisters are out of bounds.'

'First I've heard of it. Unless, of course, you have dishonourable intentions.'

85

'She's the kind of girl you court, not mess around with.'

'Ask her to dance, Jordan.'

'You think I should?'

'As you so obviously want to, yes.'

'I might just do that.'

'What about the one you jived with?'

'Judy? She lives in Carlton Terrace too.'

'Anyone's girlfriend?' Brian tried to sound disinterested.

'No one I know anything about. But she's fit.'

'Meaning?'

'Well able to put anyone who steps out of line back in place.'

'Now that's a challenge.'

'I can't see her...'

'Jordan, I don't need anyone to hold my hand. I've been around a dance hall before and I'm quite capable of asking a girl to dance, including the redhead when she reappears.'

'In that case, see you.'

Brian took another long pull at his pint, then realised it was his fourth and it was only nine o'clock. If he didn't slow up he'd be waking with a hangover and that was no way to impress a new landlady. He stood back as the familiar melody of 'Twilight Time' filled the room.

Martin was dancing with Lily but if he was besotted he was showing no signs of it. He was holding her at arm's length and their conversation was too animated to be romantic. Adam hadn't wasted any time in getting Martin's sister out on to the floor. He glanced at the table where Lily and Martin's sister had been sitting in the hope of seeing the redhead again and did a double-take. A girl was sitting alone there, an exceptionally well-endowed blonde judging by the amount of flesh bulging from the top of her dress. And what a dress! She could have escaped from Ladies' night in the officer's mess to slum it with the masses.

'One of those, six of the other,' he murmured to himself, quoting one of his father's favourite phrases. If he'd been moving on and out of Swansea he might have opted for the blonde, but he sensed she was trouble. He looked around again and saw the redhead leaving the other end of the bar with two orange juices. As he watched, she carried them to the table where the blonde was sitting. Almost falling over his feet in his eagerness to get to her, he rushed to their table.

Helen was finding it increasing difficult to sit within the confines of her hooped petticoat, watching her friends dance and smiling insincerely at the room in general without receiving any offers herself. After dancing with Judy, Adam Jordan hadn't left Katie's side – which really hurt. The knowledge that tall, blond dreamboat Adam Jordan preferred small, nondescript Katie to her in all her finery stung more than her pride. To add insult to injury, Martin had claimed Lily the moment he'd spotted her and Judy had found herself a dark, good-looking stranger who evidently knew both Martin and Adam, judging by their exchange of conversation between dances.

'By yourself?'

She made a face. 'Hello, Jack.'

'That's no way to look at a man who's come to ask you to dance.'

She remembered her mother's admonition; 'You stay away from Jack Clay, he's a bad lot' and decided the warning lent him new charm. 'All right.' Careful of her petticoat, she rose to her feet.

'That's some dress. It must have taken hours to sew on those beads.'

'I don't sew.'

'I thought every woman sewed.' He pulled her close and looked down her bodice.

'Not me.' She straightened her arms, pushing him away from her.

'Funny isn't it,' he commented after a few minutes silence. 'You and me, living so close and this is the first time we've danced.'

'Nothing funny about that.' She looked at him, really looked, for the first time. She knew his brother Martin better because he'd been a friend of Joe's before Joe had won a scholarship to grammar school and Martin had been sent to the secondary modern. Jack had the same dark features, black curly hair and eyes as Martin, and was, if anything, more handsome, but there was something hard – dangerous – almost brutal about Jack that was missing in his older brother. She recalled some of the stories she'd heard, that Jack had been toughened but not broken by his two years in Borstal. That since his release he'd done nothing but get into trouble; fights, dodgy business and worse – whatever 'worse' was.

'I could take you home.'

'You could, but I'm going with the girls.'

'On the bus,' he scoffed. 'I'd take you home on my bike.'

'Push bike,' she sneered.

'Motor.'

'Bought it?'

'No, stole it.'

'From the way people talk, I wouldn't put it past you.'

'I earn good money on the building site; I can afford to buy whatever I want. So what do you say?'

'I say no thanks.' Suddenly conscious of his hand on her naked back and his legs pressing against hers, she moved away from him again.

'You all right?'

'Hot.'

'Then why don't we cool down with a drink?' Taking her hand, he led her towards the bar. 'What's it to be?'

She blushed and turned away as the barman studied her cleavage. 'Something long and cool.'

'Gin and tonic and half a bitter.'

She drew him to one side. 'I'm not supposed to drink.'

'You're over age.'

'Just.'

'Then get it down you.' Paying the barman, he handed her the gin. 'Let's find somewhere quiet where we can sit and talk, and I can tell you about my bike.'

'Here is fine.' Helen sat at the nearest table. Judy had returned to their table with the stranger. The orchestra was playing her current favourite, 'Red Sails in the Sunset', Lily was still dancing with Martin, only closer than before; Katie and Adam were behind them. As she watched, Adam moved his head down to Katie's and kissed her on the cheek. Taking the gin and tonic, she emptied the glass in one gulp.

'You were thirsty.'

'Yes, I was,' she replied defiantly.

'I'll get you another.'

'The bar's crowded and they'll be calling last orders soon.'

'I know the barman.'

'In that case, thank you.' She smiled as she looked into his eyes. 'Tell you what, Jack, as you can't take me home, how about we go outside for some fresh air?'

'And when we want to get back in?'

'After another of these, I wouldn't want to come back in.'

He picked up her glass. 'I'll meet you round the corner by the cliff.'

'I'll be waiting.'

'So, Judy Hunt, you like dancing, you come here most Saturdays, you're a trainee hairdresser and you live in Carlton Terrace.'

'I can give you a rundown on my friends as well if you like. It'll save you having to ask them to dance.'

'I'm more interested in you.' Brian gave her the full benefit of his most winning smile.

'So, Brian...'

'Powell.'

'Now you know all about me, what about you?'

90

As Judy looked up at him she wondered how she could have ever thought fair boys more attractive than dark.

'I've come to Swansea to work.'

'As what?'

'Sort of civil servant.'

'What sort?'

'Can I take you home?'

'You don't waste time, do you?'

'I'm new to the area, I need a guide, someone to show me where the locals go and what they do, and you're the prettiest native I've met.'

'I always go home with my friends.'

'I could take them home too.'

'All three of them?'

'Why not?'

'You wouldn't be able to handle them, they're man eaters.'

'Then how about you take me to one of the cinemas next week? My treat, tickets, ice cream, chocolates and fish and chips afterwards?'

'Sounds like I'll be sick.'

'We'll forget the chocolates.'

'I have to work.'

'First I've heard of a hairdresser working nights.'

'I have homework. I study two days a week in college.'

'Two days! If that's all, you can afford to take a couple of hours off.'

'I can't, really.'

'If it will make you feel any safer, I'll get one of my mates to take out one of your friends and we'll make it a foursome.'

'Safer? You're dangerous?'

'You obviously seem to think so judging by the number of hoops you're making me jump through just to get you to go out with me.'

'Something's amusing Judy.' Martin released Lily's hand as the music finished so they could applaud the band. 'Would you like an orange juice?'

'No, thank you.' She glanced at her watch. 'Another five minutes and I'll have to get my coat.'

'Can I take you home?'

'I've arranged to go with the others – Judy, Katie and Helen.'

'I understand.'

'I can't leave them, Martin. I promised my uncle...'

'I said I understand. I'm sorry I haven't been good company. I'm a bit preoccupied. Thinking about my future,' he clarified hastily, not wanting to go into details about his family. 'Leaving the army – job – prospects–'

'I thought they'd kept your job open in the council garage.'

'They have, but I don't want to stay there long-term. After I pass my mechanic's exams I intend to open up my own place. Do repairs, resprays, you know the sort of thing.'

'Not really.'

'I can't believe I'm talking to you about resprays. I'm sorry, I'm boring you.'

'You're not.'

'Then you won't mind if I ask you to come out

with me. Perhaps we could...'

'Lily, there you are.' Joe, Robin at his heels, both resplendent in their dinner jackets strode across the dance floor. 'We've come to pick you up.'

'It *was* a good idea of Larry's to leave the party early.' Robin leered at Lily as he moved in on her.

There was a slur in Robin's speech that rang warning bells. Lily glanced at Martin who stepped back.

'I always go home with the girls on a Saturday, Joe.'

'I wasn't going to leave them here.'

'Your car only seats five and as you have a friend...'

'One of you will have to sit on my lap,' Robin slid his arm round her waist. 'And I think it should be you.'

'This one's spoken for, Robin.' Joe calmly removed his friend's hand.

'Hardly,' Lily asserted forcefully, looking at Martin who refused to meet her gaze.

'Come on, Lily,' Joe broke in impatiently. Compared with Larry's party he was, if not exactly on home territory, on familiar ground, and he intended to press the advantage for all it was worth, especially in front of Robin. 'Let's go,' he ordered abruptly, 'Larry's waiting in the car.'

'If you're giving two people a lift, you really won't have room for us.'

'If the other girls are as small as you we'll have room for lots.' Robin breathed brandy fumes into her face.

'I won't go without the others.' Lily looked

around for Judy, Helen and Katie.

'They'll be along in a minute.'

'I have to get my coat and as Judy and I have the tickets the others won't be able to get theirs without us. Helen's not sitting at our table. Why don't you look for her, Joe, while Judy and I go to the cloakroom? Martin...' She turned but he had already gone.

Drunk, Larry rested his head against the back seat of Joe's car and waited for the world to stop spinning. As it steadied, he glanced towards the cliff. A girl was standing in front of it. A tall girl, with pale-blonde hair, white arms and shoulders in a dress that had no top. Deciding there was only one reason why a girl would stand half-naked outside a ballroom late at night, he dug into his pocket and pulled out a crushed five-pound note he'd extracted from one of his birthday cards. Slowly, cautiously, so as not to send his head spiralling again he fumbled with the door catch. A couple of seconds later he succeeded in opening it. Humming the opening bars of 'I'm in the Mood for Love' he staggered towards his unexpected birthday present.

'All alone, little lady?' His tongue was suddenly too large for his mouth.

'I'm waiting for someone,' Helen countered primly, moving away.

'Me.' He lurched beside her, steadying himself against the cliff. 'And I've arrived.'

'I hardly think so.' Realising he was drunk, she tried to head back to the safety of the ballroom but he slumped over her, effectively imprisoning her between his arms. Bending his head to hers he kissed her full on the mouth.

Nauseated by the reek and taste of stale brandy, salmon and sour cream on his breath she forced her fists up and pushed against his chest with all her strength, but heavier than her he continued to pin her to the cliff wall. Fighting for air, she brought up her knee and dug her stiletto into the toe of his shoe.

As the point hit home, he moved back just enough for her to free one of her hands. 'I'm wearing handmade shoes you bitch!' he bellowed as she hooked her fingers into his hair and wrenched his head away from hers. Slamming her back against the cliff with one hand, he plunged his free hand into her bodice.

Stunned by the blow, the back of her head and neck stinging from the impact of the rock, her cry for help was reduced to a whimper. She began to shake uncontrollably.

Encouraged by her trembling, his fingers closed round her breast. 'Fiver do it?' He tweaked her nipple as he dragged her further into the shadows.

'Let me go,' she begged.

'You want it. Girls like you always do. I have the money. I bet you don't see five pounds from one week to the next.' He delved for the note.

As his hand slid into his pocket, she lashed out again with her foot but he was ready for her. Side stepping to avoid the point of her heel, he made no attempt to stop her toppling backwards. His watch strap caught on the bra cup inside her dress. A resounding tear was accompanied by the ominous rattle of beads falling on to tarmac.

Finally finding her voice she screamed, clutching her torn bodice as the bra cup fell from his wrist.

'You were the one who wanted to play rough.' He stood back as she struggled to her feet. 'Now that's a sight to get a man going.'

Helen glanced down. Her left breast hung exposed above the torn dress. She crossed her arms tightly. 'You ... you beast!' Swinging her right hand back, she slapped him hard across the face.

He caught her hand and held it high while stroking her naked breast with the back of his fingers. 'Very nice.' He waved the note in front of her eyes, 'but service first, payment later. How about another kiss.' Pulling her towards him, he crushed her body with the weight of his, pinning her arms to her waist before kissing her again. As the woollen cloth of his dinner jacket scratched her bare skin she realised the other side of the bodice had fallen to her waist.

Terrified and panic-stricken, the animal instincts of her childhood fights with Joe kicked into play. Sinking her teeth into his cheek, she kneed him in the groin. Recoiling, crying out in pain, he released her wrist. She crossed her arms again and tried to run to the safety of the ballroom.

Anger overriding caution, he followed. Catching her by the waist, he hurled her back against the cliff. 'I want my money's worth...'

Helen opened her mouth and shrieked 'Help' with all the strength and force she could master. Suddenly Jack was in front of her. Dropping the drinks in his hands, he raised his arm and aimed his clenched fist directly at her assailant's jaw.

CHAPTER FIVE

'Lily, there you are.' Ignoring the protests of the other ten-thirty-curfew girls crowding around the cloakroom hatch, Judy bulldozed her way through to her friend. 'Excuse me,' she snapped at a girl with dyed, blue-black hair who deliberately tried to block her progress by elbowing her in the chest.

'And excuse me for living,' the girl bit back tartly.

'I have her ticket,' Judy lied. Pushing two tickets into Lily's hand, she looked around. 'Where's Helen?'

'Last I saw she was with Jack.'

'Jack Clay! Her mother will fry her alive.'

'Not if Joe finds her before she stays with Jack long enough for her mother to hear about it.'

'Joe's here?'

'He came to take us home but he has another boy with him who's been drinking and one waiting in the car.'

'He came to take you and Helen home,' Judy corrected, 'Katie and I are catching the train.'

'With Adam Jordan and Brian Powell?'

'What if we are? And there's no need to look at me like that.'

'I'm not looking at you like anything.'

'Come on Lily, I know you. What's wrong with us going home with Adam and Brian Powell?'

'Nothing.'

'You don't even know Brian.'

'He's our new lodger.'

'And you saw him first, is that what you're saying? God, this is Helen and Adam all over again...'

'It's not Brian,' Lily contradicted firmly, 'It's Helen. We shouldn't have left her by herself in that dress.'

'We didn't tell her to wear it.'

'No, but we didn't stay with her either. I spent all night with Martin. Katie's been with Adam–'

'And what a surprise that was. "Wouldn't say boo" Katie Clay landing the best-looking boy in Carlton Terrace. That's one in the eye for Helen.'

'That's nasty, Judy. Thank you.' Lily took the coats the attendant handed her.

'It's what Helen deserves after the way she carried on tonight, trying to spoil our evening. And seeing as how I danced the first dance with Adam, Helen probably wants to scratch my eyes out along with Katie's. But so what, we're her friends not her keepers.' Judy took the last two coats and fought her way back to the door. 'Is she very angry with us?'

'She wasn't pleased when you danced the first dance with Adam.' Lily made a beeline for Katie who was hovering anxiously in the foyer.

'I can't help it if he preferred to dance with me and before you say another word I'm not as nice as you. There's no way I'd turn down a boy like Adam Jordan because a friend staked first claim. Besides, even if I had refused to dance with him, there's no guarantee he would have asked Helen.

He had the whole of the rest of the evening to dance with her and he didn't leave Katie – not that I saw.'

'You haven't found Helen?'

'No.' Lily handed over the old, navy-blue school mac that Katie had chopped to three-quarter length in a futile attempt to make it look fashionable.

'You girls have to get a move on if we're going to get a seat on the ten-thirty train.' Adam took Katie's coat from her and held it out, ready to help her on with it.

'Joe's looking for Helen. He's offered us a lift in his father's car.' Lily checked her watch, then caught a glimpse of Joe standing with his friend talking to a group of boys at the bar. They obviously hadn't expended much time or energy on the search for Helen.

'I thought you were in a hurry to catch the train, Judy,' Brian prompted as he joined them.

'I am, but we've lost Helen.'

'She can't have gone far in that dress,' Adam commented.

'Perhaps she's in the Ladies and we missed her, Judy...' Lily looked up as a shout echoed in from outside.

'Fight!'

'Look at...' A chorus of wolf whistles drowned out the rest of the cry.

'Why do I think that's something to do with Helen?' Lily tore through the door, closely followed by Judy and Katie.

'Stay back.'

'That's my brother!'

'All the more reason for you to stay back, Clay.' Pushing Martin behind him, Brian slipped off his jacket as he ran towards the cliff face. Fighting his way through the encircling crowd, he thrust his coat at Helen who was cowering, white-faced and shivering, beneath a rocky outcrop. Muttering, 'cover yourself up', he turned to a boy who was standing over another lying on the path in an evening suit. Guessing Martin's brother wouldn't be wearing a dinner jacket, Brian checked his injuries weren't too severe before examining the man on the ground. His face was bloody and he was groaning but his eyes were open and Martin thought he could detect a touch of theatrical display in the agonised cries.

Sensing the one still standing was about to move in again, Brian gripped his arm and held him back. He spotted Adam on the fringe of the crowd and shouted, 'Call the police and an ambulance. The rest of you, on your way,' he ordered, with more authority than he felt.

'Bloody spoilsport!' a boy called from the circle of onlookers.

'Less of that language.'

'Or...'

'He'll arrest you.' Forcing his way through, Roy tipped his helmet back on his head and eyed the boy who'd sworn. 'You're Ned Davies's son, aren't you?' The boy shrank behind his friends. 'Come on, now,' Roy coaxed softly. 'You heard the man. Break it up. You've all got homes and beds to go to, and at this time of night you should be safely tucked up in them.'

There was a moment's hesitation before those on the edge of the crowd began to move away. After that the rest were quick to disperse.

Roy crouched beside Larry. 'You all right, son?'

'Do I look all right!' Larry sat up and spat blood from his mouth. 'My face is a mess, my dinner suit ruined...'

'And your flies open,' Roy stated flatly. 'Your name?'

'Why?' Laurence demanded.

'I'm a police officer, son.'

'Laurence Murton Davies.' Larry hastily fastened the buttons on his trousers before glaring at Jack. 'My father will have you in court for this.'

'We'll see about that, boy. Either of you care to tell me what happened?' Roy looked past Jack to where Helen, now wrapped in her own coat, was sobbing on Lily's shoulder. There was something pathetic and ridiculous in the sight of the tall, well-built girl being supported by the diminutive Lily, but Roy didn't laugh.

'He' – Jack pointed at Laurence – 'attacked the girl I was with.'

'That right, Helen?' Roy asked.

Helen's cries grew louder and more incoherent.

'Either of you see anything?' Roy looked from Brian to Martin.

'We heard people shouting after the barman called last orders. I came out and saw these two fighting. The girl's dress was already torn,' Brian answered.

'So you were too late to see exactly what happened.'

'It's bloody obvious,' Jack broke in angrily, picking up the remains of Helen's dress from beneath the cliff face. 'Look at this. He ripped it off her...'

'All I did was kiss her and she was willing enough.' Staggering to his feet, Laurence reeled and vomited on the path.

'Steady, boy.' Roy helped him on to a low wall. 'You're best sitting down.'

'I was ready to pay her.' Laurence opened his hand; the crumpled five-pound note lay in his palm.

'You filthy, swine!' Jack dived towards Laurence but Brian was quicker. Blocking his path, he held him firmly in his grip.

'Jack, please,' Roy murmured in his hypnotically smooth voice. 'You're in enough trouble as it is, without courting more. Helen?' Reaching out, he patted her shoulder. 'What have you got to say about this?'

Shrinking from Roy's touch, grasping Lily as though her life depended on maintaining her hold, Helen's cries escalated into hysteria.

'We have to get her home, Uncle Roy,' Lily pleaded as Judy and Katie helped her support Helen.

'The ten-thirty train has gone,' Adam announced, sticking close to Katie.

'My mother'll kill me.'

Roy waved as an ambulance came clanging down the path. 'Not when I explain, Judy.' He gazed in exasperation at the new crowd forming around them. 'Brian, see Mr Laurence Murton Davies into the ambulance. You too, Helen.'

'No! Not with him. I won't go anywhere with him!' Helen dived back, dragging Lily with her.

'What you got, Roy?' the ambulance man asked as he climbed out of his cab.

'Possible concussion, hysterical girl who may have been attacked.'

The man looked from Laurence to Helen. 'As they're conscious we'll take them both.'

'Girl won't go into the ambulance with him.'

'Then it has to be the concussion. Sorry, Miss,' the man apologised to Helen. He drew Roy out of earshot. 'She'll be seen quicker if you get her to the station and send for the police doctor. It's chaos in Casualty. We've got over twenty injuries stacked up from a fight in the Dockers Club.'

Roy removed his helmet and scratched his bald head thoughtfully. 'Brian, go into the Pier. Warn the manager we'll need to borrow his office and their storeroom for a few minutes, then phone the station and ask them to send a man to the hospital to look after Mr Laurence Murton Davies, and a car and a Black Maria here. Martin, you stay with your brother. We'll sort this out in town. Joe, how nice to see you.' He greeted Joe expansively as, oblivious to the fight and his sister's plight, Joe strolled towards his car with Robin. 'Why don't you come back to the Pier with the girls and me? It looks like your sister could do with a stronger shoulder than Lily's to cry on and given the circumstances I think yours might be the most suitable.'

'You didn't say you'd become a copper,' Martin reproached as he returned to the office after telling Adam he wouldn't make it back to his place.

'You didn't ask.' Brian replaced the receiver on the telephone in the manager's office.

Jack was sitting quietly, but Brian noticed that he looked towards the door every few seconds. 'I'm going to clean myself up.'

'You're not going anywhere,' Brian warned as Jack left his chair.

'I'm a mess.' Jack fingered his blood-spattered shirt and jacket.

'You are, but those bloodstains are evidence.'

'I need a slash.'

'Then I'll go with you.'

'I don't need a bloody nursemaid.'

'You do, while you're involved in a possible criminal case.'

'That's right; hang me, just because I threw a punch at a rich bastard in a monkey suit. Never mind that he deserved it.'

'No one's accusing anyone of anything, Jack.'

'Yet,' Jack sneered.

'I'll go with him,' Martin offered.

'No...'

'What's the matter, Brian?' Martin enquired acidly. 'Don't you trust me?'

'I trust you.' Emulating Roy's relaxed attitude in the hope that it would diffuse the tension between him and the Clays, as it had done between Roy and the crowd outside, Brian perched on the edge of the manager's desk. 'But you have to realise it could go hard with Jack if he doesn't put his side of things sooner rather than later, and the mess on his face and clothes is part of that. It might help prove that he took sufficient share of the punishment to plead self-defence, should the other party accuse him of unprovoked assault.'

'I didn't take much punishment but I gave plenty,' Jack boasted. 'This' – he fingered his bloodstained shirt – 'Is crache blood.'

'Talk like that won't help, Jack,' Martin warned.

'It won't make any difference either, no one will listen to me.'

'I'm listening.'

'A copper listening to a Clay who's been to Borstal? That's a first,' Jack mocked.

'Even if I didn't respect your brother, it's my job to get to the truth of what happened out there. Still want to pee?'

'I can wait.' Jack leaned against the wall.

'Want to tell me what happened?'

'You really want to know?'

'I wouldn't have asked if I didn't.'

'Helen suggested we went outside.'

'Helen – that's the girl with the dress?'

'Without one,' Martin interposed drily.

'We were dancing; she was hot. I bought her a drink.'

'What kind of drink?'

'Gin and tonic – two of them but she didn't drink one. I dropped it when I clocked that bastard.'

'Christ, Jack, she's under age,' Martin interrupted angrily. 'And if she drank you must have...'

'She's eighteen, I checked, and I only had a couple of beers.' Jack turned on his brother.

'That's not the point. Think how it looks, gin and tonic...'

'Only one.'

'I've seen you with a couple of beers inside you.'

'Not since I was fifteen and I've learned how to take it since then.'

'You had one drink, Helen suggested you went outside, then what?' Brian pressed, breaking up the argument.

'She went ahead while I went to the bar to get more drinks.'

'They let you take glasses outside in this place?'

'No, but I know the barman. Why?'

'Because broken glass can be classed as an offensive weapon. You sure you didn't use them on Murton Davies?'

'I told you, I dropped them when I saw Helen trying to fight him off.' Jack's voice hardened. 'And after I dropped them, I thumped him. I suppose you'll tell me now that I have to pay for the glasses.'

'You're sure she was the one who suggested you went outside.'

'It was her idea.'

'You didn't see her talk to that man in the dance hall?'

'You were there. How many blokes did you see in dinner jackets?'

'Two.'

'One was Joe Griffiths, Helen's brother,' Martin explained.

'But the man you hit wasn't in the ballroom?'

'Not that I saw.' Jack met Brian's steady gaze.

'And this Helen you were with didn't know him?'

'All I can tell you is when I went outside his flies were open and he was trying to get on top of her. She was screaming her head off. There wasn't time for introductions, even if she did know him.'

'And her dress?'

'How many times do I have to say it? The bloke I clobbered tore it off her.'

'You saw him tear it?' Brian persisted.

'Yes.'

'Then it looks like a clear case of Sir Galahad to the rescue.'

'What's the betting no one else will see it that way when a Clay's playing Sir Galahad?' Jack retorted acidly.

'Any of you girls see what happened?' Roy asked as he escorted them into the storeroom.

'They were with her, they must have...'

'You'll get your chance to talk later, Joe.' Roy pointed to a couple of chairs outside the door. 'But for now, you and your friend sit and behave like good boys until the Black Maria arrives.'

'I've nothing to do with any of this, I didn't see a thing so I may as well leave you to it,' Robin slurred, backing towards the door.

'And you are?' Roy rested his hand on Robin's shoulder as he squinted at the piece of paper Brian had handed him after seeing Laurence Murton Davies into the ambulance.

'Robin Watkin Morgan.'

'Robin Watkin Morgan, do you know Laurence Murton Davies?'

'I wouldn't say know,' Robin hedged. 'Joe just

happened to be giving both of us a lift, that's all.'

'Where to?'

'Pardon?' Robin looked at him blankly.

'You said Joe was giving you a lift. Where was he taking you?' Roy glanced into the storeroom before closing the door on the girls.

'Home.'

'Which is?'

'Gower Road. My father is Dr Watkin Morgan. You must have heard of him, Constable?'

'I have.' Roy set his mouth into a thin hard line. The one thing guaranteed to set his teeth on edge was people trying to intimidate or curry favour with the police by using their position or influence. It annoyed him even more when it wasn't their own position or name they used and he knew the senior police surgeon, Dr Watkin Morgan, well enough to suspect that he wouldn't be pleased at the thought of his son cavorting down the Pier, drunk. 'And Laurence Murton Davies?'

'What about him?'

'Is he staying with you?'

'No.'

'Then where were you taking him?' Roy looked at Joe.

'He came along for the ride. It's his twenty-first, he'd had one too many...'

'Then he was drunk?'

'Not exactly.'

'Let's get this straight, Joe, he was in your car. You were giving Robin a lift home and Laurence Murton Davies had come along for the ride, although in your words "he'd had one too many"?'

'That's about right,' Joe agreed sheepishly, realising his explanation sounded ridiculous.

'So you intended to drive Laurence Murton Davies home afterwards?'

'I hadn't thought that far.'

'Then do some thinking now,' Roy advised harshly, 'because that's your sister in there. And in case you hadn't noticed, she's in a bit of a state. From initial appearances it appears to me that your friend Laurence has had something to do with that.'

'It can't be Larry. It has to be Jack Clay. Everyone knows what he is.'

'Constable, as I said, I'm nothing to do with this so if I can get a taxi...'

'You can get one from the station, Mr Watkin Morgan. There are one or two points I'm not clear on and you may be just the person to set me straight.' Walking into the storeroom Roy closed the door behind him.

'We'd just got our coats when we heard the row outside, Uncle Roy.' Lily's arms were round Helen who was sitting with her face buried in her hands.

'We only got there a minute or so before you, Mr Williams,' Judy chipped in.

'Helen?' Exasperated by the silence that greeted his question, Roy turned to Katie. 'Did you see anything?'

'I saw Helen talking to Jack in the ballroom,' she ventured courageously, shocked by the blood on Jack's clothes and Larry's assertion that her brother had attacked him. She knew better than

109

anyone how wild Jack could be, but she refused to believe him capable of assaulting anyone – even crache in a dinner suit – for no reason.

'And Helen wasn't upset then.'

'She was smiling.'

'Did any of you girls see Helen leave the dance hall?'

They looked at one another.

'No,' Judy answered, 'but I saw Jack standing at the bar by himself when I went to get my coat.'

'Which was how long before you went outside?'

Judy looked at Lily. 'A couple of minutes.'

'About five,' Lily concurred.

The manager stuck his head round the door. 'The Black Maria and car are here.'

Roy ushered the girls through the door and into the back of the car. After asking the officer driving the car to wait, he saw Joe, Robin, Jack and Martin into the Black Maria with Brian.

'You not coming with us, Roy?' the driver of the Black Maria asked.

'No, I'll bring the girl to the station as soon as I've seen the others home. Tell the sergeant I'll be right behind you.'

'If anyone should go with Helen, it should be me,' Joe muttered mutinously.

'I'll look after her, Joe.' Whether Roy had intended to sound critical or not, Joe took his words to mean 'better than you.'

'We're not going to the police station are we, Mr Williams?' Katie asked in a small voice as they sped down Mumbles Road towards Swansea.

Roy turned from the front passenger seat and

smiled. 'No, love, I'll drop you home but you and Lily may have to make statements tomorrow.'

'Statements...'

'It's nothing to worry about. You just tell me what you saw.'

'I didn't see anything that happened outside.'

'But you did see what happened inside. It will be all right,' Roy reassured, 'You can make the statement in our house and your Mam can be there.'

'My mother will have a fit at the sight of me coming home in a police car.'

'I'll explain Judy.'

'What about me?' Helen gasped hoarsely between sobs.

'I'm sorry, Helen, but you're going to have to come down to the station with me so we can sort out what happened back there.'

'My father will kill me.'

'Oh, I doubt he'll do that, love,' Roy reassured.

'Leastwise, not until you've paid for that dress,' Judy whispered in Helen's ear as Roy turned back to give the driver directions.

'We're well ahead of the time it would have taken you to walk from the train stop,' Roy murmured as they turned the corner into Carlton Terrace. 'Right, as yours is the first house, Judy, I'll see you inside.'

Lily squeezed Helen's hand in an attempt to comfort her as her uncle walked Judy to her front door. He was inside only a few minutes.

'Is Judy's mother angry?' she asked as he returned.

'No, love, none of this is your fault. You next, Katie.'

Shaking, Katie crept out of the car and followed him down the steps to her basement.

'Got your key, love?'

'Isn't it in the door, Mr Williams?'

'It is. Bad practice that, anyone could walk in.' Knocking loudly, he turned the key and stepped down into the kitchen. Annie was hunched over the table.

'Annie?' He blanched as she turned her face to him. It was a raw mass of bloody, beaten flesh, her blood-flecked eyes sunk so deeply into the swollen tissue above her cheekbones he doubted she could see.

'I – I – fell over, Roy,' she mumbled thickly. 'Hit the sink...'

Walking over to her, he wrapped his arm round her shoulders. She cried out and he saw her right arm hanging purple and limp from her shoulder. 'Come on, love, I'll take you to our house.'

'I can't – the boys – Ernie–' She didn't even ask what he was doing bringing Katie home.

'Katie, pack whatever you and your mam need for the night. You're spending it in our house. Go on, love,' he prompted when she hesitated.

'Dad...' She didn't need to say any more.

'I'll check.' Roy walked to the door that led to the passage.

'He's out,' Annie whispered thickly. 'He woke up and went out. We thought he'd sleep through the night but he didn't ... and I fell over...'

'I know, Annie. You don't have to tell me how clumsy you are. I've seen it since the day you moved into the street.' Helping her out of the chair, he scooped her into his arms as she fainted.

'When the ambulance comes you'll go with Annie, Norah?'

'If I do that, Roy, who's going to stay with the girls?'

'They're sensible enough. They proved that tonight.'

'But Ernie...'

'I'll alert the patrols to keep an eye on the place. It might be as well if you warn Lily to keep the door locked and bolted, and at the first sight or sound of Ernie to ring 999, but I doubt he'll come here, not to a policeman's house after what he's done.'

'And Brian?'

'Remind Lily to ask who's there before opening the door.'

'Roy...'

'Sorry, Norah, I've got to get to the Griffithses. They'll want to come down to the station.'

'That Helen Griffiths,' Norah began heatedly, 'she's nothing but trouble. I'll not have our Lily...'

'We'll talk about it in the morning, love. Lily and Katie have had enough to cope with for one night. And ring the station before you leave the hospital. I'll get a car to pick you up and bring you back here.' Roy stepped over the low wall that separated the Griffiths' house from theirs and rang the doorbell. He rang it three times before giving up and returning to the car.

'Do you know where your mam and dad are?'

he asked Helen.

Her sobs had subsided since the other girls had left the car and he couldn't help thinking that her tears had been more for the benefit of her audience than any injury or shock she'd sustained. 'Mam's in the theatre. Dad's at some old boy thing.'

'Dynevor School?'

'I think so.' She began to cry again at the prospect of seeing her father.

'That's being held in the Mackworth Hotel,' the driver said.

'We'll telephone from the station.' Roy recalled some of the rumours he'd heard about Esme Griffiths as he climbed into the front passenger seat of the car. If they were to be believed she spent more time in Swansea Little Theatre than she did with her family. The evening's events had rather borne that out. No mother worthy of the name would have allowed her daughter to go to the Pier in a dress like the one Helen had been wearing. Little wonder the girl was running wild and attracting the wrong kind of attention.

He glanced back at Helen, hunched and miserable on the back seat of the car, and felt an unexpected pang of pity. He'd have a few words with John and Esme Griffiths when they came down to the station. What was the point of having money enough to give your children everything they wanted if you didn't take the time and trouble to guide them on the right path?

'Tell us exactly what happened,' the sergeant barked.

Helen began to cry again, this time softly and quietly.

'The truth.' The sergeant looked from the girl to Roy. He was aware he sounded harsh and intimidating but he wasn't used to questioning young girls. Signalling to Roy to step outside, he closed the door and glanced up and down the corridor to make sure they couldn't be overheard. 'Do you think she was raped, Williams?'

'No, sir. But only because there wasn't time. The girl's dress had been ripped off her and Murton Davies's flies were open when I got there. In my book that makes his intentions obvious. Young Clay told Powell the girl was struggling with Murton Davies when he left the ballroom with the drinks. He also says he saw Murton Davies rip her dress, which suggests Murton Davies had just attacked her.'

'I phoned the hospital.'

'Is Murton Davies all right?'

'Oh, yes. Minor bruises and contusions. He's also drunk as a lord but then he might as well be one. You have heard of the Murton Davieses?'

'Yes, sir,' Roy answered carefully.

'His father's already been on the line screaming for his son's attacker's blood.'

'And the girl his son tried to rape?'

'I'd be very careful who you relate that version of events to, Constable Williams.'

'His friends admit he was drunk. The girl was screaming and trying to fight him off. Clay saw him tear the girl's dress. His flies were open. How much more evidence do we need?'

'Murton Davies's solicitor is at the hospital.

From the boy's version of events, it appears he and the girl got a little over-amorous, the girl's dress got caught on his watchstrap and he accidentally ripped it.'

'You believe that, sir?'

'I believe in youth and high spirits, and a girl crying rape when she thinks she's about to be exposed as a tart. We'll have to wait for the doctor's report, but there appears to be no real damage done to the girl that I can see, and you know the Murton Davieses. The father's Grand Master this year. He can call on some pretty strong connections.'

'That doesn't alter the facts of the case, sir.' Roy knew damned well it did, but he wasn't going to stand by while Jack Clay's and Helen Griffiths's more likely version of events were swept aside without a single protest.

'You know how difficult it is to prove these cases one way or another. Between you and me, if the boy did tear her dress deliberately she would have got no more than she deserved,' the sergeant pronounced caustically. 'Parading down the Pier half naked on a Saturday night. Her dress might be in shreds, but by all accounts there wasn't enough to cover the bits that mattered before it was ripped off her. Has she said anything to you about why she left the ballroom?'

'Not to me, Sergeant, but Jack Clay mentioned she was hot...'

'I bet she was. The Murton Davieses' solicitor suggested she's a professional streetwalker.'

'She's barely eighteen.'

'We've picked up younger.'

'I know the girl and her family. They live next door to us.'

'In Carlton Terrace?'

'That's where I live, sir.' Roy tried not to let his exasperation show. He knew what the sergeant was thinking. No family in Carlton Terrace could possibly rank as consequential in the scheme of Swansea politics or importance as the Murton Davieses.

'The solicitor also suggested that both the girl and the boy who attacked Murton Davies had been drinking. He said something about smashing glasses over his client.'

'It appears the girl had one gin and tonic, sir. The boy she was with, Jack Clay, brought out a second and dropped the glass when he went to help her fight off Murton Davies.'

'Allegedly fight off, Constable. And as he admits he bought her two gin and tonics even if we can't prove the streetwalker charge, we may get her on drunk and disorderly.'

'You want me to charge her, sir?'

The sergeant bristled at the disapproval in Roy's voice. 'Not yet, but we'll keep it in mind. I think the best thing we can do from everyone's point of view is sweep the whole thing under the carpet. I can't see the Murton Davieses wanting a scandal any more than the girl's parents or the lad who attacked him. What's his name?'

'Clay, Jack Clay, sir.'

'Sounds familiar.'

'It should.'

'There we have it. A wild one, eh.' The sergeant

stood back and thought for a moment. 'There's no doubt she arranged to meet this Clay outside?'

'She hasn't said, but witnesses inside the ballroom corroborate Jack Clay's story, so it seems likely, sir.'

'That puts a whole new complexion on things. In my experience couples only leave a ballroom to do the one thing they can't do inside. It could be she is a professional after all. Arranged to meet one chap, then another comes along, smarter, wearing a dinner jacket, more money in his pocket...'

'I don't think either her or Clay had more than a couple of kisses in mind, sir. That path's too public. Not the sort of place a professional would choose a few minutes before closing time when the entire area is about to be flooded with people leaving the Pier to catch the ten-thirty train back to Swansea.'

'Sarge?' a young constable opened the door that led to the public desk. 'Miss Griffiths's father is here.'

'Doctor here yet?'

'On his way, Sarge.'

'Send him in as soon as he gets here.'

'And Mr Griffiths?'

'Better tell him to come in.'

CHAPTER SIX

'What happened, Roy?' White-faced, John Griffiths didn't even see the sergeant as he rushed through the door. 'Is it one of the children ... Esme...'

At a nod from the sergeant, Roy beckoned John towards an interview room further down the corridor. 'Come in here, John, and I'll explain.' Roy opened the door on a cubicle that stank of cheap disinfectant mixed with other odours that didn't bear thinking about. Deliberately slowing his pace to accommodate John, Roy still had to wait for him after pulling two upright utility chairs from under a steel table.

'Please, who is it?'

Roy waited for John to sit, then took the chair opposite. 'There was a fracas down the Pier. Helen's dress was ripped. Two boys had a bit of a punch-up, probably over her but it looks like neither she nor them are hurt – not seriously,' he amended, remembering the blood on Larry's face and Jack's suit. 'But one of the boys has been taken to hospital and we've sent for the doctor to check out Helen and the other one to be on the safe side.'

'If Helen's hurt or upset, Esme should be here.'

'Do you know where she is?'

'The theatre.'

'We sent someone down there; it's locked.'

'There's probably an end-of-run party. Her cousin, Dot – Dorothy Ellis who lives above her hat shop in Eversley Road – generally organises them.'

'I know the place, we'll send a car.' Roy looked up as Brian knocked and opened the door. 'You still here, boy?'

'Just keeping Martin company. The sergeant asked me to tell you the doctor's here and he wants him to examine Helen first.'

'We're on our way.' Roy rose from his seat.

'Martin? Martin Clay's involved in this?'

'Only as a witness to the fight,' Roy replied. 'Helen's next door. If anyone can sort out this mess, she can. You go ahead, I'll see to that car.'

Helen was sitting, shivering, on a chair wrapped in her coat and a blanket.

'Helen?'

She burst into yet another paroxysm of noisy tears as her father walked into the room.

'What happened, love?' John sat on the chair beside hers.

Embarrassed, ashamed and more upset by her father's solicitude than she would have been by his anger, she plucked at the stitching that hemmed the grey blanket, shredding it.

'The boy your daughter was with insists she was attacked, Mr Griffiths,' the sergeant answered for her.

'Were you?' John asked, horrified.

'It was horrible,' Helen wailed.

'There's only one way to settle this, Mr Griffiths, and that's a full medical examination. We'd 'appreciate your consent.' The sergeant handed him a form and a pen.

'Is that really necessary?' John glanced across at a screen in the corner and saw a man place a doctor's bag on a couch behind it.

'Given the hysterical condition of your daughter and her inability to answer the simplest of questions an examination is our only recourse,' the sergeant replied resolutely. 'It may provide us with the evidence we need to proceed if she has been attacked, and medical attention should she require it.'

Helen hid her face in her hands again, rather than meet her father's questioning gaze.

'The form, sir.'

John attempted to read the paper the sergeant had given him. The words wavered on the page.

'You sign there, sir.' The sergeant indicated a line.

John looked at Helen again. 'Helen?'

As her sobbing escalated the sergeant broke in, 'Believe me, sir, we've tried everything to get through to her.'

John glanced from the sergeant back to his daughter. After a few interminable seconds he scribbled his signature. 'You'll wait for her mother to get here.'

The door opened and Roy entered the room.

'You've tracked down Mrs Griffiths, Constable Williams?'

'I'm afraid not, sir.' Roy couldn't bring himself to meet John's eye. 'She wasn't in Eversley Road.'

'Dot...' John began.

'The shop and the flat above it were locked.'

'Then she must be home.'

'They tried there on the way back, there's no one at your house.'

'In that case you won't mind if we go ahead with the examination, seeing as how we have your permission, sir. The sooner it's over the sooner we can take whatever measures are necessary.' The sergeant's tone brooked no argument.

'Come on, John, I'll find us a cup of tea,' Roy guided him out of the room. 'And then you can talk to Joe.'

'Joe's here?'

'He was in the Pier when it happened but he's fine. You can see for yourself.'

'You have a woman officer on duty?' the doctor asked the sergeant, as Roy closed the door.

'Not at this time of night but I've seen the procedure often enough.'

'Right, young lady.' The doctor turned to Helen. 'Behind the screen, remove all your clothes and lie on the couch.'

The next ten minutes were the most humiliating and embarrassing Helen had ever experienced. As she lay on the examination couch, eyes tightly closed but not enough to stop the tears trickling down her cheeks, the doctor poked and prodded her body as though she were a specimen on a slab. And the whole time he examined her he talked to the sergeant over his shoulder – about the weather, the prevalence of drink-related fights at the weekend and, the ultimate mortification, her.

'There's a scratch on her right breast. Do you want a photograph?'

'Might as well.' The sergeant's voice, brusque, deeper than the doctor's, fell harshly on her ears as he leaned over the couch to view the mark. Helen cringed as the coarse material of his uniform trousers brushed against her bare legs. 'Could that have been made by a watch strap?'

'Possibly. It's not deep.'

Helen winced as the doctor ran his hands over her right breast and pressed down.

'Does that hurt?'

'Not really,' she whispered.

'Her knickers and suspender belt are intact but her stockings are in shreds.' The sergeant's pen scratched over his notebook.

'Right, young lady, you can dress.'

Realising the doctor was no longer touching her, Helen opened her eyes. The doctor had moved to a sink in the corner, where he was washing his hands.

'Just your knickers,' the sergeant qualified as he went to the table to get a camera. 'I need to photograph that breast.'

That breast, not *your breast.* The sergeant's dismissive tone stung as Helen turned her back and scrambled into her knickers under cover of the blanket.

'No doubt about it, a virgin,' the doctor murmured but not too low for Helen to hear as the sergeant focused the camera and waited for the flash to charge.

'You surprise me. Sit on the couch and drop the blanket to your waist.' The sergeant clicked the shutter.

'And apart from the scratch, not a mark on her. Your desk sergeant said something about a boy.'

'He has cuts and bruises. He's down the corridor.'

'I'll find it.' The doctor glanced at Helen as the sergeant took a second photograph. 'If you were my daughter you wouldn't sit down for a week. You had a lucky escape tonight, young lady. Go out in a dress like that again and you might not be so fortunate. One of the constables said you come from a respectable family. They won't be regarded as quite so respectable if they have to visit you in an unmarried mothers' home.'

'He's right,' the sergeant added. 'Put your coat on. I'll get your father back in here and then perhaps you'll finally tell us the truth.'

Roy paused as he walked behind the reception desk. Following the duty sergeant's orders, officers were still interviewing Jack Clay to see if he would change his story to bring it more in line with the one telephoned in by Larry Murton Davies's solicitor. After hearing both, he doubted it was going to happen. 'Still no sign of Mrs Griffiths?' he asked the duty constable.

'The patrols have checked out both the addresses you gave us twice, Roy. If you've any other suggestions I'll get the boys to call.'

'When can I take my brother home?'

Roy looked across to see Martin sitting next to Brian in the public area. 'When our enquiries are complete, Martin.'

'All he was doing was defending Helen.'

124

'Doctor's examining her now. We'll know more when he's finished. Why don't you go home.'

'I'm not going anywhere without Jack.'

'Powell, you're off duty.'

'No harm in sitting with a friend; besides, I'm a potential witness.'

Roy decided it wasn't the time or place to tell the boy he wasn't doing himself any favours with the brass by sitting with the brother of a suspected felon. Leaving them, he returned to the corridor. The sergeant was showing John into the examination room. Roy caught a glimpse of Helen sitting hunched in her coat. The sergeant closed the door on John and joined Roy.

'I'd appreciate it if you sit in on this one, Constable Williams.'

'I know the family, sir.'

'That's why I want you in there. Tell me, off the record, what do you think happened?'

Roy took his time over answering. The sergeant didn't hurry him; Roy habitually thought out every word before he opened his mouth, which was exactly why so many officers sought his opinion – and advice – but this time Roy knew he was being used to find holes in Murton Davies's solicitor's argument.

'Jack Clay's a wide boy, sir, but I can't see him going near crache in a dinner jacket let alone attacking one unless he, or someone he knew, was being threatened.'

'Then you don't think Clay attacked this girl and Murton Davies came to the rescue?'

'Is that what the Murton Davies's solicitor is saying now?'

'Clay agrees he arranged to meet the girl outside the ballroom. He could have got carried away.'

Roy shook his head. 'He didn't have time to do more than take the drinks outside and jump on Murton Davies. It's obvious, sir, he was protecting the girl. Besides, a good-looking boy like Clay doesn't have trouble getting girls to go out with him. And every rapist I've come across avoids public places. Jack Clay would know that most youngsters leaving the Pier choose to walk past that cliff face rather than take the steep climb to the top of Limeslade. And the bar in the Pier was already closing as he left. Jack would have realised he had only a few minutes at best before the crowds followed. But it's my guess Murton Davies doesn't mix with the kind of youngsters who go down the Pier so he wouldn't know any of those things.'

'Did you know it was Murton Davies's birthday?'

'Someone did mention it, sir.'

'Young lad like that high-spirited, a few drinks, if the girl led him on...'

'Everyone's agreed she was in the ballroom and he wasn't. So there's little chance of her leading him on, sir.'

'Unless she did her leading on outside. But when we get down to it, it's no more than Jack Clay's and the girl's word against Murton Davies.'

'Was she raped, sir?'

'She's a virgin, so you're right about her not being a professional. The only mark on her is a scratch on her breast, which was more than likely caused by the watch strap.'

'Then we've a case against Murton Davies.'

'His solicitor has agreed to drop the assault charge against Clay if we drop all charges against his client.'

'And you're happy with that, sir?'

'I think it's best. The one thing Murton Davies and Clay agree on is Clay threw the first punch so it will be as well if Clay and the girl forgo any idea of counter charges.' He looked at Roy. 'You'll persuade them, Williams?'

'And there you have it, Mr Griffiths. The doctor made a thorough examination. Your daughter is a virgin, which rules out the possibility that she was raped. He also confirmed she is unhurt apart from a slight scratch on her breast which was most likely made by the watch strap of the young man she was with.'

For Helen, the word 'virgin' was the final straw after the indignity of the medical examination. She burst into tears again.

'All we are left with is the possibility that your daughter was subjected to an indecent assault.' The sergeant took a deep breath before facing Helen. 'Miss Griffiths, were you assaulted tonight?'

Helen's sobs grew louder.

'Is that a "yes" or a "no" Miss Griffiths?' The sergeant drummed his fingers on the table. 'As you see, Mr Griffiths, it was your daughter's inability to answer simple questions coupled with the circumstantial evidence that led me to believe a medical examination necessary.'

'Circumstantial evidence?' John repeated in bewilderment.

'I wouldn't have allowed a child of mine to go out in public wearing a dress like that.'

'I didn't mean to...'

'What dress, Helen?'

Roy picked up the torn dress from the examination couch and handed it to John. The ruined bodice flopped down over the skirt.

Recognising it as part of the warehouse's new and expensive winter collection, John rose to his feet. 'You took this from the warehouse? Did you?' he repeated softly when Helen refused to answer.

Staring down at the floor she nodded wretchedly.

'And how did the bodice get torn?'

'That horrible boy attacked me,' she whimpered, struggling to control herself.

'Who... ? What boy? My God...'

Roy motioned John back into the chair. 'Helen, don't you think it's time you told us what happened?'

'That boy attacked me and Jack.'

'Jack Clay!' John's face darkened in rage.

'I'm going to be sick.'

Quicker than the sergeant, Roy picked up the bin and thrust it under Helen's mouth, just in time.

'So that's it; you keep me here half the night, then you say I can go?' Jack's voice rose precariously as he confronted the sergeant.

'You should thank your lucky stars that Mr Murton Davies isn't pressing charges. Well-respected family the Murton Davieses.'

'And mine isn't?'

'Come on, Jack.' Martin took his arm. 'Time to go.'

'He's right.' Brian laid his hand on Jack's shoulder.

'Martin?' Roy stopped him, as they were about to walk through the door.

'Now what?' Jack demanded.

'Jack, please,' Martin pleaded wearily. 'Go on with Brian, I'll catch you up.'

Roy waited until he and Martin were alone in the passageway. 'When I dropped Katie off I found your mother in a bit of a state.'

'What kind of a state?' Martin didn't know why he was asking. He already knew.

'She said something about your father coming round and her falling against the sink.'

Martin closed his eyes tightly. 'I should never have left her.'

'You can't be with her twenty-four hours a day, boy. Norah has taken her to hospital. Katie was upset by seeing your mother hurt and all this nonsense so I thought it best she spend the night with Lily in our house.'

'I'll go to the hospital.'

'They won't let you visit at this time of night. Chances are, they'll have kept your mother in, but if they haven't, Norah will have made up a bed for her. Best to leave seeing her until the morning.'

'Thank you, Mr Williams.'

'Go carefully,' Roy warned as Martin stepped through the door into the chill early-morning air. Martin knew he wasn't warning him about what he might meet in the street.

'Up to bed, both of you,' John ordered bleakly as he opened the front door.

'Dad...'

'Bed, Joe, I'm in no mood for talking this out now.'

Helen needed no second bidding. Clutching her coat close to her, she ran upstairs. Joe hesitated for a moment, then followed.

John dropped the brown-paper carrier bag that held the ruined dress and closed the front door. He glanced at his watch. Two o'clock and his wife's camel-hair coat still wasn't on its hanger on the hallstand. Somehow it was easier not to question the late hours Esme kept when he could pretend to be asleep in his attic bedroom.

Unfastening the buttons on his lightweight Burberry he tossed it over the newel post at the foot of the stairs and limped into the parlour. He winced as he switched on the lights. Esme had recently redecorated 'contemporary' style and he loathed it.

The house had been his grandparents'. He had moved in with them after his parents' early death and hadn't realised how much he loved the place until Esme had used the easing of postwar rationing restrictions as an excuse to introduce the latest decor and replace the oversized, solid Victorian furniture with spindle-legged, flimsy fashionable pieces. Perhaps it had been as well that both his grandparents had died before he had married so they hadn't witnessed his wife's modernisation of their home.

Refusing to make any concessions to the age or style of the house, Esme had called in a carpenter to board over the doors. Acid-etched and stained-glass panels had disappeared beneath sheets of hardboard nailed to within an inch of the door edge and framed with beading. The carved banisters on the stairs had suffered a similar fate. Then all the woodwork had been painted to 'complement' the new multi-primary colour schemes, although he failed to see how bright-orange and red skirting boards comple-mented anything.

The parlour, now renamed 'lounge' had under-gone the most radical change. It had been on the gloomy side with nets, Rexene-upholstered three-piece suite and a massive chenille-covered table, but it had also been a haven of tranquillity. Now, even the iron-framed and tiled grate he had once toasted bread in had been torn out, replaced by a recessed square set a foot above the floor to house an ugly gas fire. The lino was crimson, the nylon carpet square, green and purple intersected by black lines 'Picasso style', and the back-aching three-piece suite upholst-ered in an itchy grey and black nylon tweed that picked at the skin around his fingernails.

And it wasn't as though he could sit anywhere other than this newly decorated 'lounge'. The dining room had suffered the same indignity, the walls painted purple, the furniture replaced by an uncomfortable steel-and-Formica 'dinette' suite.

Even the old kitchen at the back of the house had lost its range and been transformed into a 'kitchenette', 'ette' being the new appendage to almost every word that applied to household furnishings.

Occasionally, when he overheard housewives' conversations in the warehouse he felt as though the whole world had gone diminutive. The only room on this floor that had retained its original name was the scullery, but it had cost him a small fortune to replace his grandmother's copper boiler and mangle with the latest washing machine and electric wringer.

Esme's and the children's bedrooms were also 'contemporary'. Only the three rooms in the attic, one of which he slept in, had escaped Esme's thirst for change. The basement, at his insistence, held all the old furniture that he had categorically refused to throw out.

Loosening his bow tie, he went to the cocktail cabinet and pulled down the flap. Lights sparkled on highly polished mirrors, sending infinite rows of gold squiggle-decorated glasses into the distance as the tinkle-plonk music-box strains of 'Stranger in Paradise' filled the air. Reaching for a bottle of whisky left over from Christmas he poured himself a stiff measure.

'I didn't expect to find you up.' Esme appeared in the doorway, a frothy concoction of feathers and netting perched on her immaculately styled blonde permanent wave, her duster coat open, revealing a narrow brown cocktail frock.

He closed the door of the cabinet. 'And I didn't expect you to be so late.'

'Malcolm organised an end-of-run party. We got talking.' She shrugged her shoulders in a well-rehearsed gesture. 'You know how time goes.'

'Malcolm?'

'Our new leading man. I have mentioned him, but you obviously weren't listening. He recently joined the English department at the training college.' She stood, waiting.

Careful to rest his glass on one of the half-dozen Formica coasters chosen to match the carpet, he helped her out of her coat and carried it into the hall.

'Hang it up properly; you didn't get the shoulder seams straight last time,' she called after him as she unpinned her hat.

He hesitated as he returned, staring at her, while he searched for the right words to tell her about Helen and the police station.

'When you've finished studying me, I'll have one of those.' She pointed to his whisky as she reached for the cigarette box set on a side table.

'I thought you always held your last-night parties at Dot's.'

'Malcolm's bought a place in Belgrave Gardens. It's more comfortable and convenient than Dot's flat.' She crossed one elegant, silk-clad leg over the other as he poured her a drink.

He slammed the cabinet door to silence 'Stranger in Paradise'.

'I wish you'd told me where you were going.'

'It was one of those spontaneous things. None of us knew where we'd be until we were there.'

'You could have telephoned.'

'You were in the Mackworth.'

'Only until eleven.'

'Don't tell me you missed me.'

'I didn't, the police...'

'Police ... Joe!' She dropped her glass, spilling whisky over the sofa. He watched the stain sink in as it spread, hoping it would ruin the upholstery, and provide an excuse to have the suite re-covered.

'Joe is fine, and Helen – now.' He couldn't resist adding the last word or making it sound like a reproach. 'Helen was taken to the police station. She was attacked.'

'Attacked!' Esme dabbed ineffectually at the stain with her handkerchief. 'My God...'

'She wasn't hurt, not seriously, but she was badly shocked. The police doctor examined her. He confirmed she's still a virgin.'

'You allowed a doctor to examine her intimate...'

'I had no choice. Helen was hysterical, you were nowhere to be found.'

'You're blaming me for this?'

'No one's blaming you for anything, Esme. From what I can gather, a boy attacked Helen outside the Pier Ballroom and tore her dress, another boy came to her rescue and stopped him but because the boy who attacked her was Larry Murton Davies...'

'Joe was going to a party at the Murton Davieses' tonight. Larry's twenty-first. There's no way Larry would have been down the Pier,' she contradicted, finally lighting her cigarette.

'Joe was with him – not when Helen was

134

attacked, of course...'

'Joe knows about this?'

'He went to the station with Helen. There's no doubt about it, Esme. The boy Helen was with hit Larry Murton Davies and from all accounts saved her from a lot worse than having her dress torn.'

'What boy?'

'Jack Clay.'

'One of the Clays in the street! The one who went to Borstal! My God, the Murton Davieses will never invite Joe to their house again.'

'Helen was attacked by Larry Murton Davies and all you're concerned about is whether or not the Murton Davieses invite Joe to their house again? If Joe hasn't the sense to tell them to go to hell after this, then I'll do it for him.'

'You said Helen's fine, she wasn't hurt...'

'I said she was shocked. It could have been much worse.'

'But it wasn't!' she exclaimed, her voice rising in hysteria. 'You've never grasped that it's who you know that's important in this town. Joe had an invitation to a party at the Murton Davieses. He had no need to go down the Pier...'

'He went there to pick up Helen and her friends.'

'You let him have the car?'

'I wasn't using it.'

'Joe – the university, his career – this could affect everything I've ... he's worked for. Why on earth did you allow the police to...'

It was the first time since their marriage that John had seen his wife flustered. 'I didn't allow the police to do anything. I wasn't even there when Joe and Helen were taken to the station. They sent an officer to the Mackworth to get me.'

'Then it will be all over town tomorrow that Joe and Helen were arrested. You fool,' she hissed, needing to blame someone.

'Joe wasn't arrested, he was supporting his sister and it's Helen you should be concerned about.'

'Helen's always looking for trouble. And that's entirely your fault. You spoil her. Where's Joe?'

'Upstairs in bed. As is Helen.'

The relief on Esme's face was palpable. She drew heavily on her cigarette. 'If you hadn't given Joe the car, the chances are Larry Murton Davies would have asked him to stay over. He has a sister two years younger than Joe. Emily's a debutante; she came out in London, has been presented to the queen...'

'I couldn't give a damn about debutantes. We're talking about Helen.' He noticed Esme's hand was shaking and realised Helen wasn't the only one in shock. 'In my opinion the police only advised me not to take it any further because of the name Murton Davies.'

'Knowing Helen, nothing happened. That girl overdramatises every situation.'

'She took a dress from the new winter ball gown collection. The blue beaded strapless...'

'You allowed a girl of that age...'

'I allowed her to do nothing, Esme. I didn't even know she had it. It was torn off her – the police would like to believe accidentally, caught on Murton Davies's watch strap, although I have my doubts. Jack Clay saw her half naked, struggling with Murton Davies, assumed the worst and waded in.'

'And who is Jack Clay to come to Helen's defence?'

'It appears he was with her.'

'Idiot girl has absolutely no people sense. If I'd had my way we would have moved out of this street years ago and then there would have been no way that Helen would even know Jack Clay. It's obvious she set out to make an exhibition of herself. And Joe risked everything...'

Helen hugged her knees to her chest as she crouched against the boarded-in banisters on the first floor and listened as her mother's voice grew more and more piercing in escalating anger. She could hear every word as clearly as if she had been in the lounge and the tirade confirmed what she had suspected for years. That her mother didn't love her, or care what happened to her – that she only cared about Joe.

'Helen?' Joe loomed in the doorway of his room, a shadow only fractionally darker than the gloom of the landing. 'What are you doing out here?'

'Listening,' she confessed wretchedly.

'They'll calm down.'

'Mam won't, not this time.' She began to cry, softly, weakly as the events of the night finally hit home.

'Come on, back to bed.' Joe helped her from the floor and led her into her bedroom. 'It won't seem as bad in the morning.'

'Yes, it will. You saw all those people staring. Everyone thinks I'm a slut.'

'They won't when I'm around, because I'll set them straight. And I'll sort out Larry. Murton Davies or not, he won't get away with what he did to you tonight.'

'If you fight him it will only make things worse. He thought I was one of those girls you can buy. Nothing can change that.'

'He was drunk; he didn't know what he was doing. He made a mistake no one will ever make again, I promise you.'

'You can't look after me for ever.'

'I won't have to. People soon forget gossip, Helen.'

'Not gossip like this.'

'Get some sleep. You'll be able to put everything into perspective in the morning.' As Joe closed the door on his sister he reflected that unfortunately Helen was right. No one loved a piece of salacious gossip more than Swansea people. The older generation would tut tut and shake their heads. Young girls would be warned to stay away from Helen – and boys? If his friends' behaviour was anything to go by, they'd give her a wide berth in public and try to get as close as they could to her when no one was looking, in the hope of seeing even more of her than the crowd had down the Pier.

Silence, grey and intimidating, hung over Carlton Terrace as Brian, Martin and Jack rounded the corner.

'I don't start work until Monday,' Brian began hesitantly as Jack walked on ahead.

'So?' Martin whispered, conscious of the noise of their footsteps reverberating over the pavement.

'Maybe we could do something tomorrow. You could show me Swansea. I have a bike. You could ride pillion.'

'I don't know what it's like in Pontypridd, but round here coppers aren't everyone's favourite people. It doesn't pay to be seen with one.'

'I thought after Cyprus...'

'You thought wrong. Didn't you see the way your colleagues stared at you when you sat with me tonight? Roy Williams tried to warn you off, but you wouldn't listen.'

'We're mates.'

'Coppers don't have mates, especially mates called Clay. If you don't believe me, look at the way Jack was treated.'

'We had to be sure of the facts.'

'Can you look me in the eye and tell me honestly that the facts played any part in Jack's release. What happened back there was one big cover-up by the people who can afford monkey suits.'

'Jack's free.'

'Only after a grilling, and if someone had persuaded Helen to say that Jack, not the other boy, had attacked her Jack would be in a cell right now.'

Brian fell silent. He wasn't proud of what had happened to Jack in the station but he had also been extremely glad that he hadn't been dragged any further into what could have turned out to be a very messy case. 'So that's it,' he said finally, 'two years' friendship down the drain, just because I'm a copper.'

'That's it, but thanks for what you did tonight,' Martin muttered grudgingly as he followed Jack down the steps to their basement.

CHAPTER SEVEN

Katie stirred restlessly in the bed as someone tried the front door. Seconds later there was a knocking. Sitting bolt upright, Katie whispered, 'Lily?'

'I heard the key turn, so it's either Brian or Auntie Norah,' Lily reassured her as she stepped out of bed and pulled her dressing gown over her pedal-pusher pyjamas.

'You'll ask who it is before opening the door?' Katie's voice was hoarse from the tears she had shed earlier.

'Of course.' Opening the door, Lily switched on the landing light and ran downstairs on bare feet. The hall tiles were icy to the touch and she wished she'd stopped to find her slippers. 'Who is it?' she called out, trying to decipher the shape through the stained-glass panel.

'Brian Powell.'

She drew back the bolt on the door and opened it as far as the chain would allow.

'Do you always lock your lodgers out at night?'

He blinked against the light and the sight of Lily: prettier in her dressing gown with her face scrubbed clean of make-up and her dark hair loose, tumbling round her sleep-flushed face, than she had been dressed up in the ballroom.

'Auntie Norah had to go to hospital with Katie's mam and Uncle Roy is working, so Katie and I are alone in the house.' Releasing the chain, she pulled her dressing gown high around her throat and retreated to the foot of the stairs.

'Well, you don't have to worry now.' He stepped inside and took off his coat. 'I'm here to protect you,' he added facetiously.

'Auntie Norah left bread, ham and cheese on the kitchen table for your supper. She asked me to tell you to help yourself to anything you want, but I think she'd appreciate it if you put what you don't eat back in the pantry.'

'Thanks for the warning but although I grew up in Pontypridd I was brought up in a fairly civilised manner.'

'I wasn't suggesting...'

'I know you weren't Lily. I was teasing. Now go back upstairs before you catch your death.'

'Goodnight, Brian.'

'Goodnight,' he called after her. 'Did you say Katie was with you?'

'Yes.' She turned back, glad she wasn't alone in the house with him. There was something unaccountably disturbing about his dark good looks.

'You can tell her the trouble has been sorted. It was all a misunderstanding; there'll be no charges, and Jack and Martin are already home.'

'Thank you.' She raced upstairs and into her bedroom, closing the door as Brian went into the kitchen.

'I heard him tell you about Jack and Marty. Ow, you're freezing,' Katie complained as Lily crept in besides her, still wearing her dressing gown.

'Sorry but it's cold out there.' Lily sat up as she heard Brian on the stairs. He walked past their door and into the front bedroom. 'He couldn't have eaten anything. Auntie Norah will be disappointed. She thinks all men have appetites like Uncle Roy.'

'Do you like him?' Katie asked.

'I don't know him, but I do know that Judy really wanted to go home with him.'

'He seems nice, a bit like Martin. Do you think Jack really hurt that boy?'

'No more than he deserved to be hurt,' Lily pronounced decisively. 'I think he was trying to attack Helen before Jack jumped on him.'

'I was afraid Jack might have to go to gaol.'

'For helping Helen?'

'You always want to believe the best of everyone, Lily. Didn't you see the way people were looking at Jack? He's been to Borstal. Everyone thinks he's a bad lot...' Katie faltered as a tear rolled down her cheek.

'I don't think Uncle Roy or Brian believed Jack was in the wrong for a minute, but they couldn't say anything down the Pier because policemen have to be seen to be impartial. I told you not to worry.' Lily hugged Katie's thin shoulders. 'Uncle Roy can sort anything. Remember the time Jack got caught stealing cigarettes? Uncle

Roy cleared it with Mr Phillips so all Jack had to do was apologise and deliver papers for a month.'

'Mr Phillips even kept Jack on afterwards and paid him for his paper round, but beating up a boy who can afford a dinner jacket is a bit different from stealing five Woodbines.'

'It's all over now.'

'Do you think Helen will still talk to us?'

'After wearing that dress tonight it's more likely to be the other way round,' Lily murmured, recalling her aunt's tight-lipped comments about their friend. 'But there's no use in worrying about things we can't do anything about.' She used one of her uncle's favourite expressions. 'Let's try to sleep.'

'I won't until your Auntie Norah gets back with news of Mam.'

Lily lay back on her pillow and tried to think of something they could discuss that would take Katie's mind off her family. 'What did you and Adam talk about?'

'The army. He and Marty were together for a while.'

'Did he ask you to go out with him?'

'No, but he offered to take me home.'

'I'm sure he would have asked you to go out with him if he had brought you home on the train.'

'I'm not. He was nice and everything, but he wasn't like Joe Griffiths with you or Brian with Judy.'

'And what's that?'

'Gooey-eyed.'

'Joe wouldn't give a girl like me a second

143

glance. He has his university friends. You saw him in that dinner suit.'

'And the way he was watching you. Helen's right, I've never seen him look at any girl the way he looked at you tonight.' Katie snuggled further down under the covers. 'He's bound to ask you to go out with him.'

'That doesn't mean I will.'

'Why not? He's good-looking.'

'Good looks aren't everything. Would you go out with Adam if he asked you?'

Katie recalled her mother's face when she was carried into the ambulance, her father's crude and casual brutality. The noises that came from her parents' bedroom the nights he didn't work, her mother's weak cries, her father's angry shouts. 'No,' she whispered into the darkness. 'No, I don't want to go out with anyone.'

'Not ever, not even with Adam Jordan?' Lily asked in disbelief.

'Not ever,' Katie echoed. 'All I want is a good job and a small flat of my own – perhaps not my own. I could keep house for my brothers, especially Jack. He needs someone to look after him, not like Marty.'

'You'll change your mind when you meet the right boy.'

'I don't think so,' Katie maintained solemnly. 'Some women are meant to be spinsters and I'm one of them.'

'I'll talk to you in five years when you're married with three children.'

'I won't change my mind, Lily. You'll see.'

Jack glanced around the kitchen. 'It's not like Mam to leave this place in a mess.'

'Constable Williams told me Mrs Evans took her to hospital and rather than leave Katie alone here he thought it best she spend the night with Lily.'

'Why?'

'Dad came round and gave Mam another beating. Constable Williams knows there's no saying what Dad would do if he came back drunk and found Katie here alone.'

'We shouldn't have left Mam.'

'That's what I said to Constable Williams, but as he pointed out, we can't be with her twenty-four hours a day.' Martin walked through the kitchen and opened the door into the passage. His parents' bedroom door was open. His father lay face down on the bed, snoring, his muddy boots spreading filth over the faded rayon eiderdown. Fighting his initial urge to haul him off the bed and beat him to a pulp, Martin closed the door quietly and returned to the kitchen.

'The old man in?'

'Yes, which is why I'll be out of here first thing tomorrow. Taking a teacloth from the drawer in the kitchen table, Martin began to dry the dishes his mother had stacked on the wooden draining board.

'If you find a place...'

'When, and as soon as possible, I'm moving you, Katie and Mam out.'

'And if Mam won't go?'

'After what happened tonight, I'll make her.'

'Want some tea?' Jack picked up the kettle.

'I want to talk. Why the hell did you arrange to meet Helen Griffiths outside the Pier tonight?'

'Like I told you and your copper mate, she said she wanted some fresh air.'

'You only had to look at what she was wearing to know she was trouble. Every other boy there gave her a wide berth.'

'I felt sorry for her.'

'That's rich, a Clay feeling sorry for a Griffiths.'

'As you said, no other boy would go near her – or girl that I saw. She was by herself most of the night. You were with Lily, Katie was with Adam, Judy had gone off with your copper friend...'

'So you decided to go to her rescue.'

'I didn't know things were going to turn out the way they did.'

'Sometimes I wonder if you go looking for trouble.'

'Not me, I like the quiet life.'

'That's not what I've heard. Do yourself a favour, Jack, stay away from Helen Griffiths.'

'That's one warning I don't need. After tonight I wouldn't touch her with a septic barge pole.'

'Glad to hear it.' Martin stashed the last of the dishes in the rickety dresser and flung the towel on to the stand. 'I'm for bed. I don't suppose you fancy creeping into Mam and Dad's room and filching the alarm clock? I want to be out of here by eight.'

'On a Sunday?'

'I'll go round the newsagents and read the cards in the windows to see if there's any adverts for rooms to let.' He looked around the kitchen. 'Furnished if possible. We don't want to take anything from this place. There's memories here I'd like to bury once and for all.'

'Want some company?' Jack asked tentatively.

'Yes – yes, I would. If we split up we're bound to find something by the end of the day.'

'I'll get the clock.'

Esme didn't bother to knock at Helen's door in the morning. She walked straight into her room. Still in her pyjamas, unwashed, hair uncombed, Helen was curled on her windowsill. 'I know all about last night. What have you got to say for yourself?'

'Nothing,' Helen whispered so quietly that her mother didn't hear her.

'I asked you a question, Helen.'

'The boy attacked me...'

'By boy you mean Larry Murton Davies?'

'That's what Constable Williams called him.'

'Whatever he did, you led him on. You do realise that, don't you? It's entirely your own fault. You took one of the most expensive dresses from your father's warehouse – a dress totally unsuitable for a hop down the Pier. You set out to expose yourself and ruined the dress in the process. And you haven't a single word to say in your defence. Have you any idea of the damage this will do to our reputation as a family, not to mention yours?'

'The doctor...'

'Carried out a medical examination, your father said.' Esme sat on the end of Helen's bed and reached into her pocket for her cigarettes. 'It appals me that the police thought that necessary.

147

They obviously had you down as a streetwalker and believe you me, men don't court or marry streetwalkers – or girls who've been the subject of gossip.'

'I didn't mean for it to happen.' Helen burst into tears; she simply couldn't help herself, although she knew they wouldn't have any effect on her mother. Esme had always regarded any kind of emotional display as a sign of weakness.

'No doubt, but from what the police told your father, half of Mumbles saw you naked last night. What's the use of a doctor certifying you're untouched when you've made an exhibition of yourself? And to think of all the advantages your father and I gave you. Private school, coaching, dance, music, art and elocution lessons – I had hoped that you would learn to mix with decent people and in time marry the right kind of man, but that has gone by the board now. Any man who gives you a second glance will have only one thing on his mind and it won't be an engagement ring.'

'I'm sorry,' Helen choked out between sobs.

'Yes, well, it's spilt milk and that's for sure. Your only hope is to stop going out, except to work, that's if they'll still have you. In six months or so...'

'Six months!' Helen stared at her mother, aghast at the suggestion.

'At least that.' Esme flicked her ash into a cut-glass hairclip tray on Helen's dressing table. 'And in the meantime just hope and pray this doesn't affect Joe's reputation – because if it does, I won't ever forgive you.'

'They kept your mother in, Katie.' Norah told Katie the news as soon as the girls ran downstairs in the morning. 'She's broken her arm in a couple of places, fractured her skull and her cheekbone. She's also cracked her jawbone and ribs and has a few bruises, but the doctor who saw her last night said there's no reason why she shouldn't be as good as new after a couple of weeks' care in hospital and a month or two's rest at home,' she added, stretching the truth.

'Can I see her?'

'This afternoon, Lily and I will walk to the hospital with you and until your mother comes home you'll be staying with us. I settled it last night,' Norah said firmly, forestalling any argument.

'Thank you, Mrs Evans, but what about my brothers?'

'They're grown men; they can manage on their own for a few weeks. Good morning, Brian,' Norah turned to greet him as he walked into the dining room. 'Did you sleep well?'

'Yes, thank you, Mrs Evans.'

'You stayed in the police station with Jack...' Katie began nervously.

'As I told Lily last night, he's fine, Katie. There'll be no charges.'

'But that boy...'

'Everyone agreed it would be better to drop the whole thing.'

'So nothing's going to happen to Jack?'

'Nothing, he's home, you can see him.'

'After breakfast,' Norah interrupted. 'The

potato pancakes will need turning, Lily. Katie, if you'll be kind enough to cut the bread, two slices each makes ten but bring the loaf in. We may need more.'

'Yes, Mrs Evans.'

Norah waited until she was alone with Brian. 'After we've eaten, would you go to next door's basement and ask Martin and Jack to call in here as soon as they can? My brother will want a word with them.'

'About last night?' Brian asked, slightly mystified.

'Their mother had an accident; he'll want to see them about that. Now we don't stand on ceremony in this house, the tea's made. Why don't you pour yourself a cup.'

'Constable Williams.' Joy's face was stern, her voice cold as she opened her front door to see Roy on her doorstep. 'You've called about last night.' She spoke loudly for the benefit of the milkman who was delivering bottles next door.

'Morning, Mrs Hunt, Constable Williams.' The milkman tipped his hat before spending longer than necessary picking up the empty bottles and arranging his delivery on the doorstep.

'Morning, Sid.'

'Morning,' Joy acknowledged briefly.

'Mrs Hunt, the duty sergeant down at the station asked me to let you know that everything's been cleared up. We won't be needing statements from Judy or the other girls about the fight they witnessed outside the Pier last night,' Roy answered in an equally loud voice.

'If you'd care to come in, Constable, I've just made a pot of tea.'

'Thank you, Mrs Hunt, but I've just come off shift. I have another call to make and my sister will be expecting me for breakfast.'

'And Helen?' she murmured quietly as the milkman returned to his truck.

'Is probably very shaken this morning.'

'I've told Judy she's not to associate with her any more.'

'Norah said the same thing last night, but I think you're both being a bit hasty. That girl will need her friends more than ever after yesterday.'

'I won't have Judy jeopardising her reputation by being seen with Helen. A widow with a young daughter to bring up can't be too careful...' She turned aside, unable to meet the look in Roy's eye.

'Thank you for your offer of tea, Mrs Hunt. Good morning.' Straightening his helmet, Roy walked past the milkman. Joy watched for a moment, then closed the door. She loved Roy dearly but this time she was certain he was wrong. Helen Griffiths wasn't fit for decent company. If he chose to allow Lily to carry on seeing the girl, that was his and Norah's business. She would do everything in her power to make sure Judy never spoke to or was seen with Helen again.

Roy had to bang on the Clays' basement door a full ten minutes before Ernie opened it. Red-eyed, dishevelled after sleeping in his clothes, his thinning hair standing on end, his breath smelling like a mortuary in a heatwave, he glared balefully at Roy through gummed-up eyes. 'What do you want?'

Roy pushed his way in and looked around the kitchen. It was tidier than it had been the night before when he had helped Annie and Katie out through the door, but a privation that stemmed from more than lack of money screamed from every chipped, worn surface and cracked piece of china.

'Annie's in hospital.'

'What's the silly bitch done now?' Ernie scratched his backside, then reached for his cigarettes. Pulling a crushed packet of Senior Service from his trouser pocket he stared at a few strands of tobacco, all that was left in the bottom of the silver foil.

'If I had to make a guess, I'd say run into your fist.'

'You want to be careful. I could sue you. That's defamation of character, that is. My Annie...'

'Your Annie will be dead if she carries on living with you.'

'She didn't say I hit her.' There was a glimmer of fear in Ernie's eyes. 'Did she?' he challenged. Roy remained silent, watching Ernie's apprehension grow. The fact that Ernie was afraid Annie might betray him was enough to give Roy hope that one day she would make the official complaint he needed to prosecute the man.

'Did she?' Ernie coughed up a gob of phlegm and spat in the sink.

'She's in a bad way this time.' Roy avoided the question.

'How do you know?'

'I found her here last night when I brought Katie home. Norah called an ambulance and the hospital telephoned the station this morning.'

'What they want to do that for?'

'They have to notify us of any unexplained injuries. It's the law. Annie has a fractured skull and broken and cracked bones. Last night her right arm and face looked as though a steam-roller had run over them.'

'She's clumsy.'

'The only clumsy thing she ever did was marry you, Ernie.'

'You've no right...'

'I've every right. I couldn't call myself a man, much less a constable, if I sat back and watched you kill her without lifting a finger.'

'But she didn't say a word about me hitting her.' Ernie stared at Roy, daring him to state otherwise.

'Her jaw's wired. She can't say much.'

'So she hasn't made a complaint.' Ernie smiled triumphantly, revealing a row of blackened and crooked teeth. 'If she had, you'd have had me down the station by now.'

'She'll see sense one day.' Roy wished today had been that day but even beaten, humiliated and exhausted by pain, Annie had persisted in perpetuating the myth that she'd fallen and hit her face on the sink. If it had been up to him, he would have persevered in the hope of persuading her to change her story, but the doctor and his sergeant had insisted he limit his questioning to no more than ten minutes.

Hard-won experience and common sense dictated the sergeant's handling of the situation. 'Domestics' were notoriously difficult to prosecute. Most victims were intimidated, coerced or coaxed into dropping the charges by their assailant long before their case reached court and as Annie wouldn't even admit to being assaulted to begin with, he was working against impossible odds.

'I warn you, Roy, keep your nose out of my affairs.' Ernie opened the door.

Roy stood his ground. 'Until Annie's well enough to come home, Katie stays with us.'

'The hell she does! She's my daughter.'

'Annie asked Norah to take care of her. She wants it that way. Any argument from you and I'll send Katie out of Swansea.'

'Think you're so bloody big in that uniform, don't you? Well it doesn't cut any ice with me. I remember you when your arse was hanging out of your trousers and your family didn't have two halfpennies to rub together...'

Roy turned his back and walked away. His only thought was with the boys. He hoped Jack and Martin had left for the day. He couldn't imagine where they'd gone but anywhere had to be better than what passed for their home.

'It was an accident, Annie, pure and simple. You slipped on some water and fell against the sink. The sort of thing that can happen to anyone.'

Annie struggled to open her swollen, bruised eyes, the only points of colour in her bandaged face.

The rubber-tipped legs of Ernie's chair

154

squeaked as he dragged them over the highly polished lino closer to Annie's bed. 'It won't happen again, Annie.' Reaching out, he took her work-roughened hand in his. 'I'll give up the drink.'

Annie mumbled something that sounded suspiciously like, 'You've promised that before.'

'This time I mean it,' he snarled. A nurse sitting at the desk in the middle of the ward rapped hard with her knuckles as his voice sharpened. 'I'll turn over a new leaf, you'll see,' he whispered in a more conciliatory tone. 'Come on, Annie. For better for worse, that's what you always say and we've had some good times.' He straightened his tie as the nurse left her station to attend to a patient on the opposite side of the ward. 'Do you remember all those picnics on Kilvey Hill? Catching the bus to Oxwich, swimming and looking for crabs and winkles on the rocks, you, me and the kids. The boys digging that enormous hole and little Katie falling headfirst into it. I had to fish her out...'

Annie turned her face to the wall. She remembered only one walk on Kilvey Hill when they were courting and a single trip to Oxwich with the Sunday school when the children were small. Ernie wouldn't give them money for the outing the following year and shortly after that the boys had refused to go to church.

Ernie glared as a cleaner clanked past with an enamel bucket and mop. 'I'm not surprised you're too tired to talk with the racket they make in here. It will be different when you come home, you'll see. We'll have another picnic. Perhaps

155

even go back up Kilvey Hill. It's still warm enough. We could take a trip up there next Sunday if you're out of here. We may find some late blackberries. Remember that jam you used to make? It had a real tang to it, not like the shop-bought slops you put on the table these days.' He shifted uneasily and his chair squeaked again. Annie turned back and watched him. He was brushing down his trousers. He'd washed and shaved for the occasion as well as donned his best – and only – suit. 'Come on, Annie, you're my girl, try to remember.'

'Your wife probably finds it difficult to remember anything, Mr Clay. Her injuries are severe. We've had to give her a large dose of painkillers to enable her to cope with the discomfort.'

A young doctor stood at the foot of Annie's bed.

'I can see that.' Ernie bit back defensively.

'I'd like to discuss your wife's condition with you when I've finished my rounds. Shall we say ten minutes from now in the ward office?'

'You can say what you bloody like. You don't look like a proper doctor to me. You're too young...'

'Ernie,' Annie pleaded through numb and swollen lips.

'I'll be there,' Ernie capitulated. As the doctor walked away he squeezed Annie's hand. 'You've not been talking to anyone?'

She winced as she shook her head.

'That Roy Williams came calling this morning – he said to let me know you were in here. Bloody Nosy Parker! He insisted you wanted our Katie to stay with Norah until you came out. Well, I soon put him right on that. Her place is at home, looking after me and the boys.'

'No!'

'You all right, Mrs Clay?' The doctor returned. Lifting her left arm he took her pulse.

'Of course she's not all right,' Ernie shouted. 'Look at the bloody state of her.'

'I'll have to ask you to leave, Mr Clay, you're upsetting the patient.'

'That's my wife!'

'And my patient. Do I have to call a porter? The ward office is this way, Mr Clay.' The doctor walked alongside Ernie. Opening the door, he blocked the corridor with his body leaving Ernie little choice but to enter the office.

'Take a seat, Mr Clay.' The doctor moved his own chair between Ernie's and the door. 'We're concerned as to how your wife sustained her injuries.'

'She fell.'

'So she says, but I've checked her medical records and she seems to meet with far more accidents than the average woman.' The doctor lifted a file from the desk and opened it. 'January 1949, she broke her left arm in two places.' He raised his eyes and looked at Ernie. 'A difficult thing to do, even falling down stone steps, which is what she said she'd done. July 1949 cuts and bruises to her back, apparently sustained when hanging out washing on a wet day. Again, a strange thing for any housewife to do.'

'We live in a basement, there's nowhere else for her to hang the washing.'

'Christmas 1949,' the doctor continued, 'cuts and bruising around the eyes. She walked into a door.' He flicked through the pages at random. 'February 1950, June 1950, two incidents during December 1951 – I could go on and on. Your wife has required hospital treatment on thirty-five separate occasions since your demob from the army in 1946.'

'She's clumsy.'

'Don't you think it peculiar that she didn't require any treatment for injuries resulting from her clumsiness during the war? But of course, you were away then, weren't you.'

'What are you suggesting?'

The doctor looked Ernie coolly in the eye. 'Nothing as long as her injuries were accidental.'

'She hasn't said any different, has she?'

'No,' the doctor conceded.

Ernie left his seat and jabbed his finger at the doctor's white coat. 'I want her home.'

'She won't be fit to resume her domestic duties for some time, Mr Clay.'

'That won't matter; we have a girl to help her. Her place is with me and her children.'

'Not until I release her, Mr Clay, and I won't be able to do that until her bones have mended and that is going take quite some time.'

'We'll see about that.'

'You wouldn't want to put your wife at risk, Mr Clay, would you?' The doctor crossed his arms and stared back at him. After a few moments he rose from his chair and stepped aside. Pushing his way past, Ernie stomped through the door and down the corridor.

'I tried to make Mam leave last night, Mr Williams, but all I succeeded in doing was making things worse for her.'

'I doubt you did that, Martin. You've always done everything you can to help your mother.'

'Not this time.'

'What happened isn't your or Jack's fault but the situation can't be allowed to carry on. I spoke to the doctor this morning. Your mother might not survive another "fall" like the one she had last night.'

'What about the police?' Jack demanded belligerently. 'Why don't you protect her instead of going after innocent people?'

'Get your mother to make a complaint, Jack and we'll do plenty. But until she signs a statement our hands are tied.'

'And he can carry on beating her.'

'While she insists her injuries are the result of accidents and continues to live with him, yes.'

'I thought that if I found rooms she might leave him but Jack and I looked all over this morning. There were a couple advertised in the newsagents but only for single blokes. We need somewhere big enough for Mam, Katie, Jack and me.'

'Those girls all right?' Roy asked as Norah walked in with a fresh pot of tea.

'They're upstairs in Lily's room, sorting out accessories to go with Katie's new costume for her interview tomorrow.'

'Even if you found rooms, Mam wouldn't move into them, Marty.' Jack pushed his chair back from the table and stretched out his legs. 'You heard her yesterday. She won't leave him. He hits her about and she won't have a word said against him.'

'Well, your mam won't be home for a while yet and there's always the chance someone in the hospital will talk sense into her. Meanwhile, your Katie is fine here.' Norah poured their tea, rested the teapot on the stand and lifted the milk jug and sugar basin from the tray. 'So why don't you boys find somewhere for yourselves? That is, unless you want to stay at home.'

'Not on your – Nellie,' Jack hastily amended a word he sensed Norah would object to. 'But we don't want to move too far from Katie in case she needs us.'

Norah didn't have to ask what the boy meant. They couldn't be sure Katie was safe from their father's violence, even in a policeman's house. She looked at Roy.

'I know what you're thinking and it won't work,' Roy interceded.

'Why not?'

'Because it's too close to Ernie, that's why not.'

'It's as big as the place Ernie's renting now, should Annie and Katie decide to move in with the boys later.'

The decisive tone in Norah's voice warned Roy further argument was useless. She had thought the situation through and found the solution. The risk of her remedy bringing trouble into the house counted for nothing, set against Annie's, Katie's and the boys' troubles. 'The rooms are a mess,' he protested lamely.

'What rooms, Mr Williams?' Martin asked.

160

'Our basement. It's not up to much, three rooms and one of those is a sort of kitchen cum bathroom. We had a bath plumbed in and a gas water heater put above it during the war when an evacuee family lived there. There's an outside toilet but I don't need to tell you any more. All the basements in the street are much of a muchness.'

'You'd rent us your basement?' Martin questioned excitedly.

'We've used it as a dumping ground for everything we didn't want but considered too good to throw out for years. It needs a good clear-out.'

'But it would be perfect. And, as Mrs Evans said, there'd be room for Mam and Katie if they wanted to join us.'

'One step at a time, Martin.' Norah passed him the sugar. 'I think Katie would be better off up here with Lily and me, until your mam comes home from hospital.'

'And before you make up your mind one way or another, you'd best take a look at the place. It needs decorating as well as sorting.'

'I did some painting in Borstal,' Jack enthused.

'Tell you what.' Norah gave the boys a rare, tight smile. 'If you decide to take it, how about we give you the first month rent free in exchange for clearing and decorating the rooms?'

CHAPTER EIGHT

Helen wiped the last of the pans, pushed it into the stove to dry, slammed the oven door and looked around the kitchenette. Everything appeared clean and pristine but she didn't doubt her mother would find fault, just as she had done all day and, looking back, for as long as she could remember. Predictably, her father had chosen to inform her privately how disappointed he was at her behaviour before taking refuge in his customary reticence. If past experience was anything to go by, he'd forget – or pretend to forget – all about it in a few days and go back to loving her as unconditionally as he always had. She'd expected worse from her mother, but even Joe had been taken aback by the hostility and venom of Esme's reaction. There hadn't been a single word of sympathy for Laurence Murton Davies's attack on her, or the medical examination she'd been subjected to, only cold condemnation for stealing the dress and making the family the focus of scandal and gossip.

She couldn't help but contrast her relationship with her mother with that of Lily and her Auntie Norah, or Judy and Joy Hunt. Judy and Lily discussed everything from make-up, fashion and hairstyles to boyfriends and sex with the women who had brought them up, and she envied them that close intimacy. Even when it came to important things like the facts of life, she'd had to rely on Lily and Judy for the details which Norah and Joy had shared with them.

Revelling in her misery, Helen raked up every painful memory. Like all the times her school concerts had clashed with her mother's rehearsals and her father had sat alone when everyone else had two parents to watch them perform. The horrendous rows whenever she had wanted to buy grown-up things like make-up and stockings; there had even been a fight over her first bra, her mother insisting she didn't need one long after girls half her size had been wearing them.

It was almost as though she hadn't wanted her to grow up. As a child she had hoped things would change when she was older. Her mother was smart and sophisticated. Like Joy Hunt she enjoyed going to the theatre and cinema, but the longed-for invitations to join Esme on her out-ings had never materialised. Instead of accom-panying her as soon as she'd been old enough, as Judy did Joy, she'd been relegated to the Cinderella role of clearing up whenever the daily wasn't around, receiving the same sneering criticism for her effort whether she did the job properly or not.

Her father was different. She loved him and was certain he loved her, which made his present disappointment in her difficult to take. But knowing he would forgive her made her ache all the more for a kind word from her mother.

Uncertain how to cope with the intensity of Esme's rage, Joe had cleared off half an hour after

163

breakfast, using the excuses of picking up the car he'd left in Mumbles the night before and a non-existent Sunday study group to ignore her plea for support. The midday Sunday meal had been a silent, strained affair. Hardly anything had been eaten and Esme had left the house before dessert, announcing she was going to visit her mother before news of last night's events spread to Langland. With a parting shot to Helen to clear up, she'd run to catch the bus. Her father had muttered something about stocktaking and walked out a few minutes later.

Wishing that a friend – any friend – would knock at the door so she could talk about the way she felt and last night, Helen untied her apron, hung it on the peg on the back of the door and wandered restlessly from room to room. She picked up objects and set them down again without really seeing any of them. Normally on a fine Sunday she would have called on Lily, Judy and Katie. They would have taken the train down to Mumbles and walked along the seafront in the hope of seeing someone they knew – preferably male and good-looking – and afterwards visited one of the Italian cafés for ice cream. But even if she'd felt like going out and facing people – and she didn't – both her parents had been adamant. If she dared leave the house they'd send her to stay with her mother's great-aunt who lived in an isolated farmhouse in the wilds of Carmarthen-shire. The threat wasn't an idle one. Her mother had talked of sending her there anyway and she had a feeling it was only her father's intervention that had prevented the ticket from being bought.

She curled up on the windowsill of her room and looked down at the garden three floors below. Her father's vegetable plot was ready for harvesting and it was an indication of the uproar in the house that he wasn't working on it. All this trouble – all this upset – was entirely her fault. Her mother was right. No decent boy would look at her again. Only ones like Laurence Murton Davies who wanted to paw her and do disgusting things... She shuddered at the humiliation of the medical examination, the contempt in the sergeant's face as he'd photographed her breast.

Resting her chin on her knees she sunk her head on her arms and cried harsh salt tears that burned her eyes and dried her throat. It would be better if she were dead. Then she would no longer be a disgrace to her mother and Joe. How did people kill themselves? Hanging? She stared up at the light fitting. The electric cord looked flimsy; if she tried to tie herself to that it would be bound to break, probably bringing half the ceiling down and bare wires with it. She might even be electrocuted. She'd heard someone say that when a person was electrocuted their flesh fried and smelled like bacon.

She could hang herself from the stairwell. Just the thought made the hairs prickle on the back of her neck. She had always been terrified of heights. She could never bring herself to step off into nothingness, which was ridiculous when she considered she was plotting ways to put an end to her life.

There were pills. Mrs Bootley from the Promenade whose husband had run off with their next-door neighbour had killed herself that way. Leaving the sill she went into the bathroom and inspected the cabinet. The sum total of medicines amounted to half a dozen aspirins and a packet of laxatives but there were several bottles marked 'poisonous if ingested'. Hair preparations, perfumes, disinfectant – but what if they didn't kill her, only hurt her in some hor-rible painful way, or turned her into a mindless cabbage? She had read about a child who had drunk poison that had damaged her stomach and made her life a misery. And poisons weren't certain. She wanted something that would make her mother realise she had been serious and knew there was no chance of being saved.

She pictured her funeral. The curtains closed in the front windows of the house, the cortège leaving, her father, inconsolable in grief, her mother throwing herself on to her coffin, showing her more affection in death than she had ever shown her in life. Joe and his friends in suits and black ties looking suitably sombre at the graveside as her coffin was lowered into the earth … she could put her head in the oven. Then she remembered her mother's new stove was electric.

Wandering back downstairs she went into the kitchen. A knife? She opened the drawer, took out the largest of the carving knives and ran her thumb down the edge. Deciding it was blunt she replaced it in the drawer. Then she saw blood drip from her hand on to the floor. Picking up a tea towel she ran to the cold tap to staunch it. The blade was so big; she doubted she could bring herself to plunge it into her heart but she could cut her wrists. Wasn't that the way Hollywood film stars killed themselves? Her history teacher had said something about Romans doing it in the bath because hot water made the blood run faster. But that would be messy if she kept her clothes on and too many people had seen her naked last night for her to want to make a spectacle of herself again – even in death.

She stared at the knife then went to the pad next to the telephone in the hall and scribbled

I couldn't bear to live with the disgrace I've brought on you. I'm sorry,
Love Helen.

Taking the knife, she unbolted the door in the hall that led to the basement and the back garden. She would cut her wrists, but not in the house where her mother could accuse her of making a mess. She would do it outside where the last thing she would see was the endless blue sky and the clouds just like – like – she had a vague recollection of reading something similar in a book but she couldn't remember which one.

'Mrs Evans mentioned you were moving in down here. I thought you might need a hand.' Brian stood at the door at the foot of the staircase that opened into Roy Williams's basement and waited for Martin to tell him to shove off.

'We need all the hands we can get. Mr Williams said there was a mess down here and he wasn't joking.' Martin kicked aside a box of old newspapers. 'It looks as though it's been used as a dumping ground by the entire street, not just this house.'

'How many rooms are there?' Brian stepped back as Martin tossed a broken wooden clothes horse down the passage.

'Three and, as you see, all packed full of junk. Apparently there's everything we need some-where beneath this lot and after we've excavated it Mrs Evans said she'll give us enough bed linen and towels to be going on with.'

Brian glanced around the corner and saw a sink, stove and bath ranged along the walls. 'A kitchen and two bedrooms?'

'That's it.

'How much rent you paying?'

'Nothing for the first month but we have to paint and decorate the place. The rent will be a pound a week after that.'

'How about I pay ten bob a week straight off for one of the rooms and give you a hand with the decorating?'

'Why would you do that? You've got it cosy upstairs. All home comforts, meals laid on, wash-ing done...'

'And my every move watched. Supposing I find a girl?'

'I thought you did last night.'

'Give me a chance. Let's just say Judy's more my style than Maria was.'

'Even so, you're still a copper and you shouldn't mix with criminals, and whichever way you look at it, your lot regard Jack as one.'

'How about you let me worry about "my lot".'

'And if you catch Jack doing something he shouldn't?'

'Like beating up the crache?'

The irony wasn't lost on Martin. 'What do you say, Jack?' he asked as his brother walked in from the garden where he'd been building a bonfire.

'About what?'

'Brian moving in and paying half the rent. It would mean us sharing a room but we could save some money for Mam to buy the things she'll need when she comes out of hospital.'

'You want us to share this place with a copper?'

'I'm not a copper off duty.'

'A copper's a copper in the buff or his uniform, the pub or on the beat.'

'He helped you last night,' Martin reminded.

'And afterwards I heard you tell him to sod off.' Jack picked up the clothes horse.

'I'm thick-skinned.'

'I've noticed.' Jack threw the broken wooden frame out of the door.

'I work shifts, you'd hardly know I was here.'

'We could use the money.' Martin picked up a crate of empty beer bottles.

'I'd find the extra.'

'Where?'

'Round and about.'

'That's what I'm afraid of. It might pay to have a copper in the house to keep an eye on you.'

'Suit yourself, you always do.' Jack kicked a path through the rubbish in the passage.

'You'll have to move out when my mother and Katie move in,' Martin warned, handing the crate to Jack.

'Thanks. At least that'll give me a breathing space. How about I start clearing the front room?'

'Find a bed and it's yours.'

Joe strolled through Mumbles towards the café where Helen and her friends usually stopped for ice cream. Glancing in the window, he saw Judy, Katie and Lily sitting at a table. He pushed open the door, hesitated, then put his head down and walked away. After the events of the previous evening he wasn't certain of the reception he'd get from any of them.

Lighting a cigarette, he wandered into the amusement arcade and watched a crowd of young boys empty their pockets into the machines. Recalling the sour taste the loss of his allowance had brought when he'd been their age, he turned on his heel and headed for the beach. The tide was coming in, the sand almost covered. Soon the water would be lapping at the pebbles. Since childhood he'd loved the sucking, slurping noise the waves made as they ebbed and flowed among the rocks. Sitting on the sea wall, he looked out across the bay towards Port Talbot and thought about Larry. He didn't need to talk to him to know how he'd treat last night's incident. He could almost hear his braying laugh: 'If it had been anyone's sister other than your own, Joe, you would have been ogling her tits along with the rest of us. No harm done!'

'No harm done.' It was what Larry, Robin and even he had said dozens of times, after one of Larry's 'larks'. Like when Larry had propped a ladder against the window of the bathroom outside the girl's hostel in the training college and tried to peer in through the skylight before almost breaking his neck when the ladder went crashing to the ground. Or the time he had dived into the Watkin Morgans' swimming pool and pulled down the top of Angie's French pen pal's swimming costume. The time he'd...

He could go on and on. Never once had he or Robin suggested Larry's pranks were juvenile, in poor taste, or had upset the girls Larry targeted. And to his shame he realised that if Larry had torn the dress off anyone's sister other than his own last night, he might even have thought the incident amusing. But then he'd had to look at Helen's face this morning and listen to the names their mother called her, all the while knowing that nothing that had happened was Helen's fault, apart from the initial purloining of the dress. Jack Clay had been right to tackle Larry, he was only sorry Jack hadn't given him a more thorough going over. But then, that might have resulted in Jack being returned to Borstal as punishment for doing what he should have done: protect Helen. Worst of all was his mother's blind assumption that he was mixing with the cream of Swansea society. She was completely unaware that most of the people she regarded as the 'cream' assumed they had the right to ride roughshod over any and everyone with less money and influence than they, and that included him, Helen and probably their father.

The one thing he was sure of was he didn't want to see Larry again, because if he did, he'd more than likely pick up where Jack Clay had left off. But where did that leave him? Ostracised by the in-crowd dominated by Larry and Robin that his mother had been so pleased he'd infiltrated, and still cold-shouldered by the boys in the street he had played with as a child because he'd been to grammar school and university.

'Hello, Joe.'

Suddenly and acutely aware of the scent of Lily of the Valley, he turned to see Lily standing beside him.

'I'm sorry. I didn't mean to disturb you but I wanted to ask after Helen.'

'You coming, Lily?' Judy called as she and Katie walked down the steps on to the narrow strip of beach, all that was left above the tide line.

'In a minute. You go on, I'll catch up.' Folding her skirt beneath her, Lily sat on the wall beside him. 'Is Helen very upset?'

'What do you think?'

'I'd be, but I'm more of a coward than Helen.'

'Helen's not brave, just stupid. No girl in her right mind would have worn that dress to the Pier last night.'

'I did wonder if we'd pushed her into it.'

'Egged her on?' he asked in surprise.

'Not exactly. But she showed it to us before we went out and we tried to persuade her to wear something else.'

'And suggesting to Helen that she shouldn't do something is the best way to get her to do it.'

'I'm sorry.'

'It's hardly your fault.'

'But you must feel dreadful after bringing that

boy to the Pier in your father's car.'

'Yes.' He climbed to his feet. 'But I'd rather not talk about him or what happened last night.'

'Of course. I'm sorry.'

'Stop apologising.'

'Tell Helen I was asking after her, will you, please.' Jumping down from the wall, she went to the steps.

'Lily.' He followed, catching up with her as she reached the beach. 'I didn't mean to be short with you. It's just that after last night I'm so angry I don't know what to do with myself.'

'Uncle Roy always tells me to bite my big toe when I feel like that.'

'I can't imagine you ever being this frustrated.'

'I'm good at hiding my feelings.'

He took a deep breath. 'I love the sea. I'm still angry, yet I can look at those waves and almost forget all the rows and arguments at home.'

'Were your parents furious?'

'With Helen for taking the dress. She's been locked up as a punishment. Forbidden to go anywhere except work for six months so you won't be seeing anything of her unless you call, and that's only if my mother lets you in.'

'Poor Helen,' Lily murmured, deciding it wasn't a good time to tell Joe that she and Judy had been ordered not to talk to or visit her.

'So, to change the subject, this isn't last night and I'm not taking you home, but would you like to go out with me?'

Speechless, Lily stared at him in amazement. She hadn't believed Helen's assertion that he was after her for an instant.

'Is that look a "yes" or "no"?'

'I'm only allowed down the Pier and to the pictures with Judy and Katie.'

'Are you telling me that because you don't want to go out with me?'

'I've never thought about going out with you,' she replied, not entirely truthfully.

'Because you don't like me.'

'Because you're Helen's brother.'

'And that means.'

'You've taken me by surprise.'

'So I have to start slowly. I have to work tomorrow – a small part in a play being broadcast on the radio.' He couldn't resist the boast. 'But how about the pictures on Tuesday? *Roman Holiday* is on at the Carlton,' he added as an incentive, recalling that he had once overheard Lily tell his sister that Gregory Peck was her favourite film star.

'I'd like to see it,' she confided shyly, 'but I'd have to ask Auntie Norah.'

'So that's a "yes" if your aunt agrees.'

'Yes.'

'I'll call and ask her permission, if you think it would help.'

'It might.'

He closed his hand round hers. 'The view is better out there.' He pointed into the bay where two or three small yachts were circling buoys. 'One of my friends has a boat. We took it out last weekend. It was glorious.'

'I've never been in a yacht.' She wondered if the friend was the one who'd torn Helen's dress. 'Only a boat on the lake in Singleton Park and once in Roath Park in Cardiff.'

'Then I'll have to wangle you an invitation next time we go. When would be the best time to meet you on Tuesday?'

'If my aunt agrees.'

'If she agrees. How about when you leave work? We could have coffee and cake in the Kardomah and fish and chips on the way home.'

'A proper date.'

'A proper date.' He smiled. 'I know Mrs Evans and Constable Williams are old-fashioned but I hope you don't expect this to be the beginning of an old-fashioned courtship.'

'I don't expect it to be the beginning of anything, Joe.'

'You haven't been out with many boys.'

'I haven't been out with any boys.'

'And I haven't been out with a girl quite like you before, so this is going to be a new experience for both of us.'

Jack Clay was staggering down the path, bent double under the weight of a monstrous iron umbrella stand, when he saw something move in the garage next door. Not wanting to believe his eyes he dropped the stand and craned his neck. Helen was sitting on a crate just inside the door. Running to the garden wall, he scrambled over it, landing slap in the middle of John Griffiths's prize-winning dahlias. 'What the hell are you doing?' he cried, rushing into the garage and grabbing the enormous knife Helen was using to saw her wrist.

'Jack!' She leapt to her feet, only to sink back on

to the crate.

'I'm not surprised you feel faint.' Grabbing her hand, he probed the cut with his fingers. 'You're lucky you haven't cut anything vital.'

'And you'd know about that,' she muttered weakly.

'Boys were always doing stupid things like this in Borstal. Here.' Pushing her head between her knees, he wrapped a none too clean handkerchief round the wound.

'I haven't cut a vein?' she mumbled.

'No, you haven't. And you're a fool for trying. Why on earth are you trying to kill yourself?'

'To put my family out of their misery.'

'Wouldn't it be easier to run away from home?' Holding one end of the handkerchief between his teeth he knotted it firmly into place.

'It would if I had somewhere to run to.'

'There's always somewhere.'

'Not for me. Not after last night when half the people in Swansea saw me naked. My mother says I've blighted my brother's life as well as my own.'

'He looks like the type who'll survive.'

'You don't know him. He's in university. He mixes with all sorts of smart people, important people...'

'Like the bastard who tried to jump you.'

'I wanted to thank you for coming to my rescue but I didn't see you – not after they took me to the police station. I wanted to but...'

'Fat lot of good I did both of us.'

'That boy, he would have ... he wouldn't have stopped if you hadn't hit him.'

'And he got away with jumping on you and tearing your dress to shreds, and I nearly got charged with assault. That'll teach me to try to save girls from the crache. In future I'll let boys in dinner suits do whatever they want.'

'I tried to tell them what happened. How you helped me.'

'If you hadn't they'd have probably locked me up and thrown away the key,' he acknowledged grudgingly.

'I'm sorry. I behaved like an idiot.'

'Not as much of one as now.' Relinquishing his hold on the back of her neck, he tossed the knife on to a workbench behind them.

'Haven't you ever felt like giving up?' She struggled to sit up.

'Never.' He grinned cheerfully. 'It's too much fun annoying people.'

'I wish I could think like you.' Unable to keep her emotions in check a moment longer, she burst into tears.

Wretched, with red eyes and nose, in grease-stained pedal pushers and cotton top, her face streaked with dust and tears and devoid of make-up, Jack found Helen more appealing than in all her painted glory and expensive frock. He had earned more clips round the ear from his father for bringing home starving cats and stray dogs than he had for stealing. Upset, abandoned, Helen needed someone and, as her family had so obviously rejected her, that left him.

Conveniently forgetting his promise to Martin that he wouldn't touch her with a septic barge pole, he put his arm round her. She turned and sobbed on his shoulder as though her heart was breaking.

'Hey, nothing's worth this,' he protested, embarrassed by her flood of emotion.

'But don't you see, my mother's right, no one will ever want to go out with me. Not after what happened last night. I may as well die; I have nothing left to look forward to...'

'You kidding. A girl like you? Anyone would be proud to have you for a girlfriend.'

'No, they wouldn't,' she wailed.

'I would.'

'Really?' She stared at him, her tears distorting his face, making it wobbly and fuzzy around the edges.

'Really,' he echoed. And then he kissed her.

'Do you have to go home right now?' Joe asked Lily as they followed Katie and Judy along the beach. 'If you don't we could go back to the café...'

'Back?' She looked at him in surprise.

'I saw you there earlier,' he admitted.

'Why didn't you come in?'

'I could buy you a coffee, and Judy and Katie,' he offered hastily, not wanting to admit that he'd half expected her to rebuff him. 'Or another raspberry ripple if you want one. Then I could drive you home. I left the car at the Pier last night.'

She couldn't help smiling. He must have watched them in the café for a while to note exactly what they'd been eating. 'I'm sorry, Joe, but Auntie Norah expects us back for tea and

Katie wants to help her brothers. They're moving into our basement and they asked her to give them a hand to clean it after they've cleared out the rubbish.'

'Next Sunday, perhaps.'

Sensing he was reluctant to go home, she said, 'You could come to tea if you like. Auntie Norah wouldn't mind.'

'But she's not expecting me.' He knew how his mother would react if he brought home one of his university friends without warning, giving her no chance to stock up on food or arrange the dining room to its best advantage.

'She always makes too much food.'

'I could buy some ice cream on the way as my contribution,' he suggested, wanting to make a good impression.

'It will melt. Aunt Norah doesn't have a fridge.'

'Lily?' Judy turned round. 'You catching the train?'

'If you walk to the Pier I'll give you a lift.'

'And if I walk to the train stop I'll save myself a quarter of a mile.'

'Lazybones,' Joe teased.

'It's all right for those who are used to parking themselves on their rear ends all day in university,' Judy retorted. 'Try being a hairdresser. We don't get a chance to sit down all week. I'm on my feet from breakfast until teatime, Monday to Saturday.'

'Poor, Judy.'

Picking up a clump of seaweed, Judy threw it at him. He laughed as he pulled it out of his hair, refusing to be riled in front of Lily.

'Well, I'm for the train, next one's leaving in ten minutes.'

'If you don't mind, I'll go back with Judy, Lily. My brothers will probably be ready for my help by now.'

'Lily?' Joe asked, clearly hoping she'd opt to walk to the Pier with him.

Lily looked from Joe to her friends, realising the decision was more momentous than a simple choice between whether to walk and drive, or take the train.

'As I sit down all day too, I could do with the exercise so I'll go to the Pier with Joe. Do me a favour, Katie, tell Auntie Norah I'll be along shortly and I'll be bringing Joe to tea.'

Judy raised her eyebrows.

'Come round after tea,' Lily invited in an attempt to play down the implication of her staying back with Joe. 'You can inspect Katie's outfit for tomorrow.'

'And give me some advice on my hair,' Katie pleaded.

'If you like I'll wash and set it for you,' Judy offered.

Lily waved and turned back to Joe. He held out his arm. She hesitated for the barest fraction of a second before taking it.

'I must look a mess.' Helen smoothed back the hair that had come loose from her ponytail.

'Killing yourself is a messy business.' Jack wiped the tears from her face with his thumbs.

'You making fun of me?'

'You'll get used to it.'

180

'I've heard about you, Jack Clay, and your tarts. You might have saved me – twice – but that doesn't mean I'll go out with you.' Even as her anger burned she found herself wishing that he wasn't quite so good-looking.

'You could be *the* tart if you like.'

'What's that supposed to mean?'

'What I said.'

'Are you asking me to be your girlfriend?'

'There's a vacancy.'

'For how many?'

'I only go out with one at a time. More gets complicated.'

'And you'd know how complicated, I suppose.'

'Let's say I've tried it without much success. Would another kiss help make up your mind?'

'No.' She left the crate. Catching her hand, he pulled her back.

'You'd be getting a good-looking boyfriend, unlimited motorbike rides and...' He bent his head to hers again.

Summoning all her strength, she tried to push him away but he held her wrists in an iron grip. 'No more kisses,' she remonstrated, as he grazed her lips with his.

'Why?' He moved on to nuzzle the nape of her neck.

'Because it reminds me of that horrible boy last night.'

'Give me a chance and I'll help you forget him. So how about it?' Raising his head, he gazed into her eyes. 'Me and you?'

'My mother would kill both of us if she found out. She went berserk when she discovered it was you who rescued me last night.'

'Ten minutes ago you wanted to kill yourself to get away from her.'

'You don't understand...'

'Yes, I do, you're ashamed to be seen with me.'

'I'm not. But I couldn't bear any more rows at home. You've no idea what it's like.'

'I can imagine,' he murmured drily.

'But we could see one another secretly. No one ever comes down to our basement. We could meet here without anyone being any the wiser.'

'Sneaking around isn't my style.'

'It will only be until I leave home. I'm starting work next week. As soon as I save enough I'm moving into a bedsit. Then we can go wherever we like.'

'Together?'

'Anywhere you want. Rub my mother's nose in it.' She sensed him wavering. 'Look, you can see my bedroom window from here. It's on the second floor, the one on the left. We could have a signal. If it's safe for you to come to the basement I could put something on the sill.' She thought rapidly. 'A candle.'

'You expect me to hang around the back lane every night in the hope that you might be able to put a candle in your window? I may not have a girlfriend at the moment but I do have a life. Skiffle group practice, overtime...'

'It's not going to work, is it?' She shivered, sensing her only chance of living any kind of a life until she left home slipping away from her.

'How about pinning a number to the back of your curtain? Eight o'clock means you can meet me down here at eight, nine at nine...'

'And once I'm here, I can lock the basement door from the inside so no one can get down from the house.'

'I'd prefer a girlfriend I could take out and show off.'

'And I'd prefer to be taken out and shown off, but I'm in disgrace.'

'Not with me.' Leading her back into the shadows he kissed her again, only this time she was prepared. As his mouth closed on hers, she met his lips. His hands were warm on the small of her back, as he pulled her even closer. Her limbs grew weak as his hands slid downwards over her hips.

'Jack! Jack! Where the hell are you?'

He drew away from her. 'Marty and I are moving into the basement next door and it looks like he can't do without me for five minutes.'

'So it appears.' Her voice grated, oddly hoarse.

'I have skiffle group practice tomorrow. I won't be in until ten. That's too dark to see anything.'

'If the house is empty I'll come down to the garden and wait for you.'

'Ten o'clock, you'll hear my bike engine.'

'I'll be here if I can.'

He kissed her again.

'Jack!' Martin's voice sharpened in exasperation.

'Your gate to the back lane locked?'

'Yes.'

'Then I'll climb the wall.'

'What will you tell Martin?'

'The truth. That a mate needed help. Until

tomorrow.' Hauling himself up on his hands, he swung himself over the wall that backed on to the lane. A few minutes later she heard the garden gate open next door.

'I could hear you in Mansel Street, Marty. What's the problem?'

'Where the hell have you been? This fire could have got out of control.'

'But it didn't. I built it too well for that.'

'You still left it. Where have you been?'

'Helping a mate.'

'With everything that needs doing here!'

'He only needed a hand for ten minutes...'

'You've been gone more like half an hour. You're holding us up. A shed-load of rubbish needs shifting from the passage.'

'I'm there.'

As Jack's voice grew faint, Helen hugged herself. She had a boyfriend. A secret boyfriend. First thing tomorrow she'd start on the basement. Shift the furniture round in the room with the biggest window, make it cosy and comfortable, clean it until it shone spotless. Take down her record player; make some pictures for the walls. She would explain that if she was going to be locked up for six months she'd need her own sitting room. Her mother wouldn't care unless she thought she was enjoying herself. She would have to learn to keep the miserable expression on her face and that wouldn't be too hard in front of her parents. From now on all her smiles would be Jack's. She really, truly wasn't alone any more. And it felt wonderful.

'Helen.' Joe was in the hall as she reached the top of the stairs. 'What's this?' He held up the note she'd written earlier.

'I was going to run away.' She hid the knife behind her back.

'It reads more like you were thinking of killing yourself.'

'I wasn't thinking straight.'

'And now?'

'I decided I had nowhere to run to.' She darted into the kitchen.

'You won't do anything stupid?' he asked earnestly.

'Not any more,' she answered blithely, sliding the knife back into the drawer.

CHAPTER NINE

Norah checked the hem of Katie's skirt, pulling it first one way, then another. 'Turn round, Katie, slowly mind.'

Katie rotated in front of the full-length mirror in Norah's workroom.

'You look every inch the successful secretary.'

'You're not just saying that to make me feel better?' Katie studied her image in the glass. The costume Norah had made her had wiped out her entire savings plus all the birthday money her mother had scrimped together and she needed reassurance that it was worth it.

'No, I'm not just saying it, you look wonderful,

so grown-up.' Norah brushed away a tear as she stroked the fine charcoal-grey wool of Katie's jacket. 'It's a pity your mother isn't here to see it on you.'

'I'll wear it when I visit her on Wednesday, but if I don't get this job it will be a complete waste.'

'As your mother said when she chose the material, you had to have a birthday present. And even if I do say it myself, that jacket fits as well as any I've seen coming out of a bespoke tailor's. Lily's hat, gloves and bag complement it perfectly.'

Katie continued to eye herself critically and decided Mrs Evans was right. The mid-calf-length full skirt and tight-waisted jacket skimmed her thin figure, emphasising her tiny waist yet adding inches where she needed them most on her bust and hips, and the sheen on the wool was one that came with quality. Her white cotton blouse was bleached clean, freshly starched and ironed, the plain black clutch bag, bracelet-length cotton gloves and black pillbox hat businesslike. The only problem was she didn't feel in the least bit like herself.

'You'll get the job,' Lily said from the doorway.

'You came.' Katie beamed.

'Told you I could take an hour off.' Lily looked Katie up and down. 'You're perfect, apart from the hat.'

'You and Judy said it looked good yesterday.'

'We were wrong. Looking at you now, I think the beret would be better. I won't be a minute.'

As Lily ran upstairs, Norah reached for the clothes brush and gave Katie's costume an unnecessary going over. She was proud of Lily's dress sense. Her foster-daughter seemed to know instinctively what was right, what wasn't and how to cut cost without marring the overall effect. But she was prouder still when other girls asked for – and took – Lily's advice.

'Ready?'

'Apart from the butterflies doing the rumba in my stomach,' Katie replied.

'Here,' Lily returned, stood behind Katie and unpinned her hat. 'I know a bank isn't quite like a solicitor's but I've seen the girls go into the Mansel Street offices in the morning. They're well dressed but in a businesslike not "going out" way.' She handed Katie the beret. 'This is plain and a bit young, but that's exactly the look you should be aiming for when applying for your first real job.'

'There you are, love,' Norah said briskly. She didn't know the difference between working in a bank or a solicitor's but Lily had been in an office for six months and, as far as she was concerned, that made Lily an authority on what shorthand typists should wear.

'Your hair needs redoing.' Lily opened her bag and pulled out her comb.

'There's no time.'

'Your interview isn't for another half-hour. It's a five-minute walk from here to Thomas and Butler's. Sit!' Pulling a chair in front of the mirror, Lily pushed Katie into it, unclipped her ponytail, combed out her hair and twisted it into a French pleat at the back of her head, which she secured with a couple of pins she took from her own hair.

'There, just like the picture of Audrey Hepburn in *Roman Holiday*,' she declared as she pulled the beret on to Katie's head and adjusted it.

Katie bit her lip as she studied her reflection in the mirror. Lily was right; the black beret did look better.

'Put the gloves on – perfect,' Lily declared. 'Don't worry, Auntie Norah, I'll get her there in one piece.'

'I know you will, love.'

'See you later.' Lily kissed Norah's cheek.

'Try not to bite your lips before the interview, Katie,' Norah warned, 'or you'll ruin your lipstick. And good luck, not that you need it,' she called after them as Lily opened the door.

'Thanks for coming home to help me dress.' Unaccustomed to her peep-toe, high-heeled shoes – a birthday present from her brothers –Katie clung to Lily's arm as they rounded the corner and headed down the hill into Verandah Street.

'I had an hour coming to me. Mr Collins made me work through yesterday's lunch hour.' Lily made a face. 'He knocked a pile of papers from one of the desks, spent ten minutes ranting about the amount of filing cluttering up the office, then ordered me to clear all the surfaces.'

'Lily...'

'You're worried how it will go. Well, don't.'

'That's easy for you to say. You've a good job.'

'There are days when I wonder. "Lily, get the tea, Lily, clear the cups, Lily, take the post round the desks, Lily, this needs delivering to the other side of town, Lily, get us a bun while you're out." And once in a blue moon, "Lily, this is only for the files so you can type it." After six months of being at everyone's beck and call I'm still not allowed to type anything destined for clients and they won't let me take dictation. Another couple of months and I'll forget most of the typing and all of the shorthand I ever learned.'

'But you've never worked anywhere except an office.'

'I worked in the Milkmaid.'

'When you were in tech, and only on Saturdays and holidays, that's not like washing dishes in a café all the time.'

'Katie, stop worrying. You came top of your evening class.'

'That's the point. It was evening class not a proper tech or school of commerce.'

'All the more reason for Thomas and Butler to take you on. You've proved you've got what it takes to stick at something.'

'But a solicitor's office...' Katie's voice trailed as she looked across the road at the massive Victorian building that dominated the corner of Mansel and Christina Streets. 'I can't imagine working there. Not after the café.'

'Now look at me,' Lily ordered. 'Just as I thought, hair, lipstick, beret, gloves, shoes, costume all perfect. And...' She bent her head close to Katie's. 'Is that Norah's perfume I smell? The special one she keeps for Christmas and birthdays?'

'She said I should wear it for luck.'

'It never fails. Now walk in there and stun them

into giving you the job. You deserve it after getting the certificate. And think how good it will feel to give your mother the news on Wednesday.'

Katie tensed herself as she crossed the road. She glanced back. Lily was standing on the pavement, watching her. She waved, then squaring her shoulders and holding her head high, just as Miss Crabbe, her shorthand tutor, had advised when applying for a job, she headed for the gate that separated Thomas and Butler's frontage from the pavement.

The little confidence Lily had imparted deserted Katie the minute she opened the door and stepped into an oak-panelled reception area that could have swallowed her mother's kitchen ten times over. A glamorous woman sitting behind a desk gave her a vacuous professional smile. 'Can I help you, madam?'

Katie broke into a cold sweat. 'I'm here for the interview,' she blurted nervously, instantly thinking of a hundred better ways she could have introduced herself.

'And you are?'

'Clay. Katie Clay.'

'We've been expecting you, Miss Clay.'

Katie's pulse raced. Was it her imagination or was there a hint of reprimand? She looked for a clock to check if she was late. If only Lily hadn't insisted on redoing her hair. Perhaps it would have been better if she had worn the hat not the beret. It would have been dressier...

'Miss Clay?'

'Sorry,' Katie apologised, conscious she hadn't

been listening.

'Mr Thomas and Mr Butler will see you shortly. Would you like to take a seat while you wait?'

'Thank you.' Feeling clumsy and awkward, Katie walked over to a semicircle of chairs grouped around a low table set with a neatly arranged fan of magazines. She would have liked to have picked one up, but lacking the courage to disturb the display, she studied the room instead. The light-oak wall panelling looked and smelled as though it received a daily polishing of beeswax and the floor, an elegant shade darker than the walls, was so highly buffed that Katie was terrified she'd turn her ankle when she left her seat. Every single piece of furniture matched the panelling. Behind the receptionist's pale-oak desk stood a row of pale-oak filing cabinets. A porcelain vase fashioned to resemble twin sticks of bamboo held an arrangement of cream carnations. Sepia pen-and-ink sketches of Swansea landmarks hung at regular intervals around the walls. Katie recognised Swansea Castle or rather its few remaining walls, the Museum, the Glynn Vivian Art Gallery, the old Guildhall – everything looked so clean, so ... so 'de luxe', as Mrs Petronelli would have said, that she couldn't imagine touching anything, let alone working in the place.

What on earth had made her think that she could land a job in a solicitor's office as grand as this? As her last traces of hope evaporated, she began to tremble. She also realised her feet hurt. Her shoes had fitted her when she'd bought them so why were they tight now? Her heels and toes were stinging with a pain she knew from experience would result in blisters. She told herself she could bear it. She'd have to bear it – just as long as she didn't limp when they called her in. That would be the final humiliation. They might think she had borrowed someone else's shoes for the interview because she couldn't afford her own.

Lifting the flap of Lily's clutch bag, she surreptitiously pulled out her mirror to check that the discreet sprinkling of powder she'd dusted on to her face hadn't disappeared, or the lipstick she had applied so carefully a quarter of an hour before had wandered on to her teeth. She wished she had the courage to ask the receptionist if she could go to the Ladies. If there was a larger mirror she'd be able to check that the beret and her hair were still all right and the seams on her nylons straight.

'Miss Clay?'

Katie had thought the receptionist's black skirt, blue blouse with black velvet ribbon tie and short curly hairstyle the height of sophistication but she paled into insignificance against this new apparition. Dressed in a navy tailored suit with mid-calf, pencil-slim skirt and light-grey blouse, the young woman exuded self-confidence. Her blonde hair was swept neatly behind her ears, her make-up glossy, her perfume subtle, yet effective enough for Katie to pick up from six feet away.

No matter how much she earned, Katie knew she'd never achieve that degree of sophistication or the deftness of touch that had led to the choice of exactly the right accessories: Gold button earrings, discreet and tasteful, complemented by a gold lapel pin and a half-hoop of diamonds on the third finger of her left hand. Katie wasn't surprised she was engaged. She could imagine men vying to be seen with her, and not the sort of men who lived in Carlton Terrace either. Rich men with well-paid jobs who drove new cars and owned houses. No rented rooms with outside toilets or shared bathrooms for them – or her.

'I'm Isabel Evans.' The secretary held out her hand.

Katie stumbled to her feet, one shoe getting in the way of the other. 'Pleased to meet you.' She fumbled awkwardly with her cotton gloves, dropping one as she realised her hands were damp. Isabel picked up the glove for her before shaking her hand.

'Mr Thomas and Mr Butler will see you now. If you'd follow me.'

'Thank you.' Clutching her bag and the envelope containing her certificates and testimonial from Miss Crabbe, Katie slipped, spraining her ankle and tearing the thin strap that held her left shoe together above the peep toe.

'Are you all right, Miss Clay?' Isabel was at her side. The receptionist left her desk and between them they helped her to her feet. Katie fought back tears of pain and mortification.

'Oh, dear, your shoe...'

'It's all right, I'll get a cobbler to stitch it.'

'It looks new,' Isabel observed. 'If I were you I'd take it back to the shop. If you'd like to postpone the interview, I'm sure Mr Thomas would understand.'

'I'm fine,' Katie lied.

'If you're sure.' Isabel supported Katie's arm as she opened the door that led from the reception area to the offices. 'Mr Thomas looks stern,' Isabel whispered, 'but he's fair and Mr Butler is charming.'

Instead of calming Katie, the confidence set her nerves jangling even more.

'Would you like to wait a moment before going in?'

Not trusting herself to speak, Katie shook her head. Isabel opened another door and guided her down a second corridor. Tensing herself yet again, Katie breathed in Isabel's clean, cool scent and tried to forget her bungling start to the interview. If she walked carefully, Mr Thomas and Mr Butler might not notice her broken shoe and if they were as nice as Isabel suggested, perhaps she would even forget this interview was such a milestone. There was no way she could tell her mother and Norah she'd failed after the cost of the evening classes and the work they'd put into her costume.

'Is this your first interview?'

'For an office job. Does it show?'

'No,' Isabel prevaricated. 'I remember being incredibly nervous when I went for my first position.'

'Honestly?'

'Don't worry, you'll be fine. Your references are very good.'

'You've seen them?'

Isabel nodded as she tapped on a door, opening it at a brisk 'Enter'.

'Good luck.' She left Katie to walk into the room alone.

Two men sat behind the largest desk Katie had ever seen. One was middle-aged, well-built, imposing with thinning grey hair and a pepper-and-salt moustache; the other young and slightly built with red hair.

The older man peered short-sightedly at her over a pair of half-moon reading spectacles. 'Miss?' He checked the paper on his desk.

'Clay,' the younger man supplied, smiling at Katie.

'Yes, sir,' Katie stammered nervously.

'You don't have to call either of us "sir"; you're not in the classroom now, Miss Clay. Mr Thomas will do. And this is Mr Butler.'

'Yes, Mr Thomas, Mr Butler, thank you.' Katie gripped Lily's handbag tighter. She had no idea why she was thanking them.

'Sit down, girl, sit down,' Mr Thomas muttered impatiently shuffling his papers. 'You've applied for the position of office junior?'

'Yes, Mr Thomas.'

'It appears from your certificates and college references that your typing and shorthand speeds are excellent and, most important, also your spelling. You went to night school?'

'Yes.'

'Why?'

The question took Katie by surprise. 'Because I had to leave school at fourteen,' she blurted uneasily, 'and I wanted qualifications that would get me a better job.'

'Your teachers didn't think you were up to passing the matriculation?'

'No, Mr Thomas, they were pleased with my work but my father – my family – needed the money so I had to leave.'

'And you work in a café at present.'

Katie stared at the application form in his hand. It was hers, she recognised her handwriting and as she'd detailed her entire history on it she couldn't understand why he was asking her questions she'd already answered.

'Yes, sir,' she muttered, forgetting to call him Mr Thomas.

'And what exactly is it you do in this café. It is the one opposite the Grand Theatre?'

'Yes, Mr Thomas. I clear tables, wash dishes, serve behind the counter and wait tables when we're short-staffed.'

'Take the money,' he barked.

'No, Mr Thomas, one of the family works the cash register.'

Mr Thomas frowned and Katie had the feeling he'd decided her present employers didn't regard her as trustworthy enough to handle their money.

'Are you happy there?'

'Yes, Mr Thomas.'

'Then why do you want to leave?'

Well drilled by Miss Crabbe, Katie refrained from listing her real reasons. That she wanted to work in a clean office instead of the hothouse, chip-fryer atmosphere of the café. That she longed to do more challenging work than skivvying. That she wanted more to look forward to than promotion to waitress when she'd only have to remember which people had ordered what food and writing out bills. And most important of all, she wanted to earn more money than she could in a café. Money enough to take her out of her family's basement and enable her to buy nice clothes, perm her hair and give her the same air of sophistication as Isabel Evans. Money that would secure her independence so she need never be reliant on a man to keep her.

'I would like to work in an interesting position where I could use the skills I've been taught in evening class and hopefully acquire new ones,' she chanted parrot-fashion.

'You do know what this job is?'

'Yes, Mr Thomas.' Disconcerted by his piercing stare, she concentrated on a point somewhere between his and Mr Butler's heads. 'It's office junior.'

'I don't know what your idea of an office junior's duties are, Miss Clay, but in Thomas and Butler they make the tea, run errands and copies off the duplicating machine and do the filing. You do know what filing is?'

'Yes, Mr Thomas. Storing documents in alphabetical order.'

'You've done it?'

'Miss Crabbe explained it, Mr Thomas, in evening class.'

'So you've no actual experience.'

'Miss Crabbe kept our typing and shorthand exercises in a drawer in files in alphabetical order. When we finished one we were allowed to replace it and remove the next.'

'A drawer, not a filing cabinet.'

197

'Yes, Mr Thomas.' Katie recalled the bank of pale-oak filing cabinets behind the receptionist's desk and wished she'd never mentioned Miss Crabbe's single drawer.

'You don't help out in the office of the café by any chance, do you?'

Katie sensed that Mr Butler had meant to be kind, but lost for words she stared down at her hands. The nearest thing to an office they had in the café was the shelf under the till where they stored receipts, invoices from suppliers and the cigar butts Mr Petronelli could never bring himself to throw out. 'No, sir,' she stammered after an embarrassing pause.

'That's unfortunate.' Mr Thomas pulled his chair forward. Lifting the file in front of him, he rapped it down on the desk. 'So you've no experience and you've just passed your examinations.'

'With distinctions in shorthand, typing, English and spelling,' Katie interrupted eagerly to show what she could do, after all the talk of what she couldn't.

'I can read, Miss Clay,' Mr Thomas snapped, making her feel more inadequate than ever. 'But you've no experience of office work.'

'I learn quickly.' Katie dared a second interruption because she sensed the job she'd pinned all her hopes on slipping from her grasp.

'I don't doubt you do.'

'And my shorthand and typing speeds will improve with practice.'

'Our juniors do very little typing and no shorthand. We have secretaries for the skilled work.'

'I would be happy to work my way up, Mr

198

Thomas. All I need is a chance to prove myself.'

'It's an office junior we want, Miss Clay, not an ambitious "would-be" secretary. Frankly, if we have a vacancy at senior level we advertise the position as suitable for the holder of an accredited school of commerce diploma. You've met our Miss Evans.'

'Yes, Mr Thomas.' Katie looked down at her hands again. She didn't need Mr Thomas to remind her there was no way she could compete with the likes of Isabel Evans.

'She not only has a diploma from a school of commerce but also from Lucy Clayton.'

Katie remained silent – she had never heard of Lucy Clayton.

'One last thing, what sort of wages were you hoping to earn?'

'Miss Crabbe...'

'Ah, your mentor, or is it oracle?' He laughed at his own joke but Mr Butler remained straight-faced.

Failing to understand the significance of Mr Thomas's remark, Katie ignored it. 'She suggested one pound ten shillings a week would be fair for girls with our qualifications but I would be prepared to work for less if there were prospects.' Katie dug her nails into the palm of her hand. Everyone in night school had warned her that wages were tricky, ask too little and you could find yourself working for less than the going rate, too much and you wouldn't get the job.

'Well, Miss Clay, Thank you for your time.' Mr Thomas left his seat, effectively ending the interview.

'Thank you for seeing me, Mr Thomas, Mr Butler.'

'As we have more people to interview, we'll inform you of the outcome in due course.'

'Yes, thank you.' Holding the envelope she hadn't opened and her bag, she rose slowly, balancing her broken shoe precariously on her sprained foot.

He pressed a buzzer on his desk. 'Miss Evans will see you out.'

Katie hobbled to the door with as much dignity as she could muster. It opened before she reached it.

'See Miss Clay out, Miss Evans. Then I have some letters for you to take before we interview our next applicant.'

'Yes, Mr Thomas.' She closed the door. 'That wasn't too bad, was it?' she asked as she helped Katie to the front door.

'It was dreadful.'

'If you don't get the job, look on it as practice for the next interview. It might be for a better job that pays more.'

Katie tried to return Isabel's smile, but she couldn't help feeling that the secretary had sized up her prospects the moment she'd broken her shoe. And even if Isabel was wrong, she'd rather work in the café for the rest of her life than face another ordeal like the one Mr Thomas had just put her through.

Philip Butler left his chair, picked it up and carried it across to the back wall of his uncle's office. 'You've already given the job out.' It was a statement not a question.

'A chap in the Chamber of Commerce has a daughter just out of Gregg's. He has a business but won't take her into it. Not that I blame him for that, it's notoriously difficult to work with family. Her mother's a decent sort of woman, knows how to talk, dress and present herself, so the daughter will be more our sort.'

'Then why advertise the job and get the hopes up of poor girls like that? She was practically dying of nerves.'

'Which will go against her no matter what job she applies for. If she's like that at an interview just think what she'll be like when she has to work.'

'You didn't make it easy for her.'

'I wish your mother had never sent you to that blasted university. All you've done since you've come back is spout socialist ideals. Do yourself and me a favour, Philip, grow up! Thomas and Butler is a well-respected firm. People look to us to lead the way. We can't take on an unsuitable girl just because you feel sorry for her. And after talking to that one I'm not sure she should be aiming any higher than the café she's already working in.'

'I think...'

'You think! I've been meaning to say this since you joined Thomas and Butler. Just because your father and I set up this firm together, don't go assuming that you have an equal partnership.'

'My father...'

'Your father is dead, Philip. I offered to buy out his share. Your mother convinced me I should take you on instead. But unless you cure this sentimental streak and start behaving like a professional, I will press her to accept my offer. The next interview is in one hour. Be prompt.'

'I'm not sure I want to sit in, if you've already promised the job.'

'Do you want to continue working here?' Richard Thomas stared at Philip. 'Fine, I'll see you then. Now, if you'll excuse me, I have letters to write. Someone in this firm has to bring in enough to cover the overheads.'

'Hey, Katie, you look smart.' Adam ran to catch up with her as she hobbled across the road. 'What's the matter?' he asked as they reached the pavement and he saw tears in her eyes.

'I've broken my shoe.'

'So you have and twisted your ankle by the look of it. Have you been to the doctor's?'

Adam's kindness coming on top of Mr Thomas's brusque interrogation was too much. Katie burst out sobbing as she clung to the arm he offered her.

'I had to take a couple of hours off to go to the dentist. I've just left. Come on, I'll help you home.'

She shook her head fiercely.

'Then how about we go down the café opposite the Albert Hall and have a cup of tea?'

Too upset to argue, Katie allowed him to lead her away.

'Two teas and two sticky buns please, George,' Adam called as he pushed open the door to the café. 'And plenty of sugar in one of the teas, my friend here has twisted her ankle.'

'So I see.' George picked up a rag and soaked it under the cold tap behind the counter. 'Here.' He handed it to Adam. 'That might bring down the swelling.'

'Thanks, George. Katie...' Adam looked across to see her tears still falling thick and fast. 'Look, if it hurts that much I'd better take you home.'

'It's not my ankle,' she burst out between sobs.

'Then what?'

'You're being kind and that man was horrible.'

'What man?'

'Your tea, miss, and help yourself to all the sugar you want.'

George pushed the bowl in front of her. 'And here's two of our stickiest buns. If I were you I'd eat first to make sure you get at least one bite. Adam's a terror when he gets in front of those. I've seen him eat six in a row.'

'Thank you.' Katie managed a watery smile.

'That's better.'

'I'm sorry. I don't know what came over me. I had this interview for an office job and it went wrong.'

'Is that all.' Adam lifted her foot up alongside him as he slid into the booth opposite her.

'All!'

'I take it you wanted the job.'

'More than anything.' She glared at him. 'And don't you dare sneer at me, Adam Jordan, just because you're working in the Land Registry and I'm in a café. I could work in an office if I was given the chance.'

'Of course you could work in an office and I'm not making fun. My mother told me you came top of your class in night school. Look, I know what you're going through. I never thought I'd pass my Civil Service entrance.'

'But you did.'

'Eventually. But it wasn't easy and by the time I'd finished the last examination I'd begun to wonder if I'd be better off labouring like my father.'

'You don't mean that.' Katie blotted her tears with her handkerchief.

Adam bit into one of the buns. 'Yes, I do,' he reiterated decisively. 'I know there's no career prospects labouring, but unlike me, my father's never had to worry about making a mess of things and losing his job. I'm terrified someone in work is going to realise that I've no business being in the Civil Service. That saying about "the higher you go the further you fall" could be prophetic where my career is concerned.'

'I've never thought about it that way.'

'Take my cousin, Tom. He has absolutely no ambition beyond his guitar and music. He, Jack Clay and a couple of the boys formed a skiffle group last year. They've got their first engagement on Saturday, a youth club dance in St James's church hall but Bill Haley and the Comets couldn't be more pleased with a booking at the Albert Hall. I envy them their dreams of success.'

'I haven't got anything besides work either. This was my big chance to get out of the café and I messed it up.'

'There'll be other interviews.'

'There won't, because that's the last job I'm applying for. I won't risk going through another experience like that again.'

'What on earth did this man say to you that was so horrible?'

'That I had no experience.'

'Well, you haven't, have you?'

'There was no need for him to say it the way he did. As if all I'm good for is café work.'

'I'm sure he didn't mean it that way, Katie. He was probably looking for someone who was used to working in an office because they don't have time to train you in the things that can't be taught in night school.'

'Do you think so?'

'I think there's a right job waiting for everyone. You'll find yourself an office job or it will find you, if that's what you really want. Now drink your tea.'

'After I've paid for it.' She fumbled in her handbag.

'My treat, if you'll come out with me.'

'Just the two of us?'

'Why not?'

'I'd prefer to go out in a crowd.'

'Brian's asked Judy out. We could make it a foursome.'

'I'd still have to ask Mrs Evans. I'm staying with her and Lily until my mother comes out of hospital.'

'I'll check with Brian, and there's the dance on Saturday. I know it's only a youth club, but Tom and the others can do with all the encouragement they can get. It would be great if you could get the other girls to go as well.'

'I'm not sure about Helen but I'll ask Lily and Judy.'

'So, it's true?'

'What?'

'That Helen's parents have locked her up after Saturday.'

'Knowing Helen, it won't last long. Her father never stays angry with her for more than a day or two. No one does.' There was a touch of envy in her voice.

'I don't know why, she's not half as nice as you – or pretty,' he added quietly, after checking George wasn't in earshot.

'Oh, yes, I'm really pretty with tears blotching my make-up and a swollen ankle.'

'I don't say things I don't mean, Katie. Have you got time for another tea?'

'I ought to go back to Auntie Norah's. She'll want to know how the interview went.'

'I'll walk you. If Brian's in I'll talk to him about fixing a date. Shall I call in on you afterwards?'

'If you like.' She hadn't meant to sound quite so offhand but there was something about Adam Jordan – his blond good looks and quiet self-assurance – that made her uneasy and she couldn't quite say why.

CHAPTER TEN

Norah was peeling potatoes in the kitchen when Katie hobbled in. She looked up, smiled, and when Katie didn't return her smile or volunteer any information, she ventured, 'How did it go?'

'Terrible. They didn't want me.'

Drying her hands on her apron, Norah picked up the kettle and filled it. 'I'm sure they didn't say that to your face, Katie.'

'They said they'll let me know.'

'It couldn't have been that terrible. You were gone a long time, you must have a chance.'

'I was gone a long time because my shoe broke. I twisted my ankle and bumped into Adam Jordan. He took me to the café down by the Albert Hall and they gave me a wet towel to bring the swelling down.' Kicking off her broken shoe, she lifted her swollen foot.

'That looks as though it needs an elastic bandage. Sit in the easy chair and rest your leg on this.' Norah moved a kitchen chair in front of her.

'The man who interviewed me practically told me I hadn't got it because I've no experience.'

'It's your first interview, love,' Norah murmured sympathetically from the depths of the cupboard where she was rummaging in the First Aid box. 'It's not so easy to get a job when you're starting out and haven't had a chance to prove yourself. Our Lily had to make three applications.'

'She made three applications, but she still got the first job she interviewed for.'

'And you'll get the right job for you, you'll see.' Emerging with a roll of crêpe bandage, Norah sat on the kitchen chair, gently drew Katie's foot on to her lap and gingerly prodded the swollen joint. 'This is a bad sprain, you'll need to take it easy for a day or two.'

'I have to work.'

'Not tomorrow.'

'They'll dock me a day's pay. Mam needs the money.'

'Not in hospital.'

'There'll still be bills.'

'Which are your father's responsibility.'

'Dad was right,' Katie declared miserably. 'Mam should never have spent all that money on shorthand typing lessons. I'm not going to get an office job in a million years. All I'll ever be good for is washing dishes.'

Wise enough to realise that anything she said would only make Katie feel worse, Norah finished bandaging the girl's foot, washed her hands and set about making tea. She wasn't so old that she couldn't remember a time when assurances that everything would turn out well only seemed to make disappointments a hundred times worse.

'I think we've covered everything, Miss Griffiths.'

'Thank you, Mr Thomas, Mr Butler.' Helen left her chair as Richard Thomas pressed the buzzer on his desk.

208

'We'll see you at eight thirty Monday morning.' Richard eyed Helen from beneath his bushy eyebrows.

'Yes, Mr Thomas. Thank you Mr Thomas.' Helen's heart sank. For all his brusque, businesslike air there was something creepy about Richard Thomas. A touch of the 'sneaky old grubby eyes' as Judy had christened the middle-aged men who slyly watched them and other young girls changing on the beaches around Gower.

He had scarcely allowed her to say a word. After a cursory glance at her certificates he had outlined her future duties, incidentally referring to his staff in an arrogant, derogatory way that suggested he had no compunction about bullying even the most senior of them.

The door opened and Isabel Evans walked in.

'Miss Evans will show you around the office, Miss Griffiths. Miss Griffiths starts with us next Monday as office junior, Miss Evans.'

'Yes, Mr Thomas. Congratulations, Miss Griffiths.'

'Thank you,' Helen murmured.

Accustomed to anticipating Mr Thomas's wishes, Isabel held the door open. 'If you'd come this way, please, Miss Griffiths.' She stepped back so Helen could precede her down the corridor to the General Office and reception area.

'Miss Mair Miles, our receptionist. Miss Miles, this is Miss Helen Griffiths. Miss Griffiths will be joining us on Monday as office Junior. Miss Griffiths, Miss Cynthia Allen and Miss Belinda Jenkins, our secretaries...'

Helen's grin almost became a grimace as the names of her prospective co-workers washed over her. There were a bewildering number of them, a receptionist, a telephonist, a senior secretary, two junior secretaries and a typist. Mr Butler nodded briefly to her as he walked through reception to the opposite end of the building. His smile was reserved for Isabel. Was it her imagination or did a pitying look pass between them. She wondered what had happened to the last office junior; she couldn't help noticing that there wasn't a secretary young enough to have been promoted recently from the position.

'You've a job where?'

'Thomas and Butler,' Helen whispered hesitantly. After Sunday she had thought Esme couldn't get any angrier, but her mother's face was contorted – ugly in the intensity of her rage. 'Dad did tell you...'

'He didn't or I would have put a stop to it. Your father has absolutely no sense. And I wouldn't count on starting work there if I were you. I don't know what he was thinking of.'

Confused, Helen charged upstairs.

'More problems?' John asked, as he hobbled into the hall in time to hear Helen's bedroom door slam.

Esme turned furiously on him. 'How dare you arrange for Helen to work in Thomas and Butler's?'

'I told you...'

'You most certainly did not.'

'I did, and even if I didn't mention their name

they are a well-respected firm. They're not only my solicitors. Your own mother...'

'Precisely,' she broke in cuttingly. 'Not only your solicitors but also my mother's. Didn't it occur to you that I wouldn't want Helen working there?'

'No.' He shuffled over to the sofa. It was raining and on wet days his scars ached unbearably, not that he ever complained about the pain to Esme. He looked up at her. 'Is there something you know about Thomas and Butler's that I don't?' he asked quietly.

'Of course not.'

'Then why shouldn't Helen work there?'

Refusing to meet his eye, Esme fumbled with the cigarette box. She had never revealed the identity of Joseph's father to John and wouldn't have, even if he had asked outright. But he hadn't, not when she'd announced she was pregnant shortly after their marriage, or on the day Joseph was born when simple arithmetic would have made it clear there was no way he could have fathered her son.

Damn Helen for wanting a job and damn John for organising her one in the only office in Swansea she didn't want Helen working in. But there was no way she could tell him the reason that lay behind her objections without betraying the secret she had kept for over twenty years.

'Why, Esme?' he repeated softly.

'I would have thought it was obvious. Thomas and Butler deal with my mother's affairs and Joseph's trust fund.'

'Helen's starting as an office junior, not junior

partner. Her duties will hardly include dealing with sensitive documents. Your family's or anyone else's.'

'I suppose you think I'm overreacting.' She forced herself to look at him. 'Helen will be meeting the public. After what happened on Saturday she'll be exposed to gossip of the worst possible kind.'

'And the best way to deal with that is ride it out until it's forgotten.'

'I might have known you'd take that attitude.'

'Esme...'

'I'll see if Mrs Jones has actually remembered to prepare the vegetables for the evening meal for once.' She almost ran into the kitchen, leaving John bewildered, confused and – suspicious.

He'd never asked Esme about Joe's father because he'd always assumed he'd been one of her 'set'. A boy too young to marry. For the first time he wondered if Joe's father had abandoned her because he already had a wife. Peter and Amelia Butler had been his mother-in-law's closest neighbours and Esme had babysat for them. Was Joe the result of the old cliché, the young virile husband with a wife recovering from childbirth and an attractive babysitter?

Like most of the businessmen in the town, Peter Butler had been a member of the Chamber of Commerce, but unlike the others, he'd been consistently polite and pleasant, always asking after Esme and Joe. Had he asked out of guilt at abandoning them? Did Joe resemble him? He tried to picture Peter but could only recall unremarkable features, brown hair and Esme's uncharacteristic grief when she'd heard of his early death in a boating accident.

He would have to broach the subject with Esme again when she wasn't so distraught and Helen and Joe were out. If only she'd said something. Now Helen was working with Peter's son he knew he should push it, but he had never managed to persuade Esme to talk to him when she didn't want to and he had a feeling he wouldn't succeed now.

At the end of the working day Richard Thomas poured his customary whisky, left his desk and stood in front of the window. Sipping slowly, he watched the shop and office workers trudge up the hill from the town centre. He had almost forgotten Esme Griffiths – Harris – as she was, until John Griffiths had asked in a Chamber of Commerce lunch if anyone knew of an office junior vacancy that might suit his daughter. To his own amazement he had buttonholed John at the bar afterwards and offered the girl a job. Even now he couldn't say exactly what had prompted him to do it. Curiosity to see Esme's daughter? A desire still to be seen as a benefactor to his old friend's family? As executor of Esme's father's will he'd had cause -and later – excuse – to visit Esme's mother almost every day. Esme had been a schoolgirl, a virgin and a very pretty girl. He might even have been tempted to forget the twenty-five-year disparity in their ages if he hadn't been married.

He put the thought from his mind, just as he'd done over twenty years ago. He had been married then and was still married. Daisy was exactly the kind of wife that suited him and his needs, domesticated, dutiful, obedient and decorative, a competent hostess with none of the new-fangled ideas of female emancipation that set his teeth on edge. And she had agreed before their marriage – albeit reluctantly – when he had informed her he didn't want children.

When Esme became pregnant he arranged a private abortion, expensive, discreet. No one would have been any the wiser if she had gone along with it. Instead, she'd avoided him and created a scandal by marrying seventeen-year-old John Griffiths after a whirlwind courtship. At the time he'd felt almost any other option would have been better for her. If she'd felt so strongly about having the child, she could have gone to a Salvation Army home and had it adopted. As it was, he'd felt duty bound to keep a discreet eye on the boy after the first time he'd seen him in his grandmother's house.

Joseph had been a solemn three-year-old with dark eyes and hair and an intelligent look he was convinced the child had inherited from him. A son any father would be proud of. Shortly afterwards he began to filter more money into the trust fund Esme's aunt had set up for Joseph than the old woman had seen in her lifetime.

He had continued to monitor Joseph's career from a distance. He knew he had a part in a radio play being broadcast that night, a practically unheard-of honour for a temporary student researcher. If only he'd realised when he was younger how proud a man could be of his child's achievements, but he and Daisy had lived the life he'd chosen – unencumbered, sophisticated, with holidays they would never have been able to afford if they'd had to pay school fees...

A knock at the door interrupted his reverie.

'Come.' He looked at Philip in surprise. 'I assumed you'd left for the day.'

'You do know that girl you just took on is the one involved in the incident with Laurence Murton Davies on Saturday night.'

'Are you absolutely sure?' Richard was adept at concealing shock.

'I didn't see her because I was at the hospital but I recognised the name. I rang the station and they confirmed the address.'

'You should have said...'

'What?' Philip questioned acidly. 'You'd already given her the job.'

'You told me you'd settled the Murton Davies incident.'

'Not the gossip. That girl...'

'Looks and sounds right for this office. But mention it to Isabel and tell her to keep a close eye. The first sign of trouble and she's out through the door. Thank you for bringing the matter to my attention. You will go over the Roberts case files tonight?'

'I have them in my briefcase.' Philip closed the door as he left the room.

Richard recalled what Philip had told him about the incident on Saturday night. It wasn't difficult for him to imagine Helen naked, even given the amount of padding in women's under-clothes. She appeared to have much the same figure as her mother had had when he'd known her. He wondered if she had the same temperament. Esme had been fifteen when he'd seduced her – not that it had been difficult – and afterwards ... he smiled fondly at the memory. Who would have thought that an outwardly ice-cool blonde exterior could have concealed such a sensual nature?

John Griffiths glanced around the bar of the White Rose. Seeing Roy Williams sitting in a corner he limped over to his table. 'Can I get you another, Roy?'

'I was thinking of going home. It's been a long changeover shift but seeing as how you're already holding my glass I'll let you twist my arm.'

John went to the bar and ordered two pints of best bitter.

'I'd like to talk to you about Saturday night.' John looked around to make sure no one could overhear as he returned and set two full glasses on Roy's table.

'Don't ever quote me but that was a mess and not very well handled by the force. I'm sorry.'

'I'm only sorry Helen was foolish enough to put herself in a position where a boy like Murton Davies could take advantage of her.'

'We've all been young and foolish in our time,' Roy commented philosophically. 'You do know it's Jack Clay you should be thanking. There's no saying what might have happened if he hadn't stuck his oar in.'

'I know.' John looked down into his glass. 'Is Murton Davies really going to get off scot-free?'

'I'm afraid so. For all our sakes I hope he's learned his lesson and there's no next time for some other innocent girl.'

'Bloody crache!' John swore with uncharacteristic vehemence.

'If we had charged him and it had gone to court, Helen would have had to go into the witness box. I've seen similar cases and the girl never comes out unscathed. People like the Murton Davieses can afford to buy the best legal advice. By the time their barrister had finished with Helen, she – and the jury – would have felt as though she was the one on trial.'

'She shouldn't have worn that dress,' John concurred, 'but Murton Davies shouldn't have ripped it off her either. Tell me, what would you have done if it had been your Lily?'

'Killed the bastard.'

Roy spoke so flatly that John couldn't be sure whether he was serious. 'I wish Helen would calm down. She's putting years on me.'

'And every boy who saw her in that dress on Saturday night.'

'Esme won't allow her out of the house and the girls haven't been round. I suppose they've been warned not to talk to her.'

'Norah and Joy Hunt will change their minds in time. A couple of weeks and the whole thing will be forgotten.'

'Not by me – or Helen. She's going to pay for that dress if it takes her ten years. As for Norah and Joy, I can't say I blame them. If one of Helen's friends had behaved the way Helen did last Saturday I would have forbidden Helen to see her again.' John sipped the froth off his pint. 'I trust this job of hers will make her think a bit more about others and less about clothes, make-up and having a good time.'

'Helen's got a job?'

'In Thomas and Butler's as an office junior. Heaven only knows why Richard Thomas didn't cancel the interview after last Saturday. He must have heard what happened. According to my secretary, half of Swansea is talking about young Murton Davies and what he did to Helen. And on top of Saturday there's the question of Helen's qualifications. They leave a lot to be desired. She failed more than half her examinations first time round.'

'So why do you think he gave her the job?'

'I know you won't let this get any further, Roy, but I asked around the Chamber of Commerce. Richard Thomas offered. I assume because he was a close friend of Esme's father and Esme's godfather. He looks after my affairs and a trust fund Esme's aunt set up for Joe. But for all that, the offer surprised me. Richard never struck me as the sort of man to do anyone a favour unless there was something in it for him.'

'I see.' Tight-lipped Roy picked up his pint.

'What's wrong?'

'Nothing.'

'Come on, Roy, we've known one another for years, something's wrong. What is it?'

'Office junior, you say, Thomas and Butler.'

'Nothing wrong with that is there? Or do you know something about Thomas and Butler I don't?' he asked warily, recalling Esme's reaction to the news.

'Annie's girl Katie had an interview for that job this afternoon. It didn't go well. The senior partner as good as told her there and then that she wouldn't get it because she lacked experience.'

'I didn't know little Katie had been to tech.'

'She hasn't. Annie went out scrubbing pubs by day and sewing for Norah at night to scrape up the money to send her to night school. The kid did well, came top of her class in every subject, distinctions all the way. Annie even bought some good-quality cloth, so Norah could make the girl a new costume for the interview. That's why I'm sitting here. All Norah and Lily did through tea was commiserate with Katie. I don't think they ate more than a mouthful between the three of them. It was enough to put me off my food. So deciding I was better off out of the house for an hour or two, I came down here. It's impossible to listen to the radio through a chorus of female voices.'

'You say Katie got top marks in her year?'

'In all her subjects, or so I understand from Norah.'

'Shorthand and typing?'

'The lot, Norah said, whatever "the lot" is.'

'Don't suppose she'd consider taking a job in the warehouse? My secretary's getting married at the end of the month. I was going to advertise next week, but if Katie can start on Monday my girl can train her up. If she likes the work and can cope with it, I'll keep her on.'

'You know the situation there...'

'I know Ernie's put Annie in hospital again, the boys have moved into your basement and Katie's staying with Norah and Lily. You're a braver man than me. I've often thought about helping Annie and the kids, but I've never taken it further than thought. I remember Ernie from school. I was three years below him and, fortunately, never attracted his attention but I do remember him flattening anyone who got in his way.'

'Yet you're prepared to offer Katie a job.'

'That's different, that's just work.'

'Ernie could just as easily make a scene in your warehouse as on my doorstep.'

'Not with the number of men I've got working for me.'

'You do know that with Ernie the way he is and Martin and Jack only earning apprentice's and labouring wages, Annie relies on Katie's money.'

'I'll see Katie all right. You and Norah know Annie better than me, Roy. Can't you persuade her that she and the girl would be better off without Ernie? He must drink double his wages every week and the extra has to come from them.'

'If Annie's thinking of leaving Ernie, she's keeping it close to her chest. I saw her yesterday and nothing will shift her from the story that she tripped and hit her face on the sink. She'll go back to Ernie, she always does, and knowing Katie, she'll not let her mother go back alone. But if the girl gives up the café to work for you, there's no way they'll take her on again if you decide not to offer her a job at the end of her training. Her present wages may be grim but they're better than no wages at all.'

'If Katie's not up to the work I won't keep her on in the office but I can always use an extra pair of hands in the warehouse. I'll find her a place there. What do you think!'

'I think you should ask her. Another?' Roy picked up their glasses.

'I shouldn't, but our house is as miserable as yours by the sound of it. Helen has hardly said a word the last couple of days. Joe's working in Alexandra Road and Esme's in the theatre, auditioning for a new production.'

'She's keen.'

John realised Roy's casual remark was a criticism of the amount of time Esme spent away from home but he couldn't think of a word to say in her defence.

'Drink up.' Roy emptied his own glass. 'And while I think of it, has Joe told you he's taking Lily out tomorrow? Full marks to the boy. He came round to ask Norah's permission. She agreed, but warned him that if he upsets our girl he'll have to answer to me.'

John gave a wry smile. 'I think he already knows that, Roy, and speaking for myself I couldn't be more pleased. Nice, sensible girl, Lily.' He could have added 'unlike Esme' but then he had never been publicly disloyal to his wife and had no intention of starting – yet.

'That wasn't too horrendous, was it?' Robin asked Joe after the producer had signalled 'off air'.

'No,' Joe agreed tersely, folding his script as he

turned away. Since Robin had tried to absolve himself of all responsibility for Larry on Saturday night, he could barely bring himself to look at, let alone talk to, his friend. He also wanted to sound nonchalant and casual for the benefit of the producer and the rest of the cast, as though his five doorman's lines hadn't cost him several anxious hours and a sleepless night.

'Good work, people.' The producer opened the door to the studio.

'Right, I'm for home.' The leading actor reached for his jacket.

'No drinks?' Robin looked to the rest of the cast. 'You're welcome to come back to my place. We could have an impromptu pool party,' he added by way of incentive. 'How about it, Geraldine?'

'I have to go through tomorrow's script.' Geraldine was blonde, attractive and six years older than Joe and Robin. An experienced professional who had delivered her thirty lines with considerable confidence and aplomb.

'Then how about a lift home?' Robin pushed.

'You don't know where I live.'

'I'll take you anywhere.'

'London?' She picked up her handbag from a table at the back of the studio.

'You want to go to the station?'

'You don't give up, do you, boy.' To Robin's chagrin she tickled him under the chin.

'Don't say I didn't offer.' He turned to the door.

'How about as far as Sketty.'

He beamed triumphantly. 'As it's an MG you'll

have to sit on Joe's lap. Or better still, he can drive and you can sit on mine.'

'I have to go home,' Joe demurred, furious with Robin for behaving as though Saturday night had never happened.

'Oh, come on, I want to talk to you about Larry. You do know no one's talking to him?'

'No.'

Geraldine looked coolly from Robin to Joe. 'Do I get my lap?' she interrupted.

'Of course.' Robin took her arm as they left the studio. 'My house has a pool. It's a beautiful evening, we could swim, have a few drinks. What do you say?'

'I'll be too busy going through tomorrow's script to babysit.'

'Babysit?'

'Little boy your age, that is what you wanted, isn't it?'

'You're beginning to sound boring.'

'I can always take the bus.'

'I wouldn't dream of it. Here.' Robin tossed Joe his car keys as they reached the front door.

'I'm not coming with you.'

'I need to talk to you, Joe. Please?'

It was almost impossible to fight Robin when he was in one of his conciliatory moods and Joe was curious what – if any – punishment was being meted out to Larry, but there were practicalities to consider. 'I won't be able to get home afterwards.'

'I'll drive you. Come on, Joe. Be a sport.'

Unable to come up with another reason why he shouldn't go with Robin, Joe pushed the keys into his pocket and followed him out on to Alexandra Road.

Helen checked her watch as she brushed a layer of dust from the sofa in the front room of the basement. The place was a mess and there wasn't time to give it more than a cursory dusting before the magic hour of ten. She'd hidden in her room until her mother had ordered her to lay the table for the evening meal. Not daring to broach the subject of her job again, she'd cleared the dishes after her mother had left for the theatre, cleaned the kitchen and hovered around upstairs until her father went to the pub, unfortunately not early enough for her to have a really good go at the basement.

Walking to the back door, she shook out her duster while listening hard for the roar of Jack's motorbike's engine. 'Please don't let him stop in a pub,' she whispered. 'Please ... please ... please...'

Someone must have answered her prayers for a few seconds later the unmistakable noise of a motorbike resounded from the lane that ran at the back of the terrace. She checked her watch again. Half past nine. He must be eager to see her to leave a full half-hour before practice normally ended. Racing down the path, she reached the bottom of the garden as a dark shape emerged from the back of the garage next door.

'Hello, it's a nice evening,' she called over the garden wall.

'It is, but cold for young ladies to be out without a coat.'

She peered into the gathering twilight. 'Jack?' she murmured hesitantly.

'Brian Powell. We've met, Miss Griffiths, but I don't think we've been formally introduced.' He stepped closer and extended his hand over the wall. 'How do you do?'

Roy opened the door quietly and trod as lightly as he could down the passage, but he needn't have bothered. Norah was sitting in an easy chair in their kitchen-cum-living room, hemming a skirt for a customer. 'I thought you'd be listening to the wireless in the parlour with the girls.'

'This needs finishing. Your supper's on the table.'

He lifted the cloth on a plate to see beautifully cut and presented ham sandwiches.

'The mustard's in front of you.'

'I don't deserve a sister like you.'

'You don't.' Norah bit the end off a thread, and reached for the cotton reel on the small table next to her. 'But I can't say I blame you for taking refuge down the pub with all that wailing earlier. Not that Katie knows anything for certain one way or the other, and there'll be no peace in the house until she does.'

'Katie's right, she hasn't got the job.' Roy sat at the table picked up a knife and reached for the mustard pot.

'You can't possibly know that.'

'I met John Griffiths in the Rose. He didn't know Katie had an interview at Thomas and Butler's, but he told me Helen had and she'd been given the junior's post.'

'That girl!' Norah laid down her needle in indignation. 'She wouldn't get a place in a bus queue on her own merit. This is Esme Griffiths pulling strings again...'

'Before you say another word it might be for the best.'

'How can you even think that! Helen only has to click her fingers to get whatever she wants. Money, clothes, and look what that led to on Saturday night. John is far too lenient on her. That girl's never been disciplined in her life. Mark my words, there'll be more trouble there. Besides, poor Katie needs the money far more than Helen Griffiths with her overflowing wardrobe and pocket money that would keep a family of four in food for a week.'

'When I told John that Katie had applied for the junior's post and was upset because she didn't think she'd got it, he offered her a job in the office of his warehouse. His secretary is leaving but she'll have time to train Katie before she goes. Two pounds five shillings a week for a month's trial. If Katie's not up to the work he'll find her a place in his warehouse; if she is, he'll keep her on in the office and up her wages.'

'John offered Katie a job?' Norah stared at Roy in disbelief.

'She can start when she likes. As far as John is concerned, the sooner the better. He suggested she go round there for a chat, but it is only a formality. The job's hers if she wants it.'

'Good for John. I always did like that man. Well?' Norah peered at Roy over her glasses. 'What are you waiting for? Call the girls and tell

Katie to go round there.'

'Now?'

'It's not yet ten o'clock, or has John Griffiths had even more to drink than you?'

'We had two pints,' Roy remonstrated mildly.

'Some might believe you, I don't. Go on, Roy. Find the girl and make her day, if not her week. She's had nothing but bad news since she came home to find Annie in a mess on Saturday night.'

'Could I do with a swim!' Robin sighed, watching Geraldine disappear down Sketty Road.

'Cold shower more like,' Joe observed caustically as he pulled away from the kerb.

'She is so ... so...'

'Hot?' Joe suggested.

'It was hot in that studio.' He looked across at Joe. 'You want a dip?'

'I don't want a late night. I have an early start in the morning.'

'Ah, ha, you've been shunted on to *Thought for the Day*. That'll teach you to be nice to vicars.'

'It'll be a new experience.'

'Working on *Thought for the Day* is the kind of experience I never want to have.' Robin craned his neck to catch a last glimpse of Geraldine. 'I don't have to go in until six o'clock tomorrow evening. One hour from now I intend to be tipsy, two hours from now drunk. Very, very drunk. In fact, so drunk I won't be able to crawl out of bed until five tomorrow afternoon, that way I might succeed in avoiding my parents for the next twenty-four hours. You wouldn't believe the lectures I've had since Saturday.'

227

'You told your parents what happened?'

'The duty police surgeon was on the phone to my father first thing Sunday morning. God! The sparrows hadn't even woken up. You can always count on the doctors in this town to tell one another everything. If you want to spread a rumour forget the newspapers, just whisper it into the medical grapevine.'

'What did he say?' Joe asked, recalling that Helen had been forced to undergo the indignity of a medical examination.

'That Larry behaved as no gentleman would and should have been put in the cells and left to rot.'

'What do you think?'

'That I'd be doing pigs a disfavour by saying Larry behaved like one. Even allowing that he was drunk and didn't know Helen was your sister, he shouldn't have treated any woman the way he treated her. Everyone I've talked to has said the same thing. As of Sunday morning, Larry's been officially, universally and publicly shunned by all who matter, including and especially my people.'

'You're not just saying that because Helen is my sister?'

'We all have sisters. And it's not only Angie my father is concerned about. I have been expressly forbidden to socialise or even communicate with Larry because Larry has, and I quote, "embraced evil, become embroiled in the devil's ways and is likely to sway me from the paths of righteousness", or something along those lines. My father goes in for biblical language when he lectures on moral rectitude.'

'My father will be pleased to hear that no one wants to know Larry. I think if he had been able to get to him on Saturday night he might have killed him.'

'And you?'

'I've decided to jump Larry on the first day of term.'

'Larry's not worth being sent down for, or the aggravation I've been subjected to. Endless, boring lectures from my mother on how to treat females as ladies and it was no better when I escaped to the billiard room. All I got there was my father telling me that no gentleman ever forces his "companionship" on a woman, much less rips off her dress. And then came the worst bit; he poured out the whisky and after a couple of glasses got all chummy and suggested that if I ever have an overwhelming, uncontrollable urge he knows a woman he can fix me up with.'

'How embarrassing. What did you say?'

'It's what I didn't say. I could have begun with the night we picked up those tarts outside the Museum.'

'You didn't tell him about that!'

'What do you take me for.' Robin looked sideways at Joe as he slowed the car and changed down a gear. 'You've never talked about that night.'

'Because I'd rather not.'

'If you promise to keep your mouth shut, I'll tell you something.'

'About Larry?'

'Me. I paid that woman two pounds but I

didn't let her near me. I couldn't. She was old, ugly and covered in sores. It was horrible. I couldn't even bring myself to kiss her.'

Joe burst out laughing. 'My experience wasn't any better.'

'Then you didn't do anything either?'

'Not that night.'

'I've been thinking. What Larry did to your sister was foul and he shouldn't have done it to any woman but forgetting all that, I think it – I mean sex – has to mean something. When all's said and done we're not bloody animals.'

'This coming from the man who was panting after Geraldine five minutes ago?'

Robin sat silently as Joe drove through the gate to the garaging and parking area in front of his house. 'You ever done it?' he asked suddenly.

'What?'

'Stop being so bloody obtuse. Slept with a girl.'

'I've played around.'

'We've all played around. I got Emily to take off her blouse yesterday.'

Joe stared at him, as much taken aback by the revelation as the fact that Robin got Emily to undress for him.

'Just her blouse. And I needn't have bothered. The man who built the vaults in the Bank of England probably designed the corset she was wearing underneath it. Park by the door. As I intend to spend tomorrow in bed nursing my hangover, you may as well borrow the car.'

'Don't be silly.'

'I told you I intend to get drunk and sleep away most of the day. You can pick me up in the

230

evening and drive me to work.' Robin left the car and slammed the door. He rang the bell. 'Damn, I forgot.' He patted his pockets. 'Pops and Mums have taken Angie to some boring party or other. They gave Mrs John the night off and it looks like I've forgotten my keys. Come on, let's go round the back.'

Picking up the spare key from its hidey-hole behind a loose brick in the garden wall, Robin unlocked the door to the sun lounge at the rear of the house, switched on the inside and outside lights, pulled off his pullover and slung it on one of the cushioned rattan chairs. He gazed at the long narrow pool that filled the area between the patio and the lawn.

'Thank God we've the place to ourselves. I can't wait.' Kicking off his shoes, he left them where they lay. It never ceased to amaze Joe just how carelessly Robin flung his clothes around the house. If he'd done the same his mother would have shouted at him for a week. But then the Watkin Morgans had a live-in housekeeper as well as a maid, while his mother, as she was so fond of telling his father, had to put up with a daily, and an incompetent one at that.

'Bring the whisky and a couple of glasses, will you,' Robin shouted, as he dived naked into the deep end of the pool.

Joe didn't need a second invitation. One of the best things about his friendship with Robin was the Watkin Morgans' hospitality and the way they encouraged him to treat their home as his own. It had taken him a while to become accustomed to the blasé attitude ex-public schoolboys like

Robin had to nudity but now he had no qualms about joining in Robin's all-male swimming parties.

Tossing his clothes on to a chair in the sun lounge, he dived to the bottom of the pool. As the cool, clean water closed over his head he was filled with gratitude towards Robin. Not only for his friendship but for the way he had dismissed Larry. He hated any kind of unpleasantness and it would be far easier to ignore Larry along with everyone else than to confront him.

CHAPTER ELEVEN

'I don't have to go to an interview?'

Roy tried not to smile, lest Katie think he were laughing at her. 'Not in an office, but Mr Griffiths would like a word with you.'

Katie glanced at the clock. 'Now?'

'It's late but not that late.' Norah knew there was no way Katie would settle until she heard the job was hers from John Griffiths.

'We walked up from the pub together so he's in now.'

'I wouldn't be disturbing him?'

'I don't think so.' Roy prised the lid off one of Norah's cake tins and foraged for a rock cake. 'He said Mrs Griffiths and Joe were out.'

'I could see Helen while Katie talks to her father.'

Norah frowned at Lily.

'Just talk, Auntie Norah,' Lily pleaded. 'There's no harm in that. Joe said she wasn't allowed out. I can't stop thinking about her. She must be feeling just awful, and lonely,' she added, sensing her aunt wavering.

'All right, you can go, but I want both of you back in this house before half past ten. You've got work tomorrow, Lily. Katie, take one of the walking sticks out of the stand in the hall. Whatever you do, don't put any weight on that ankle or you'll find yourself in bed for a week. And, Lily, not too sympathetic with Helen, please. She did take that dress from her father's warehouse without asking.'

'We heard you on the radio, Joe, you too, Robin. The play was good.'

'Emily, Angie, clear off, we're not fit to be seen,' Robin shouted as Emily Murton Davies and his sister walked out of the sun lounge on to the patio that bordered the pool.

'We listened to every word.' Angela draped herself elegantly along a deckchair, hiked up her skirt and crossed her long, slim legs to display them to their best advantage. 'The doorman was wonderful. He spoke completely in character and really made you believe in him as a doorman; the chauffeur, on the other hand, was dreadfully wooden.'

'I couldn't give a damn what you thought of the play. Clear off, both of you.' Robin looked for something he could throw at his sister but seeing nothing within reach, he gave up and swam to the side of the pool to join Joe who was pressing himself rigidly against the side.

'Neither of you has anything we haven't seen. We've both been to life-drawing classes.'

'For God's sake, Angie, I'm your brother.'

'Joe isn't.'

'All the more reason for you to go inside.' Joe moved closer to Robin as Emily walked down the side of the pool, presumably in the hope of getting a better view.

'Help! We're drowning.'

'There's no one to hear you, Robin. Mums and Pops are still at the party and from the jolly state of Pops and the way they were both enjoying themselves they won't be home for hours.'

'So you intend just to lie there.' Joe flushed crimson as Angela coolly parried his scowl.

'Only until you come out of the water.' She picked up a towel from the deckchair next to hers. 'Then, I'll dry you off.'

'These are my certificates and Miss Crabbe – that's my teacher in night school – wrote a testimonial.' Katie's hand shook as she handed John Griffiths the envelope Richard Thomas had barely glanced at.

'Thank you, Katie, please, sit down.'

'My marks were good.' Katie perched on the edge of the uncomfortable sofa in the Griffithses' lounge and tried to look anywhere other than at Helen's father as he scanned her papers. The skin on one side of his face was purplish red, blotched, puckered and heavily scarred, his left hand skeletal and clawlike. She'd never been so close to him before but, strangely, she wasn't

234

repelled by his disfigurement as she'd expected to be, more fascinated in some peculiar way. Realising most people would react as she was, she made a conscious effort not to stare.

'Not just good but excellent.' John replaced the papers in the envelope and handed it back to her.

'But I have no real experience of office work, only my classes in night school, Mr Griffiths.'

'You're not supposed to emphasise your short-comings when you apply for a job, Katie.'

Unnerved by his cautionary advice and even more by his gentle smile, she fell silent.

'I gather you have worked,' John prompted, finding her lack of confidence endearing, particularly when contrasted to his daughter's surfeit of self-assurance before last Saturday.

'Just in the café, Mr Griffiths, and Mr Thomas from Thomas and Butler's more or less said that didn't count. So are you sure you want me to work for you?'

'I am sure your Miss Crabbe didn't tell you to ask that question at a job interview, Katie, but as we're being honest, no, I'm not sure I want you to work for me.' In an attempt to put her at ease John deliberately left the lounge door open as he sat in a chair opposite her. 'And I won't be sure until you have worked alongside my secretary for a few weeks. If you cope you can have her position when she leaves at the end of the month. If you can't, I'll find you a place in the ware-house. Is two pounds five shillings a week while you're training all right?'

'Yes, Mr Griffiths.' Katie's eyes sparkled in the lamplight.

'Will you be able to start on Monday?'

'I should think so, but I'll have to give notice in the café.'

'Let me know. The sooner you start the better from my point of view because there's a lot for you to learn. I don't know what you're used to but we work long hours in the warehouse. Eight till six, five days a week and eight till one on Thursdays. Occasionally, at busy times of the year, like Christmas and the end of the summer school uniform rush, there'll be overtime but you'll get an extra hourly rate to compensate.'

'I wouldn't mind working on for nothing...'

'I'm an employer, Katie, not an exploiter. Would you like to ask me any questions?'

Katie racked her brains in an effort to come up with something intelligent, but too excited to think of anything coherent, she shook her head. 'I don't think so but thank you, Mr Griffiths.'

'Then hopefully I'll see you next Monday. If you can't make it, drop in and let me know when you can start.'

'I'll call in on my way home from work tomorrow night. I'll know by then.'

'By the noise I'd say Helen and Lily are in the kitchen. Why don't you join them?'

'Thank you, Mr Griffiths, and thank you for the job.'

As Katie left the room John went to the cocktail cabinet, opening and closing it quickly to minimise 'Stranger in Paradise,' a tune he was rapidly coming to hate. Taking the whisky bottle and glass he had snatched, he sat back and basked briefly in the warm glow that engulfed him whenever he made a charitable donation or managed to help someone less fortunate than himself. But after a few moments all thoughts of Katie were forgotten as he tried to make sense of the welter of conflicting emotions Esme had generated.

The more he contemplated his marriage, the more he wondered if Esme had ever cared for him, or if he had merely been a solution to a problem. His inability to pinpoint her where-abouts on Saturday night had brought home to him just how far they had drifted apart. Esme had been keeping late hours for years, but it had been humiliating when he'd been forced to admit publicly that he didn't know where his wife was at one in the morning. And the blame wasn't entirely hers. He had chosen not to question Esme as to where she went and what she did a long time ago, because it had been easier to continue with the pretence that their marriage was fine rather than confront the reality that she no longer loved him. That's if she ever had. The only wonder was she had married him at all – but then perhaps there hadn't been another naïve, trusting fool around at the time.

He had been at his most vulnerable. His grandfather and grandmother had died within six weeks of one another. Lonely and totally alone for the first time in his life, he had divided his time between the house and warehouse – domestic and business chores – scarcely thinking about either. Then, like a rainbow breaking over a desolate landscape Esme had burst into his life.

He recalled the first time he had seen her,

dressed in school uniform, a ridiculous, pleated gymslip that had made even her slim figure appear plump. She and her aunt had visited the warehouse to look for unseasonable clothes to take them through a cruise her aunt had booked as a reward for Esme's exceptional performance in the school matriculation examinations. He had shown them to the ladies wear section and, after they'd made their choice, Esme had pressed him to buy a ticket to a charity ball her mother had helped organise. Expecting to be ignored, or at best sidelined among her other admirers, he had almost torn up the ticket – but hadn't.

She had been nineteen, cool, blonde and stunningly beautiful in a white silk gown and her mother's pearls; he had been seventeen, crippled and ugly, yet, to his amazement, from the moment of his arrival in the Mackworth Hotel, she had singled him out. Flattered, scarcely daring to believe his good fortune, by the end of the evening he would have done anything she asked of him. He could no longer recall their courtship, the exact sequence of events or how it had happened, but within a month he had found himself a married man and six months later the father of a premature baby boy.

Fortunately he'd had no close relatives to question Joseph's paternity but his few friends and neighbours hadn't been slow in suggesting that Esme had used him. Apart from their stinging remarks and attitude to Esme, he genuinely hadn't minded. His disfigurement had tempered his romantic nature, forcing him to become a realist. On the few occasions during adolescence when he had dared to dream of marriage and children, the reflection staring back at him from the mirror every morning had shattered his fantasies. By the time Esme entered his life he had long been convinced that all women – and men – found him repulsive. And yet against the odds, he had found himself married to a beautiful and intelligent woman.

It didn't take him long to discover she wasn't easy to live with, but everyone he spoke to said the same thing. It was difficult to adjust to married life after free and easy bachelorhood. His single life had been brief and anything but easy. However, he'd reasoned Esme's might have been better and he almost persuaded himself she had to feel something for him. After all, she had chosen him to be the father of her child.

For almost two years Esme had been home to greet him at the end of every working day. She had cooked his meals, cleaned the house, washed his clothes and even shared his bed. Shy, diffident, he had hoped she found their lovemaking as satisfying as he did, but he had never found the courage to broach the subject. Looking back, those years between Joe's birth and Helen's conception had been the sum total of their marriage. Joseph had been a happy and contented baby he had been proud to acknowledge as his son. But when Esme returned from hospital with Helen in her arms she asked him to move out of their bedroom until she recuperated from the birth.

Sensitive to her needs, he had agreed and carried his clothes up to one of the attic bedrooms. When he had tentatively suggested that he move back a year later, Esme had protested she was still unwell. He left the matter for six months, by which time Esme announced that the doctor had warned her another pregnancy would kill her. When he had tried to bring up the subject of birth control, she closed every discussion with the insistence that none was one hundred per cent reliable. Helen had been two years old the last time he had tried to discuss anything resembling a personal life with his wife.

Esme had continued to keep the house in apple-pie order and, as the business flourished, improved their lives. She employed a daily to relieve her of the housework, and her involvement with the Little Theatre and her nights out with Dot – a feature from the day they returned from their fortnight's honeymoon in London – increased from one or two a month to three or four and sometimes even more a week as well as most of the weekends. Publicly and privately she was polite, mannered – and distant – towards him. He missed the intimacy of their early married life but made excuses for her absences to their children and himself on the pretext that, as she worked so hard in the house all day, she was entitled to pursue her hobby in her free time.

But after Saturday night he didn't doubt that rumours would spread from the police station throughout the entire town, that's if they hadn't already. The question was, should he carry on ignoring Esme's absences and nights out, allowing every friend, acquaintance and business contact to laugh, mock and pity him, or confront her and risk hearing her confirm his worst suspicions, perhaps shattering his life and their children's irrevocably?

'Angie, if you and Emily don't go into the house this instant I'll tell Mums about this.'

'No, you won't, because you'd have to admit you were swimming in the buff and you know she doesn't like it.' Angie lay back in the deckchair and filched a cigarette from a box on the table next to her. 'Em, pour yourself a drink and get one for me please, while you're at it.'

'Babycham?' Emily took two bottles from the rattan cocktail cabinet in the sun lounge and held them up, either side of her face.

'I'd *love* a Babycham.' Angie parodied the advertisement.

'And we'd love you two to disappear into the house,' Robin called from the pool. 'It's bloody freezing in here.'

'Especially when you can't move a muscle,' Joe added heatedly.

'I wouldn't have invited Joe back here if I'd known you were going to tease him.'

'We're not teasing. The male nude is part of our art course and we're searching out as many examples as we can to carry out an in-depth study.' Angie took the drink Emily handed her.

'If I stay here a minute longer my examples are going to freeze and drop off, so study away.' Heaving himself up on his arms, Robin left the pool. Emily screamed. Angie tossed him a cushion from one of the chairs. Holding it in front of himself, Robin threw a towel into the water close to Joe. 'As these are no ladies you don't have to behave like a gentleman. Right, Emily, do you want to make a detailed sketch right now?' Lurching towards her, he laughed as she ran off into the hall. 'That proves it,' he called after her. 'You're all bluff.'

'Beast!' Angie pouted as Joe followed Robin out of the pool, the towel dripping round his waist.

'Spoiled your fun?' Joe didn't even try to conceal his irritation.

'Well, as the sights are under wraps' – Angie gazed coolly at the wet towel that clung round Joe's hips, bringing a flush to his cheeks – 'I may as well get the sandwiches Mrs John left for supper. Not that you two deserve them.'

'Out,' Robin snapped sharply as he reached for a dry towel.

'You're shivering, Joe. How about a whisky to warm you up before I go?' Angie held up the bottle.

'You determined to give me pneumonia?'

'Nursing you better could be fun – for both of us.'

'Out!' Robin repeated, exchanging his cushion for a dry towel and throwing the wet cushion at her.

'I can take a hint.' Angie followed Emily into the house.

Pulling the blinds that screened the sun lounge from the hall, Robin locked the door and briskly towelled himself. 'You'll have a drink?' He reached for his father's whisky.

'No thanks, I'm working early tomorrow and it's time I dusted off my books. I can't believe it's our last year in Uni.'

'The telling one.' Robin made a face as he poured himself a drink. 'I don't know why you're worried. You're bound to get a first, everyone's blue-eyed boy.'

'I wish.' Drying himself quickly, Joe reached for his underpants. Even with a closed blind and a locked door between them he didn't trust Angie. 'I take it Emily's not part of Larry's disgrace.'

'That would hardly be fair.'

'I suppose it wouldn't,' Joe conceded grudgingly.

'Emily's a nice girl.'

Joe raised his eyebrows.

'All right, I admit I fancy her.'

'You want to take off more than her blouse?'

'A fellow could do worse.'

'You're going out with her?'

'Give me a chance, she's only just got back from London.'

'But you will?'

'Probably. We could make it a foursome. Angie's keen on you.' Abandoning his glass on the coffee table, Robin pulled on his underpants and trousers.

'She has a funny way of showing it.'

'You decent?' Angie called from the other side of the door.

'Just about.' Robin unlocked it, as Joe buttoned his shirt.

'Sandwiches and coffee for those who don't want to steal Pops's whisky.' Angie handed the heavy tray to Joe.

'I take it the party wasn't any good.' Robin

pulled Emily down on top of him as he fell into a chair. She sat on his lap, squealing as he tickled her.

'It was boring. Everyone was talking about Larry's disgrace.'

'He wasn't there?' Joe set the tray on a side table.

'He's been exiled to great-uncle Charles's house in Cardiff,' Emily gasped between shrieks. 'Stop it, Robin.' She slapped his wrist. 'I'm sorry, Joe. I heard it was your sister's dress he ripped. I wish Larry hadn't got stupid drunk. I'm not sticking up for him or trying to excuse what he did but he was well out of it at the party. He probably didn't have a clue what he was doing by the time he got to Mumbles.'

'Probably,' Joe muttered non-committally. Pulling on his sweater, he reached for the car keys in his pocket and held them up. 'You sure about this, Robin.'

'Yes, but don't go yet.'

'If I don't, I'll never get up in the morning.'

'I'll walk you to the car.'

'There's no need, Angie.'

'I want to. Besides, I could do with some fresh air.'

'Didn't you walk back from the party?' Robin asked.

'We called a taxi.'

'See you tomorrow around five, Joe.' Robin poured himself another whisky.

'I'll be here.'

'I'll only be working for a couple of hours, if you hang around we could...'

244

'Sorry, Robin, I have plans tomorrow night. See you.' Stepping through the french doors, Joe walked around the side of the house.

'Plans that involve a girl?' Angie queried, running to catch up with him.

'Plans that involve my sister.' Joe was surprised how easily the lie rolled off his tongue. 'She is very upset.'

'Give her my best wishes and tell her I'm sorry.'

'She doesn't know you.'

'That doesn't mean she won't.' As they reached a gap in the shrubbery she grabbed his hand. 'Are you very cross with me for teasing you?' she asked, pulling him back.

'I'm not a great one for practical jokes.'

'It was meant as a bit of fun.'

'Like Larry with my sister.'

'I didn't jump on you or tear off your clothes.'

'It wasn't funny, Angie.'

'I'm sorry. Don't be such a grumps. Give me a chance and I'll show you just how sorry.' Standing on tiptoe she kissed him, pushing her tongue into his mouth. Before he realised what was happening he found himself kissing her back. As she pulled him deeper into the gloom beneath the close-growing rhododendrons her fingers trailed over his fly.

'Angie!' He retreated quickly, hitting his head on an overhanging branch.

'I've shocked you?'

'Nice girls...'

'Don't think about sex like nice boys?'

'You weren't like this before you went away.'

'Only because I didn't know what I wanted

before I went away. It took London and France for me to realise how special you are. And eight weeks of missing you for me to want you this much.'

'And an entire summer for me to get over you,' he murmured warily.

'We're not over, Joe. We're just beginning.' She pushed him back against the boundary wall.

'Robin...'

'Is besotted with Emily. Let's go to the summerhouse. You can see the sea from there.'

'I know,' he murmured thickly as she touched him again.

'Joe...'

'I really do have to go, Angie.' Turning on his heel he almost ran back up through the bushes to the front of the house.

'You don't have to be kind, I know everyone thinks the worst of me.' Helen lifted her chin defiantly, challenging Lily to say otherwise as they sat either end of the window seat in the kitchen that her father had categorically refused to allow her mother to rip out.

'No, they don't,' Lily demurred.

'But you don't want to go round with me anymore. You've made that obvious; none of you called here yesterday and Joe said he saw you, Katie and Judy in Mumbles.'

'It wouldn't have made any difference if we had called. Your mother won't allow you out.'

'You still could have called,' Helen persisted illogically as Katie walked into the kitchen. 'Did my father give you a job?'

'Yes, isn't it wonderful, he...'

'Has done more for you than his own daughter.' Helen knew she was being unfair but she couldn't help herself. She didn't want to be fair. She wanted to hurt and humiliate someone – anyone – the way her mother, the police and the police doctor had hurt and humiliated her.

'Helen, you have a job in Thomas and Butler's. Can't you be pleased for Katie?' Lily chided, as Katie's eyes welled.

'Why should I be pleased for her when none of you even called round to ask after me yesterday? All I did was stand outside the ballroom. Stand, mark you. I didn't say a word or put a foot wrong, just stood there. And after I get attacked by a maniac who tears my dress and bruises my arms I get punished by being locked up. And what do my friends do? Come and sympathise? Oh, no, not them. They go off down Mumbles for ice cream and a good time.'

'Be reasonable, Helen, what else could we have done?' Lily asked.

'Sit here with me.'

'Your mother wouldn't have let us in.'

'She was out so she wouldn't have known.'

'We didn't know she was out.'

'No one cares what happens to me.'

'We do,' Lily contradicted earnestly. 'Your mother will soon calm down and then you'll be able to come everywhere with us again.'

'You don't know my mother.' Helen sat back and crossed her arms. Conscience pricked by the tears in Katie's eyes, she muttered, 'I suppose as my father has to have a secretary, it may as well be you.'

'You don't mind?'

'It's nothing to do with me who he employs.'

Lily checked the time. 'Time we were going.'

'Careful you don't stay with the scarlet woman too long.'

'Now you're being silly. We promised Auntie Norah we'd be back in the house by ten thirty. I've work in the morning.'

'I suppose I'll see you the next time you feel like making a charitable visit to the outcast.'

'We'll come again as soon as we can,' Lily replied diplomatically.

Helen stayed in her seat as Lily opened the door.

''Bye, Helen.' Katie followed Lily down the passage.

''Bye, Katie, 'bye Lily,' Helen shouted after them. 'I'm sorry...' She looked up to see the front door already closed. Clenching her hands into fists, she grabbed a cushion from the window seat and hurled it across the room. It hit the dresser, knocking over a black, white and red vase her mother had bought the week before.

'What was that, Helen?' her father called from the parlour, as she scooped up the pieces and wrapped them in newspaper.

'A milk bottle, Dad.'

'You all right?'

'Going to bed,' she snapped. 'There's no point in my staying up.' Hiding the newspaper-wrapped fragments beneath a pile of potato peelings at the bottom of the bin, she ran up the stairs, slammed her bedroom door and threw herself on her bed.

If Jack really cared for her he would have left his skiffle group practice early and met her in the garden. He should have realised she'd wait for him from nine o'clock on. Did he love her or didn't he? Or was he just playing stupid games? The ex-Borstal boy putting one over on the respectable girl next door – only now she wasn't quite so respectable. Had he only asked her to be his girl so he could treat her like that horrid Larry Murton Davies? Like a ... a common tart, as her mother had said. She fingered her lips remembering Jack's kisses – warm, tender – and the way they had made her feel. He had to love her after kissing her like that – didn't he?

Had he turned up after she'd left? Or hadn't he any intention of coming at all? Surely he realised she couldn't hang around the garden all night waiting for him – not after Brian had seen her.

Lying face down on the bed, she pulled at the fringes on her candlewick bedspread. He loved her – loved her not – loved her – loved her not ... She was still holding the fringes when she woke the next morning, fully dressed and lying on top of her bedclothes. Loved her – loved her not–

'You look ridiculous,' Esme commented as Helen appeared at the breakfast table in one of Joe's old rugby shirts and a torn pair of pedal pushers.

'As I'm not allowed to leave the house until I start work next Monday I thought I'd put my prison sentence to good use and clean the basement.'

'Sounds like an excellent idea to me, young

lady.' John helped himself to a piece of toast. 'But you don't touch any of the furniture down there.'

'Only to clean it, Dad, I promise.'

'Don't go thinking that once you've sorted the rooms you can have your friends round there,' Esme warned. 'You've been locked in for a reason.'

'You don't have to go over it again,' Helen muttered.

'Just as long as you realise you've done wrong.'

'I'm not likely to forget it seeing as how you remind me every five minutes.'

'How dare you...'

'I don't want to hear you speaking to your mother like that again, Helen. Helen...' John shouted after her as she flounced out of the room and stamped up the stairs.

'Aren't you being a bit hard on her,' Joe remonstrated as he reached for the butter. 'After all, she didn't do anything...'

'No, Joseph?' Esme broke in quietly. 'Only stole one of the most expensive dresses from the warehouse, a totally unsuitable dress that incited a boy to treat her like a streetwalker, incidentally ruining her reputation and holding the entire family up to ridicule.'

'Esme...'

'And we all know whose fault that is, don't we, John?' Esme's voice remained soft, modulated, as she turned on her husband. 'You've spoiled her since the day she was born. Let her get away with whatever she wanted to do, without sparing a thought for the consequences of her actions. If it wasn't for me I dare say you would allow her to forget even this. Don't you see, what happened on Saturday night is a direct result of your indulgence. If she is ever to learn how to behave or have any kind of a respectable life...'

'I've got to go.' Pushing his toast into his mouth, Joe reached for the jacket he'd hung on the back of his chair.

'You sit down and eat your breakfast properly.'

Joe hesitated long enough to make his mother wonder if she was losing her influence over him.

'I forgot to ask, Joe, how did it go last night?' John asked, changing the subject in the hope that it might lighten the atmosphere.

'Fine,' Joe replied tersely.

'I listened to the play, it was excellent.' Esme poured herself a second cup of coffee and reached for her cigarettes.

Joe bit into a piece of toast as though he were punishing it.

'I saw Roy Williams last night. He mentioned you'd asked Lily out.'

'Lily from next door?' Esme narrowed her eyes.

'She's a nice girl, Esme.'

'No one has any idea where she came from or who her people were.' Esme frowned at her son. 'Joseph, we've given you opportunities I could only dream of. You mix with the finest Swansea has to offer, you meet clever, well-educated, attractive girls from the best families and yet you ask an abandoned evacuee – a nobody – to go out with you. It simply doesn't make sense.'

Pushing his plate aside, Joe left the table.

'Please.' Esme laid her hand on Joe's arm. 'I'd like an explanation.'

251

'There is none to give other than that I enjoy Lily's company and would like to get to know her better.'

'Better than Robin's sister?' Esme queried archly.

'I'd prefer to spend my free time with Lily. There's nothing wrong with that, is there?' he demanded, daring his mother to say otherwise.

Esme drew heavily on her cigarette. 'As long as you remember it is just "spending time".'

'What more can I offer any girl at the moment than my time?'

'I don't like the way you said "at the moment". Get serious about a girl like Lily and she could drag you down. You need the right wife where you are going in life, Joseph. Someone from a family with contacts that will help you in your career; a girl who has been brought up to be socially competent, who knows how to dress and talk, a good hostess...'

'There's more to life than kowtowing to influential people and empty social fripperies, Esme.'

Esme and Joe stared at John in amazement. It was the first time he had dared interrupt one of their arguments.

'Lily's a decent girl and if Joe chooses to go out with her, or even marry her, I for one would be delighted.'

'Don't you want Joseph to get on in life?'

'I want him to be happy.'

'And you think he'll be happy married to a girl with hardly any education? No social graces, no ambitions...'

'Are you describing Lily or me, Esme?' John raised his eyes and looked at her. When she remained silent he continued, daring to say exactly what he thought to her for the first time in years. 'If I've made you unhappy, or thwarted your social ambitions, Esme, I'm sorry. I really am. But then you haven't exactly made me happy either, so please feel free to leave any time you want.'

She stared at him incredulously. 'After all these years ... I've no money, no training...'

'You can keep your allowance. The offer is on the table, it's up to you whether you accept it or not.' He walked into the hall, scarcely believing what he'd said. His hands were trembling, his heart thundering, but he felt a strange sense of elation. He'd done it. He'd actually taken the first step to free himself from Esme and a marriage in name only that had placed a stranglehold on his life for the last eighteen years.

Hands on the back of his chair, eyes focused on the floor, Joe heard his father take his coat from the stand and open the front door. He sensed his mother watching him. Embarrassed for her and his father, he couldn't bring himself to look at her. Turning to the door, he followed his father out of the house.

John had only just closed the door on the driver's side of his car when he saw Joe leaving the house. Winding down the window, he hailed him. 'I'll give you a lift.'

'I'm only going to the studio and I'm already late.'

253

'You'll be two minutes quicker in the car.'

Capitulating, Joe opened the passenger door.

'I'm sorry you had to see that, Joe.'

'Dad...'

'Please let me finish and when I have, I don't want to hear another word on the subject from you. I'm sorry your mother and I have problems, but they are nothing to do with you. I will love and support you and Helen for as long as you need support and afterwards I will always try to be there if either of you need my help.'

'Dad...'

'I just wanted you to know that.' John stopped the car outside the BBC building. 'Now, you'd better go inside before you are late.'

CHAPTER TWELVE

Helen waited until the front door opened and closed a third time before venturing out of her bedroom. Leaving the breakfast table for the daily to clear, she went down to the basement. Trying not to think about Jack, she dragged the rugs outside and beat them on the line until her arms ached. She dusted the furniture and swept the floorboards in the front room that had a window overlooking the garden. She carried down her record player and records, arranged them neatly on a side table and pasted photographs she'd cut from magazines on to the back of old rolls of wallpaper she had found in one of the wardrobes. Finally she cleaned the window, pinned her collages to the wall and carried the rugs back in.

The sofa and easy chairs that had been in the parlour during her childhood were covered with a slippery uncomfortable dark-green material she didn't like, so she scavenged some old striped blankets from the top of the airing cupboard and draped them over the seats. They really didn't look too bad once she'd set the old, squashy tapestry cushions on them.

Standing in the doorway, she surveyed her handiwork. The room looked clean, bright and inviting: a place she would enjoy sitting and listening to her records in. She hoped Jack would think so – if he ever saw it. Racing upstairs, she discovered the daily had left and no one else was at home. Toying with the eight and nine she had drawn on cards, she decided to take a chance and pinned the nine to the back of one of the curtains in her room. Then, just in case, she opened a tin of spam, cut a pile of sandwiches and wrapped them in greaseproof paper. Placing them in a carrier bag together with a couple of slices of fruit cake and a bottle of lemonade, glasses and plates, she carried them downstairs, hiding the bag behind the sofa.

She caught sight of herself in the hall mirror as she returned upstairs. Her mother was right, she did look a sight, but it was nothing a bath, fresh clothes and make-up couldn't cure. And then – then what? Her heart raced. She wasn't at all sure what a clandestine evening with Jack – if he came – would bring. Hopefully some excitement to dispel the boredom. And if he didn't turn up?

She dispelled the thought from her mind. He hadn't turned up last night because Brian was in the way. She had told him she couldn't risk being seen with anyone. He was only thinking of her – that had to be it. He'd only been thinking of her.

'Mrs Evans didn't want me to go in to the café today because she thought I should rest my ankle but I couldn't let Mr Petronelli down. I thought I could do the washing up just as well sitting down but it was hopeless at break time because I couldn't walk quickly enough to cover for the waitresses. So when one of the other girls said her sister could start work in the café right away, Mr Petronelli agreed I could leave at the end of the day. That means I can start here first thing tomorrow morning if you want me to, Mr Griffiths.' Katie stood uneasily in front of John Griffiths's desk in the warehouse office. She felt shabby and grubby, and knew she smelled of the café kitchen, an unappetising mixture of fish, chips and cooking fat.

'That's good news, Katie. As I said, you have a lot to learn.' John Griffiths peered at her over the rim of the reading glasses he wore when he worked on the account books. 'If you have time I could show you around now and introduce you to everyone. Then it might not seem so strange when you come in tomorrow morning.'

'I'd like that, Mr Griffiths.'

John rose from his chair and slipped his jacket on over his shirtsleeves and braces. 'This, as you've probably gathered, is my office. And the lady who showed you in' – he opened the door that connected to the outer office – 'is Rosie Thomas, my soon to be married secretary. Rosie, this is the young lady I told you about, Katie Clay.'

'Pleased to meet you.' Rosie smiled and looked into Katie's eyes as she shook her hand, and Katie felt as though Rosie was genuinely glad to see her.

'The offices, as you see, haven't been decorated in years; there never seems to be a good time to refurbish them. They're not very grand but they are functional and hold everything we need to hand.'

Katie looked around at the battered steel filing cabinets and shelves filled to overflowing with ledgers and boxes of papers. Neither office was anywhere near as luxurious as Thomas and Butler's but she felt more at ease in them.

'This is where I meet our suppliers' representatives.' John indicated an alcove off the main office that held a comfortable three-piece suite and a table half hidden under piles of brochures. No neat fan of magazines that would need constant rearranging, Katie noted gratefully. 'This corridor leads to the Ladies and Gents toilets, the back staircase down to the loading bay and yard.' John pointed out the various doors as they walked down the passage that opened out of Rosie's office. 'And this is the main warehouse.' Holding the door for her, he stepped forward. Katie followed and found herself on a glasswalled staircase that overlooked the ground floor. 'Three floors.' There was unmistakable pride in

John's voice. 'Ladies', gents' and children's fashions, handbags, shoes, luggage and haberdashery on the ground floor. Furniture on the first and household linens, tableware, china, silverware, baby goods and jewellery on the second.'

'I had no idea your warehouse was so big, Mr Griffiths.'

'It's deceptive when you look at the frontage.'

Katie followed him down the stairs and into the fashion department. She stared at rail after rail of dresses, costumes and blouses. 'I've never seen so many clothes.'

'The one thing I insist on is that all my staff, even the ones who work in the stockroom, are well-dressed and well-spoken. Our customers are important people and it's vital that they are extended every courtesy when they patronise Griffiths's Wholesale.'

Katie looked down at her shabby black skirt, threadbare and rusty from washing, and her old school blouse. 'These are my café clothes, Mr Griffiths. I have a costume, a new one. Mrs Evans made it for my interview at Thomas and Butler's.'

'You'll need more than one outfit, Katie. Everyone does, that is why I encourage my staff to open a five-shilling-a-week account. Once open, they can have a five-pound voucher to spend in the warehouse and, as all staff purchases carry a thirty-per-cent discount, five pounds can go a long way. Why don't you look around now and I'll send Rosie down to help you open one and choose some things. Rosie knows what sort of clothes are suitable for the office. She also has very good dress sense,' he hinted tactfully.

'I'm not sure, Mr Griffiths. Mam hates debt...'

'But this wouldn't be debt, Katie. Think of it this way, you'll be earning two pounds a week instead of two pounds five shillings. And two pounds is considered reasonable for what you'll be doing, isn't it?'

'It's more than I hoped for,' she assured him hastily, lest he think her ungrateful.

'So you'll be earning two pounds, plus a few clothes. Shall I send Rosie down?'

'Please, Mr Griffiths, thank you.'

'And after you've finished shopping, I'll drive you back to Carlton Terrace.'

'There's no need, Mr Griffiths, really.'

'You can't go far on that ankle. I know what it feels like to try and push yourself beyond your physical capabilities.'

'Thank you, Mr Griffiths.'

As Katie watched him limp back towards the office she envied Helen her father more than ever. Not only because John Griffiths was kind and generous, but because he was easy to talk to and understood her problems without even having to ask her what they were.

Joe loved the sense of intimacy mixed with fantasy and expectation the cinema conjured every time darkness closed around him in an auditorium and lights began to flicker on the screen. His love affair with films had begun when his father had taken him to a matinee performance of *Snow White and the Seven Dwarfs* to celebrate his third birthday. Losing himself in the colour, images, music and story, he had sat enthralled, not wanting to leave even after the final credits had rolled and the lights had come up.

But with Lily everything was different. As the lights dimmed he looked to the screen, only this time he couldn't bring himself to concentrate for more than a few seconds at a time. Lily, not the story being played out in front of him, filled his senses. He was acutely aware of her sitting beside him. Her cool, clean scent, a mixture of Lily of the Valley, medicated shampoo and Camay soap, was more beguiling and alluring than all of Angela's expensive perfumes. He found himself listening intently for the small sighs of her soft, shallow breaths. He stole sideways glances while she followed the film and, as darkness settled once again after the intermission at the start of the main film, revelled in the soft feel of her hand that he had dared to take into his.

He couldn't recall ever feeling this way before, not even at the height of his passion for Angela, and it had never been enough for him simply to sit next to Angie. He had wanted more – and always more than she had been prepared to give. He'd humiliated himself by running after her last winter and doing everything she asked of him, yet even when she'd reduced him to the status of pathetic, besotted slave and the butt of their combined friends' jokes, she had only been prepared to give him a few chaste kisses. And she'd made him beg for those. There had been a single memorable, abandoned occasion when they'd both drunk more of the wine her father had laid down for Robin's twenty-first birthday than had been good for them, and she'd allowed him to grope at her breast through several layers of cardigan, cotton blouse and thick brassiere. But he'd been so drunk he'd assumed he'd dreamed the whole thing the following morning and would have continued to do so if she hadn't reprimanded him for taking advantage of her.

He wondered if he felt the way he did towards Lily simply because Angela had let him know she was available. Did the poet in him prefer the ideal of unrequited love? He stole another glance at Lily, rapt, engrossed in the film and, as his feelings towards her intensified, an image of them making love flooded unbidden to his mind. He could almost feel the texture of her skin beneath his fingertips, the teasing, silken brush of her hair as it swept across his face, the sweet taste of her lips, moist, warm as they opened...

As his body responded to the pictures he conjured, Lily turned her head and smiled. His face burned. Staring intently and blindly at the screen, he released her hand and tensed every muscle in an effort to control himself, terrified she would read his thoughts – and despise him for them.

When she looked back at the film, he slowly, gradually began to breathe again, all the while hating himself for thinking of Lily that way. Already he'd decided that he wanted more from her than sex. And if he were fortunate enough to engender the same overwhelming feelings in her he would happily forgo all the poetic misery of unrequited love in favour of fulfilment.

Calmer, he reached for her hand again and was reassured by the answering pressure of her fingers on his.

'You all right, Joe?' she whispered close to his ear.

'Fine.' Careful to keep his gaze fixed on Audrey Hepburn, he lifted her hand and kissed her fingertips. He knew she was watching him but he preferred not to look at her. Occasionally imagination coupled with anticipation could heighten even perfect pleasure.

Helen turned the page in her book and read the top line. Recognising she hadn't understood a single word, she began again, then realised she didn't have a clue who the characters were or what they were doing. Exasperated, she threw the book across her bedroom. It fell against the wardrobe, splitting the spine, before landing in a welter of loose pages on the floor.

Damn her mother and damn her father for effectively locking her in the house when they were both out enjoying themselves. It was half past eight. She had switched the nine to an eight after her mother had left the house but there had been no sign of Jack. She had watched carefully for him from her window, not daring to stand out in the garden lest Brian, Martin, or Constable Williams saw her and realised who she was waiting for.

Leaving her bed, she sat on her windowsill and looked out. She could go downstairs, climb the garden wall and – and what? Half the people in the street would be sure to inform her mother if they saw her and even if she took the risk where could she go and what could she do?

Lily was at the pictures with Joe, all lovey-dovey, and that would be the end of their friendship because everyone knew that once a girl started going out with a boy all she wanted to do was coo at that boy even on Saturday dance nights. Besides, her mother had informed her at teatime that last night's visit from Katie and Lily must have been a fluke, down to her father's offer of a job to Katie, because it was common knowledge in the street that Mrs Hunt and Mrs Evans had forbidden Judy and Lily to see, or be seen with, her. And as Katie was staying with Mrs Evans, presumably that meant she had lost even the most malleable of her friends.

Twilight was gathering thick and fast, reminding her that winter was on its way. It felt as though even the seasons were conspiring to depress her. Tempted to scream from boredom, she left the windowsill and paced her bedroom floor. Twelve steps one way, thirteen the other. Unlucky thirteen, certainly for her. She needed to get out of the house, to breathe fresh air. No one could blame her for that. Not even Brian. And the garden was still hers whether Jack wanted her to be his girl or not.

Tearing down the two flights of stairs, she opened the basement door and ran to the door set in the wall at the far end. There was a tree, a gnarled old apple that hadn't borne any fruit in years. It had seemed huge when she and Joe had been children. They had spent hours climbing it, generally when her mother hadn't been around to complain about the state they were getting their clothes into. She stretched up and hooked her hands round a branch.

'If you're just standing there doing nothing, I don't suppose you'd give me a hand.'

She whirled around to see Jack's head above the five-foot wall that separated the gardens. 'You scared the living daylights out of me.'

'Sorry, but I'm desperate. I'm trying to repair my bike and I need another pair of hands. Martin's in night school, Brian's working and when I looked in upstairs, Mrs Evans and Katie were surrounded by bits of paper and cloth, and I didn't like to disturb them.'

'I put a number in my window.'

'I know, eight. I only saw it ten minutes ago. I stayed back at the yard to try to fix my bike. When I couldn't, I had to wheel it home.'

'I see.'

'It's the truth, Helen. You going to help me or not?'

'Give me a hand and I'll climb over the wall.'

'Wouldn't it be easier to walk round?'

'It would but our garden door is locked and I haven't the key.'

'Give me a minute.' Humping a crate from the garage, Jack stacked it against the wall, stood on it and leaned over, extending his hand to Helen. Taking it, she nimbly walked up the wall and balanced precariously on the row of jagged stones that topped it.

'Don't you dare jump, you'll break your neck.'

She landed beside him before he could say

another word. 'It wasn't that far down,' she gasped, winded by the fall. Her ankles and knees hurt but she would have died rather than admit it.

'You're an idiot.'

'Only sometimes.' Fighting the pain in her ankles, she rose to her feet. 'Right, what do you want me to do?'

He opened the back door of Roy Williams's garage. Light flooded out into the garden, sending shafts into the still air, highlighting mosquitoes. 'Hold a nut in a monkey wrench while I try to loosen it. At the moment all it's doing is going round and round.'

'What's a monkey wrench?'

'This.' He slammed the tool into her hand. 'Come over here.'

Resenting his tone, she hesitated before doing as he asked. Ten cramped, irritating minutes later she was beginning to long for the boredom and solitude of her room.

'Don't loosen your grip, not now. It's finally shifting!' he exclaimed crossly.

'I'm not.'

'You bloody well are...'

'I didn't come here to be sworn at.' Dropping the wrench, she leapt to her feet and went to the door.

'Bloody girls, you're all the same. No sticking power.'

'And what's that supposed to mean, Jack Clay?'

'What I said. We're almost there and you have to walk out in a huff.'

She glared at him and he glared back. It

reminded her of one of the stupid contests they used to have in school when the person who looked away or blinked first lost the game.

'You were the one who swore. And you didn't even apologise.'

'Why should I when you're going anyway.'

'Say sorry and I might not.'

'And you still might.'

'Try me and see.'

He turned back to his bike. 'I thought you agreed to be my girl,' he muttered.

'That was before you stood me up last night.'

'I was here. You weren't.'

'I saw Brian – I thought he was you.'

'You spoke to him?'

She nodded.

'That's all I need. If he says anything to Martin...'

'So now you're ashamed to tell your brother about me.'

'You're the one who doesn't want anyone to know about us. And if you must know, I promised Martin I wouldn't have anything more to do with you after last Saturday. You did get me into a pile of trouble. Martin and I were in the police station for most of the night.'

'That's right, rub it in just like my mother. Helen Griffiths – nothing but trouble...'

'Just like Jack Clay.' He smiled up at her.

Cautiously returning his smile, she retrieved the wrench and clipped it back on to the nut.

'Thanks.' He set to work again.

'So how do you like living next door?' she asked.

'Well enough.'

'I heard your mam's in hospital.'

'The whole bloody street knows, and who put her there.'

'I hope she'll be better soon.'

'So do I. There, that's it.' Freeing the bolt, he unscrewed it. 'That needs some work doing to it before I put it back on.' He wiped his hands on an oily rag.

'Great tennis racket.' She lifted it down from a shelf.

'Prehistoric more like, but Constable Williams wouldn't let us throw it out when we sorted the basement.'

'I suppose you'll be going out on Saturday night.'

'Not to the Pier. My skiffle group's playing in St James's.'

'I wish I could go.'

'But you won't be able to.'

'Not this time but my mother can't keep me locked up for ever.'

'When she lets you out again she won't want you going out with a Clay.'

'I thought we sorted that out on Sunday. She can't stop me from going around with whoever I like.'

'Come off it, Helen. Don't tell me you haven't had second thoughts since then.'

'I haven't. That's why I was so mad when you didn't turn up last night or tonight.'

'I'm here now.'

'So you are.' She looked at him, wondering if was going to kiss her again.

'I've been thinking...'

'Here it comes.'

'Be honest, Helen. The only reason you wanted to go outside with me on Saturday night was because you were too embarrassed to carry on sitting in the Pier in that dress.'

'I'm sorry I wore the dress but I'm not sorry I agreed to meet you – apart from what happened afterwards, which wasn't your fault.'

'Really?'

'If you think any different you're an idiot. You're a good-looking boy, Jack Clay.'

'You're not so bad yourself.'

'So?'

'So what?'

'Why not come round.'

'Now?'

'No, next week,' she snapped in exasperation. 'I've spent all day cleaning our basement so we'd have somewhere to sit. I put my records and record player in there and made sandwiches.'

'So, a Griffiths really is asking a Clay out?'

'More like in. What do you say?'

Joe helped Lily on with her coat, then stood back to allow those who'd left their seats just before the closing credits to stampede ahead of them. Taking Lily's hand, he joined the tail end of the queue moving up the aisles and into the foyer. 'Fish and chips?' he asked, entwining his fingers with hers.

'I'm not hungry after that coffee and cake in the Kardomah.'

'Then you're more easily satisfied than most girls.'

'So you have been out with a lot of girls.'

'A few.' He tried not to sound condescending. 'But then I'm older than you.'

'You make it sound more like thirty years than two and half.'

'Sorry, I find it difficult not to think of you as a child.' As they stepped into the street he released her hand and slipped on his own overcoat.

'Because I'm short.'

'Because you're Helen's friend.' He gave her hand a slight squeeze as he caught it again. 'You're not sensitive about your height, are you?'

'No,' she lied, 'but I'd give anything to be tall like Helen.'

'Anything?' He raised his eyebrows.

'Now you're teasing me.'

'I'm sorry.'

'That's the second time you've apologised since the film finished. It doesn't feel right, does it.'

'What?' He looked up and down the street in search of inspiration. If Roy had been anything other than a policeman he would have taken Lily into a pub. But he suspected that if Roy Williams discovered he had taken Lily into a pub, this first date would also be their last. He could hardly take her into a café or restaurant if she didn't want to eat, unless they went to one of the small Italian-run places where the proprietors genuinely didn't seem to mind serving customers only coffee or tea late at night and they were all everyday sort of places. He wanted to take her somewhere special. The only problem was where...

'Us going out together.'

His blood ran cold as he turned to her. 'I've bored you.'

'Don't be silly; I've had a lovely evening. I enjoyed the visit to the Kardomah and the film but it's obvious you think of me as a child and Helen's friend, and I think of you as Helen's brother.'

'I don't think of you as a child,' he protested.

'You just said you did.'

'I didn't mean now. I meant – I don't know what I meant, Lily. It was just something to say. It's a bad habit of mine to blurt out the first thing that comes into my head whenever there's a gap in the conversation. Are you sure you don't want a meal? It doesn't have to be fish and chips, we could find somewhere that serves something else.'

'I'm really not hungry.'

'Just a coffee, then. I did tell your aunt we'd be going for a meal after the film,' he reminded.

'All right, one coffee. But only one, I have work in the morning.'

'So do I, but it's only just ten o'clock, surely you don't go to bed this early.'

'No, but I have things to do.'

'Slap a mud pack on your face, wind curlers into your hair, take out your teeth and soak them in a glass.'

'I don't do any of those things.' She smiled mischievously. 'Except for the teeth.'

'So you do have a sense of humour.' He steered her round the corner to a café set conveniently close to the bus station. The air was thick with cigarette smoke, the atmosphere hot and steamy after the cool of the street, the front tables packed with bus crews on break, polishing off plates of sausages, beans, eggs and chips. He stood in the doorway until his eyes became accustomed to the smoke, then spotted an empty corner table in the back that afforded a little privacy.

'Sure you wouldn't like anything with your coffee?' He helped her off with her coat as the waitress came to take their order.

'Nothing, thanks.' She sat with her back to the wall and watched him as he hung their coats on the stand. Half the women in the room were staring at him but he appeared to be oblivious to his good looks and the attention he was attracting. A plus for her, but she couldn't help feeling that something wasn't quite right. That he should be with one of his university girlfriends, not her.

'What you said earlier about me being Helen's brother.' He offered her a cigarette as he sat opposite her. 'Could it be that you need persuading not to think of me as your brother too?'

'I don't smoke and no, I can't even begin to imagine what having a brother or sister is like. It's just that...' Her voice trailed as she realised how ridiculous her thoughts would sound put into words.

'What?' He smiled encouragingly.

'I always assumed that the first boy to ask me out would be a stranger. Someone I'd never seen before, not a boy I'd known most of my life.'

'And a stranger would be better than me.' He leaned back to enable the waitress to put two of the coffees that were only served in the Italian cafés on the table. Thick and creamy, the tops

271

frothing with steamed milk.

'It would be easier to exchange small talk with someone I didn't know.'

'If it's small talk you want, let's start with the plot of the film. Handsome, sophisticated, debonair writer meets beautiful girl with a mysterious past she refuses to discuss or explain. Beguiled, captivated, he falls in love, only to discover the girl is a princess and for ever unattainable. See the similarities?'

'I'm no princess.' She laughed.

'But you do have a mysterious past.'

'Only when it comes to my real family.'

'You can't be sure that the blood in your veins isn't blue.'

'With a name like Sullivan?'

'Irish royalty who fled after the Cromwell invasion.'

'To the East End of London?'

'I'm trying to invent a romantic background for you.'

'That doesn't fit the facts.'

'Tell me what you know and I'll do better.'

She spooned sugar into her cup and stirred her coffee. 'I was three years old when I was evacuated. Auntie Norah kept the label pinned to my coat when I arrived in Swansea. It had my name, Lily Mary Sullivan, an address in London that no longer exists because it disappeared in the Blitz and a square that meant special consideration. When Auntie Norah asked, no one was able to tell her what the special consideration was. Fortunately for me, she took a chance that it might not be too serious and gave me a home anyway.'

'You never found out more?'

'I plagued the life out of Auntie Norah as soon as I was old enough to understand that my parents didn't want me back, but by then Auntie Norah and Uncle Roy were the only family I could remember and I think I would have hated having to leave them, even if someone had come looking for me. Auntie Norah made enquiries on my behalf and discovered that my mother had died during the war, probably in the Blitz. No one seemed to know anything about my father other than his name. As he never turned up for me at the end of the war I suppose he must have been killed too.'

'How about you're the last surviving member of the French royal family, guillotined during the reign of terror? The descendant of a child entrusted to an Irish nanny who smuggled it across the Channel and...'

'Into the East End.'

'You're obsessed with the East End. It's not a stumbling block.'

'Everyone I've met who has been there says it's anything but a salubrious area.'

'A poor Irish nanny wouldn't be able to afford a Mayfair address.'

'I can see you have a great career ahead of you when you get your degree: Joseph Griffiths – or should it be Josephine? – romantic novels and fairy tales a speciality.'

'I could do worse than spend my working life in a fantasy world.' He reached across the table for her hand.

'You wouldn't be able to pay your bills.'

'So beautiful and so prosaic.'

'I take it that's a poetic way of saying I'm a realist.'

'If you're worried about paying the bills – don't. I'll have more money than even I'll be able to spend, because everyone who can read will want to escape into the worlds I'll create.' He gazed intently into her eyes, watching the gold flecks glitter with reflected light.

'Then you do want to become a writer.' She was conscious of talking purely for the sake of saying something. She had never felt so peculiar or quite so out of her depth before. The old familiar Joe she thought she knew so well seemed to have vanished, leaving an intense stranger in his place. A man she suddenly felt she knew nothing about.

'I already am.'

'Helen showed me your poetry.'

'And?'

'I'm not sure I understood it.'

'I'll give you a line-by-line breakdown any time you like.'

'You want to write books as well as poetry?'

'Eventually.' He squeezed her fingers lightly. 'When I've lived enough to have something to write about.'

'You wouldn't have to know a great deal about life to write a film like the one we've just seen.'

'On the contrary, you'd have to know what it is to fall in love – and lose the person you love, and that is everything.'

'It's so unfair to think that a princess can't marry the man of her choice because he's a commoner.'

'I'm already amending your life story. How about noble or intellectual instead of royal blood? Russian political prisoners banished to Siberia by Stalin entrusted you to an Irish nanny who gave you her name to conceal your real identity...'

'How about you walking me home?' She suddenly realised that the bus crew closest to them had fallen unnaturally silent, because they were listening intently to Joe.

'You really are determined to stop me from giving you an interesting background.'

'It's interesting enough.'

'Why settle for reality when fantasy is so much more satisfying?'

'Because reality is what you wake up to every morning.'

'Not if you're a poet.'

'So if there's something in life you don't like, you simply weave a story to blot it out.'

'You understand me perfectly.' Leaving the table, he reached for her coat and helped her on with it, before paying for their coffees and escorting her through the door.

'What's your earliest memory?' she asked as they stepped into the street.

'Dad bringing my mother home from the hospital with Helen.' He drew her close to him as they walked through the town.

'How old were you?'

'Two.'

'I wish I could remember something before I came to Uncle Roy's and Auntie Norah's.'

'Be grateful nothing as traumatic as Helen

happened to cause you to remember.'

'That's unkind.'

'I remember being horribly, insanely jealous. Masses of Mum's relatives and friends visiting, cooing into her cradle, smothering her with presents and ignoring me.'

'I'm sure it wasn't like that.'

'Whose memory is this?'

'Does it worry you that I don't know anything about my family?' she asked suddenly.

'No.'

'I could be illegitimate.'

'So?'

'Some people think that's a disgrace.'

'They should realise that we're living in the twentieth century not Dickensian times.'

'My parents could have been horrible...'

'No, they couldn't.'

'How do you know?'

'Because they had a daughter like you.' Drawing her into a shop doorway, he cupped his hands round her face and kissed her.

CHAPTER THIRTEEN

'Watch my father's dahlias this time,' Helen whispered as Jack leapt into the soft earth of the flowerbed.

'You should have warned me before I jumped.' Lifting his foot, he brushed a clump of crushed blooms from the thick crêpe sole of his boot.

'Quick, before someone sees us.' She ran up the path and under the asbestos canopy to the back door. Darting up the passage, she locked the connecting door to the rest of the house before showing Jack into the front room.

'Are all your family out?'

'Yes.'

'Then why are we whispering?'

'I have no idea.' As she'd already pulled the curtains, she turned on an old-fashioned, pink-shaded table lamp that bathed the room in a muted – and she hoped – romantic glow.

'Great.'

'You like it.' She switched on the Dansette record player she'd stacked ready with her ten favourite 45s. Lifting out the carrier bag she'd hidden behind the sofa, she set it on the table, laid out plates, tumblers and knives, and arranged the food she'd brought down earlier.

'I like the look of those sandwiches.'

'I wasn't sure you'd be hungry but I made them just in case.'

'I'm glad you did, I'm starving.' He sat on the sofa and reached for a plate as the strains of the Inkspots singing 'Unchained Melody' filled the room.

'Want some lemonade?' she asked, uneasy now she was finally alone with him. The same chill was running down her spine as last Saturday, when she'd caught sight of herself in the mirror in the Ladies room in the Pier. She couldn't help wondering if it was a forewarning that her craving for excitement might lead to a situation she'd regret later.

'I'd prefer beer.'

'I haven't any.'

'Then lemonade will have to do,' he mumbled through a full mouth. He glanced at her as he helped himself to another sandwich. 'If you're waiting for me to apologise for hogging the food, you'll wait a long time.'

'I made them for you. I've eaten.'

'I wish I had. This living with my brother and Brian isn't the same as being at home when my mother had tea on the table when I got in.'

'You've got your freedom. I'd give anything for that.'

'Seems to me you're doing all right.' He looked around. 'Your own space, your own things, doing pretty well what you want...'

'Inside the house.'

'With visitors like me, you've no reason to go out.'

'You can't be here all the time. And I start work on Monday.'

'In a solicitor's. Katie told me you'd got the job she tried for.'

'I didn't know she'd applied...'

'It wouldn't have made any difference if you had. You'd have got the job without even bothering to turn up for the interview. It's a different world for people like you. Word in the right ear and you get whatever you want.'

'And what's that supposed to mean?' she demanded angrily as Doris Day's 'Secret Love' crashed down on the turntable to replace 'Unchained Melody'.

'Just making sure you realise girls like you don't

go around with boys like me before we go any further.'

'I thought we'd sorted that out?'

'And if your mother and father walked in on us right now?'

'My father would be upset but he wouldn't say very much. My mother would say a lot, and...'

'Kick you out,' he finished for her.

'Probably send me to a home for wayward girls.' She flushed at her lack of tact.

'From what I hear they're not as bad as the ones for boys.' He demolished another sandwich in two bites.

'Of course, you've been in one.'

'I like the way you said that, as if it hadn't been a talking point in the street for two years. "Wild Jack Clay got put away, boy with his nerve got what he deserved."'

'Did they treat you very badly?'

'From what I gather from Marty and Brian, being in Borstal is no worse than being a National Service conscript in the army.'

'Did they lock you in a cell?'

'Only at night, or if you went barking mad.'

'You don't mind talking about it?'

He shrugged his shoulders. 'It happened. It's no big deal. I lost a couple of years of my life that I wouldn't have done very much with anyway. I was hardly the star scholar in school.'

'All the same...'

'Face it, Helen. Your mother would go spare at the thought of us together. I'm a Clay, my father's an alcoholic who beats his wife, I'm a no-good who's been to Borstal. You're a Griffiths, brought up in the lap of luxury.'

'Call this luxury...' she began warmly.

'You've never had to eat bread and scrape, or watch your mother go out scrubbing to put even that on the table. Or hidden under your bed when your father comes home drunk and starts smashing the place up, so terrified of showing your face you wet yourself rather than go to the lavatory, all the while praying that when he's finished with the furniture he won't start on your mother – or you.'

'And that makes me a snob.'

'In my book,' he replied candidly.

'Then why did you come round?'

'For the sandwiches.' He heaped another two on his plate.

'You didn't know I'd have food.'

'Snobs always do. Tea and cucumber sandwiches in the afternoon.' He mimicked her mother's accent so accurately she almost hated him.

'Why don't you just go?' She opened the door.

'Because I don't want to.' He pulled her down on the sofa beside him. 'Is this what you asked me here for, Helen?'

Setting his plate on the table, he kissed her. He tasted of lemonade mixed with bread, butter and Spam. Her initial reaction was one of distaste but even as she raised her hands and closed them into fists ready to thrust him away, he pushed her gently down on to the sofa. Her head sank into the cushions on the armrest as his tongue entered her mouth. She was acutely aware of his heart beating above hers, the sensation of his body pressing against hers through layers of clothing. She closed her eyes as a most peculiar consciousness coursed through her veins. Half excitement – half fear–

Breathless, heart pounding, she opened her eyes as he moved away from her. Sitting back at the opposite end of the sofa, he winked at her before reaching for another sandwich.

'You...'

'Don't tell me you didn't enjoy that, or weren't expecting it.' A mischievous light flickered in his dark-brown eyes. 'And when I've finished these sandwiches there'll be more.'

'Jack Clay...'

'Having you for a girlfriend is going to be fun as well as dangerous.'

'I can't risk you staying more than another five minutes,' she warned, suddenly afraid of what could happen if he stayed longer. 'I have to clear the plates and wash them before my mother notices they're missing from the kitchen.'

'That's all right, we can do a lot in five minutes.' Reaching for her, he kissed her again.

Half hoping, half dreading another kiss lest one of the neighbours saw them and passed comment, Lily turned shyly to Joe as they reached her front door. 'Thank you for a lovely evening.'

'I enjoyed it too. I'll pick you up from work on Thursday, the same time as tonight.'

'Yes, please.'

'What would you like to do?'

'We could go for a walk. Perhaps down Mumbles,' she suggested tentatively, not wanting him to spend any more money on her. He was a student; she was working; yet he hadn't allowed her to pay for a single thing during the evening.

'Then we can discuss what we're going to do on Saturday.'

'I promised Judy and Katie I'd go to the St James's youth club dance with them. Jack Clay's skiffle group are playing there.'

'Youth club!'

'Pretty unsophisticated after your university parties.' She smiled, taking the sting from her words. 'But as you reminded me earlier, you are older than me.'

'I suppose I deserved that. Keep next Sunday free and we'll take that trip down Gower.'

'I will.'

'Thank you, Lily.'

She braced herself for another kiss but he vaulted the wall. Unlocking the door, she stepped inside to his whispered, 'Goodnight, sleep well.'

'Kettle's boiled. Fancy some tea?' Jack asked, as Martin walked into the kitchen of the newly whitewashed basement that they and Brian had transformed into a fairly comfortable living room.

'If you make it.' Martin dumped his bag of books on the table and fell into the nearest easy chair.

'Rest your weary legs, why don't you,' Jack sniped as he reached for the teapot.

'Brain more than legs. God that class was hard going tonight. I'm not sure I can stand another couple of months of night school as well as work.'

Martin glanced at Jack as he set the kettle back on the stove. 'You're looking pleased with yourself.'

'Fixed my bike.'

'You said you couldn't do it without help.'

'Just call me a genius.'

'With lipstick on his collar.'

Jack glanced in the mirror Brian had hung above the sink. The collar of his blue shirt was smeared with unmistakable pink blotches.

'Caught you.'

Jack thumbed the mark. 'It's passion pink and jealousy will get you nowhere.'

'Who is she?'

'No one you know.'

'You expect me to believe that?'

'She helped me fix my bike.'

'Then she must be desperate – or stupid.'

'Evening.' Brian walked through the door and removed his helmet.

'Aren't you supposed to say "evening all"?'

'You've been watching too many police films, Jack.' Sitting in the chair opposite Martin, Brian began to unlace his boots. 'You making tea?'

'Now you're turning me into a slave as well.' Despite his grumbles Jack reached for a third cup.

'Ah, but you make such a good one and seeing as how you're up, pass us the tin of biscuits.'

'We haven't any.' Jack sugared Martin's tea and handed it to him.

'I bought one this morning, it's in the cupboard.'

'So you have. Tea maker gets first pick.' Jack

opened it and selected two chocolate ones before handing it over to Brian.

'This is cosy.' Removing his boots, Brian stretched his toes towards the single-bar electric fire as he rummaged in the tin.

'Almost as good as having a wife to order round,' Martin teased.

'That's the last favour I do for either of you two, for the next month,' Jack growled as he handed Brian his tea and settled comfortably in the third chair.

'Jack was just telling me about his new girlfriend.'

'Nice shade of lipstick,' Brian commented.

'Passion pink,' Martin goaded.

'I never thought I'd see a police helmet on the kitchen table of a place I was living in,' Jack interrupted in an effort to change the subject.

'You thought we sleep in them?'

'I thought you lot were robots that came fully dressed. Wind up, point in the right direction and off you go and harass innocent people.'

'Not funny, Jack,' Martin warned with a sideways glance at Brian.

'I have a sense of humour.' Brian leaned back in his chair. 'Granted not much of one after the shift I've just done, the miles I've walked and the way my feet feel, but it's still there.'

'So, who have you arrested today?'

'No one, as it happens. I've been out on patrol to familiarise myself with Swansea. It's a bit like being on a building site.'

'Courtesy of Hitler's bombs.' Martin dunked a digestive in his cup.

'It needed knocking down.'

'Eaten razor blades today,' Brian enquired of Jack, 'or are you always like this?'

'If he was, he wouldn't have found himself a girl.'

'Lay off, Marty,' Jack snapped, growing testier by the minute.

'How about a game of cards?' Brian suggested.

'Fine, if anyone knows where to find them.'

'There's a pack in the bedroom. I'll get them.'

'You like to live dangerously,' Brian murmured, after Martin left the room.

'How do you mean?'

'The blonde bombshell next door. It's none of my business...'

'That's right, it is none of your business.'

'Friendly warning, that's all.'

'As a copper,' Jack sneered.

'As a mate. It's easy to see she's keen on you, but she's trouble, Jack.'

'According to everyone else around here so am I, so we're well-matched.'

'Who's well-matched?' Martin asked as he returned with the cards.

'Us, in this flat,' Brian answered. 'Just take a look, anyone would think we've been living together for years.'

'Well?' Katie demanded as Lily switched off the light, threw off her dressing gown and climbed into bed beside her.

'Well what?'

'Aren't you going to say anything about your date with Joe, other than "I had a good time"?'

'There isn't anything else to say. We had coffee and cake in the Kardomah, saw *Roman Holiday*, which you must see first chance you get, and went to a café.'

'You must have talked about something besides the film. Did he tell you he loved you? Did he kiss you? Are you going out with him again?'

'If I'd known you were that interested, I would have invited you along.'

'Lily...'

'All right, we talked about nothing much that I remember but he did ask me out again on Thursday evening and we'll probably go somewhere on Sunday.'

'"Probably" doesn't sound very romantic.'

'It *was* our first date,' Lily reminded heavily.

'So why didn't he kiss you or sweep you off your feet?'

'Do you think that happens outside of films and books?'

'The kissing does.'

'As you're obviously dying to know and won't go to sleep until you do, yes, he did kiss me.'

'What did it feel like?'

'Katie!'

'Nice – horrid – I've tried but I can't imagine a big wet mouth on mine. What if his teeth are bad or his breath smells?'

'Joe has neither problem.'

'Helen said the first boy who kissed her put his tongue in her mouth and it tasted foul.'

'I was there when she talked about it.'

'Joe didn't try to do that?'

'No.' Lily smiled, as she recalled the warm, soft,

surprisingly gentle sensation of his lips on hers, the feel of his body against her own...

'But he did put his arms round you.'

'Why don't you go out with Adam Jordan and find out what it's like to date a boy for yourself?'

'Because he hasn't asked me and I don't want to. Did you like it?'

'What?'

'The kiss and Joe pawing you, of course.'

'Joe didn't "paw" me as you put it. That sounds horrible and Joe and his kiss were anything but.'

'So you did like kissing him?'

'I didn't mind.'

'I would.' Katie shuddered as she burrowed deeper beneath the bedclothes. 'I can't imagine what it feels like to actually want to kiss a man.'

'The right man will change your mind.'

'I'll never change my mind. Do you ever wonder what it would be like to sleep with a man in the same bed? To allow him to do all the disgusting things men want to do with women to you. Just the thought of taking all my clothes off in front of a man makes me feel sick without trying to imagine him actually touching me.'

Remembering the severity of Katie's mother's injuries and her aunt's damning observations on the way Ernie Clay treated his wife, Lily thought carefully for a moment before speaking. 'Auntie Norah told me it can be wonderful when you love the man and he loves you. She said living with the right person, knowing you're not alone and won't be ever again, is like nothing else in life. And although her husband was killed in the war she still feels he's with her. That's why she's never wanted to get married again.'

'So you do want to sleep with Joe.'

'Katie, I was talking about Auntie Norah and her husband, not Joe and me.'

'But you must think something of him to have gone out with him tonight, and when he kissed you, didn't you wonder what it would be like to sleep with him?'

'No, I did not.'

'Then you've never thought about sleeping with a man?'

'Only in general, after Auntie Norah told me the facts of life. I certainly haven't thought about it with Joe.' Lily crossed her fingers, hoping Katie couldn't tell she was lying.

'So you're not in love with Joe.'

'After only one date?'

'Some people say they only had to look into someone's eyes once to know they'd met the one person they wanted to spend the rest of their life with.'

'No doubt across a crowded room. You've been reading too many *Woman's Weekly* romances.'

'If you don't feel that way about Joe, then why go out with him?'

'Because he's the first and only boy who has asked me and I like him.'

'Like, not love, so if someone better-looking comes along you'll drop him and go out with them.'

'The minute Gregory Peck knocks on the door.'

Katie started to laugh. 'Can you imagine it, "Sorry, Joe, can't go to the pictures with you tonight, Mr Peck's called in his Rolls-Royce to take me to the Savoy.'"

'Sh,' Lily hissed although she was laughing as much as Katie. 'We'd better go to sleep before Auntie Norah shouts at us for keeping her awake.'

They both closed their eyes. Katie's breathing soon fell soft and quiet but no matter how hard Lily tried to relax, sleep eluded her. She raked over every single detail of her evening with Joe. His eagerness to please – she suspected that if she'd asked him to buy her the whole range of cakes on offer in the Kardomah he would have. Then there was the odd way he had looked at her in the cinema. He had thought her engrossed in the film but she hadn't been too engrossed to watch him. And afterwards in the café he had been keen enough to press her to go out with him again – but he'd also admitted he'd been out with other girls.

Where were they now? Where she would be a week or two from now – a memory for Joe to smile over when he took out his next date or the one after that? One evening didn't give her any rights over him, so why did the thought of him with other girls, especially kissing them, hurt so much?

'Want to go to the pictures?' Martin asked Jack as they left the hospital after visiting their mother.

'I have skiffle group practice.' Jack checked his watch. 'But I've time for a quick pint.'

'All right, one pint, but you're buying.'

'Why not you?'

Still arguing, they crossed the road and walked

289

down the street towards the Bay View, an old Victorian pub that overlooked the town end of the beach.

'Mam looked rotten,' Jack said flatly as he carried the beers over to the table Martin had commandeered.

'Hardly surprising, considering what she's been through.' Martin tried to sound casual as he sipped the froth off his pint, but he had been as shaken by his mother's appearance as Jack. And it wasn't just her injuries – although they were worse than even he'd imagined – it was the distant, detached way she'd greeted them, barely opening her eyes, too weary to talk – almost to breathe – as though life itself was too much for her. 'I could kill the old man,' he burst out suddenly and savagely.

'She wouldn't thank you for it. I don't think she even listened when we tried to persuade her to move in with us when she leaves the hospital.'

'Mrs Evans and Katie may have better luck. That's why I gave you the nod to leave early. Mrs Evans seems pretty determined to get her to move in with her for a couple of weeks' convalescence.'

'Do you think for one minute that Mam will listen to her?'

'There's no good brooding about it until she's ready to come out. And you heard the doctor. It won't be for weeks yet. Have you seen the old man?'

'No. Why?'

Martin eyed Jack over the top of his glass. 'Because I wouldn't put it past you to have a go at him.'

'As I just said, what would be the point when Mam sticks up for him no matter what he does to her? Although, now I think about it, it's surprising he hasn't been round to try to get one of us back. He never could bear to clean up after himself.'

'He wouldn't dare knock on the door to Roy Williams's house.'

'He's not scared of Constable Williams or anyone else when he's drunk. When he's sober is another matter. Then he snivels like the coward he is. Marty, would you give up the flat and move back home if Mam does insist on living with him again?'

'No, and as I've said, I'd lock her up if she tried.'

'You couldn't do that.'

'I'll not allow her to take Katie. The girl's a bag of nerves. Move her back in with Dad and she'll have a breakdown.'

'It's a bloody mess all round, isn't it. Another pint?'

'I thought you said you only had time for one.'

Jack glanced at his watch. 'I can squeeze in another if you twist my arm.'

'Consider it twisted. My shout, I think.'

'Pass the salt.' Esme's request was snapped out in a staccato that announced she had neither forgiven her husband for telling her she was free to leave, nor her son for taking Lily out.

As Helen picked up the cruet set and handed it to her mother she checked the time on the new orange and purple dining-room clock. Ten minutes past seven – only one minute had passed

291

since she had last looked. She was having trouble concealing her impatience. What if her mother decided to spend an evening home for once? Her father and Joe wouldn't think to look in on her if she spent the entire evening in the basement but her mother was bound to come poking and prying, especially if she suspected she was enjoying herself. And Jack had agreed to come round at ten. Only this time he was going to jump the wall and walk to the back door to lessen the risk of anyone seeing them together.

'You're dressed up to sit around the house, Helen,' Esme reproved suspiciously.

'I had a bath and changed earlier. I was filthy after cleaning out the other two rooms in the basement.'

'As no one ever goes in the basement I can't see why you bothered, or why you had to put on that pale-blue shirtwaister. It shows every mark.'

'It will wash.'

'Mrs Jones has more important things to do than your unnecessary washing and ironing.'

Hoping for support, Helen looked at her father. He was staring down at his plate, poking at his ham salad in a desultory fashion, apparently oblivious to her presence and the conversation.

'I'm going mad, locked in this house. I wanted to do something useful. Nothing wrong with that, is there?' Helen tilted her chin upwards.

'There's plenty, young lady, if you think what your antics led to last Saturday night.'

Crumpling her napkin into a ball, Helen threw it on to her plate and knocked over her chair as she ran out of the room.

'Playing happy families is getting to be a habit around here.' Joe pushed his plate aside and lifted Helen's chair upright.

'Where are you going?' Esme asked as he headed for the door.

'Robin's. We've arranged to study.'

'Take the Rover.' Fishing the keys from his pocket, John tossed them over.

'Thanks, Dad.' Striding into the hall, Joe grabbed his coat.

Esme gazed in disgust at her children's plates. 'I don't know why I bother.'

'You don't.'

'I beg your pardon?' She looked carefully at John.

'Mrs Jones does.'

'I do the shopping, I make all the arrangements...'

'I'll clear up, Esme.' He left the table. 'We can't have you being late for the auditions, now can we.'

The sharp retort on the tip of Esme's tongue remained unspoken. 'And you?'

'Kind of you to ask. I expect I'll find something to amuse myself with as I have done every evening for the last twenty years.'

'If you object so much to my involvement with the theatre, why haven't you said anything before?'

'Would it have made any difference if I had?' He looked up from the table and into her eyes.

'Of course it would have. You're my husband...'

'Am I?' As he continued to watch her he realised he felt nothing for her, nothing at all.

Whatever there had been between them, even if it had been only one-sided, had disappeared, leaving indifference in its wake.

'What kind of talk is that?' She was conscious that she was talking too quickly and loudly to conceal the fear that he would ask her for a divorce, a social stigma guaranteed to make any woman an outcast, even one as indispensable as she believed herself to be to the Little Theatre. Divorcees were regarded as 'fast' by respectably married women and easy game by men who would never dare make a pass at someone else's wife – in public.

'We've never done things together in the way most husbands and wives have.'

Suspecting that he was referring to their separate bedrooms as much as their independent social lives, she chose to ignore the inference. 'We have the children...'

'They're grown-up, Esme.'

'Helen...'

'Is no longer a child, no matter how hard you try to keep her one.'

'Me! Saturday night...'

'She made a mistake she might not have made if you'd taken the trouble to talk to her about the kind of things most mothers discuss with their daughters. Boys, clothes, make-up...'

'She's impossible. I try to guide...'

'You shout, not guide, Esme. Have you talked to her about Saturday?' he pressed. 'I mean really talk, not lecture, laying down even more rules and punishments.'

'You think she should be allowed out to make a

spectacle of herself again?'

'I think the surest way to get Helen to repeat her mistakes is to lock her up and force her to go sneaking behind our backs.'

'I'll not allow her out of this house...'

'Then I will. Keeping her from her friends will only make her all the more determined to defy us.'

'We should discuss this.' She glanced at the clock.

'But not now, you'll keep people waiting and more important people than your own daughter,' he mocked.

'The auditions tonight are for the next production. If you want me to stay home I'll ask the committee to find another director for the play. I'll spend more time with you and Helen...'

'And play the martyr. No thank you.'

'I'm trying to do what you want.'

'That's just the problem, Esme,' he said wearily, lifting the tray on to the table. 'After twenty years of marriage there is absolutely nothing that I want to do with you.'

Helen crouched on the landing, her face pressed against the boarded-in banisters, listening hard. She'd heard her father offer Joe the car keys and caught a glimpse of the top of her brother's head as he left the house, but since then everything had been quiet. She'd caught a few distant murmurs of conversation, but they'd been too faint for her to make out the words. Suddenly the ringing click of her mother's stiletto heels resounded across the lino in the hall. Shrinking back, she darted into her bedroom and closed the door just as her mother ran upstairs and into the bathroom. A few minutes later Esme returned downstairs and Helen crept out of her room again.

The bathroom door was open, the air redolent with Chanel No. 5, her mother's favourite perfume. The clatter of dishes downstairs suggested her father was clearing the table. Her mother never lifted a finger once she was dressed to go out. A rustle of fine wool cloth lined with silk came from the hall as Esme removed her camel-hair coat from the stand. Not daring to look lest she be seen, Helen counted off the seconds, imagining her mother adjusting her coat, setting her hat on the back of her head, pinning it into place. Reaching for her three-quarter-length brown leather gloves, checking there were no wrinkles round her fingers and, the final touch, tying her brown silk scarf round her throat... Before she had finished picturing everything the front door opened and closed.

Heaving a sigh of relief, Helen charged downstairs and into her father who was taking his own coat from the stand.

'I'm going to the pub. Finish up in the kitchen for me, Helen.'

He didn't even wait for her to reply before following her mother out of the door.

Helen cleared the dining room and kitchen in record time, scraping the leftover ham salad and chips into the pig-swill bin, washing and drying the plates with more abandon and less care than her mother would have approved off, wiping the smears she had missed with the tea cloth.

296

Slinging the stained tea cloth into the linen bin in the scullery, she untied her apron and hung it on the back of the door. It wasn't even eight o'clock. She had plenty of time to steal some of her mother's Chanel and redo her make-up and hair. She hesitated as she walked past the door to the lounge. Sneaking in, she opened the cocktail cabinet, starting at the sound of 'Strangers in Paradise'. She closed the door quickly before realising there was no one besides herself in the house to hear it.

Opening it again she studied the contents: half-empty bottles of whisky and sherry that would certainly be missed, a full bottle of gin and at the back a second untouched bottle, probably Christmas gifts from warehouse suppliers who weren't aware that neither of her parents drank gin. She had enough money saved in her room to replace one. She could persuade Joe – no, not Joe – Jack, who had made it clear on Saturday that he was accustomed to going into off-licences and pubs, to buy another. Taking the bottle, she closed the cabinet and ran downstairs.

CHAPTER FOURTEEN

'Katie, Lily?'

'Isn't that Adam Jordan calling you?' Norah asked as they left the hospital.

Lily looked across the road and saw Adam running to meet them.

'Martin, Brian and I were just going into Joe's Ice Cream Parlour,' he panted, lying through his teeth. He had bumped into Martin and Brian in the Bay View and they had been on their way to the White Rose with thoughts of beer not ice cream on their minds. 'Would you like to join us? My treat. You too, Mrs Evans,' he added hesitantly.

'I'm a bit old for ice cream in the evening, thank you all the same, Adam, but I'm sure the girls would like one.' Norah sniffed the air in front of him. 'You haven't been drinking by any chance, have you?' she enquired sternly.

'Only half a pint, Mrs Evans. After work.'

'You sure?'

'Absolutely, Mrs Evans.'

'In that case the girls can go with you.' Norah gave him a look that told him she didn't believe a word he'd said. 'I was going to call in on Mrs Lannon anyway, Lily,' Norah reminded, pre-empting any protest. 'She wanted to be measured for a skirt.'

'If you really don't mind walking back on your own, Auntie.'

'I'd welcome the peace.' Norah glanced at Katie who was close to tears. Annie hadn't been well enough to say more than a few words. The doctor had taken them aside and warned them her injuries weren't healing as fast as he would have liked, which had upset Katie as much as seeing her mother vacant-eyed and withdrawn. Norah suspected Annie's problems were as much psychological as physical. In Annie's position she wouldn't be in a hurry to leave the caring environment of the hospital and three square meals a day for the uncertainties of life with Ernie.

'We'll see the girls get back safely, Mrs Evans,' Adam promised.

'Before half past ten,' Norah cautioned. 'They both have work tomorrow.'

'Knickerbocker glories all round?' Adam suggested, hoping to impress Katie with his generosity, as they crossed the road to where Martin and Brian stood waiting.

'A small strawberry ice-cream would be about all I could manage,' Lily demurred. 'Auntie Norah's teas don't leave room for much supper.'

'Katie?'

'The same please.'

'Marty?'

'Just coffee, thanks.' Martin's stomach was revolting at the thought of ice cream after all the beer he'd drunk. He'd meant to go home after Jack had left the Bay View but he'd run into Brian who persuaded him to have 'just one more' that had somehow become another two. He wasn't exactly drunk but he was also aware that he wasn't exactly sober either.

'Same for me too, please, Adam,' Brian called after him as they walked into Joe's. 'Judy not with you?' he asked as they sat down, although it was patently obvious she wasn't.

'It's her night for evening class.'

'So, where have you girls been?'

'Visiting Katie's mam in hospital.' Lily saw Martin pale and changed the subject. 'So are you going to see Jack play on Saturday in St James's?'

'Jack's in a play?' Martin queried as Adam laid a tray of coffees and ice cream on their table.

'His skiffle group are playing in the Youth Club dance. Hasn't he said?' Adam handed the girls their ice creams.

'He hadn't told me they had a booking.' Martin made a resolution to respect Jack's privacy less and interrogate him more. Perhaps if he'd made it his business to do so a few years back, he might have saved his brother from the disgrace of Borstal.

'There are still tickets left. The girls are going.' Adam winked at Katie who turned aside.

'Can you get me one?'

'Make it two.'

'Consider it done.'

'We could walk there with you, girls.' Martin reached for the sugar.

'How about we meet the three of you here about half past seven, have a coffee and go on to the youth club?' Brian suggested.

'That's fine by me,' Martin enunciated carefully lest he slur and Lily suspect he'd been drinking.

'By the three of us, you mean Katie, Judy and me?' Lily picked up her spoon and dipped it into her strawberry ice cream.

'And Helen,' Adam added. 'If she can make it. I heard her mother won't let her out.'

'What do you think, Katie?' Lily looked at her friend.

'If it's all right with Judy, it's all right by me.'

Lily noticed that Katie hadn't responded to Adam's smile. She also noticed that Adam couldn't stop looking at her friend.

'Then it's a date. You'd better eat up girls, if we're going to get you home before Norah's curfew.'

'What a racket,' Adam complained as a motorbike roared past.

'Idiot deserves to get killed.' Something made Martin turn around. He was too late. It was already out of sight. The uneasy feeling grew in the pit of his stomach. Jack wouldn't be such an idiot as to drive flat out down St Helen's Road, especially after drinking two pints of beer earlier. Would he?

'Sandwiches and gin. I thought you didn't drink.' Jack joined Helen on the sofa in the basement.

'I stole it from my father's cabinet so I'll have to replace it. I was hoping you'd buy a bottle for me. I have the money.' She opened her purse.

'Give it to me later. I'm starving.'

'I'm beginning to think that's your middle name.' She felt ridiculously shy with him considering the kisses they'd exchanged the evening before. 'How's your mother?'

He shrugged his shoulders.

'You did see her tonight.'

'How do you know?'

'Joe mentioned Lily was going to visit with Katie. Your mother's not any worse, is she?'

'She's not good. I suppose you know why she's in there.'

She nodded.

'I'd rather not talk about it.'

Sensing she'd blundered into forbidden ground,

Helen picked up the bottle of gin. 'Want some gin and lemonade?'

'Don't mind if I do.'

Taking two tumblers she poured gin into one of them. Not having a clue how much a normal measure of spirit was, she didn't stop until the glass was half full and the bottle a quarter empty.

'You've never drunk gin before.'

'Is it that obvious?'

Taking the glass from her, he tipped half the contents into the second tumbler. 'I suggest we top them up with lemonade and keep topping up, otherwise you'll be too drunk to stagger upstairs and I'll never make it back over the wall. Cigarette?' He opened a packet and offered her one.

'I don't smoke.'

'You don't like it?'

'I've never tried.'

'Not even round the back of the bike shed when you were twelve?'

'We didn't have a bike shed at my school.'

'Don't know what you're missing.'

'I don't like the smell and if my mother came down here it would be the first thing she'd pick up on.' To her relief he closed the packet without removing one.

Handing her one of the glasses, he lifted the other and touched it to hers. 'To us.'

'To us.' Taking a long draught of the gin and lemonade she smiled at him, waiting for his kiss. She wasn't disappointed. Taking the glass from her hand, he set it together with his own on the table.

'How about we make ourselves more comfortable.' Kicking off his shoes, he pushed her back on to the sofa and lay beside her.

'This feels...'

'Right?'

His kisses coupled with the gin sent her head swimming. She was conscious of his hands on her face, her neck...

'That is absolutely enough, Jack Clay!' Removing his hand from the inside of her dress and the outside of her bra cup, she climbed over him, leaving the sofa and retreating to the door.

'I saw more than your bra last Saturday.'

'Only because my dress was torn.' Helen fastened the top button on her shirtwaister. 'And you won't be seeing any more of me in future.'

'Make a bet on that?' He grinned.

'Yes.' She opened the door.

'Where are you going?'

'Upstairs.'

'You said your family won't be home for hours.'

'They won't.'

'Then come back here.'

'No.'

'You afraid?'

When she didn't reply he held out her glass. 'Come on, don't spoil things.'

'It's you who spoiled them.'

'By putting my hand on the outside of your iron-padded bra?'

'It's not iron...'

'It felt like it. I thought we drank to us.' Picking up their glasses he drank half the contents of his own, while offering her hers.

'You trying to get me drunk?'

'Don't tell me you've never been drunk either,' he mocked. 'Face it, Helen, you just don't know how to enjoy yourself.'

'And you do, I suppose.'

'Better than you by the look of it. What's the matter, don't you trust yourself?'

'I don't trust you.'

'That's a fine thing for a girl to say to her boyfriend. Surely I don't have to teach you the facts of life, or do you still think babies are found under gooseberry bushes?'

'Decent people...'

'I'm not decent people – I'm dangerous, remember.' He patted the sofa beside him as she finally took her glass from him, but she sat in the chair opposite.

'Haven't you ever wondered what it's like to make love?'

'No.'

'That's a fib. Girls talk about it all the time.'

'Only the girls you know.'

'I know you well enough.'

'No, you don't.'

'I know you wouldn't let any other boy kiss you the way I just did.'

'I could have another boyfriend,' she challenged.

'I haven't bumped into anyone else creeping over your wall.'

'They come late at night when you're in bed.'

Leaving the sofa, he knelt in front of her and rested his face on her knees. 'Would it be so awful for you to admit you like kissing me?'

She looked into his eyes and felt herself drowning in their depths. 'No,' she whispered in a small voice.

'Then how about picking up where we left off.'

'I don't want to have a baby.'

'There are ways of preventing that.'

'You've...' Steeling herself to ask the question uppermost in her mind, she blurted, 'You've made love to other girls?'

'Hundreds, and none are pregnant.'

'You're lying.'

'Perhaps.' He slid his hand up her skirt, past her stocking tops, slipping his fingers beneath her suspenders on to her naked thigh.

'Don't.' She grabbed his hand, holding it firmly in her own. 'I won't go all the way.'

'I know you won't.'

'So, what's the problem,' he coaxed, unbuttoning her dress with his free hand. 'The curtains are pulled, the door locked, no one will ever know what we've done – or haven't.'

'I'll know.'

Reaching up with his free hand, he pulled her head down to his and kissed her again. 'You can't lose your reputation a second time, Helen, so why not enjoy all that being a bad girl offers.'

'Because...'

'Because what?' he murmured, sliding his hand higher.

'I go to night school on Tuesdays and Fridays, but I'm free tomorrow. We could go to the pictures or something,' Martin suggested diffidently to Lily as they rounded the corner from Craddock Street into Carlton Terrace.

'I'd like to, Martin, but I'm going out with Joe tomorrow night.'

'I wouldn't have asked if I'd known you were going out with Joe Griffiths.'

'It's not like he's my boyfriend or anything; we've only been out together once. We're just friends.'

For the first time Martin found himself wondering whether Lily was as artless as she appeared, or a scheming little flirt out to get two men circling round her.

'I'll be seeing you on Saturday,' she continued brightly when he didn't reply.

'Yes.'

Taken aback by his brusqueness, she looked ahead to where Katie was walking with Adam. He reached for her hand, but Katie either didn't see it or deliberately walked away.

''Night girls, don't forget to mention Saturday to Judy.' Brian dashed down the steps to his door.

'We won't,' Lily assured, as Martin followed him without looking back at her.

'See you, Adam.' Katie ran to the door, reaching it before Lily, leaving Adam to look after her with a wistful expression that reminded Lily of the abandoned dogs in the animal shelter in Singleton Park.

'You annoyed Angie by pushing off the way you did on Monday night.' Robin drew back his cue, balanced it carefully between his index finger and thumb, and pitched it forward, sending the balls scattering over the table.

'I had work to do.'

'Pull the other one.'

'And an early start in the studio.' Grinding a cube of chalk over the tip of his cue, Joe studied the position of the balls as he moved to the other side of the table.

'She thinks you're still upset because she suggested you went your separate ways in the summer.'

'I'm trying to take a shot.'

'Tell me to keep my nose out of your affairs, why don't you.'

'How about we talk about you and Emily.' Joe potted the ball he'd been aiming for and smirked triumphantly at Robin.

'We did it.'

Joe whirled round.

'Last night. In my bedroom before Mums and Pops came home.'

'You and Emily...'

'Surprised me too, but I sort of got carried away and she went along with it.'

'And if she gets pregnant?'

'Give me credit for some sense.' Robin patted his pocket. 'I paid a visit to the barber the moment I sensed which way the wind was blowing there.'

'What's the barber got to do with it?'

'"And would sir like anything else? Hair preparations, comb, brush ... French letters..."'

'No barber's ever offered me those.'

'That's because you insist on going to your father's. And for the record, they don't ask, just offer the extras. It's up to you to tell them what you want. Here.' Robin took a small cardboard packet from his shirt pocket and tossed it across the table. 'Three feather-light...'

'You don't have to come out with the advertising spiel. I have seen them before.'

'For a minute, there, you had me wondering.'

'I never thought that a girl like Emily...'

'A girl like what?' Robin demanded indignantly.

'A nice girl.'

'Emily is a nice girl. And we're living in the 1950s not the 1850s, thank God. Haven't you heard it's all right for women to enjoy sex these days – and take it from me, they do, if you push the right buttons.'

'And when she wants to get married?'

'Years from now.'

'Whenever, what's her husband going to think when he discovers she's not a virgin?'

'You sound like my mother's maiden aunt.'

'A girl's reputation is everything...' Joe began hotly, thinking of his sister and Larry.

'As is her sex appeal. And I've been enhancing Emily's every way I know how. I may even end up marrying her myself.'

'And if you don't?'

'If her future husband has any sense, he'll be grateful to me for breaking her in.'

'You're disgusting.'

'God save me from the bourgeoisie and their petty bloody morality.'

'You want us to be as immoral as the select few, so there'll be more women available for you to practise on.'

'Now you're telling me I'm an aristocrat!'

'There might not be a title, but look at this place and the way you live.'

'I admit we're comfortably off. Last time I looked that wasn't a crime. But you can't exactly plead poverty either. You go to university the same as me. Your allowance is the same. Your trust fund is bigger...'

'What do you know about my trust fund?'

'Wake up, Joe, this is Swansea, everyone know's everyone else's business.'

'So, I'm beginning to find out.'

'There's no need to go into a huff. I'm not the one who did the prying.'

'But you move in circles that do.' Joe took his next shot, missed the ball and sent his cue skidding across the baize.

'Steady, my father's only just had this table re-covered.'

'And if I bugger it, he'll just have to re-cover it again, won't he.'

'What the hell's got into you?'

Joe stacked his cue on the stand. 'I'm surprised a socially acceptable family like yours puts up with their son slumming with the likes of me.'

'For Christ's sake, Joe, all I was trying to say is you give more credence to outmoded, archaic rules than me or, fortunately for me, Emily.'

They stared at one another for a moment. 'Tantrum over?' Robin handed Joe back his cue.

'I can't bear the thought of people discussing me behind my back.'

'They do that wherever you live. And if you don't want the size of your trust fund talked about, I suggest you have a word with your solicitor. He has a loose mouth, especially after he's had a few drinks.' Robin took and missed his next shot.

'That breaches client confidentiality.'

'Now you want to sue your solicitor – take my advice, Joe, vent your frustrations on something else. Preferably shaped like this.' Resting his cue in the crook of his elbow, Robin sketched a large-bosomed woman in the air with his hands.

'So, what was it like?' Joe asked, keeping his eyes fixed on the table.

'Gentlemen don't talk about it. Leastways not when they do it with girls they care about.'

'Then you do care for her.'

'That's a given. Despite what you think of me for seducing the gorgeous Emily, I may yet marry her... But not this week.'

'Next?' Joe enquired caustically, shooting his cue.

'We have known one another most of our lives.'

'But you've only just started seeing her.'

'In every sense of the word.' Robin walked round the table. 'Girls look good in their under-wear but *so* much better out of it. I even brought up the subject of weddings and we're agreed neither of us is in a hurry to walk down the aisle. There are too many other things to think about. My career – when it gets started – hers. She's going to art college with Angie and wants to finish the course even if she never works. And then there's a house, furniture, so many boring things to settle. We both want to have fun before we start trawling round department stores and estate agents. She fancies going skiing at Christmas. Her people have friends who have a chalet in Switzerland. If you're with Angie by then, you could come with us. You know what parents are. They'd be happier at the thought of two girls going off with two boys. It preserves the illusion of single-sex bedrooms and respectability.'

'I have no intention of going out with Angie – or sleeping with her – to suit you and Emily.'

'I thought you were hooked on her or was that some other friend I saw moping around all summer, mooning over his lost love?'

'Leave it out, Robin,' Joe snapped irritably, childishly pleased when Robin missed his shot.

'Whisky?' Robin went to the decanter on the sideboard.

'Doesn't your father ever complain about the amount of his booze you drink?'

'He doesn't keep a check on it. If he did my mother might realise just how much he drinks all by himself. Keep them,' Robin said carelessly as Joe tried to hand the pack of French letters back to him. 'I've plenty and you never know when they might come in useful.'

Concerned lest someone walk in and see the packet lying around, Joe stowed it in his shirt pocket. 'These aren't foolproof.'

'They are if you use them properly.'

'That's not what I've heard.'

'You don't believe that rubbish about the government putting pinholes in one in every dozen to keep up the population.'

'How naïve do you think I am?'

'After that outburst earlier I was beginning to wonder. So, you taking Angie out soon, or what?'

'What's it to you?'

'Nothing, except that she asked me to put in a good word for her. Girls tell one another everything. It's a bit like follow my leader. Now that Emily's tried it little sister won't be far behind and you could be the lucky recipient. If you are, you're so upright and moral, you'd marry her even if Marilyn Monroe flung herself at your feet the next time you left the house. And that would give me a decent brother-in-law I could get on with, not to mention help me with my career in the BBC.' Robin stood back and watched Joe line up his next shot.

'You're talking rot.'

'You're a high flyer, I'm a plodder. I don't mind. Pops has the pull to get me into the organisation. Eventually, you'll be in a position to keep me there.'

'Angie really asked you to talk to me?'

'She did. And if you know anything about Angie, that should tell you how desperately fond of you she is. She's never run after a boy before in her life. And speak of the devil.'

'You didn't say she was in the house,' Joe reproached as voices drifted in from the hall.

'You didn't ask. She's been plotting some girl thing or other in the drawing room,' he shouted for the benefit of whoever was in the hall.

'Charity concert for the benefit of the Children's Fresh-Air Fund, not girl thing,' Angie corrected, opening the door and looking at them. Joe glanced into the hall, it was packed with what seemed like a horde of chattering girls in pastel frocks, bright-red lipstick and high-heeled

312

stilettos that were making machine-gun noises on the tiled floor.

'Hello, boys.' Half a dozen of them crowded in behind Angie.

'Goodbye, girls.' Robin moved to the door.

'Say goodbye nicely, Robin,' Angela chided.

'Goodbye nicely.'

'Isn't he a scream,' Emily shrieked at no one in particular.

'A hoot.' Angie smiled at Joe and arched her eyebrows. 'If you're staying for supper, Joe, I'll warn Mrs John.'

'He'll be staying for breakfast if you don't leave us in peace to finish this game,' Robin interrupted.

'See you later, Robin,' Emily cooed, backing into the hall.

'Joe?' Angie waited, hand on doorknob.

'I'll be out after the game.'

'Then I'll tell Mrs John to set an extra place.'

He faltered as he looked into her eyes. 'Please, Angie,' he capitulated, 'if it's not too much trouble.'

'No trouble, Joe, no trouble at all.'

'What the hell...' Martin was jerked out of sleep by a banging on the front door that resounded down to the end room that he and Jack had organised as their bedroom.

'Need you ask?'

Martin opened his eyes to see his brother balancing on one leg while he thrust his other into his jeans.

'What time is it?' he barked above the pounding

313

on the door. 'After twelve. The old man can't be working tonight and by the racket he's making I'd say he's pissed.'

Martin leapt out of bed. 'You're not going to the door.'

'You want him to wake the entire street?'

Grabbing his dressing gown, Martin pushed ahead of Jack, but Brian reached the kitchen before either of them. Opening the front door, Brian stepped forward. Red-eyed, swaying on his feet, Ernie would have fallen flat on his face if Brian hadn't held him stiffly at arm's length.

'Who the hell are you?' Ernie's eyes rolled alarmingly in his head as he tried – and failed – to focus.

'I think you're the one who should be introducing himself,' Brian replied in his detached police officer's voice.

'You're not my bloody son.'

'I'm glad to say.'

'Bastard!'

'I have to caution you...'

'Jack, where's bloody Jack...' Gripping the doorposts, Ernie swayed precariously forward. 'There you are, you stupid moron. I've come for my money.'

'What money?' Tying his dressing-gown belt, Martin stepped in front of his father, preventing him from advancing any further into the room.

'Rent money. The stupid cow next door...'

'As neither of us are living next door, we're not paying the rent.'

'You'd see your mother put out on the streets?'

'She's not moving back in with you.'

314

'You...' Ernie swung a punch. Brian parried it before Martin had a chance. Lifting Ernie's arm high behind his back, he held him firm as he slumped forward.

'Want me to arrest him?' Brian looked from Martin to Jack. 'We've enough for breach of the peace and drunk and disorderly.'

'Which will get him what?' Martin asked.

'A cell until he sobers up, a fine if he goes to court.'

'Which he won't pay and my mother will starve herself to find money for.' Jack took his father from Brian and slung him over his shoulder. 'What's the bloody point?'

'The point is we can't have him coming round here and making that racket at this time of night.'

'Because he scares you?' Jack taunted.

'Because he'll terrify your sister even more than she is now, and possibly Lily and Mrs Evans, although in a fair contest I'd back Mrs Evans against your father any day.'

'I'll give you a hand to get him home.' Martin rummaged in Ernie's pockets for his keys. Flicking through the ring, he extracted the one he wanted and walked through the door.

'You're not going to dress?' Jack asked.

'Who'll be around at this time of night to see me?'

Brian had made a pot of cocoa and cut half a dozen sandwiches, by the time Jack and Martin returned.

'You were gone a long time,' Brian commented as Martin slung his dressing gown and pyjama

315

jacket in a bucket ready for washing, filled the sink with water and plunged his head and hands in it.

'The place was like a pigsty.'

'If it had been up to me I would have thrown him in his own filth, but this one' – Jack indicated Martin – 'insisted on changing the bed.'

'I don't like him any more than you...'

'Then why clean up after him?'

'Mam's sake, I suppose.'

'Do you have any idea when she's coming out of hospital?' Brian poured cocoa into three cups.

'No.'

'I'll move out any time you want me to.'

'There's no need. Mam won't move in with us even when she does come out.'

'You don't know that, Jack.'

'Yes I do.' Slamming the door behind him, Jack stormed off down the passage.

'I'm sorry about Jack.' Drying himself off, Martin sat at the table in his pyjama trousers and sipped his cocoa.

'In his position I'd be climbing the wall.'

'Then you do understand.'

'I try. Look it's none of my business...'

'It is when the old man comes thumping on our door at this time of night.'

'He must have been pretty desperate to ask you for his rent money.'

'Meaning?'

'Have you thought he could be about to get evicted?'

'In which case he'll have to leave the street ... and Mam won't have anywhere other than here to come back to.' Martin's face cracked into the first real smile Brian had seen on it since he'd come to Swansea. 'Powell, you're a bloody genius.'

'It's only a theory.'

'I can check the details with Mrs Lannon tomorrow. She's told me dozens of times that if it was only my father in her basement, she'd have had him put out on the street years ago.'

'Might he leave Swansea?'

Martin shook his head. 'That would be too much to hope for. Apart from his job, everyone he knows is here. Aside from a stint in the army he's never left the place.'

Brian would have offered to keep a discreet eye on Ernie Clay but he sensed it would be superfluous. He was surprised Ernie had got away with knocking on their door tonight, but then Roy was on night shift and things could get busy after the pubs closed. He suddenly understood why the rotas had been changed in the station so he and Roy were never on together.

'Thanks for the cocoa.' Martin picked up Jack's cup. 'I'll take this down for him. And thanks for persuading us to let you move in.'

'Changed your mind about coppers?'

'Keep at it and I might.'

'Thank you for the supper, Dr Watkin Morgan, Mrs Watkin Morgan.' Joe nodded to them as he left the table.

'It's a pleasure to have you here, Joseph. Any time,' Mrs Watkin Morgan gushed.

'See you tomorrow,' Robin murmured absently,

317

gazing intently at Emily.

'I'll see Joseph out.' Angela accompanied him into the hall. 'Don't forget your coat.'

'I won't.'

'There's a party tomorrow...' Angie began.

'I'm busy.'

'Your sister again.' She smiled brightly. 'Don't answer that.'

'How about Saturday?'

'Last pool party of the season here. You'll come?'

He remembered Lily was going to the youth club dance. 'I'll come.'

Standing on tiptoe, she kissed his cheek. 'I'll see you then.'

CHAPTER FIFTEEN

John scanned the letter Rosie had put on his desk before scribbling his signature at the foot of the page. 'That's it for the day?'

'Yes, Mr Griffiths.'

'You can leave now.'

'It's only five o'clock.'

'Have an hour on me. How are the wedding preparations going?'

'Fine, I think, Mr Griffiths.'

'You think,' he reiterated, looking quizzically at her.

'My mother's taken it upon herself to see to every detail.'

'Then all you have to worry about is looking beautiful on the day.'

'That's one way of looking at it, Mr Griffiths.' She picked up the letters. 'I'll get Katie to put these in the post.'

'How are you getting on with her?'

'She's keen, conscientious, works well; in fact, she typed this and, as you see without a single mistake, unlike most of my letters.'

John set his pen on his desk, crossed his arms and looked up at his secretary. 'I know you, Rosie, there's a "but" coming.'

'From a work point of view I can't fault her, Mr Griffiths, but she is dreadfully nervous and absolutely petrified of making a mistake. She also tries to clear all the outstanding business at the end of every day, which you well know is impossible. I reassure her every chance I get, but at the rate she's going she'll be a worn-out wreck before her probationary period is up. She wouldn't take a tea break at four o'clock because of the typing, and when I suggested she take one now she insisted she'd prefer to study our accounting systems.'

'But all in all you think she's up to the job.'

'More than up to it, Mr Griffiths. You picked well.'

'That's what I've been waiting to hear.' John glanced into the outer office as Rosie opened the door. Katie was sitting at Rosie's desk, head bent over the invoice book. She did look tired and drawn but was it down to the stress of the job as Rosie had suggested, or was it her father? Along with half the street he had heard Ernie banging on her brothers' door in a drunken stupor late last night and when he had seen Roy coming home after night shift, Roy had let slip that Annie Clay wasn't doing so well.

Making a mental note to offer Katie a lift home to see if he could help her in any way, he picked up the furniture catalogue he had been studying and flicked through the dining room suites. None looked as though they would last more than a couple of months of normal family wear and tear, unlike his grandmother's suite, which he had packed away in the basement – but if customers wanted contemporary style before durability and craftsmanship, that's what he would stock.

The telephone rang in the outer office. Hearing Katie answer it in a tone virtually indistinguishable from Rosie's, he left his chair and moved restlessly to the window. Now that he'd begun to consider a life without Esme all he wanted from her was his freedom, but would she give him a divorce if he pressed her? And would Joe and Helen want to live with him or their mother? The only thing he could be certain of was that if Esme did agree to a divorce she would not want to stay in Carlton Terrace, considering the number of times she had tried to get him to move out of the street.

Already Joe spent more time outside the house than in, although if he had been in Joe's position he wouldn't want to spend time at home after witnessing the ultimatum he'd given Esme. But then Joe was no longer a child. After university he would make an independent life for himself and move on to wherever his work was. And Helen?

She had seemed strange the last week. Detached, secretive, cleaning out the basement instead of fighting with Esme and demanding she be allowed out as he'd expected her to. Helen was growing up and not very well if last Saturday night was anything to go by.

Helen's problems seemed insurmountable; it pained him even to think of them. He loved her and wanted to help her, only he wasn't sure how. But if Esme left, could he cope with Helen alone?

Just thinking about it led to a vision of life without Esme. Of living alone – or possibly just with the children – of restoring the house to the comfortable, homely place it had been in his grandparents' day. Listening to the music he liked on the radio and the record player on Sunday mornings. Asking the daily to prepare the kind of food he preferred and hadn't eaten at home since his marriage. Traditional cooked dinners, with meat and three vegetables, thick, savoury gravy, roast potatoes and stuffing. And afterwards substantial suet puddings filled with apple and rhubarb, and smothered in creamy custard as opposed to the endless cold salads and fruit jellies Esme ordered. The more he considered how his life would be without his wife, the more it appealed. He would be alone but not lonely. And best of all, he wouldn't have to think about Esme any longer. Where she was. What she was doing, or who she was doing it with. He wouldn't have to concern himself whether she approved of anything he or the children did. Freedom...

'Mr Griffiths.' He turned to see Katie standing in the doorway. 'Mrs Evans is on the telephone;

she would like to speak to you.'

'To me?' He looked at Katie's white face and realised what the call might mean. 'Do you know how to put a call through to my telephone?'

'Yes, Rosie showed me.' She returned to her desk. He closed the door behind her and waited for the ring.

'We won't be getting many more evenings like this before the year's end.' Joe breathed in deeply as he stood on the foreshore of Swansea Bay and gazed out towards Mumbles Head. The sun, an enormous golden ball, hovered above the sea, floating on filaments of saffron and crimson clouds, lending the entire scene a surreal tinge, blending sand, cliffs and sky in a single-textured mass of artist's palette tints from yellow through ochre and orange to scarlet.

'No, but I like the beach in winter. When I was younger Uncle Roy used to take me on long walks, especially after a storm. You'd be amazed at the things we found washed up – tables, chairs, shoes, bricks – and when it began to get dark we'd go home, and Auntie Norah would be waiting with the fire stoked high and home-made cake and bread ready for toasting in front of the parlour fire...'

'Is that a hint that if I bring you down here in winter I'll have to arrange the welcome-back fire and food first?'

'No.' She coloured in embarrassment. 'I was just trying to say...'

'That you like walking in winter.' He caught her hand, holding it as they turned towards

Mumbles. 'Do you want to do anything when we get there? Have an ice cream, coffee, window-shop?'

'Window-shopping sounds fun.'

'Really? Most...'

'Girls you know.'

'I left myself wide open for that one.'

'Alternatively we could just walk to Mumbles, sit on the beach until the sun sets and get the train back.'

'Whatever you like.'

'Is Helen still angry with us?'

'Why should she be angry with us?'

'I mean, Katie, Judy and me. She was furious because we didn't call for her when we went to Mumbles on Sunday.'

'She couldn't have gone anywhere on Sunday. My mother threatened to send her to my aunt's farmhouse in Carmarthen if she as much as tried to set foot over the front doorstep.'

'I know, but when Katie and I tried to explain why we hadn't called she refused to listen.'

'Helen can be stupid as well as stubborn and Sunday wasn't her best day. She's calmed down since then. She's spent most of her time cleaning out the basement and all that dusting, polishing and beating of carpets has taken the edge off her aggression. I went down there yesterday. She's organised a sitting room for when you girls come round again.'

'I'll work on Auntie Norah. Perhaps she'll allow Katie and me to call on her tomorrow.'

'I'd wait until my mother was out if I were you.'

'How would we know whether she's in or out?'

'I'll come round and tell you. I'll even sit in the basement with you.'

Not quite knowing how to respond to his offer, she looked away. There was hardly anyone else on the beach. Way in the distance at the dock end of the bay a man was exercising two spaniels. Close to Mumbles she could just about make out a solitary woman with what looked like a terrier on a lead.

'We could watch the sunset from that dune.'

'We could.' Her heart began to beat faster.

Leading her towards the edge of the beach where the sand was broken by great clumps of coarse grass, he took off his mac and spread it on the ground.

'You'll get cold,' she warned.

'Not if you snuggle up close and keep me warm.' As they sat next to one another he wrapped his arm round her shoulders. 'Put your hands under my pullover.'

'They're freezing.'

Taking them, he tucked them beneath his Aran sweater against his chest. Conscious just how cold they were, she tightened her fists as small as she could.

'Keep them still.'

'Sorry.'

'And stop apologising, that's definitely your worst fault, being sorry for everything even when it's not your fault.' He blew on the tip of her nose. 'You're turning blue. I wish it were the beginning of summer, not the end. But there's always next summer.'

'Will you be here?'

'On the beach?'

'I meant Swansea.'

'Not too far away,' he murmured seriously. 'I have a lot to stay here for.'

'You'll be qualified.'

'And working, heading for the grown-up world.' As he gazed into her eyes he couldn't understand Robin and Emily wanting to prolong their courtship. He could think of nothing he wanted more than marriage to Lily. He'd even begun to plan out his life with her. As soon as he turned twenty-one he'd raid his trust fund to buy a small, cosy house with an enormous garden somewhere in the country close to the BBC in Llandaff. When he came home at night he'd close the curtains and shut out the world; they'd sit in front of the fire and watch the flames while they ate and afterwards make slow, languorous love on the hearthrug...

'Look.' An enormous tanker loomed on the horizon, dwarfing the yachts circling in the bay.

'When I was younger I used to come down here to watch the ocean-going ships sail in and out of the docks. I was so sure then that I'd leave Swansea on one of them. Travel round the world, make my fortune and return with chests stuffed full of treasure.'

'Like Dick Whittington.'

'Oh, much richer than him.' He laughed. 'My father destroyed that particular fantasy when I was eight by taking Helen and me across to Ilfracombe on a day trip. Our return wasn't at all like I imagined.'

'Uncle Roy and Auntie Norah took me on one

325

of those trips too.'

'We could go again – together.'

'I'd like that.'

'Do you mean that, or will you always see me as Helen's older brother?'

'You'll always be Helen's older brother.'

'I suppose I will,' he murmured, not thinking about what he was saying. Slipping his fingers beneath her chin, he tilted up her face and kissed her. His touch was so light, so gentle that afterwards she couldn't be sure it had happened. She drew back, ashamed of herself for expecting more after last night.

He looked into her eyes before bending his head to hers a second time, and this time the touch of his lips on hers was firmer, more assured and as his hands slid round to her back, she finally put all thoughts of his other girls from her mind.

'John...'

'Is something wrong, Norah?'

'We've had a call from the hospital.' John heard a sharp intake of breath as Norah fought to keep control. 'Annie died a few minutes ago. Roy's gone for the boys. Can you bring Katie home?'

'Do you want me to tell her?' he asked, amazed to find himself volunteering for the task.

'Whatever you think best.'

'And if she asks what happened?' John spoke quietly and calmly, in an attempt to force Norah to concentrate on practical matters.

'From the symptoms, the doctor thinks it might have been a brain haemorrhage. He said it was not an entirely unexpected complication, given the severity of her injuries, but there was nothing he, or anyone else, could have done to save Annie, even if they had known it was going to happen. As Roy said, she has taken a lot of battering over the years. Roy's bringing the boys here...'

'Don't worry about Katie, I'll get her to you as soon as I can.' John put down the receiver and picked up his jacket from the back of his chair. Checking his car keys were in the pocket, he went to the door. Katie was sitting ashen-faced at her desk. He looked at her and realised she knew. 'Get your coat, Katie,' he murmured gently.

Dry-eyed, she walked like an automaton to the coat-stand.

John picked up the telephone receiver and hit the button that connected to the warehouse floor. 'Geoff, I have to go out. You're in charge and given the time, you'll have to close up tonight... No, don't take the takings to my house...' He watched Katie button on the new grey woollen coat she had bought with the advance he had given her. She'd mismatched the top and second buttons and the hem hung uneven, lending her a quality even more urchin and orphan-like than usual. Orphan-like... 'That's right, Geoff, straight to the night safe. Take Mike and Alan along with you for security. Don't worry about up here. I'll lock the office.' He replaced the receiver.

'Katie?'

She looked so lost and forlorn; John did what he would have done if she had been his own daughter. Opening his arms, he held her tight before leading her gently out of the building to his car.

'The bastard! The bloody bastard!' Beside himself with rage, Jack slammed his fist into Norah's kitchen wall.

'Jack, come on now, there's a good lad.' Roy pulled him back. Holding Jack's wrists firmly in his hands, he examined his knuckles. 'Do that again and you'll likely break some bones, and that won't help anyone.'

As tears of pure rage, frustration and despair began to fall from Jack's eyes, Roy signalled to Norah.

'Would you and Jack like to be alone for a bit, Martin?' she asked.

'Please, Mrs Evans,' Martin accepted gratefully.

'I'll send Katie in when she gets here. If you need us before then, we'll be in the parlour.' Roy and Norah closed the door behind them.

'All that bloody effort to get rooms and decorate them! All that bloody work for nothing. Mam will never set foot in them, never see them, never know how much we wanted to get her away from him...'

'But Katie will, Jack. We have her to think about now.'

'She'll be better off up here.'

'She's our sister,' Martin reminded, trying to get his brother to think of something other than the part their father had played in their mother's death. 'We have to look after her, protect her...'

'Like we protected Mam?'

Jack's rage dissolved into tears and with them erupted years of pent-up emotion. Martin held his brother, realising that for all his anger, swagger and bravado, Jack hadn't come any distance since he was six years old and Roy Williams had caught him stealing cigarettes from the corner shop.

'How did Mam die, Mr Griffiths?' Katie asked as he turned the car into Walter Road.

'Mrs Evans told me they can't be sure yet, but the doctor thinks one of the blood vessels in her brain burst. The end was sudden and very quick. She wouldn't have felt any pain. She would have simply gone to sleep and never woken up.'

'It happened because Dad beat her.'

'No one can be sure of that, Katie.'

'I can.' She turned her small white face to his. 'Can I see her?'

'The hospital won't let you, yet. The nurses will need time to wash your mother's body and lay it out properly,' he explained, leaving out all mention of the indignities of post-mortem examination. 'When my grandmother died I wanted to see her but I had to wait two days until I was allowed to bring her body home.'

'We don't have a home...'

'You and your brothers have a lot of friends, Katie, and I'm sure Mrs Evans and Constable Williams will arrange something suitable. Whatever happens, I promise you that you will be able to see your mother before she's buried.'

'I'd like a lock of her hair. Mam had one of her

own mother's.'

'You'll be able to cut one, Katie.'

'Thank you for telling me the truth, Mr Griffiths.' Katie stared straight ahead as he pulled up outside Roy's and Norah's house. 'Most people would have tried to fob me off with lies about how Mam died.'

He laid his hand on her arm, preventing her from leaving the car. 'Take whatever time you need and if there is anything – anything – you can think of that I can do to help, you will ask me?'

'Yes, Mr Griffiths.'

John left the driver's seat and walked round to help Katie from the car.

Norah opened the door to them before they reached it. 'Your brothers are in the kitchen, Katie.'

'Thank you, Auntie Norah.' Katie ran through the hall.

'Come into the parlour, John.'

'Thank you, Norah, I will for a few minutes, if you don't mind.'

'It's good of you to bring Katie home.' Roy ushered him to a comfortable chair.

'Least I can do.' John strained his ears but no sounds came from the kitchen.

'They're best left alone. Sorry, I'd like to offer you tea, John, but the kettle's in the kitchen.'

'I think something stronger is in order.' Roy removed three glasses and a bottle of brandy from the cupboard in the alcove next to the fireplace.

'Has anyone told Ernie?' John asked.

'We couldn't get an answer at the flat. Mrs

Lannon's given him notice for non-payment of rent and he's supposed to be out by this Sunday, but no one's seen him since the boys put him to bed last night.'

'Someone will have to identify Annie.'

'I'm taking Martin and Jack down to the hospital. They wanted to see Katie before they went.'

'She wants to see Annie.'

'That might be best left until after the post-mortem.'

John bowed to Roy's superior professional knowledge of the rituals of sudden death. 'Did Annie have any insurance?' John looked from Roy to Norah. 'I'm not prying. Annie was my neighbour as much as yours and I've done precious little over the years to help her.'

'You...'

John held up his hand. 'No excuses, Norah, we both know I could have done a lot more for her and the children. Please, I'd regard it as an honour if you'd allow me to pay for the funeral, but I do have a condition. You have to tell the children it was covered by an insurance policy. I don't want them feeling they owe me anything.'

'I don't know what to say.'

'It's only money, Norah,' John dismissed. 'And money is meaningless once you've enough to live on, but it's the most important thing in the world when you can't cover the bare essentials.'

'In that case, John, we accept on behalf of the children.'

'And they'll never find out?'

'Not from us.'

'Thank you.' He sipped his brandy. 'Is Lily with the boys?'

'She's with Joe.' Norah made a face as she drank her brandy but John noticed she managed more of it than him. 'They said they were going to walk to Mumbles.'

'I could try to find them.'

'Let her enjoy the evening as long as she can. There's nothing she can do for now, and as Katie's sharing her room, she'll be with Katie all night.'

John nodded.

'But if you have time, John, perhaps you could drive the boys and me down to the hospital,' Roy suggested. 'I know it isn't far, but Jack's taken the news badly and he's unpredictable enough normally.'

'I'll be glad to, Roy. And if you need anything, or more money...'

'You'll be the first one we come to,' Roy promised, recognising John's need to be of use. The doorbell and telephone rang simultaneously. 'And you can start helping now by answering the door, while I get the phone.'

As soon as news spread of Annie's death a procession of neighbours found their way to Norah's and Roy's door. The first was Mrs Lannon, who insisted on going into the kitchen to hand Martin a key to the new lock she'd had fitted to the door of the family's old basement flat to deny his father access. After telling him to take all the time he wanted to clear the place of the family's possessions, she hugged Katie, almost hugged

332

Jack before thinking better of the idea in the face of his obvious disapproval, and joined Norah and Roy in the parlour.

The next was Joy Hunt, who sat stiffly, sipping a cup of tea Katie had made, while steadfastly refusing to look Roy in the eye. Like John, she offered money, help with Katie, and food and drink for the post-funeral meal. The Jordans came; Doris took over the kitchen and sent Adam down to the basement to see if he could do anything for the boys who had retreated there with Katie.

'Is it ever going to stop?' Jack snapped, as the doorbell overhead rang, yet again, and footsteps echoed above their heads.

'People are trying to be kind,' Martin commented absently, haunted by an image of his mother, as she had been the last time he had seen her. White, lifeless, too exhausted to talk, her face bruised black and blue, the crown of her skull, jaw, hands and arms encased in bandages. Like Jack, he burned to do something to his father but Roy's words – cool, calm, sensible – stayed with him: 'You have your brother and sister to think about now, boy. They have no one else and they need you. Forget revenge and forget your father. With luck, you may never see him again.'

'They weren't bloody kind when Mam was alive.' Jack's voice, angry and savage, cut through his thoughts.

'That's unfair, Jack.'

Both Jack and Martin turned to their sister. They were the first words Katie had spoken since they'd left upstairs.

'Mrs Evans and Mr Williams have done everything they can for us and if they didn't do more before, it was only because Mam wouldn't let them.'

'Martin, Jack.' Roy knocked on the connecting door. 'When you're ready, Mr Griffiths will take us down to the hospital.'

Adam rose to his feet. 'I'd better go,' he said awkwardly, glancing at Katie who had consistently ignored him, whether deliberately or not he couldn't decide.

'Thanks for coming round.' Martin left his chair.

'I'll tell the other boys what happened, Jack.'

'Other boys?' Jack looked at Adam blankly for a moment, then he remembered. 'The youth club dance.'

'They'll probably push the booking on a few weeks. They have a record player. Perhaps in a month or so...'

'No, I'll play on Saturday.'

'Jack, it's not important.'

'I have nothing better to do.'

'Marty?' Adam appealed.

'Jack's right, none of us is doing any good sitting around here listening to the bell ring upstairs. We may as well go.'

'Won't people think it disrespectful?'

'People can think what they bloody well please. My mother knew what I thought of her and what I'll carry on thinking of her for the rest of my life. I'll change out of my working clothes. I'll only be a couple of minutes, Mr Williams.' Jack walked down the passage towards his bedroom.

'Can, I go with you?' Katie asked Roy.

'This is only going to be a lot of forms and papers, Katie. You'd be better off waiting to see your mam. I'll arrange to have her brought back here as soon as the hospital release her body, but that probably won't be for a day or two. Once she's here you can spend as much time with her as you like before the funeral.'

'Here? To this house?'

'Norah's arranging the parlour now, Martin. She could probably do with some help, Katie, after the boys and I have left.'

'I'll come up then, Mr Williams.'

'Please, call me Uncle Roy, Katie. Mr Williams sounds funny coming from you. I'll be upstairs, Martin. Take your time. The hospital won't mind an extra ten minutes or so.'

'That should do it.' Norah surveyed the room. After firmly ushering out the last of the well-meaning neighbours, she and Katie had pushed back the chairs, lining them up against the wall to clear the rug in the centre for the trestles for the coffin. Norah had closed the curtains before they started and intended to keep them closed in the hope that the rest of the neighbours would remain at bay for a day or two, or at least until Katie and the boys had become accustomed to receiving condolences and Jack could handle sympathy with slightly better grace than he had earlier.

While she polished the chairs and side tables, Norah set Katie the task of washing every flower vase in the house and placing them on the sideboard in readiness for bouquets.

'We need to talk about food and how many people are likely to come back here after the service,' Norah said, as Katie carried in the last tray of vases. 'Mrs Jordan, Mrs Hunt and Mrs Lannon have offered to help. Do you have many relatives, Katie?' she asked, in an attempt to draw the girl out of the silence she had withdrawn into since Martin and Jack had left with Roy and John.

'No, Mam's parents died before I was born. I think she has two brothers but we haven't heard from them in years. Not even a Christmas card.'

'Do you know if they live in Swansea?'

Katie shook her head.

'The undertaker will put a notice in the *Evening Post*. If they are living in the town, hopefully they, or someone who knows them, will see it.'

'With the notices in the paper, the coffin, the cars and everything else, this funeral is going to cost an awful lot of money.'

'Yes, Katie.' Norah faced Katie head on, and prepared to tell the second-biggest lie of her life. 'It is going to be a very expensive time for you and your brothers, but your mother had an insurance policy that will more than cover the costs.'

'I never saw Mam pay an insurance man. She tried to take out a policy once, but Dad sent the man packing. He said we needed all our money for life, not death.'

'That's why she asked me to take the premiums out of the money I paid her for helping me with the sewing. So your father wouldn't find out.'

'She paid all the premiums herself?' Katie asked suspiciously.

Norah thrust her hands into her cardigan pockets and crossed her fingers. 'She did. You can have the payout yourself if you want, and you and your brothers can arrange everything. You might be able to do it cheaper...'

'No, thank you, Auntie Norah. You and Uncle Roy know more about funerals than Marty, Jack and me.'

'Unfortunately.' Norah jumped as the doorbell rang. 'Who can that be? I thought the neighbours would realise we need a bit of peace.'

Before she had time to open the door, the bell rang again, only this time whoever was there kept their finger on the button.

'They're going to run down the clockwork.'

'It's my father.' Katie's eyes rounded in fear.

'It's all right, Katie.' Norah tried to speak calmly although her own heart was thundering.

'Katie!' Ernie opened the letter box and yelled above the sound of the bell. His voice took on an ominous tone as it echoed down the passage. 'Out here this minute, girl, with your wages! Now! Or I'll come in to get you.'

'Katie, go into the kitchen, there's a good girl, and sit down before you fall down,' Norah ordered. 'I'll see to your father.'

'Please, Auntie Norah.' Katie clutched at Norah's arm in an effort to stop her going to the door. 'Please, don't go out there. Don't talk to him. Please, make him go away...'

'I can't make him go away without talking to him, Katie. It's a pity Roy's not here, he'd soon

337

sort him. But father or no father, I can't have Ernie Clay making that racket on my doorstep. Come on.' Pushing Katie ahead of her, Norah slipped out of the door into the dining room and through to the kitchen. 'I wish Roy hadn't unscrewed all the locks from these doors the last time he decorated but there's no use crying over what's gone. Get that chair and jam it under the door handle after I've left. If you hear your father in the hall, run down the steps to the garden and call to one of the neighbours.'

'Auntie Norah...'

'Do as I say, Katie, and don't worry, you're not going anywhere and most certainly not with your father,' Norah assured her emphatically as Ernie's shouts grew louder and more incoherent. As she left the kitchen, both she and Katie started at the crash of glass splintering in the inner hall.

'The chair, Katie.' Not daring to look back at the girl in case she lost what little nerve she still possessed, Norah closed the kitchen door behind her and crossed the dining room. Her mind was filled with images of Annie's face, swollen unrecognisably over broken bones, covered in cuts and bruises.

'I'm coming in...' The rattle of shards of glass showering down on to the hall tiles accompanied Ernie's threat. Resolutely, Norah continued to head towards the door that opened from the dining room into the hall. Making a valiant effort to control the hysteria rising in her throat, she placed her hand on the doorknob. Her mind worked feverishly. The only telephone in the house was in the hall. If Ernie managed to put his hand through whatever remained of the glass panel he might be able to reach inside and open the front door. Another crash – louder, more terrifying – stayed her hand. It sounded as though Ernie was battering down the door.

'Mrs Evans, you all right?'

'Brian.' Norah slumped weakly against the doorpost. 'I'm fine, so is Katie, she's in the kitchen.' She opened the door a crack to see Brian in his uniform, standing at the top of the stairs that connected the basement with the rest of the house.

'Katie's father seems to be making a habit of hammering on the doors of this house.' He looked down the passage to the front door.

Drawing courage from Brian's presence, Norah followed his gaze. The hall was carpeted in multi-coloured fragments of glass. She had loved the stained-glass panel: her mother's pride and joy, and one of the features her grandparents had paid extra for when they had bought the house new. Another crash sent the door rattling in its frame.

'I'll get you, you bitch! You're no daughter of mine...'

'He's kicking it in. You phone the police, Mrs Evans, I'll deal with him.'

Lifting the telephone from the hall table, Brian pushed it as close to the dining-room door as the cable would allow. As he walked towards the front door, Norah stepped out gingerly and lifted the receiver. Hands shaking uncontrollably, she dialled 999. The dial had never moved back into position so slowly between numbers.

'Katie!'

'Mr Clay, your daughter isn't here.' Brian's voice, calm and reasonable, fell strangely odd after the clamour of Ernie's violence.

'Then I'll have my bloody sons...'

'Believe me, Mr Clay, there's no one here.'

'You are, you lying bastard!'

Norah tried not to listen to Ernie's foul language as she dialled the final nine. She turned just as the inner hall door burst open and Ernie raced, red-faced and snorting like a bull, down the passage.

'Mrs Evans, get into the dining room and lock the door!' Brian stepped in front of Ernie in an attempt to block his path. Fit, well-built, used to giving and receiving tackles on the rugby field, Brian proved no match for Ernie's superior weight driven by alcohol-fuelled rage.

Slammed to the floor, fighting for breath, Brian mustered his remaining strength. Rolling sideways, he grabbed Ernie's foot as the man stepped over him. He looked towards the dining-room door. It was closed and a thud suggested Norah had moved something heavy behind it.

Muttering a silent prayer of gratitude, Brian braced the soles of his feet against the skirting board, holding his position and maintaining his grip on Ernie's ankle. Ernie crashed to his knees. Brian winced as Ernie's shoulder connected with his leg. Struggling to free himself from the dead weight and foul stink of Ernie's unwashed body, he fought to raise himself, reached for Ernie's arm with his free hand and hauled it high behind

Ernie's back.

'You have been caught breaking and entering. You...'

Lying on the floor behind the dining-room door, Norah heard Brian's voice, low and monotonous. The room grew dim around her as though black clouds had blotted out the sun. She was vaguely aware of the door to the kitchen opening behind her and Katie crying out, her voice shrill in fear.

Her body seemed to be shrinking. Darkness continued to creep insidiously inwards and downwards from the walls and ceiling. She turned, tried to reach out to Katie, wanting to reassure her that everything would be fine, that neither she nor Brian would allow her father to reach her, but all she could see was Katie's mouth opening in a silent scream.

CHAPTER SIXTEEN

'So, what kind of rings do you like?' Joe asked Lily as he drew her towards the window of the best – and most expensive – jeweller's shop in Oxford Street.

'I've never thought about it.'

'You wear a signet ring.'

'That Auntie Norah bought me for my fourteenth birthday.' Joe lifted her hand to inspect it. 'Plain, elegant, gold, engraved with your initials, I approve. I don't like fussy rings set with lots of

341

small stones, or ostentatiously large, coloured gemstones.'

'Isn't this a bit odd?'

'What?'

'Us looking at rings.'

'I think it's important to check tastes in furniture, books, music, films and jewellery as soon as you start going out with someone. It would be appalling to discover after two or three years of courtship that they like orange and purple colour schemes while you only like beige, cream and white, or they adore marcasite jewellery when you absolutely hate it.'

'You like beige cream and white?'

'No, too bland. So which ring do you like best?'

'That one.'

'Top tray on the left, third one along on the second row.'

'How did you know?'

'Stylish and very beautiful, like you.'

'I'm not used to compliments. I never know how to respond.'

'Try smiling and being polite, because I intend to pay you many more.'

As they moved away from the shop, he slipped his hand round her waist. 'My father is lending me the Rover on Sunday. We could make a day of it, get up early, be away from the house by eight...'

'On Sunday!'

'Nine?'

'How about nearer ten.' Amazed by how close to him she felt after just two outings and several shameless kisses, she made no objection as he left his hand round her waist. She felt wonderfully, supremely happy. Colours had never seemed so bright nor the town so full of friendly people.

'We could go to Rhossili and walk over the causeway to Worm's Head.'

'Is there a low tide?'

'I'd have to check.'

'And if there isn't?'

'There's a great café there where we could have lunch.'

'I could pack a picnic.'

'We could eat that for tea.'

'How long do you intend for us to stay out?'

'Years. I think I'll kidnap you. There are caves on the Gower no one knows about except me.'

'Really?'

'Why did I have to get myself a sceptical girlfriend?'

'I have no objection to visiting a cave, for an afternoon,' she added cautiously.

'I suppose that will have to do.' His face fell serious. 'When term starts I won't have this much free time, you do realise that, don't you. It won't mean that...' He searched for the right words.

'What?'

'That I like you any the less,' he compromised, deciding there had to be a better place than the centre of bomb-flattened and cleared Swansea on a Thursday night to tell her how much he loved her. The clifftop overlooking Three Cliffs and Oxwich at sunset would be perfect. He imagined himself opening a box, taking out the ring set with a single, exquisite diamond solitaire

that they'd just seen, slipping it on to her finger...
Shaking himself back to reality, he tightened his grip on her waist. 'About this Saturday. Do you really have to go to this youth club thing with the girls?'

'I promised I would.'

'And a promise is a promise.'

'For me it is.' She made a note to seek out Martin before Saturday and tell him there was something more between her and Joe than friendship after all. She liked Martin. It was better he knew as soon as possible, although she guessed that he had suspected it even before she did, judging by his reaction when she'd told him she was going for a walk with Joe.

'There's a party at my friend's house. You'd be welcome.' He tried not to imagine Angela's reaction if he turned up with Lily, but it would prove to Angie once and for all that they were over and he really wasn't interested in what she was offering.

'I couldn't let down the girls, Joe.'

'In that case I'll come to the dance with you.'

'A youth club!' she exclaimed dubiously. 'You sure you want to?'

'It will seem like the Ritz with you there.'

As they stepped round the corner of Walter Road into Verandah Street, he looked around. No one was in sight. Bending his head to hers, he kissed her, longer and even more passionately than he had on the beach, secure in the knowledge that there was no danger of him getting carried away in a public place.

'Tomorrow I'll come round and tell you when

the coast is clear in our house so you and Katie can visit Helen – and me.' As he bent his head to hers again, footsteps resounded on the pavement. Lily turned to see Adam Jordan hurtling towards them.

'Adam, is anything wrong?' Lily stepped back as he almost charged into Joe.

'Mr Williams – said – you'd – gone – for – a – walk...'

Adam jerked out the words as he struggled to regain his breath. Placing his hands on his knees, he crouched over and gulped in air.

Lily looked into his face as he straightened up. Without waiting for him to reply, she pulled her hand from Joe's and raced up the street.

'Whatever it is, it could have waited,' Joe admonished. 'Another five minutes and we would have been home.'

'Who are you concerned about,' Adam gasped, 'yourself or Lily?'

'Lily,' Joe snapped, furious that Adam had even asked.

'Then go after her.'

As Joe ran off, Adam leaned against the wall and took a deep breath that dried his throat and scorched his lungs. He knew he should go back in case he was needed for any more errands, but not wanting to witness Lily's pain after seeing Katie's, he stayed where he was.

Lily didn't stop running until she reached the crowd around her door. It was only when they parted to allow her through that she saw the police cars. Jack was crouched on the doorstep, holding a shovel to the floor for Martin, who was sweeping glass fragments from the inner hall into it.

Dropping the brush, Martin went to meet her. 'Your uncle is inside.'

'What happened?' Lily asked in bewilderment, looking from the shattered door to the glass littering the hall floor.

'Our bloody...'

'Your uncle is waiting,' Martin interrupted, giving Jack a warning glance. Deliberately ignoring Joe who raced up behind her, he took Lily's hand and led her around the debris through what was left of the inner door and into the parlour.

Lily blinked, adjusting her eyes to the bright light after the twilight outside. All the furniture had been pushed against the walls and the room seemed to be full of people and noise. Half a dozen policemen were standing around; Mrs Lannon was handing out cups of tea from a tray on the side table. Her aunt and Katie were nowhere to be seen.

'Lily, love.' Roy left his chair next to the fireplace. Abandoning his tea on the floor, he gave her a bear hug. 'Come into the kitchen.'

'I'll be ready whenever you are, Roy.' A young policeman headed for the door.

'I'll be with you in a few minutes.' Roy walked Lily into the kitchen to find Doris Jordan washing a sink full of cups and saucers.

'I'll get out of your way, Constable Williams.' Drying her hands in her apron, she bustled through the door.

'Uncle Roy...'

'Sit down, Lily, love.' He almost pushed Lily into the nearest chair. 'Your Auntie Norah had a heart attack.'

'Heart attack.' Lily repeated the words; she could even feel her lips mouthing the syllables but no sound emerged from her mouth as her mind struggled to cope with the implication. 'Is she...'

'She died, love. The doctor said it was quick and painless. If she'd survived she would have been an invalid and you and I know how much she would have hated that.'

A single large tear escaped Lily's eye and rolled down her cheek. She could feel it, damp, poised on the edge of her jaw; then she was conscious of another crawling down her face – and another – 'I should have been here. I should have taken more care of her...'

'No daughter could have done more for Norah than you, love.' Roy crouched in front of her chair and took her hands into his. 'She loved you very much, you know that.'

Lily nodded dumbly.

Roy reached into his tunic pocket for his handkerchief and wiped the tears from her face. 'I haven't done that since you were six, and fell off your bike and scraped your knees.'

'Why didn't you send someone to come and get me?'

'Adam went.' He sat back on his heels. 'I'm not sure where to start but it's as well you hear all of it, love. I warn you, there's a lot more and none of it good.'

He tried to find the words to tell her as gently

as he knew how about Norah, Annie and Ernie, knowing that no kindness on his part could soften the devastating effect the events of the evening would have on their lives – or his conscience. He would never, never forgive himself for choosing that particular moment to take Martin and Jack down to the hospital to identify Annie Clay.

His sergeant and colleagues had done all they could to persuade him that he couldn't have done anything more than Brian Powell, if he had been in the house. The doctor had known about Norah's weak heart and confided that she had insisted her condition be kept from him and Lily. Trying to sympathise, he'd added that Norah could have had an attack at any time – when she'd been hauling a shopping bag up from town, sewing at her machine or scrubbing the kitchen floor.

Only it hadn't happened at any time. Norah had died when Ernie Clay had been hammering down their front door and just thinking about Norah drawing her last breath to the clamour of Ernie's violence was enough to generate murderous thoughts in Roy's mind. During his years in the force he had arrested a fair selection of the town's lawbreakers, thieves, rapists and several murderers, but this was the first time he had felt like killing a man in cold blood. What was even worse was the knowledge that Ernie might not even go to prison. In his eyes the man had committed murder twice in one day and a week or two from now he would probably be walking the streets of Swansea, free to attack his sons, daughter, or any other unsuspecting soul he chose.

'I have to go down the station love.' Roy repeated himself twice before Lily understood. 'You'll be all right with the neighbours while I'm gone.'

'Yes.'

'I won't be long, half an hour at the most. I want to see what can be done.'

'With Katie's father?'

'Brian was here and I was first on the scene. We have to make statements. Katie and Judy are in your bedroom. You can sit with them...'

'Could you please explain to them that I'd rather be alone for a while?'

'I'll try, love, but people will want to make tea.'

'I'll go upstairs.' She thought of Katie, suspected she'd need her, but then Katie had Judy and her brothers. 'Do you think Auntie Norah would mind if I sat in her room?'

'No, love, I'm sure she wouldn't. Come on, I'll take you up.'

Joe was waiting in the hall as Roy helped Lily to the stairs. Roy shook his head and Joe understood. The boy held Lily's hand briefly, then allowed her uncle to lead her away.

Norah's room was neat, clean and, by Helen's mother's 'contemporary' standards, pitifully cluttered and old-fashioned. Feeling as though she were trespassing, Lily closed the door behind her and looked around. The doilies under the Victorian porcelain dressing-table set of candle-sticks, hair tidy, brush-and-comb tray and trinket pots had been crocheted by Norah's grandmother. The set itself had been a wedding gift to Norah's mother. The enormous Victorian bedroom suite had been bought by Norah's grandparents and installed when the house was new.

Lily smoothed the crocheted cotton counterpane and fingered the top border of the fine Egyptian linen sheet. If she lived to be a hundred she would never be able to make a bed as neatly and wrinkle-free as Norah. Under the pillow she found Norah's flowered winceyette nightgown. Norah had worn winceyette summer and winter for as long as she could remember, insisting that a woman of her advanced years needed a little comfort. Lifting the faded gown to her face, she held it against her cheek. It felt soft, warm, and smelled of the lavender water Norah used. Until this moment she had never thought of Norah's age, despite the number of times her foster-mother had referred disparagingly to her advancing years.

Sinking down on to the dressing-table stool, she stared at the clutter on the bedside table: Norah's things, intimate appendages of her daily life. A tiny wooden tub filled with the pins Norah used to secure the bun she wore at the nape of her neck, which no amount of imagination could rechristen a chignon. A pair of reading glasses was sandwiched in her current bedtime reading. Lily picked up the book. It had come from the lending library in Alexandra Road, an ancient copy of a Marie Corelli. Next to it stood a small bottle of French scent that looked expensive, which was probably why Norah had never opened it.

Clutching the nightdress and Norah's book, Lily curled up on the chaise longue at the foot of the bed. Somehow it seemed sacrilegious to disturb Norah's pristine bed-making. She opened the book at the first page. Norah had only read half of it; she decided that she would start at the very beginning and read every word Norah had. But when she began the first sentence she couldn't see the book for tears.

Doris Jordan crept up the stairs and knocked quietly at Lily's bedroom door. Joy Hunt emerged a few seconds later. Holding her finger to her lips, she looked back into the room and nodded to Judy who was sitting at Katie's bedside, before closing the door softly. 'Katie asleep?' Doris asked.

'At last. That medicine the doctor gave her seems to be working.'

'Lily?'

Joy moved to the top of the staircase. 'She's in Norah's room. Roy looked in on her when he came back. He asked me not to disturb her.'

'Poor lamb. He's right to let her rest while she can, with what she's got to wake up to. I could wring Ernie's neck with my bare hands when I think of sweet little Katie trapped in the dining room with Norah, while that maniac battered down the door. Who knows what would have happened to Katie as well as Norah, if that nice young policeman hadn't been here.'

'It doesn't bear imagining,' Joy agreed. 'But it's the girls we've got to think about now.'

'They can hardly stay here with Roy. After all

351

it's not as if he's a relative of either of them, not by blood.'

'Katie's brothers are downstairs.'

'But the basement isn't the house. It's obvious the girls are going to have to move out before people start talking.'

'What people? Roy is a mature man…'

'And they're innocent young girls. Who knows what could happen if they stay with him.'

'He's done a good job of raising Lily so far.'

'Norah raised Lily, not Roy. There's no way he would have been allowed to take her in if Norah hadn't been living with him. It's not right for a man to be alone in a house with young girls.'

Realising Doris was only saying what most women in the street would soon be thinking, if they weren't already, Joy decided further objections were best kept to herself.

'I'd take them in if I could, but with Adam home there's simply no room. But you and Judy have that great big house to yourselves.'

'Our basement and attic are let.'

'That still leaves you with three bedrooms on the first floor. Katie shares with Lily here.'

'I work – I couldn't possibly look after the girls.' Joy racked her brains in an effort to come up with more reasons why she couldn't take Roy's foster-daughter and Katie into her home.

'It's not as though they are babies who need looking after,' Doris Jordan protested. 'They'd be no trouble.'

'Lily is Roy's responsibility and Katie has her brothers.'

'Poor Martin's only just twenty-one and bringing home an apprentice's wage. You can't expect him to take on Katie, or that tearaway brother of his. Mark my words, after this Jack Clay will be back in Borstal before the year is out.'

'The boys seem to be managing fine.'

'Only because they don't have to look after Katie.'

'Katie has a job, she's bringing in a wage, she can look after herself.'

'I doubt it, without Norah. Do you know if Roy and Norah formally adopted Lily?'

'No.'

'If Roy didn't, the courts aren't going to look kindly on a man of his age looking to adopt an eighteen-year-old after all these years.'

'I suppose not, but whatever decisions there are to be made it will be Roy who makes them,' Joy countered, wanting to put an end to the conversation.

'He'll need help.' Doris glanced into the parlour as they reached the hall. 'Little did Norah think when she sorted that room out earlier that she was doing it for her own funeral.'

'There's nothing either of you can do so you may as well go to bed.' John stood in the doorway of the kitchen, and faced Helen and Joe who were sitting either end of the window seat.

'We're not children, Dad.'

'I know, Joe,' John agreed patiently.

'Lily might need me.'

'I've just come from next door. She told Roy she wants to be alone. Given the shock she's had, I think that's understandable.'

'I might be able to help her.' Helen left the seat.

'I'm sure you will, Helen, but not right now. Everyone's left except Judy who is staying the night with Katie. It's obvious that Roy and Lily would rather come to terms with Norah's death in their own way and the Clay boys have made it perfectly clear that they would like to be left in peace in their basement.'

'I'll say goodnight, then,' Helen said sharply, peeved at being dismissed.

'Lily and Katie will probably be glad of a visit tomorrow.'

'I'm not allowed out,' Helen reminded.

'Even before this happened I told your mother that I think you've learned your lesson. And now, your friends need you.'

'You'd let me visit them?'

'As long as you realise how much pain they'll both be in.'

'Yes, Dad.' Helen only just stopped herself from skipping out of the door by reminding herself that Annie and Norah were dead.

'I don't know how close you are to Lily, Joe, but she may appreciate a visit from you too,' John suggested, as Helen closed the door.

'I intended to call first thing tomorrow.'

'Preparation for your final year going all right?' John filled the kettle. He'd drunk far too much tea as it was, but he felt the need to do something.

'I'm doing my best.'

'No one can ask you to do more.'

Joe turned to his father and asked the question uppermost in his mind. 'Is Mum going to leave?'

'You'll have to ask her that, Joe.'

'But you want her to.'

John hesitated for a fraction of a second before answering. 'Yes, Joe. Yes, I do.'

'Helen?' Joe tapped Helen's door and tried the handle. It was locked.

'What do you want?' she called from the other side of the door.

'Just wondered if you felt like a talk.'

'I'm tired.'

'In the morning, then.'

'Perhaps.'

He walked on to his own room. After stripping to his underwear he took one of his set texts from his shelf. Crawling between the sheets, he tried to lose himself in the tragedy of *The Mayor of Casterbridge* but thoughts of Lily kept intruding into his mind. He loved her, he was absolutely certain of it. And after the way she had kissed him on the beach earlier he was almost as certain that she loved him. His body grew warm at the memory of their embraces. He had been looking forward to Sunday – then he remembered Norah and the grief-stricken look on Lily's face as she had walked away from him, and started guiltily. He and Lily had so many Sundays before them. Norah had none.

Closing the book, he tossed it to the floor and switched off the light. Pre-sleep dreams of Lily and their future together were infinitely preferable to anything Thomas Hardy had written.

Just as he'd finished furnishing their dream living room in blue and cream, he heard a floorboard creak overhead as his father climbed to his bedroom on the top floor. Later he heard the clack of his mother's high heels as she walked into the lino-floored bathroom down the passageway. Later still he heard a stair creak. Putting it down to the house settling, he turned over and returned to his dreams of Lily – and the green and gold bedroom they would share.

Helen just simply *knew* that Jack would want to see her. Locking her door, she switched off her light, sat on the windowsill of her bedroom and waited. She answered Joe when he called to her, glanced at her alarm clock when she heard her father walk up the attic stairs, and still the lights shone from next door's back windows over the empty garden. When the luminous hands on her watch pointed to just after eleven she saw Jack, clearly outlined in a shaft of light from Mrs Evans's kitchen window. He walked down to Roy Williams's garage and opened the door. Sitting on an old crate, he picked up a tin of polish and a rag, and began to clean his bike.

The hands on her watch had never crawled more slowly. Eventually she heard what she had been waiting for – the sound of her mother opening and closing the front door. Watching intently, willing Jack to stay in the garage, she waited through the longest half-hour of her life. Pulling a thick sweater over her pedal-pusher jeans and striped top, she grabbed her shoes and crept to the door in her socks, opened it a fraction and peeped out.

The house was in silence and darkness. She

pushed her door just wide enough to slip out and closed it quickly behind her. Stealing along the landing, she tiptoed down the stairs. The third stair from the bottom creaked loudly enough to wake everyone in the house and set every dog barking in the street – but miraculously it didn't.

Slipping the latch on the door that opened on to the basement stairs, she edged through it, slid the bolt home behind her, felt her way down the narrow staircase, through the door at the bottom, and fumbled towards the front room. Careful to close the curtains before switching on the light, she turned to the door – and screamed.

'Quiet!'

'Jack, you terrified me. How on earth did you get in?'

He opened his hand, revealing a length of wire. 'Picked the lock. I'm a dab hand at it.'

'You're a burglar.'

'Not any more. I only broke in because I wanted to see you. I was going to your bedroom.'

'Please, don't ever, ever do that. If my mother saw you she'd call the police and demand they lock you up. She'd send me away. We'd never see one another again.' She threw her arms round his neck. 'And I couldn't bear for that to happen.'

He drew away from her and she blanched at the whipped expression in his eyes. 'I'm sorry about your mother. I hardly knew her but she seemed a nice person.'

'Too bloody nice.' There was none of his customary rage in his voice, only a heart-rending anguish as if his mother's death had sapped his spirit. 'You still got that gin?'

357

'It wouldn't help.'

'No, it wouldn't,' he echoed, remembering his father's last drunken rage when he had turned up on the doorstep of their basement.

'My father said I can go out...'

'Not with me.'

'To see your sister and Lily tomorrow. It's a beginning, Jack.' His pain was excruciating to watch. She wanted to gather him up and soothe away his anguish with assurances that everything would come right for him again. That he was going to survive his mother's death and she would do all she could to help him get through it. Then, in a single moment of blinding clarity, she realised his attraction no longer lay in his status as forbidden fruit. Their relationship might have begun that way, but the risks he had been prepared to take in seeking her out at a time like this said more about what he felt for her than all of Shakespeare's eloquent speeches.

'You're cold. Let's push the cushions to the top of the sofa and cover ourselves with blankets.' Lighting the small lamp, she switched off the overhead light.

He made no objection as she pulled the striped blankets from the easy chairs and tucked them around both of them. Lying with her back to the sofa cushions, she circled her arms round his chest and laid her head on his shoulder. In an attempt to stop him shaking, she drew her body along the length of his, covering his legs with her own, caressing his face with the tips of her fingers. 'I love you, Jack,' she murmured, throwing all caution to the wind as he kissed her.

'Where's Jack?' Brian asked, as he walked into the basement to find Martin sitting alone at the table, a stone-cold cup of tea in front of him.

'In the garage polishing his bike. He said he needed to think. I know just how he feels.' Martin turned a white, strained face to Brian. 'I don't seem to have had a minute to myself since Roy Williams told me Mam died. And now this, with the old man. What's going to happen to him?'

'I don't know.'

'For Christ's sake, Powell, you're a policeman. You must have some idea,' Martin shouted furiously.

'He's been charged with breaking and entering, criminal damage and assaulting a police officer. He didn't steal anything so it's just forced entry and a broken door, and as I'm not hurt beyond a few cuts and scratches he could get away with a fine or, given a tough magistrate, a couple of weeks prison.'

'Mrs Evans is dead.'

'Of a heart attack, which is natural causes. When I left the station the brass were toying with the idea of trying a manslaughter charge but I doubt it will stick. It's my guess they'll keep him in the cells for as long as they can...'

'I can't believe he's going to get away with what he's done. My mother...'

'Never made a complaint.' Brian unbuttoned his tunic, sat on a chair and unlaced his boots.

'My father killed my mother and Mrs Evans just as surely as if he'd kicked them to death.'

'Morally, you're right, Marty. Legally is another

matter. And the courts are only interested in the law. Constable Williams has applied for a restraining order to keep him away from this house, street and area, so he shouldn't be round again.'

'And when he gets too drunk to know where he is?'

'We'll arrest him. Breaking a restraining order is an offence.'

'I can't believe you won't do anything.'

'Not won't, can't. There's a difference.' Kicking off his boots, Brian took Martin's cup, poured the cold tea down the sink, filled the kettle and put it on to boil. 'Have you any idea what time it is?'

Martin looked at him blankly.

'It's two in the morning. Why don't you try to get some sleep.'

'Mrs Evans and Constable Williams take us three in when my father batters my mother senseless. My mother dies as a result of the battering, my father kills Mrs Evans and you expect me to sleep?'

'Nothing that happened today is your fault.'

'No?'

'No, Marty,' Brian countered forcefully, reaching for the teapot. 'And with all the arrangements that have to be made tomorrow, someone has to be on the ball. I can't see Constable Williams or Lily up to it. That leaves you, me and Jack. How long has he been in the garage?'

Martin looked at the clock but nothing registered. 'Ten minutes, maybe an hour, I don't know.'

Brian made the tea and poured Martin a cup.

'Take this to bed, I'll get him.'

Walking out into the garden, Brian went to the garage. He opened the door and switched on the light. Jack's motorbike, battered but gleaming, was parked where he usually left it. Relieved that Jack hadn't ridden off like a lunatic to wrap himself round the nearest lamp-post, Brian closed the door. As he started back up the path he noticed a dim light burning in the basement window of the Griffithses' house. Perhaps there were other paths of destruction just as dangerous and more certain than a late-night motorbike ride after all.

Helen held Jack for what seemed like hours until he finally stopped shivering. Sliding his hands to her waist, he pulled up her sweater. She sat up and helped him remove her sweater and top, waiting until he slipped the hooks on the back of her brassiere. When he removed his own pullover, shirt and vest, she tossed their clothes on to a chair before snuggling back down beside him. She had done no more than the last time they had been alone together, but she still gasped at the sensation of his bare skin against hers. It was such a wonderfully warm, intimate and deliciously illicit feeling. As he thumbed her nipples, teasing them to hard, scrunched peaks, he kissed her with a ferocity that left her reeling.

Slowly, tantalisingly, his hands slid from her breasts to the waistband of her pedal pushers.

'Jack,' she protested, as he flicked the side button, slid down the zip and caressed the flat of her stomach.

'Take them off,' he demanded hoarsely.

'I...'

'Are you my girl or not?'

Wanting to prove how much she loved him, she kicked off her pedal pushers and knickers beneath the blankets.

'I want to see you.'

Before she could stop him he tossed the blanket aside. Sliding his fingers between her thighs, he forced her legs apart. As his jeans joined her pedal pushers at the end of the sofa he eased himself on top of her, taking his weight on his elbows.

'Jack...' she protested, terrified of what was about to happen.

'Look at me.'

Obediently she gazed into his eyes.

'You said you loved me,' he challenged.

'I do.'

'You don't have to be kind. I don't need charity or pity'

'*I* need *you*, Jack.'

'After this I won't ever leave you, or let you leave me. You know that.'

'Yes.' She held him tight as he pierced her body. She cried out in pain, but lost in passion he didn't stop, not until her cries had subsided into soft moans and by then he'd taken her to a place she'd never been before – and never wanted to leave.

'It will be all right, won't it, Jack,' Helen pleaded, as he moved away from her.

He didn't answer as he sat up on the side of the sofa. She grabbed the blanket and pulled it over her but not before he saw the blood that had spread from her thighs to the blanket beneath her.

'Jack...'

'It'll be all right,' he muttered unconvincingly, reaching for his jeans. Searching the pockets, he extracted his cigarettes and matches. This time she didn't try to stop him lighting up. Inhaling deeply, he blew smoke from his nostrils and handed her the cigarette. She puffed on it and burst into a coughing fit.

'What's the time?'

She looked at her watch. 'Just gone three.'

'I'd better get back before Martin and Brian call out a search squad.'

'I'll see you again?' she asked anxiously.

He kissed her briefly on the mouth. 'What do you take me for?'

'You seem so distant. You haven't said...'

'My mother's dead, I've had the most bloody awful day of my life. Then you give me the best present a woman can give a man. I don't know how I feel, Helen. I only know I'll never let you go. Not now.'

She lay back watching as he pulled on the rest of his clothes. 'Jack?'

He turned back, as he was about to walk through the door.

'I'll get another key cut for the basement door, but until I do, keep the wire.'

He smiled and she suddenly felt that no matter what happened it was going to be all right. 'I love you.'

'Love you back,' he whispered. Then he was gone.

CHAPTER SEVENTEEN

'Ashes to ashes...'

Desperately trying to emulate the impassive, fixed expression on his brother's face, Jack stood stiffly next to Martin. He braced himself as the vicar stooped, took a handful of earth from the mound behind them, and dropped it into the open grave, but he shuddered uncontrollably when the clods hailed down on to the casket lid. Much as he didn't want to, he couldn't stop himself from looking downwards as he struggled to absorb the reality that his mother was dead, her body in the coffin at the bottom of the pit, and even as he looked he felt himself falling...

Someone stepped forward and caught him as he began to sway. He saw Martin turn his head, but half carrying, half supporting him, Roy Williams drew him away from his brother, back through the crowd of sober-suited men towards a bench overlooking the site.

'I'm all right...' Even his voice sounded distant.

'Just sit for a moment, Jack.' Roy pushed him on to the seat and placed his hand on the back of his neck, forcing his head down to the level of his knees.

'I was all right...'

'There was no air with that crowd pressing round.' Roy sat beside him and looked across towards the vicar and Martin. 'I felt faint myself.'

Jack knew he was trying to be kind, he also knew he was lying. 'I want to see...'

'We'll go back when the service is over. Then you and Martin will be able to say your goodbyes in private.'

Jack leaned back against the seat and closed his eyes. 'Is Dad in prison, Mr Williams?'

'In the station for questioning.'

'You arranged it.'

'There were some things that needed to be straightened out. It seemed a good time to do it.'

'Thank you. He would have come here otherwise, and Martin and I...'

'You don't have to explain how you feel about your father to me, Jack. And you have my word that I'll do everything I can to make sure that he doesn't bother you, Martin, or Katie again.'

'But you can't lock him up and throw away the key.'

'Unfortunately not. Much as I'd like to.'

Opening his eyes, Jack stared bleakly at his brother, white-faced, hands clenched into fists in front of him. 'What's going to happen to us, Mr Williams?'

'If you mean you, Martin and Katie, nothing much, if I have my way.'

'You'll still rent us your basement?'

'Why shouldn't I?'

'Martin and I talked it over; we thought you wouldn't want any of us near you after Dad ... after the way Mrs Evans died. And there's Katie...'

'You've been listening to the gossips.'

'People are saying it's not right for Lily and

365

Katie to be living in a house full of men.'

'I know and that's why I intend to do something about it.' Roy rose to his feet as the mourners began to line up in front of Martin and the vicar to shake their hands. As he led Jack up the path towards the open grave he mulled over the wording of the question he intended to put to Joy Hunt tomorrow – just as soon as he'd buried Norah.

'Martin, Jack, can I have a word?' John Griffiths stopped the boys as they were about to step into the leading funeral car. 'I know Katie was disappointed at not being allowed to come to her mother's funeral...'

'Men only,' Jack muttered touchily, sensing criticism.

'I'm not saying you should have allowed her to come, Jack, but I wondered if you'd like to bring her back now. By the time we get to Carlton Terrace and drive out here again they will have filled in the grave. Katie can see where it is, look at the flowers and read the cards for herself.'

'Thank you, Mr Griffiths, that would be very kind of you,' Martin accepted gratefully. He'd been dreading the funeral 'tea' back at Roy's house almost as much as he had another bout of Katie's rage at not being allowed to go to her own mother's funeral.

'I'll see you there.' John climbed into his car and unlocked the passenger door for Joe. 'Perhaps you'd like to do the same for Lily tomorrow?'

'Yes, I would, thank you for suggesting it, Dad.'

'You and Lily...'

'I'm serious about her,' Joe broke in as John turned the ignition. 'I'm going to ask her to marry me.'

'You've only been out with her a couple of times.'

'I've known her most of my life.'

'Marriage is a big step to take and an enormous leap from friendship. Are you absolutely sure?'

'Absolutely sure,' Joe repeated emphatically. 'And with her future being so uncertain now Mrs Evans is dead, I intend to ask her as soon as I can and buy her an engagement ring. That would make my feelings clear and give her something settled to look forward to. Depending on my degree, which I should get, although I'm not sure about the first my tutor's tipped me for, I've a job lined up with the BBC in Llandaff...'

'You never said,' John interrupted.

'I didn't want another row with Mum.'

'Who wants you to teach.'

'Precisely. You're not angry with me for accepting it?'

'Anything but. It's an excellent opportunity in a well-respected organisation. All I've ever wanted is for you to be happy, Joe, and it seems to me you're going the right way about it.'

'I thought Lily and I could marry when I graduate. I'll be twenty-one by then so I'll have full access to my trust fund. I checked the figures and there's more than enough money to buy a house and a car.'

'So you'll be engaged for what – a year?'

'Ten months. It's a long time but I'd prefer to

put our relationship on a formal footing.'

'Because you're afraid Roy will send her away, or someone else might snap her up?'

'Frankly, yes.'

'What about Robin's sister?'

'It was never serious between us.'

'That's not the impression I had when she left for London at the beginning of the summer.'

'It was just a passing fancy. Lily is the real thing.'

John wasn't as convinced as Joe that Lily was the girl he should marry, especially after such a short courtship, but he also realised there was no way he could stop Joe asking Lily to marry him, or giving her an engagement ring if she accepted his proposal. And if his misgivings proved right, and Joe was more in love with the idea of Lily and marriage than Lily herself, a ten-month engagement would give him time to find out.

'I'm glad you feel that way, Joe, but you'd better be prepared for some argument, because your mother won't be very happy when she finds out.'

'You don't mind?'

'Like your job at the BBC, I don't mind. In fact, I'm pleased.'

'Pleased enough to argue my case with Mum?'

'I'll try, but you know as well as me that I can't promise you anything there.'

As he'd hoped, the number of mourners had dwindled in Roy Williams's house by the time John returned from his second trip to Morriston cemetery with Martin, Jack and Katie. Mindful of the coffin in the parlour that awaited burial the next day, he made his excuses to Roy who met them at the door and went into his own house. To his surprise, Esme was sitting alone in the lounge.

'I thought you were helping next door.' He went to the cocktail cabinet and poured himself a whisky.

'Not many came back after the funeral.'

'A lot more will turn out for tomorrow's.'

'Norah had a wider circle of friends,' she agreed.

'Where are the children?' Taking the glass he sat opposite her.

'With Lily and Judy next door. Helen told me you'd given her permission to go out again.'

'I told you I would.'

'She'll never learn discipline...'

'Let's agree to disagree on that subject, Esme. I think we have more important things to discuss.'

'More important than our daughter?'

'I want a divorce.'

'I'll never divorce you,' she said flatly.

'I saw a solicitor this morning. It will be easier with your consent, but if you refuse to give it, I'll still press ahead, Esme.'

'I won't leave you, or this house.'

'Not even if I bring a court case against you for restoration of conjugal rights?'

'You wouldn't dare. You...'

'Wouldn't go into the witness box and say that you and I lead completely separate lives and you haven't slept in my bed for eighteen years? Try me, Esme.'

'You want me to move back into your bedroom,

risk getting pregnant...'

'You're missing the point. I want a divorce, not you in my bed. And if you give me no choice but to use the courts to get one, I will.'

'And if you do succeed in divorcing me? What then? Where do you expect me to go, what do you expect me to do? I...'

'I'll give you the shop in Mumbles. It's freehold, a profitable concern, and there's a flat above it that I've just refurbished.'

'You forced me to live here after I was used to a detached house in Langland but you can't force me to live above a shop. I won't do it.' Her voice rose hysterically. 'I simply won't.'

'You can sell the shop, run it, or live there as you please. I'll also continue to give you half your present allowance.'

'Last time we spoke you said I could have the full amount.'

'If you prefer, you can have that and I'll keep the shop. Think about it, Esme, because one way or another I intend to get on with my life and I can't do that while I'm tied to you.'

'There's someone else, isn't there?'

'I only wish there were. If there had been I might have come to my senses and done this years ago.'

'I can't believe you're putting me in this position. You know perfectly well that no woman's reputation can survive the scandal of a divorce.'

'Not even if her husband leaves her for another woman?'

'Then there *is* someone else.'

'Not in my life.' He studied her, but if there was anyone else in hers she gave no indication that he could read. 'The solicitor suggested the quickest and simplest solution is I book into a hotel and hire a girl and a photographer. For about a hundred pounds they'll furnish me with all the evidence you'll need to divorce me for adultery.'

'You'd be prepared to go to bed with a total stranger to divorce me?'

'Pretend, Esme, like you on stage.' He couldn't resist making the comparison. 'It would leave your reputation intact.'

'Except with the people who'll blame me for forcing you to look elsewhere for what you couldn't get at home.'

'Now that would be nearer the truth.'

'And the business?'

'There isn't another warehouse like mine in Swansea. I'm prepared to take the risk that it will survive any gossip about my private life.'

'You're serious, aren't you?'

'Yes.' Finishing his drink, he left his chair. 'I'm going to the warehouse. If anyone wants me I'll be there. In the meantime I suggest you see a solicitor.' He walked out quickly so she wouldn't see how much effort it had cost him finally to confront her.

'Katie, what on earth are you doing here?' John asked, as he walked into the office and saw her sitting at her desk.

'Working.'

He took the invoice ledger from her hands and laid it on the desk. 'Not today, you're not.'

371

'But I want to, Mr Griffiths. I can't stand it...'
She burst into floods of tears and Rosie took her
in her arms.

'Help her to the sofa. I'll get one of the girls on
the shop floor to make some tea and bring up a
couple of aspirins.' Walking into his office, he
picked up the telephone and ordered tea. It
arrived a few minutes later. Shortly afterwards,
Katie's sobs subsided and he could hear the soft
murmur of Rosie's voice. He glanced up at the
clock: half past five, half an hour to go. It had
been a long day.

'Mr Griffiths, it's six o'clock.'

'So it is, Rosie. Time you were off home.'

'Katie's fallen asleep on the sofa. Shall I wake
her?'

'No, there's no need. I have another hour or
two's work here. I'll telephone her landlord and
he'll tell her brothers where she is.'

'See you in the morning, Mr Griffiths.' Rosie
picked up the post. John telephoned Roy and
followed Rosie downstairs to supervise the
closing of the warehouse. When he returned at
half past six, Katie was still fast asleep. Reluctant
to disturb her, he settled back in his office with
the account books. He had been meaning to
update them for some time and it suddenly
seemed as good a time as any.

It was half past eight when John made the last
entry. Telephoning Roy again, he told him that he
was waking Katie and would take her for a meal
to save Lily the trouble of cooking her something. He walked into the sitting area and looked

372

at Katie while she slept. Her hair was tousled over the cushion Rosie had placed beneath her head, her cheeks wet with tears. He wondered if she was even crying in her sleep.

As he watched, she suddenly opened her eyes; panic-stricken she stared up at him.

'You're safe, Katie,' he murmured reassuringly. 'You're in the office. You were upset, Rosie helped you here and you went to sleep.'

'I'm sorry, Mr Griffiths.'

'There's nothing for you to be sorry about. I'm only sorry that I woke you, but I thought you'd better eat. It's half past eight, the restaurants will stop serving in half an hour or so. I told Roy and your brothers that I'm taking you out for a meal,' he explained in answer to her quizzical look.

'There's no need...'

'I'm hungry too, Katie. Go and wash your face and brush your hair. I'll meet you downstairs in five minutes.'

John drove Katie to the Mermaid Hotel in Mumbles. It had an upstairs dining room that Esme had liked visiting in the first months after their marriage but he had been too self-conscious of his disfigurement in those days to enjoy eating out. It was strange how much time he had spent worrying about his appearance then and how he hardly ever considered it now.

'I've never eaten in a restaurant,' Katie confided as she sat tensely in the front seat of John's car. She had been in the car several times but only when Joe had been driving and always in the back seat with Judy or Helen or both of them, and much as she respected and admired her boss, the intimacy of the front seat made her uneasy.

'Then I hope this will be the first of many meals out you'll enjoy.' He parked the car in front of the hotel, helped her out of her seat and walked inside. Nodding to the receptionist in the office on the right, he led the way up the stairs and along the corridor. The waitress met them with menus at the door but as he stepped into the room he froze. Esme was sitting in the corner at a table for two. She had her back to him, a man he'd never seen before opposite her. As he memorised his features, the man reached across the table and placed his hand over Esme's in an intimate gesture that confirmed every suspicion he'd ever had about her late-night absences.

'Sorry.' He stepped back quickly, treading on Katie's toes.

'Sir?' The waitress was taken aback when he took the menu from Katie and handed it to her, together with his own.

'We've changed our minds.' Turning on his heel, he almost ran back down the stairs with Katie following in his wake. 'I'm sorry about that,' he apologised, uncertain whether Katie had seen Esme or not. 'There are other restaurants...'

'To be honest I'd prefer fish and chips, Mr Griffiths.'

'Eaten out of newspaper?' He smiled.

'Yes, please.'

'I know just the place to buy them and the perfect spot to eat them.'

'I'd forgotten what real fish and chips taste like.'

John screwed his wrappings into a ball and dropped them on the floor of the back of the car. 'Thank you for a brilliant suggestion.'

'I used to buy them on the way home on Friday nights for Mam...'

'I keep telling you it's all right to cry,' he sympathised as she turned away.

'But I hate breaking down all the time and you've been so kind.' She stared resolutely ahead as she struggled to compose herself.

'It will gradually get better, although I doubt anyone completely recovers from the loss of someone they love. I still miss my parents and grandparents. Every time I visit their graves I talk to them, tell them about my life and what I'm doing. I have no idea if they are listening, but it helps me to think that they are. Which reminds me, did your brother show you the catalogue I gave him of headstones?'

'Yes, Mr Griffiths, we chose a plain black marble headstone. I hope that will be all right, I had no idea they were so expensive.'

'And I hope you and your brothers didn't choose it on cost Katie.'

'No, it was one of the cheapest but we settled on it because it was the plainest. Mam was never one for frills and fancy.'

'Then there'll probably be some insurance money left.'

'If there is, Martin and Jack think we should set it aside for the upkeep of Mam's grave. How soon will we be able to put the headstone on her plot, Mr Griffiths?'

'Four to six months is about usual, Katie. It will

take that long for the ground to settle.'

'I miss her so much and every time I talk or think about her I can't stop crying. I feel so stupid...'

'Don't.' John handed her a clean handkerchief. 'And don't try to keep the tears in. It will only make you feel worse. There's no shame in crying. My parents were killed when I was eleven and I was still breaking down ten years after we buried them.'

'Killed – that must have been horrible.'

'We lived in Oxford Street. Our house caught fire one night when we were in bed. I was in the back bedroom and a neighbour rescued me by climbing on to the kitchen roof. But the fire was too intense for him to reach my parents. We could hear them, but we couldn't reach them. Then the ceiling collapsed on top of us. If it hadn't been for the neighbour dragging me out I would have died. As it is' – he paused for a few seconds – 'I was left as you see me now.'

'The scars on your face, your leg and arm...'

'Didn't you know I'd been crippled in a fire?'

'No, Mr Griffiths.'

'I assumed everyone in the street knew.'

'If they do, they never talk about it.'

'Which goes to show Carlton Terrace is not the hive of gossip I took it to be.'

'Mam always used to say some things shouldn't be talked about. Like people's disabilities and failings.'

'Your mother sounds like a very kind woman, Katie. I wish I'd taken the trouble to get to know her better.'

'Dad wouldn't have liked that. He didn't –
doesn't – like us talking to anyone outside of the
family.'

'Didn't, Katie. Hasn't Roy told you that he has
had a restraining order put on your father to
prevent him from even walking into Carlton
Terrace?'

'Yes,' she answered in a small voice.

'But you're still afraid of him.'

'I'll always be afraid of him, Mr Griffiths. He ...
he ... no matter what the law says, I think he
killed my mother and Mrs Evans.'

'A lot of people would agree with you on that.'

'Marty says that he and Jack can protect me but
they can't watch over me twenty-four hours a
day, any more than they could over Mam.'

'But unlike your mother you're never alone,
Katie. Think about it. You live with Lily, and even
when Roy works the night shift your brothers and
Brian are downstairs. And when you're in work
you have a whole warehouse full of people
around you.'

'I know. I'm just being silly.' She didn't sound
reassured and as he glanced at her he could see
fear lurking behind the outwardly composed
façade.

'Come on, time to take you home. Can you eat
any more of those fish and chips?'

'No, thank you, Mr Griffiths. You bought far
too much.'

'I didn't, Katie, you eat far too little.'

As he took the parcel from her she began to cry
again. He held out his arms and she clung to
him.

'I've never met anyone like you before, Mr Griffiths. You're good and kind...'

'No more than most, Katie.'

'Yes, you are,' she said fiercely. Lifting her tear-stained face to his, she kissed him hard and inexpertly on the mouth.

'Katie, you're overwrought, you don't know what you're doing.' Shocked, he held her back at arm's length.

'Yes, I do. Lily always told me that I would meet a man I would want to kiss one day. I never believed her but...'

'She meant a boy, Katie, not a married man with two children older than you.'

'I'm sorry, I've embarrassed you...'

'No, you haven't, Katie. Not at all.' He turned the ignition and reversed the car, swinging it in a wide arc until it faced the main road.

'I'm sorry...'

'And stop apologising.' He sounded harsher than he'd intended.

'Can I keep my job?'

'Of course. Let's forget it ever happened, shall we?' But even as he smiled across at her he was making a mental resolution never to put himself into a situation where he would be alone with little Katie Clay again. She might look like a child but the kiss she had just given him had stirred emotions he'd almost forgotten he possessed.

'Lily, would you butter the bread, please. And Katie if you'd slice the fruit and Madeira cake, but not too thinly,' Mrs Lannon warned, mindful of the economies Annie Clay had been forced to practise all her married life and had undoubtedly instilled in her daughter. She paused by the kitchen door to reassure herself that the girls were setting about their tasks competently before bustling into the dining room to check the progress of the buffet. The mourners were due back from Oxwich cemetery in the next half-hour and she intended to have food on the table and tea brewed before they walked through the door.

'Who decided funerals should be men only?' Katie asked, mutinously slicing a block of Madeira cake into half-inch wedges.

'I have no idea.' Lily was even angrier than Katie because it was her aunt's funeral they were missing. She'd pleaded with her uncle to allow her and Katie to attend both funerals and when he'd categorically refused, she'd begged that at least Katie be allowed to attend her mother's and she Norah's. The 'quiet word' she'd envisaged had developed into the closest to a quarrel they'd ever had, but he'd remained obdurate, insisting she and Katie remain at home 'with the ladies' on both occasions.

'Jack said it was because women faint at funerals. But I wouldn't have fainted, and I had just as much right to say goodbye to Mam yesterday as Marty and him, instead of sitting here making sandwiches for a load of people who didn't even know my mother, but could go to her funeral just because they're men.'

'Mrs Jordan sent us in here to fill the kettles and set them on the stove to boil in readiness. But I think the "grown-ups" want to talk about things we children are too young to understand,'

Judy sniped as she and Helen joined them.

'I'd rather be in here than sit with that lot. Well, I would,' Katie snapped, in response to a look from Judy. 'It's my mother and Lily's aunt who have died and everyone is treating us as if we're babies. Have you noticed the sudden silence when either of us walks into a room? And I've had more tearful hugs in the last week from people who couldn't be bothered to say hello to me when Mam was alive than I've had since I was born. And here we are, Lily buttering mountains of bread and me slicing cake as if we're preparing for a party, not mourning my mother's and Auntie Norah's passing. Damn it, every time one of the neighbours looks at us, I can almost hear them say it.'

'What?' Judy asked, taken aback by Katie's outburst and the first swear word she'd heard her say.

'Poor orphans.'

'You're not orphans, you still have...' Helen faltered awkwardly. 'Your brothers and Lily's Uncle Roy,' she finished lamely.

'Brothers can't replace a mother.' Katie cut down savagely on the cake.

'Want some help, Lily?' Judy pulled a chair up to the table.

'I suppose so.' Lily opened the drawer in the kitchen table and handed Judy a knife. Picking up yet another piece of bread, she suddenly dropped the knife she was using. 'Katie's right, this is nothing to do with her mam or my Auntie Norah. Who cares if the men have enough to eat! As far as I'm concerned they can starve – except

Uncle Roy and Katie's brothers. And your father, Helen,' she added, ashamed of herself for leaving out Mr Griffiths. He'd called every day since her aunt had died, checking arrangements had been made and, when they hadn't, taking it upon himself to complete them.

'This last week has all been about other people,' Katie agreed. 'What *they* think should be eaten after the service, what hymns *they* think are suitable to be played in the church. Marty tried telling the vicar that Mam's favourite hymn was "All Things Bright and Beautiful" but the vicar insisted it was unsuitable for a funeral and pencilled in "The Lord is my Shepherd", although both Marty and Jack told him Mam hated it. The flowers were just the same...'

'You and your brothers did get to choose your own flowers, didn't you, Katie?' Judy broke in. She had overheard Helen's mother muttering 'stupid extravagant waste' after Mr Griffiths had telephoned the florist on Katie's and her brothers' behalf.

'Marty and I knew Mam liked roses better than any other flower but...' Katie fought back the tears she'd had little control over since her mother's death. 'Some of the neighbours thought white roses a terrible waste of money. If it hadn't been for Mr Griffiths insisting that I knew my own mother best, I think Mam would have had a wreath of dandelions on her coffin.'

'Sorry.'

'It's not your fault, Helen.'

'But it is my mother's. She thinks she always knows best.'

'She means well.' Pushing the butter away, Lily sat back in her chair. 'And us moaning all the time doesn't help. Katie and I are just touchy.'

'You've every right to be.' Judy shaved the last piece of bread from the crust on the table.

'Are you going to move downstairs with your brothers now, Katie?' Helen shifted a stack of buttered bread on to a plate and started cutting the slices into neat triangles.

'Uncle Roy thinks it would be better if Katie carried on living here for the time being. He says we can talk it over again when Brian moves out.'

'Brian is moving out?'

In spite of the pain that had gnawed at her ever since Roy had told her Norah was dead, Lily managed a small smile at the look of horror on Judy's face. 'Not as far as I know.'

'Marty and Jack only let him live with them on the understanding that he'd have to leave when my mother...' Katie didn't cry but a shudder ran through her body. Lily wrapped her arm round her shoulders. The door opened and Martin and Jack walked in. Lily immediately left her chair so Martin could take her place at his sister's side.

'Judy, we're waiting for the tea,' Joy called impatiently from the dining room.

'Helen and I are sorting it, Mam,' Judy answered.

'Lily, the bread and butter?' Esme reminded, sticking her head round the kitchen door.

'Judy is bringing it out. I have to talk to Uncle Roy, Mrs Griffiths.'

'Katie...'

'Isn't feeling well, Mrs Griffiths. We're taking

her downstairs.' Martin and Jack escorted their sister through the door and headed for the basement stairs.

'Well!' Esme looked after their retreating figures. 'I thought those two would appreciate being kept busy.'

'It's all right, Mrs Griffiths.' Judy handed her a full plate of bread and butter and picked up a second from the table. 'You've still got Helen and me to boss around.'

'It went well, Lily. The hymns were beautiful and the service moving. I think Norah would have approved if she'd been there.'

'She wouldn't have been allowed to go,' Lily pointed out ungraciously, still smarting at her uncle's refusal to allow her to attend the funeral.

'I take it you've had a difficult time here.' Roy guided Lily towards the only quiet room on the ground floor, the parlour.

'No, everyone's trying to be kind but...'

'You don't have to say any more, love.'

The parlour looked empty and bereft now the second coffin had been removed. Seeing a white carnation on the floor of the bay. Lily stooped and picked it up. 'I can't believe I won't see Auntie Norah again – ever.'

'Neither can I, love.'

'The food's ready, Roy. Shall I get you and Lily a plateful?' Esme hovered at the open door in a black sack dress of moiré silk more suited to a cocktail party than a funeral. Her only concession to the occasion was a wisp of apron concocted from hand made lace and fine lawn.

Lily had always been a little afraid of and intimidated by Joe's mother. Now she felt simply irritated. 'No thank you, Mrs Griffiths.'

Esme looked expectantly at Roy.

'No thank you, Esme, I'll be out shortly.'

'Shall I ask Joy to pour your tea and bring it in?'

'Not for a minute.' Roy was having trouble keeping his equanimity. Since the moment the doctor had pronounced Norah dead he felt he had been surrounded by well-meaning, inter-fering women, hell-bent on taking over his life.

'I'll tell everyone you'd like to be left alone then, shall I?' Esme closed the door on them.

'I think she's miffed,' Lily whispered as Esme tugged the door until the lock gave a final definitive click.

'I'll pacify her later. You eaten?' Roy asked.

'No. I'm not hungry. I'll eat after...'

'Everyone's left,' Roy finished for her. 'I want our life to get back to normal too, Lily, but I'm afraid there isn't going to be a normal for us, not now Norah's gone.' He gave her a brief hug. 'You want to go in there with me?'

'Not really.'

'We'll need this room as well as the dining room, but not before the furniture's been shifted back.' He pulled an easy chair away from the wall and dragged it on to the rug, positioning it exactly over the dents the castors had made in the thick pile.

'I'm sorry, Mrs Jordan and Mrs Hunt wanted to see to it earlier, but I wouldn't let them.'

'Then how about you giving me a hand to do it now. Afterwards, you can go down to the garden and sit on Norah's bench while I make small talk and thank everyone for coming.'

'Wouldn't that be rather cowardly of me?'

'There isn't anyone here you won't be seeing again. I'll tell them you're not feeling well. If they don't understand that you need to be alone, they're not worth bothering with. Now take the other end of that table. Careful now, it might be a bit heavy.'

CHAPTER EIGHTEEN

'Katie, I've brought some food for you and your brothers.' Helen tapped the back of the basement door with the heel of her shoe to announce her arrival as she edged a heavily laden tray round the curve at the bottom of the stairs.

'I'll give you a hand,' Jack shouted. Running out of his bedroom at the end of the passage, he took the tray from Helen. Forcing her back, he kissed her behind the cover of the door.

'Want to sit with us for a bit?' Katie invited, as Helen followed him into the kitchen.

'Only if I wouldn't be in the way.'

'That has to be a first, tactful Helen.' Jack set the tray on the table.

'Jack, apologise to Helen,' Martin prompted.

'It's all right, I have tended to put my foot in it lately.'

'Is Lily upstairs?' Martin took a sandwich and opened it.

'She's sitting in the garden. I think if her uncle hadn't suggested she go out there for some peace and quiet she would have hit someone. Probably my or Judy's mother. The way they're carrying on up there with Mrs Jordan and Mrs Lannon, anyone would think they're catering for the Queen.'

'You only brought cheese and cucumber?' Jack asked, examining the sandwiches.

'And ham salad, salmon and lettuce and cream cheese and spring onions. I'll go back up for cake if you want some. There wasn't room for it on the tray.'

'Great, Helen, thanks, I'm starving.'

'Aren't you always,' she responded, without thinking what she was saying.

Martin looked from her to Jack, as his brother lifted four plates from the dresser and piled one high with sandwiches for himself. 'This is good of you, Helen, thank you.'

'Any time.' She smiled at Martin but the smile died on her lips. She had never seen him look so exhausted – or so peculiarly at her. Could he suspect that she and Jack... 'Point me in the direction of the teapot and I'll make tea.' Avoiding Martin's gaze, she looked around the room.

'It's all right, I'll do it.' Jack took his plate with him as he went to the stove.

'Brian and Judy upstairs?' Martin asked, still watching her.

'Seeing as how the "caterers" had to have someone to order around, they kindly volunteered.'

'Remind me to give Brian a gold star when he comes down.' Jack spooned tea into the pot.

'Do you think Lily would appreciate a cup of tea and something to eat?'

'I'm sure she would, Martin,' Helen encouraged, wishing him anywhere but in the same room as Jack and her.

'Give me a couple of minutes and you can take the tea out with you.'

'I'll do that.' Finally turning away from Helen, Martin looked at his sister. 'Katie, help me out here. What sandwiches would Lily choose?'

'Tell me to go away if you don't want company, Lily.' Joe stood in front of the bench Roy had set facing his flowerbed. He remembered Mrs Evans sitting on it sewing through almost every fine summer afternoon of his childhood, and he didn't want to intrude if Lily was remembering.

'Please, sit down. I'm trying to escape all those people upstairs. I would have gone to the basement with Jack, Martin and Katie but I think they should be left alone for a while.'

He sat beside her and took her hand in his.

'Uncle Roy said Auntie Norah's funeral went well.'

'It was quiet, dignified, moving, and from what little I knew of her I think she would have approved of the hymns and sermon. Which is more than I can say for the carrying on here, if the sniping that's going on between some of the women upstairs is indicative of what's been happening.'

'Katie and I really wanted to go to the funerals.'

'I see no reason why you shouldn't have. This Welsh tradition of men at the graveside and

387

women in the house is barbaric.'

'I wish Uncle Roy thought so.'

'He is a stickler for tradition. You being there would have upset him.'

'What about upsetting me and my aunt?'

'Lily, no one is going to mourn or miss Mrs Evans more than you. She knew that and you know it. I had a word with your uncle and borrowed my father's car. If you want to go out to Oxwich to see her grave I'll take you.'

'Now.' She jumped to her feet.

'If you like, but your uncle and my father warned me that some people might think us going off together straight after the funeral odd.'

'I couldn't care less.'

'That's my girl.'

'So you'll take me?'

'Yes.' He reached for her hand.

'I have to see Uncle Roy.'

'He's standing at the kitchen window.'

Lily looked up. Roy nodded and gave her the 'thumbs-up' sign.

'You don't have to go back into the house. The car's in our garage.'

'You thought of everything.'

'I try.'

'Joe, I...' Overwhelmed by emotion, she flung her arms round his neck and clung to him, burying her head in the shoulder of his suit, hoping he wouldn't see the tears that had hovered perilously close to the surface since Norah had died. He held her close, stroking the back of her head and murmuring soft, gentle words of comfort.

Standing in the kitchen window, Roy was astounded by the intimacy of Lily's and Joe's embrace. It brought home to him as nothing else could Lily's newfound status of womanhood. But the sight didn't upset him as much as it did Martin, who was watching from his bedroom window a floor below.

Abandoning the tray he'd stacked with plates of sandwiches and teas for himself and Lily on his bed, Martin continued to watch Lily and Joe, hating himself for staring, yet unable to tear himself away. Could that have been him if he'd found the courage to ask Lily out as soon as he came back from National Service? Would she have turned him down?

He'd once heard Mrs Evans say that loving someone meant wanting the best for them. Lily would undoubtedly be better off with Joe, because Joe would be able to give her everything he'd never be able to. But as he watched Joe guide Lily out through the gate at the bottom of the garden, he remembered his mother and all her trite adages about money not bringing happiness and for the first time he could see truth behind the hackneyed words. There was something about Joe of romance and books, something unworldly that made him uneasy about entrusting anyone's happiness to him. Especially that of the girl he loved more than anyone else in the world.

As they left the town and suburbs behind them and hit the open Gower Road that cut across

Fairwood Common, Joe took one hand from the wheel, slipped it round Lily's shoulders and hugged her. 'Poor you, you've had a foul time.'

'No more than Katie.'

'It will be a long time before either of you will be allowed to forget what happened and remember your dead the way you want to. Swansea will be talking about Ernie Clay, and what he did to his wife and your aunt, for years. Even at the graveside in Morriston yesterday people kept looking over their shoulders to see if he would have the nerve to turn up.'

'My uncle made sure he wouldn't. I'm not supposed to know, but I overheard him talking to your father when they were making the arrangements. By putting Mrs Clay's death in the paper with *all enquiries to undertaker*, they made certain the only people who would attend were people they knew about. Uncle Roy also mentioned that the police were questioning Mr Clay yesterday afternoon. I think he had something to do with the timing.'

'I can't believe Ernie Clay is free to walk the streets.'

'Neither can I, but my uncle told me that legally...'

'Mr Clay can only be charged with minor offences. My father explained the technicalities. But I still think there has to be a moral as well as legal side to the law.'

'Katie never wants to see him again.'

'From the way Martin and Jack were talking yesterday, they intend to make sure she doesn't. You and she are still going to live with your uncle, aren't you?'

'Of course. What makes you think we're not?'

'It's just that...'

'The street gossips are saying he's not related to us and young girls shouldn't be left with an older man.' She looked to him for confirmation and he nodded. 'He says he's going to advertise for a housekeeper, although Katie and I are perfectly capable of running the house.'

'While working full time?'

'While working full time,' she reiterated decisively, turning to the window.

They drove on in silence as the road turned down through the woods of Parkmill and back up to the coast. Turning left just before the crumbling Norman wall that enclosed the eighteenth-century manor of Penrice, they gazed out over Oxwich marshes and the enormous sweep of Oxwich Bay.

'I love this place, so did my auntie, but I never thought she would be buried here.'

'Your uncle told me his family had farmed in Oxwich for over two hundred years.'

'It still surprised us that she wanted to be buried here with her parents. Uncle Roy said that if her husband had had a grave she would have wanted to be buried with him, but he went down on a ship at Dunkirk.'

'If you believe in God, they're together now.'

'You don't believe in God?' she asked, as he turned at the end of the beach and drove up the narrow lane that led to the tiny Norman church.

'I think everyone has their own idea of God,' he answered evasively, parking the car in front of the gate. After helping her out, he led her through a small side gate, around to the beach side of the church. On a gentle rise overlooking the sea lay a mound of multicoloured flowers. They grated, incongruously garish against the old grey stone and subdued greenery of the church and yard.

She stood for a moment in absolute silence. When she moved, Joe allowed her to walk on alone. This was her last time with Norah and if he gave her that, perhaps she'd allow the rest of her life to be his.

Brian glanced through the door of the kitchen into the dining room and balked at the idea of walking in there. Every room on the ground floor was crammed with people; both newly arranged parlour and dining room filled with neighbours and elderly relatives of Constable Williams.

The ten days since Norah and Annie had died had been interminable. Sharing rooms with Martin and Jack had made him feel as though he'd been stranded in limbo. One or the other, or both of them, had vetoed every suggestion he had tried to make. Nothing could happen or be discussed, no decisions taken until 'after the funerals'. He was ashamed that during Annie's funeral the day before he hadn't felt much sympathy or grief for either of his flatmates, only relief that it would soon be over so his life and theirs could continue.

'Has the kettle boiled?' Judy bustled in with a tray full of dirty cups and an empty teapot.

'No.'

'Put it on. Mrs Jordan and my mother are

screaming for more tea.'

Brian obediently lifted the kettle from the range as Judy dumped the cups and saucers into the sink and ran the hot tap.

'I don't blame you for hiding in here. It's bedlam out there and people are saying the stupidest things. Some ghastly old relative of Mrs Evans's has just asked Mr Williams for her clothes because "our Norah always dressed nice when she was going out and promised I could have them when she passed on". Considering she's about ten times the width of Mrs Evans, I'm sure no such thing was ever said. She also cornered Lily before she made it through the door into the garden and asked her when she was going to the orphanage.'

'What did Lily say?'

'Fortunately Mr Williams overheard and answered that Lily was a little old for orphanages, considering she worked in a bank.'

'I don't think people mean to be tactless. Funerals are a strain; no one knows the right thing to say, so they blurt out the first thing that comes into their head.'

'I'm not so sure. You wouldn't believe the number of women who are insisting Norah promised them something on her death.'

'I would.' Tipping the tea leaves into the bin, he swilled the teapot out under the running tap. 'I've seen it in my own family. My half-brother and I had to escort my father's first wife out of the house after my father's funeral when we caught her pocketing my mother's spoons and china.'

'I'm sorry, I didn't know your father had died.'

393

Judy was more shocked by the idea of Brian's father having two wives alive at the same time than his being dead, but politeness overcame her curiosity and she kept her questions to herself.

'It happened three years ago. I'm used to the idea now of him not being there, but I miss him like crazy. Especially when something bad or' – he smiled at her – 'extra good like meeting you happens.'

'Extra good,' Judy echoed. 'We know nothing about one another.'

'A situation which will be remedied as soon as you go out with me.'

'Judy, isn't that tea ready yet?' Joy interrupted as she walked in from the dining room.

'Kettle's almost boiled.' Judy dried the last cup.

'As soon as it's made, bring it in and don't forget fresh cups.'

'You think people would have hung on to their cups if they wanted a refill,' Judy grumbled, stacking china on the tray as Brian made the tea.

'How do you fancy escaping down to the basement and sitting with Katie, Martin and Jack after I've carried this in for you?'

'Sounds great, but I'll have to wait until I won't be missed.'

Given the way her mother was watching her, Brian thought that moment wasn't likely to happen, but he smiled anyway. Lifting the heavy tray, he carried it through to the dining room. Joy Hunt had already cleared a space for it on the sideboard.

'Take these sandwiches round.' She pushed plates into both his and Judy's hands. 'I'm sure everyone is hungry, they're just too polite to be the first to eat and we're going to be left with mountains of food if you don't persuade them to stop hanging back.'

Judy gave Brian a look of commiseration as she headed for a corner dominated by a group of elderly women with badly fitting false teeth.

Joe walked to the sea wall and looked over the rocks to the smooth, broad sweep of the sandy bay. He savoured the moment, absorbing the scenery and composing lines of verse, secure in the knowledge that when she had said her goodbyes to her aunt, Lily would join him. The beginnings of a poem came to mind, even the title, 'The Last Goodbye'.

'Thank you, Joe.' Lily, looking lost and even smaller than usual in her plain black costume, was at his side.

He opened his arms and held her, then taking her hand, led her to the furthest point of the churchyard. 'The view from here is fantastic. It's one of my favourite places on Gower.'

'You come here?'

'As often as I can, particularly in winter. The entire history of old Oxwich is encapsulated in this churchyard. Look.' He pointed to the remains of rough limestone stonework set between the rocks on their left. 'Those are the foundations of eighteenth-century houses that were swept away by the sea. If you want tragedy, here it is.' He showed her a grave that held four members of the same family who had all died before their eighteenth birthday. 'Parsimony.' He indicated a grave marker that could have qualified as wartime utility if it hadn't borne the date 1850. 'Romance', the inscription on an even earlier stone chronicled the details of a married couple who had died ten days apart.

'They might have been killed by the same disease, perhaps cholera,' Lily suggested. 'From what I remember of Swansea history the dates are about right.'

'I prefer to think broken heart.' He leaned against the wall. 'That situation we were talking about earlier, you, Katie and your uncle.'

'There is no situation,' she countered. 'Uncle Roy is the nearest thing to a relative I have. He and Auntie Norah have always taken care of me and now we've lost Auntie Norah' – she hated herself for saying the words, as if they somehow made her aunt even more dead – 'we have to take care of one another.'

'You have me as well.' He removed a small box from his coat pocket. 'I intended to do this during a perfect sunset on the cliff overlooking Pobbles, but I should know by now that every time I plan something it never happens the way I imagined. I hope you and your aunt will forgive my bad timing, but I think it's important you know how I feel about you.' He opened the box. Inside was the single glittering diamond solitaire she had admired in the jeweller's shop just over ten days that seemed like a lifetime ago. 'I love you, Lily. Will you marry me?'

Lost for words, she stared helplessly at the ring.

'Please don't say we've only been out a few times.'

'Twice,' she murmured, finally finding her voice.

'We've known one another most of our lives and we won't be able to marry until next June when I take my degree, so it will be a fairly long engagement. And if you're thinking about money, don't. I have a trust fund, enough to buy a house of our own when I start work. Say something,' he pleaded, 'anything, that is, except no.'

'Joe, my aunt's just died ... everything is so uncertain...'

Taking her hand in his, he slipped the ring on to her finger. 'That's why I'm asking you to marry me, so you will have some certainty.'

'It fits.'

'Of course. We're made for one another.' Leaving the ring on her hand, he kissed the tips of her fingers. 'Do you love me?'

'Yes,' she whispered.

'Now I've established that, the rest will be simple. I'll find the right moment to talk to your uncle, we'll organise ourselves a wedding – a quiet one because of your aunt – and then I'll try to ensure that you live as "happily ever after" as possible.'

Judy dumped a tray of dirty cups in the kitchen. She looked at the sink, half full with cold, grey, sudsy water, and balked at the idea of scrabbling around for the plug to empty it. Opening the back door, she walked out on to the top step of the flight of metal stairs that led down to the garden and sat.

'On strike.' Brian sank down beside her.

'Hiding from my mother, Mrs Griffiths, Mrs Lannon and Mrs Jordan. I can't face another dirty cup or plate. Or all those people talking twaddle.'

'Well-meaning twaddle, Judy. You're being oversensitive.' He opened a packet of cigarettes and she helped herself to one. 'I didn't know you smoked.'

'I've just started. And the twaddle isn't well-meaning. If I hear one more woman whispering to another about the unsuitability of Roy looking after Katie and Lily I'll scream. And who is that frightful old woman with false teeth that rattle when she talks?'

'I think she's a relative of Constable Williams.'

'Judging by the way she's been ordering me around she must be a duchess. "I like more milk in my tea than that, miss, and one level spoonful of sugar, not heaped. I can tell by the taste it's been heaped."'

He slipped his arm round her waist to steady himself as he lit her cigarette, leaving it there when she unexpectedly and rather gratifyingly leaned against him. 'How are Katie and Lily bearing up under the strain?'

'When I saw them earlier they both looked like death warmed up. Mam said it's not going to hit either of them for a few days but I'm not so sure it hasn't hit them already.'

'Adam's cut up about it. He's fond of Katie and doesn't know how best to help her.'

'He can join the club. Helen and I only agreed to play serving wenches to our mothers' ladyships so Katie and Lily could escape. The kindest thing we could do for them was give them half an hour's peace and quiet away from this pandemonium.'

'Very generous of you.'

'There's no need to be sarky.'

'I wasn't, I meant it. You doing anything tonight?'

'Lying prostrate, given the amount of clearing up my mother will expect me to do here after this little lot have gone home.'

'If you have the strength to sit on my bike, we could go somewhere nice and I could lie prostrate with you.'

'Given that twinkle in your eye, chance would be a fine thing, Brian Powell.'

'So you won't go out with me?'

'I didn't say that.'

'Judy, what on earth do you think you're doing!' Joy shouted from the kitchen window.

Hastily dropping her cigarette, Judy ground it to dust beneath her shoe. 'Talking to Brian, Mam.'

'You call that talking?' Joy stepped out of the kitchen.

Brian dropped his arm from Judy's waist and rose to his feet. 'I was just asking Judy if she could think of any way we could help Katie and Lily, Mrs Hunt.'

'By we, I assume you mean you and the boys.'

'Adam, Martin...'

'I think Katie and Lily are best left on their own, Constable Powell,' Joy snapped icily.

Brian looked her in the eye. Her steely expression suggested there wasn't going to be a better time. 'I also asked Judy if she'd like to go out with me tonight.'

'Judy will be busy tonight.'

'No, I won't.'

Joy gave her daughter a look that might have intimidated a girl with less spirit. 'Do I have to remind you that you have college work to complete?'

'I'm up to date with my homework.'

'If you're busy tonight, Judy, perhaps we could go out another time.' Brian smiled at Joy, hoping his conciliatory gesture might result in a weakening of the opposition.

'I'm really not doing anything tonight, so I'd like to go out with you, Brian.'

'But your mother...'

'I'd rather not have said this in front of Brian, but frankly I'd rather you didn't consort with policemen, Judy.'

'What's wrong with policemen? Daddy...'

'Need I say more,' Joy interrupted. 'Brian, Judy is grateful for your invitation but I cannot allow her to accept it.' Turning, she walked back into the kitchen – and Roy Williams.

'Do we have to talk about this now, in the middle of Norah's funeral?' Joy lit a cigarette as Judy and Brian disappeared down the steps into the garden.

'Yes, we do. I came to look for you to tell you people are leaving and want to thank you for organising the food, and I find you screaming at Brian Powell just because the poor lad asked your daughter out. If you hate policemen so much, what have we been doing for the last ten years?'

'Bill was a policeman.'

'And a good one, as I remember, before he enlisted. Are you going to tell me he was a wife beater now, like Ernie Clay?'

'Don't be ridiculous.'

'Constable Williams, Mr Griffiths and the funeral director...'

'I'm coming, Mrs Lannon. Mrs Hunt, I'll call round later to pay you for the food.'

'There's no need...'

'Eight o'clock,' he said in a voice that brooked no argument. 'You will be in?'

'I'll be in,' she conceded, sensing that in his present mood he was quite capable of making a scene if she said she wouldn't.

'I'd rather you kept it, even if you don't want to wear it yet.' Joe pressed the ring Lily had slipped from her finger into her palm and closed her hand over it.

'No.' She handed it to him carefully. 'I'll take it back when Uncle Roy gives us his permission and not a minute before.'

'How soon can I ask him?'

'When I tell you it's all right.'

Taking the ring box from his jacket pocket, he opened it and replaced the ring on its velvet bed. 'Do you think that will be in a day or two, a week, a...'

'What did your parents say when you told them you wanted to marry me?' she interrupted.

'My father was delighted.'

'And your mother?' His silence told her all she wanted to know. 'You'll need her permission, Joe.'

'I have my father's and my mother will come round to the idea of us, given time.'

'I won't marry you without her blessing.'

Joe recalled the look on his mother's face when she discovered that he had asked Lily out instead of one of her beloved debs and changed the subject. 'Would you have preferred a trip to the jeweller's to look at the rest of their stock to me choosing for you?'

'No, I loved our ring the moment I saw it, but I never in a million years thought you'd buy it, or want to give it to me.'

'I've earned a lot of money this summer. It was just sitting in my bank account, gathering dust.'

'But an engagement...' Lily was suddenly overwhelmed by the responsibility and implication of accepting Joe's proposal.

Sensing her wavering, he kissed her. 'You said you loved me.'

'I do.'

'Then there's no problem we can't face together.'

'Except you. You're a writer, you've published poems, you're studying in university. You've been out with smart, sophisticated girls; you go to parties full of clever, wealthy people. I'm not part of your world...'

'You're all the world I want.' He stilled her protests by kissing her again.

'But I hardly know you,' she murmured when

he released her.

'That is easily remedied. We'll both make an effort to become better acquainted with one another's foibles and faults before we walk up the aisle and I'll make a start right now. Are you listening?' He smiled, waiting until she nodded. 'I like my eggs scrambled on toast in the morning. My favourite meal is steak, chips and salad. I hate tinned peaches, apricots and pilchards. I take milk and three sugars in my tea. I love animals but my mother would never let me have pets, so be warned, I'm likely to fill our house with cats and dogs. My favourite colour schemes are blue and cream, gold and green and black and white, which aren't fashionable but as I've been almost blinded by my mother's walls, which look as though Mickey Mouse has been sick over them, I'm likely to be firm on the question of how our house should be decorated. My father is Labour, my mother Conservative, which is why I tend to avoid talking about politics and when the time comes I'd like to have four children.'

'Four!'

'Not all at once. And I don't believe in working wives, so when we're married you'll stay at home, which I'm hoping will be a cottage in the country but as I intend to buy a car and teach you to drive...'

'Me? Drive a car?'

'Why not?'

'Cars are expensive.'

'I have news for you, soon-to-be, Mrs Joseph Griffiths. We are going to be quite comfortably off. I have enough money set aside in my trust fund to buy a house and two cars without resorting to paying on the never-never and my job has a good starting salary.'

'You already have a job?'

'I didn't intend for that to slip out, but yes, I do and please don't say a word about it as only my father knows at the moment. My mother isn't going to be happy. She always assumed I'd become a teacher and eventually a headmaster like my grandfather but I've accepted a post at the BBC.'

'In Swansea.'

'Cardiff.'

'Uncle Roy...'

'You'll be able to see him whenever you want. Cardiff is only an hour and a bit away by train and more or less the same by car,' he added, stretching the truth.

'We'll have to live there.'

'Near my work, yes.'

'You'll be on the radio.'

'Probably working more behind the scenes than behind a microphone but who knows, in a year or two I may be switched to television. Even my father thinks that every family in the country will buy a set in the next few years.'

'Uncle Roy wanted to get one for the Coronation but Auntie Norah wouldn't hear of it – he thinks that was because watching a screen would have interfered with her sewing.'

'You won't tell anyone?'

'Only Uncle Roy, and you asked me to.'

'I mean about the job.' He looked into her eyes, tawny gold, sparkling in the sunlight. 'I'd like to shout that you're going to marry me from the rooftops, Lily.'

'Lily can put the crockery and cutlery away as she knows where everything goes.' Esme untied her apron and folded it into her handbag. 'It's the least she can do, considering she and Katie disappeared when we most needed their help.'

Joy Hunt glanced around the kitchen and dining room. Apart from the crockery and cutlery piled high on the kitchen table, the rooms were relatively tidy.

'I could push the Hoover over the floor,' Doris suggested.

'Lily has the rest of the week off, Roy told me. She won't have anything to do besides house-work and she'll want to be kept busy to take her mind off Norah. I, however, have a home to go to and a meal to prepare for my family.'

'If they come back in time for it, Esme.' Doris smiled knowingly. 'I saw your Joe sneak off with Lily. It's obvious which way the wind's blowing there. I couldn't be more pleased for them. They make a nice young couple.'

'There's nothing going on between Joseph and Lily Sullivan,' Esme contradicted abruptly.

'Like the nothing that's going on between our Adam and Katie.' Doris beamed. 'Katie's a lovely girl but I must admit I'm none too pleased about it. Not with Ernie the way he is. I have night-mares at the thought of him smashing down our door like poor Norah's...'

'Much as I'd like to stay and chat, I have to organise our evening dinner.' Picking up her apron, Esme almost ran out of the door.

'I hope I haven't said something I shouldn't have.' Doris dried the last plate and stacked it on top of a pile on the table. 'Lily's a nice girl. I'd be proud as punch if Adam brought her home. Not that I've anything against Katie, except as I said, her father...'

'But your Adam isn't in university and you're not a snob like Esme, Doris.' Joy untied her apron and checked her hair in the mirror over the sink.

'Our Adam is in the Civil Service.'

'Somehow I don't think Esme sees the Civil Service in quite the same light as university. But I agree with you, Lily is a nice girl. I only hope she hasn't bitten off more than she can chew with Joe Griffiths.'

'Our Adam likes Joe.'

'Joe's not the problem. But I have a feeling that Esme's ambitions for him might be.'

'You knew about this!' Beside herself with rage, Esme confronted John in their lounge.

'If you're asking if I knew Joe was driving Lily down to Oxwich to see her aunt's grave, the answer is yes. I gave him the car so he could.' John calmly poured himself a whisky from the bottle he'd taken to leaving out of the cocktail cabinet so he wouldn't be subjected to 'Stranger in Paradise' every time he wanted a drink.

'How could you?'

'What, Esme?' John looked her coolly in the eye. 'Lend Joe my car, or give him my blessing?'

'She has no family, no standing, no money, she's a...'

406

'Nice girl and our Joe will be a lucky man if he gets her to marry him.'

'Admit it, John,' she bit back viciously, 'you're actively encouraging Joseph to marry beneath him just to spite me.'

'What would you have me do, Esme? Tell him to marry a deb, so he can land himself with a wife like you?'

'Joe's not your class, not your...'

'Son?' he questioned. 'After the years I've spent bringing him up and the nights I've sat in with him while you were out, I think he's as much my son as yours, whoever his father was.'

It was the first time either of them had ever mentioned Joe's real father. Esme fell silent

'Please, Esme.' He lowered his voice, trying to be reasonable. 'Can't we walk away from this marriage with our dignity intact? There's nothing between us. There never was, not from the very beginning, only I was too naïve and besotted to see it at the time.'

'I gave you Helen, I...'

'It's over, Esme. Don't make it any uglier than it was.'

Heart thundering at the finality in his quiet words, she steeled herself to look him in the eye. 'We can't divorce, John,' she pleaded in a small voice. 'Think of the children...'

'Think of the misery we'll subject them to if we carry on as we are. Please, don't make me hire a private detective. He may track you down to the Mermaid Hotel.'

'John, I...'

'I'm instructing my solicitor to go ahead. You

attempt to block the divorce and I'll hire that detective and tell him to question everyone you know, starting with your family and all the members of the Little Theatre.'

Turning, Esme ran out of the room and up the stairs. If she hadn't been quite so distraught she might have seen Helen closing her bedroom door.

CHAPTER NINETEEN

'And where do you think you're going, young lady?' Joy demanded as Judy ran down the stairs in her green shirtwaister and starched net petticoat.

'To meet Brian.'

'I told you...'

'You told me you didn't want me to go out with him but you didn't give one reason why I shouldn't, except he's a policeman. I've thought about it and decided that's not good enough.'

'I'm your mother...'

'And you taught me never to listen to other people and do what I think is right. Well, I like Brian, and I happen to think it's right for me to go out with him.'

Furious at having her own principles quoted back at her, Joy clenched her fists to contain her anger. If Judy had cried or thrown a tantrum she could have shouted her down, but the girl was right, she had brought her up to think for herself and take responsibility for her own actions. She was the one who'd made Judy old before her years but then, she had never realised that Judy's maturity would result in a situation like this. 'If Brian were a decent boy, he'd respect my wishes as your mother.' Joy hated herself for coming out with the kind of platitude she had always despised other women for resorting to.

'Why should he, when you don't respect him?'

Joy stood in front of her daughter as she picked up her handbag from the hall table. 'I absolutely forbid you to leave this house. You walk out through that door and...'

'You'll what, Mam? Throw me out? Fine, I'm earning enough to rent a room. I'll leave.'

'You earn what I pay you.'

'There are other hairdressing salons in Swansea. I could pick up my apprenticeship in any one of a dozen places and you know it. So, what's it to be? Do I go out and stay out, permanently, or do I return by half past ten?'

The doorbell shrilled, shattering the tense atmosphere. Joy glanced at the gold watch Roy had given her and realised it was eight o'clock.

'Your lover's here.'

'My what!'

'You told me the facts of life. Surely you didn't think me too naïve to see what's been going on between you two for years? And in case you hadn't noticed his uniform, he's a policeman. Just like my dad and Brian.' Judy opened the door. 'Good evening, Constable Williams,' she greeted him with exaggerated politeness.

'Hello, Judy. I wanted to thank you for your

help this afternoon.'

'That's all right. Don't rush off, Mam's all dolled up and waiting for you.'

'Pardon?' Roy looked from Judy to Joy.

'She's wearing her second-best dress and the perfume she keeps especially for you.'

'Judy...'

'I have to go, Constable Williams, I'm late already,' Judy broke in, interrupting her mother. 'But I would consider it a special favour if you try to change my mother's mind about policemen making unsuitable boyfriends.'

'Judy!' Joy rushed to the door as her daughter walked away. 'Back in this house by half past ten,' she shouted furiously. 'Not one minute later.'

Judy waved without turning her head, leaving Joy wondering if she'd heard her last injunction.

'I'm leaving.' The tick of the carriage clock on the display cabinet was deafening as Esme waited for John to comment. 'Don't you want to know where I'll be?'

'Of course.'

'There is no of course about it, you're driving me out...'

'Esme, please.' He murmured patiently. 'Where are you going?'

'My mother's. I telephoned her, told her you've thrown me out and want a divorce. She said she'd never have me back when I married you but I think she's pleased that I've finally seen sense now. Although she's not looking forward to the scandal...'

'You know full well that I wouldn't throw you

into the street, Esme; you can leave any time you want but I won't play the hypocrite and pretend I'll be sorry to see you go. Will you be taking the children?' he asked, in an attempt to limit the conversation to practical matters.

'You expect me to take them to mother's, knowing how frail she is?'

'I don't expect you to take them; in fact, I'd prefer it if you left them with me.'

'You'll continue to pay my full allowance into my bank account?'

'Yes.'

'And the shop?'

'My original offer stands, the shop and half your allowance or your full allowance.'

'And if I want both?'

'That isn't my offer.'

'You're right,' she said coldly, 'I do need to see a solicitor. I'm only taking one case, I'll send for the rest of my things.'

'You have your key; you can get them any time. I've no intention of being petty.'

'What will you tell the children?'

'That you've left.'

'I'll telephone and tell them the truth.'

'What truth would that be, Esme?'

'That you threw me out.' She walked into the hall. He heard the 'ping' as the telephone receiver was lifted from its cradle, her voice, agitated and excited, as she called for a taxi; the harsh rap of her high-heeled shoes as she ran upstairs.

Pouring himself another drink, he continued to sit and wait. Ten minutes later a taxi blared its horn in the street. Esme ran downstairs, called

411

the driver and asked him to carry her case. A few moments later the front door closed. John poured himself a third whisky as the cab drove away.

Esme had gone, finally walked out. It was what he'd been hoping would happen ever since the Saturday night the police hadn't been able to find her. But he couldn't understand the thick, suffocating feeling in his throat, the burning at the back of his eyes or why his hand was shaking so uncontrollably, spilling whisky all over Esme's nylon-covered sofa.

'Judy knows about us.'

'Us?' Roy sat in the chair Joy offered him.

'Don't be so bloody thick, Roy. Us, you and me, what's been going on between us.'

'She's a bright kid.'

'Is that all you can say, "She's a bright kid"? Look at the example we've set her. Lovers, no sign of a wedding ring...'

'Whose fault is that, Joy?'

'Mine,' she retorted bitterly, slumping on the sofa opposite him and reaching for the cigarette box on the side table.

'So what do you intend to do about it?'

'I don't know,' she shouted, still angry.

'How about you start by explaining to me why you didn't want Judy to go out with Brian Powell, just because he's a policeman.'

'I didn't want Judy to go out with Brian because of Bill. He was a policeman.'

'And a good husband and father.'

'Come off it, Roy, you know as well as I do that

412

he couldn't walk past a woman between sixteen and thirty-five without making a pass at her.'

'You knew?'

'I knew. Oh, you lot tried to keep it quiet inside your nice little boys' club down the station, but there were too many disgruntled husbands and boyfriends in Swansea for the word not to spread. Bill fooled around with as many women as he could fit into and at either end of his shifts, and it was all so easy for him. Tall, well-built, good-looking chap, they flocked around him and the job helped. Policemen work all hours, everyone knows that, and wives are expected to be understanding, not spend their lonely hours trying to work out whether their beloved is telling the truth about doing overtime, or stealing time to be with his latest popsy. You only have to look as far as you and me. Norah never questioned your comings and goings, or where you were, all those hours we spent in the bedroom over the salon.'

'Norah was my sister, Joy, not my wife and I'm not so sure she didn't know. Let's just say if she did, she didn't think it was her place to say anything to me about it.'

'I was eighteen when I married Bill, young, naïve and prepared to ignore his philandering because I didn't know how else to deal with it. It was what women of my generation were taught to do. All that advice from my mother and grandmother, "Don't rock the boat, dear. Confront him and he might walk out and where would that leave you? You have a daughter to think of. Police officer's a nice, steady job, the rent gets paid, you'll have a pension. And when all's said and done, every man does it. It's only natural. They're wanderers by instinct. It's not where they go, but who they come home to at night that matters. What do you care? If he's bothering someone else it means he's putting less on you." As if sex was some great miserable chore like the weekly wash, inflicted by men on their reluctant wives.'

Taking his lighter from his pocket, Roy leaned forward and lit Joy's cigarette. 'Brian Powell isn't Bill, Joy.'

'No, but he's a good-looking boy. Tall, dark and too handsome for any girlfriend's good.'

'It still doesn't follow that he'd be unfaithful if he and your Judy got together.'

'No, it doesn't because I intend to put a stop to it before it starts.'

'If that's what you were trying to do, you went the wrong way about it. You brought your Judy up to be independent like you. And you can't blame her now for thinking for herself, or being headstrong when she believes she's in the right.'

'I can't, can I?' She smiled wryly as she inhaled.

'That explains why you said what you did to Brian and Judy earlier, but it still doesn't explain why you've never married me. Or do you think I'm a policeman of the same ilk as Bill, a woman on every shift and two on every beat?'

'Is that what they used to say about him?'

'It was a long time ago, Joy.'

'It was, wasn't it,' she murmured, as though they were talking about someone else. 'And no, I never thought that about you, Roy. You're honest and very different from Bill. If you weren't I

414

would never have allowed you into my bed.'

'I wanted much more than just to climb into bed with you from the beginning, Joy.'

'I know.'

'I love you. I thought you loved me.'

'I do.'

'Then prove it by marrying me.'

'I only wish I could.' Her hand shook as she drew heavily on her cigarette. 'But I'm married to Bill.'

'He's dead.'

'He's alive and well, working for the Metropolitan Police and living in Balham with a barmaid.'

'Martin looked at us in a funny way.'

'Marty looks at everyone in a funny way,' Jack dismissed, as he locked Helen's basement door behind him and joined her in the front room.

'I think he suspects there's something going on between us.'

'What if he does? There's nothing he can do about it other than give me a bollocking.'

'He could tell my mother.'

'He's hardly likely to do that when it will get me into as much trouble as you. He may not like what we're doing, but I am still his brother.'

Helen switched on the light. It wasn't dark outside, but she had kept the curtains in the front room permanently closed since she had cleaned the room, using the excuse that she didn't want the furniture to fade when her father had commented. Her mother – she crossed her fingers as she thought of her – hadn't even bothered to walk down the stairs to see what she'd done.

'You have no idea what it was like for me this afternoon being that' – he clicked his fingers –'close to you and not able to touch you the way I wanted.' Grabbing her by the waist, Jack lifted her off her feet as he kissed her.

'You said you were going to get something.'

'I have.' He reached into his shirt pocket and pulled out a sliver of foil.

'Can I see it?'

'You can put it on me if you like. Bloke I got that off in work said his girl always does it for him.' He slid his hand down the crotch of her pedal pushers. 'You didn't waste any time in changing.'

'You wanted me to keep my black dress on?'

'I prefer you in dresses to trousers.'

'Only so you can put your hand up my skirt like you did this afternoon when we were sitting round your kitchen table.'

'No one saw.' Unbuttoning the waistband of her trousers, he slid down the side zip. 'One who undresses first is the winner and I've given you a head start.'

'What's the prize?' She pulled her sweater over her head.

'Guess.'

'Why did you tell people Bill had died, Joy?'

'Because I couldn't bear for everyone to know that he had abandoned me – and Judy. I couldn't have put up with the gossip, the humiliation, the pitying looks and all that hypocritical sympathy from women who'd feel superior because their husbands came home at night.'

'I would have thought you'd have got your fair share of all that when you announced his death.'

'It was a different kind of sympathy. A widow is respectable...'

'And a divorcee is not. I take it you haven't divorced him?'

'If I had it would have been in the papers. Judy would have had to grow up knowing that her father didn't want to live with us.'

'And letting her think he was dead was so much better?'

'It gave me my self-respect and her a dead hero for a father.'

'And a life built on lies.'

'You don't understand what it's like for a woman to be left to bring up a child on her own.'

'All I understand is that you think more of other people's opinions than you do of Judy or me.'

'That's not true. I did what I did for Judy – and you.'

'No you didn't. If you'd thought of us you would have divorced Bill years ago when I first asked you to marry me and we would have had ten years together as a family.' He left his chair.

'Where are you going?'

'Just going. Goodbye, Joy.' Taking his helmet from the table, he walked out of the door.

'Back to work tomorrow and I can't say I'll be sorry to go. This last week's been unreal.' Jack reached down alongside the sofa and rummaged in his trouser pocket for his cigarettes. Taking two, he lit them, passing one to Helen.

'I wish I worked on a building site.'

'You,' he mocked, 'you wouldn't last five minutes. It's hard, rough work, using your muscles from morning till night.'

'Anything would be better than endless filing and coffee-making, and putting up with sneaky old grubby eyes trying to look up my skirt every time I bend over.'

'What is a "sneaky old grubby eyes" when it's at home?' He laughed.

'It's what Judy calls dirty old men.'

'You have one in your office?'

'Mr Thomas, the senior partner. He's horrible, no one likes him. He shouts all the time and when he doesn't shout, he's all sly looks and touchy feely.'

'He touches you, you let me know and I'll punch out his lights. Like that other smarmy bugger who tried to grope you.' Turning and leaning on his elbow, Jack slid his hand over her naked breast.

'If you did, the police would lock you up and throw away the key,' she whispered, squirming as he fondled her nipple. 'Mr Thomas is a solicitor.'

'So what?'

'He's an important man.'

'I think I've proved you're worth a bit of trouble.'

'Jack.' Clamping her free hand over his, she imprisoned his legs between hers. 'I never thought it would be like this.'

'Like what?'

'Like, feeling that this is the best thing in the world and something I've been waiting all my life to happen. Like, wanting to tell you absolutely *everything* about myself and wanting to know *everything* there is to know about you. Like, not caring that I'm naked with you, and wanting to be with you every minute of every day and falling asleep next to you every night.'

'If we got our own place, all our life outside work could be like this.'

'Our own place – Jack'

'There are rooms to rent.'

'Not for people our age. You haven't even done your National Service.'

'Don't remind me.'

'Helen, Helen, you down here?' Joe's shout was followed by a banging on the door that connected to the rest of the house.

'Oh, God! That's Joe, quick.'

'You've locked the door?' Jack grabbed his trousers.

'Yes,' she hissed, picking up her pedal pushers from the floor and thrusting a leg into them.

'Then it's all right.'

'Not if he doesn't find me in the next few minutes. Here.' Bundling up the rest of Jack's clothes she threw them at him. 'Quick, get dressed and out of here. I'll tell him I was at the bottom of the garden.' Pulling her sweater over her head, she grabbed her plimsolls and ran to the connecting door.

'You're wobbling.'

She looked down. 'It's that obvious I'm not wearing underclothes?'

'Normally you're strapped in like a jelly in a mould.'

'Thank you very much.'

'Helen...'

'Coming, Joe.' Taking her time over unlocking the door, she glanced back before opening it. Jack was nowhere to be seen; she only hoped he was already lying low in the garden.

'Didn't you hear me shouting?'

'I was at the bottom of the garden.'

'Doing what?' he asked suspiciously.

'Talking to Katie.'

He looked around the door and down the empty passage. 'Dad wants us upstairs.'

'I'll come with you now.'

'The back door locked?'

'Yes.'

'I know what you're like, I'd better check.'

'There's no need.'

'I know what a scatterbrain you are.'

'I said there's no need!' She reached the door to her sitting room just before he did. As he threw it open, she breathed a sigh of relief. Jack had tidied everything away; the throws had been straightened on the sofa, and one of the chairs.

'It smells of cigarette smoke in here.' Joe walked in and turned to see Jack standing behind the door, mercifully fully dressed but to Helen's mortification holding her panties and corset.

'My, Katie, you have changed,' Joe said flatly.

'You won't tell, Mam, will you?' Helen asked Joe anxiously, as he embarked on a staring match with Jack.

'There's no time to talk about this now, Helen.' Joe was very glad there wasn't. Jack was what was known in Swansea terms as a 'hard nut' and from

420

the glint in his eye Joe suspected he'd have little compunction about using his superior strength, even against his girlfriend's brother – that's if Helen was Jack's girlfriend and not just casual recreation.

'I'm not leading your sister on.' Jack scowled, as if he'd read Joe's mind.

'I didn't think you were,' Joe replied, desperately trying not to look at what Jack was holding.

'I'm serious about her.'

Helen snatched her corset and pants from Jack, and stuffed them under the nearest cushion.

'I'm glad to hear it.'

Jack squared up to Joe.

'I suppose you think I'm not good enough for her.'

'I have other things on my mind right now, Jack, and so will Helen in a few minutes.'

'Like what?' Jack demanded belligerently.

Joe looked at Helen, not Jack, as he broke the news. 'Our mother's just walked out on us.'

'So what's going to happen now, Dad?' Helen asked anxiously.

'Nothing that should affect either of you, apart from your mother's absence and you can see her whenever it's convenient, in your grandmother's house, here, or in her own place, if she gets one. She told me she'll telephone both of you. If she wants you to live with her I'd like you to feel free to make up your own minds. It's not your or Joe's fault that I can't get on with her.'

'Can we carry on living here if we want to?'

'I have no intention of moving and there'll be a

home here for both of you for as long as you want it.'

'I want to stay,' Helen announced decisively, not only thinking of herself and her father but her proximity to Jack.

'Joe?' John turned to his son who had remained disturbingly silent throughout the watered-down explanations of 'differences of opinion' he'd given Helen for Esme's sudden departure.

'It doesn't really affect me that much, Dad. I've only one more year in university before I'll be off, making my own way.'

'But you'll still live here with us, won't you?' Helen asked, more concerned at the prospect of Joe leaving the family circle than her mother.

'No, I won't.' Joe decided that as he'd told his father and Lily about his job he might as well tell his sister. 'I've been offered a position – conditional on my getting a degree – at the BBC in Cardiff, and there's something else.' Joe glanced uneasily at Helen.

'Joe...'

'Let Joe finish what he wants to say, Helen, then it will be your turn.'

'I asked Lily to marry me this afternoon and she said yes.'

'Congratulations.' Leaving his chair, John shook his son's hand: 'I couldn't be more pleased. She's a nice girl and she'll make you a good wife.'

'And me a great sister-in-law.' Helen kissed Joe's cheek out of sheer relief that he hadn't mentioned Jack's presence in the basement.

'Lily wants to keep our engagement quiet until

422

she's had a chance to talk to her uncle which, given the funeral today, probably won't be for a while.'

'Roy's a sensible chap. She'll find a way to tell him soon and when she does I don't doubt he'll be as pleased as I am about it.'

'Mum won't be,' Helen said without thinking.

'The best advice I can give both of you is, it's your life, live it the way you want, because if you try to please everyone you'll end up pleasing no one, least of all yourselves.' After delivering the platitude, John went to the cocktail cabinet. 'How about drinks all round to celebrate? Helen?'

'Sherry, please.' She would have preferred gin but she was wary of her father's reaction if he discovered she'd developed a taste for it.

'Joe?'

'I'll have a whisky, Dad.'

John opened the cabinet, but before he could lift out the sherry and glasses 'Strangers in Paradise' tinkle-plonked into the atmosphere. Helen looked across at Joe and they both burst out laughing.

'If either of you can disable this damned music box, please do so.'

'What's it worth, Dad?' Helen asked.

'Five pounds,' John answered recklessly.

'I'll nip down the basement. I found a hammer there when I cleared it.'

'And I flew to Cyprus on a green flying pig but it was very noisy. All that squeaking and honking.'

'Pardon?' Judy narrowed her eyes as she looked at Brian.

'Hello, how are you? I'm Brian Powell, remember me? I invited you out this evening. I'm so glad I've finally caught your attention. Would you like another coffee?'

'No, thank you.' Judy pursed her lips to show her disapproval of his bad joke.

'Would you like me to take you home?'

Judy checked her watch. 'Not until half past ten.'

'Which gives us another hour. I repeat my question, would you like another coffee?'

'No, let's get out of here.'

Judy was outside, pacing the length of the Mumbles shopping centre before Brian had time to pick up his coat, let alone pay the bill.

'Where to now?' he asked as he joined her.

'Anywhere.'

'It's too dark and cold for a walk along the beach, it's too late for the pictures and that, unless I'm very much mistaken, leaves the café you've just walked out of.'

'There's always a pub.'

'No.'

'Why not?'

'Because it will give your mother yet another reason to dislike me.'

'Who cares whether she likes you or not?'

'I do,' he said firmly.

'I'm being difficult, aren't I?' she asked, challenging him to say otherwise.

He smiled tactfully. 'I take it you're not used to quarrelling with your mother.'

'She's never been unreasonable before. It's always been us against the world and now all of a sudden she's laying down the law like Ernie Clay...'

'That's a bit harsh,' he remonstrated. 'She's not thumping the life out of you, only concerned that you're taking up with the wrong sort of boy.'

'You agree you're the wrong sort?'

'I'm wonderful, but as she doesn't know me yet she might not realise it.'

'Don't you dare take her side.'

He held up his hands as though to ward off a blow. 'I wouldn't dream of it.'

'I'm sorry, I'm in a foul mood.'

'You mean you're not normally all sweetness and light?'

'Beast.'

'At least I got a smile, then, and contrary to expectations it didn't crack your face. I could invite you back to our basement. It's not salubrious, but we have tea and chocolate biscuits if Jack hasn't eaten them all. And before you think your mother was right, and all policemen want to do is have their evil way with young girls, Martin will be there. He was staying in to study tonight.'

'Then we'd disturb him.'

'He always stops working at ten to make tea. If we're quick, he can make one for us. On the other hand if he's delayed for any reason you can make it for the three of us.'

'My mother's right. All men expect women to wait on them hand and foot.'

'If women are prepared to do the waiting, who are we to argue?'

'I'm not prepared to do anything for a man.'

'So I see. Independent young miss prepared to

walk the streets until half past ten just to prove a point with her mother.'

'You think I'm being childish, don't you.'

'Have you noticed the moon tonight? It's a new one.'

'What would you have had me do, allow her to lay down the law and dictate who I can and can't see in my free time?'

'I think you and your mother have some talking to do, which is nothing whatsoever to do with me.'

'That's rubbish. You caused this argument.'

'Me?' He turned an innocent face to hers.

'It wouldn't have happened if you hadn't asked me out.'

'Thanks a bundle. Next time I'll pick the blonde or brunette. Ready for the ride back?' He climbed on to his bike.

'I know, let's go back to my house for tea instead of yours.'

'Me, face your mother after this afternoon? No thanks, I'm a coward.'

'You can't be a coward and a policeman.'

'Frankly, I'd prefer to deal with hardened criminals than independent women. They scare me.'

'Then why did you ask me out?'

'You look softer and sweeter than you are.'

'Tonight's been a disaster all round.'

'It has,' he concurred. 'But if you're very good I might give you another chance. You coming or not?' Waiting until she climbed on the back of his bike, he kick-started the engine and drove slowly out on to Mumbles Road.

Once they left the village behind, he picked up speed. Judy clung to his waist, cold, exposed and absolutely petrified. The wind rushed through her hair, knotting the ends and whipping them painfully against her face; her heart pounded so fast she felt as though it was going to burst from her chest; but oblivious to her fear he raced on, keeping his head down. Her relief was palpable when he slowed to walking pace as they rounded the corner of Craddock Street into Carlton Terrace.

'First time you've been on a bike?' he asked, seeing her tremble as she stepped on to the pavement.

'Second.'

'I wouldn't have thought it.'

'You didn't drive like a lunatic on the way into Mumbles.'

'If by that you mean I drove slower because there was more traffic around, I'd agree. But I do not drive like a lunatic.'

'You terrified me.'

'I gathered you're the nervous type from the way you hung on to me.' He unzipped his jacket and rubbed his waist. 'But don't concern yourself, I'll get my broken ribs strapped up tomorrow.'

'I hung on tight because if I'd fallen off at the speed you were going I would have been mincemeat.'

'I never went over forty miles an hour.'

'It felt more like a hundred.'

'Sorry, didn't know I had a maiden aunt on the back.'

'You set out deliberately to scare me.'

'And make you forget your mother. It worked, didn't it? You coming in for tea?'

She looked down the steps to the door of the basement. A light was shining through the glass fanlight at the top of the door. Someone was at home, hopefully Martin. She could handle him. 'All right.'

'I've had more gracious acceptances, but then you are just marking time until half past ten.' He ran down the steps and opened the door. Martin was standing in the middle of the room cradling a hysterical and sobbing Katie.

'Sorry,' Brian backed out of the door, treading on Judy's foot.

'Please, come in,' Martin pleaded. 'Judy might be able to do something we can't.'

'Men!' Pushing past Brian, Judy took Katie in her arms.

'Roy Williams called.' Martin pulled out a chair for Brian. 'My father went before the magistrates this afternoon. He pleaded guilty to drunk and disorderly, affray, criminal damage and assaulting a police officer. They gave him a two-month prison sentence. Roy said with good behaviour he could be out in four weeks.'

'Joe?' Helen knocked on his bedroom door.

'It's late and I'm trying to study.'

'I won't leave you alone until we talk.'

Setting aside *The Mayor of Casterbridge*, he climbed out of bed and reached for his dressing gown. Slipping it over his vest and pyjama trousers he opened the door. 'If this is about you and Jack...'

'Sh, keep your voice down, Dad might hear.'

'I doubt it. He's fallen asleep on the sofa downstairs. Heaven only knows how, it's about as comfortable as a bed of nails.'

'He did have rather a lot of whisky.'

'Can you blame him?'

'No.'

'Right, you've disturbed me, taken me away from my book and set me back by about three hours' concentration time. What do you want?'

'Your solemn promise that you won't tell a soul about me and Jack.'

'He's into sneaking around, is he?'

'Of course not, but Mum...'

'Isn't here, Helen. And if you ask Dad he may let you go out with Jack, but he may regard you sleeping with him another matter.'

'I...' She choked on her denial.

'I didn't think the underclothes Jack was holding were his.'

'I hoped you hadn't seen them.'

'I couldn't miss them. You didn't waste any time in jumping into the sack with him.'

'There's no need to be crude.'

'How would you phrase it, Helen?'

'I love him we...'

'Want to get married?' he suggested caustically.

'Why not? I'm older than Lily.'

'By two months, but Jack isn't as old as me, doesn't have prospects, or earn enough money to keep you. Think about what you're doing for once in your tiny life.'

'I have thought about it and I do love him,' she countered adamantly.

'Then there's nothing I can say.'

'You won't tell Dad.'

'Not unless I have to.'

'What's that supposed to mean?'

'I'll tell him if he's in any danger of finding out about you two from someone else. But I'd much rather you told him yourself.'

'Everything?'

'You could make a start by asking his permission to go out with Jack.'

'I'll think about it.'

'And if you get pregnant?'

'I won't.'

'How can you be so sure?'

'Because Jack's careful,' she flung back at him as she flounced off to her own room.

After Helen left, Joe tried to return to his book but his concentration had gone and the words on the page were simply so many meaningless symbols. Taking off his dressing gown, he returned to bed, switched off the light, and attempted to banish all thoughts of Jack and his sister from his mind and focus on Lily, the cottage they would buy, the life they would share. When sleep finally came he dreamed he was in the bedroom he had created and making love was even more wonderful than he had imagined it would be. It was only when he drew away from the woman lying beside him that the nightmare began: Angie was in his bed, not Lily, and Lily was standing in the doorway, watching them.

CHAPTER TWENTY

'Angie's complaining like mad because you didn't come to the pool party. She wants to know if you're avoiding her, or me and Emily because of that stupid business with Larry,' Robin said to Joe as they headed for the university cafeteria after their tutorial.

'It's nothing to do with her, you or Larry.'

'She thought because I was with Emily...'

'It's nothing to do with the Murton Davieses,' Joe reiterated impatiently.

'I'm glad to hear it.'

'Although Larry had better stay out of my way when he does come back.'

'Haven't you heard? He's not coming back, not this year. His father persuaded a friend of his who owns a hotel in Italy to give him a job. The official version is Larry is taking a year out to improve his Italian, the unofficial that his parents are hoping the incident with your sister will be forgotten by next September.'

'Not by me.' Joe strode through the door, picked up a tray and joined the queue at the counter.

'So, you coming?' Robin joined him.

'Where?'

'Our next party.'

'I don't have a spare minute these days, between studying and...'

'Why do I get the feeling my sister isn't going to like that "and"?'

'I'm getting engaged.'

Robin burst out laughing.

'I'm serious.'

'Now if it were me and Emily I could understand it.'

'You two still...'

'Does the sun go down every night? And you and your...'

'Lily. You've met her.'

'I have?'

'I suppose I can excuse you, seeing as how you were drunk at the time. The Pier Ballroom.'

'The small, dark girl; the looker?'

'That's the one.'

'Lucky you and poor Angie. When we going out in a foursome?'

'You, me...'

'Lily and Emily.'

'Given that Emily and Angie are best friends, I'd say never.'

'I'm not the sort to allow my sister's disappointment to get between me and my friends. How about showing her off on Saturday night? My parents are throwing a birthday bash for Angie. She'd love to see you even if you won't give her the one present she really wants. And don't give me that excuse about studying, no one studies on Saturdays.'

Joe thought for a moment. 'OK,' he agreed, deciding it was time that Lily met some of his university friends if only to prove they were no more intelligent than her, 'but only if you tell

Angie I'm engaged and bringing my fiancée.'

'Tell her yourself. She's sitting over there. She and Em came up this morning to see something in the history department, history of art and all that, so I arranged to meet them for lunch.'

'A Mr Thomas of Thomas and Butler's called while you were out, Mr Griffiths,' Katie greeted John as he returned to the office from an expensive and substantial lunch with a grateful bank manager anxious to keep the holder of one of his star accounts happy. Business was booming as John had never known it. It was as though the government's lifting of the last rationing restrictions had prompted people to rush out and spend every penny of their savings on all the consumer luxuries that had been denied them for so many years.

'Did he say what he wanted?' John asked, hoping that Esme had finally instructed her family solicitor. He hadn't heard from her since she'd walked out on him over three weeks before, long enough for guilt at asking her to leave to turn to relief that she hadn't returned. A few days after she'd left, he'd walked into the house to find her bedroom door open and her wardrobe and dressing table cleared. As a set of matching luggage had also disappeared from the boxroom, and he hadn't heard anything to the contrary, he assumed she was still with her mother and didn't want to keep contact with him. He knew she telephoned the children on a regular basis but as to their conversations – or meetings between them – Joe and Helen hadn't volunteered any information and he hadn't asked, on the principle that the situation was difficult enough for them as it was, without him piling on any extra pressure.

He, Helen and Joe had slipped into an easy routine. Mealtimes were noisier than when Esme had been home, the food simpler and more substantial. Her elegant 'contemporary' rooms had lost their pristine image as he had allowed Joe and Helen to spread their mess, and he'd even begun to toy with the idea of calling in a decorator to reverse the effects of Esme's modernising and bring the old furniture up from the basement.

'Mr Thomas didn't say, Mr Griffiths, but he left a number and asked if you could telephone him as soon as you came in.'

'Thank you, Katie. Get him on the line and put the call through to my office, please.'

'Yes, Mr Griffiths, and would you like a coffee?'

'That last brandy the bank manager pressed on me that obvious?'

'No, Mr Griffiths, I hope you didn't think...'

'I didn't think anything, Katie, and a black coffee without sugar would be perfect.'

He went into his office, closed the door, sat at his desk and waited for the call. Feeling heartless and callous, he hoped Esme hadn't decided to deny him a divorce. So much had changed since she'd left: Helen had the girls round nearly every evening. Lily split her free time between them and Joe, talking to him after he'd completed his studying for the day, and Jack Clay visited.

Grateful as he was to Jack for rescuing Helen

from Larry Murton Davies, he couldn't approve of his liaison with Helen and had told her so. Not knowing who else to turn to, he'd gone to Roy Williams for advice – not that it was easy to get Roy alone since he'd asked the widowed Mrs Lannon to live in and be his housekeeper. She had been only too delighted to oblige, popping between her own house and Roy's during the day and taking possession of the spare bedroom on the same floor Lily and Katie slept on at night, and, incidentally, as much of Lily's, Katie's and Roy's lives as she could interfere with. But all Roy would say on the subject was 'forbidden fruits are always the sweetest'. The inference was obvious – if he didn't allow Helen to see Jack she'd only go sneaking behind his back. Unable to come up with a better solution, he and Helen had settled for an uneasy truce. But it wouldn't only be Jack's visits that would be curtailed if Esme returned. Joe was happy with Lily...

The telephone rang and he picked it up. 'John Griffiths.'

'John, it's Richard Thomas. I'll cut straight to the chase. Esme has instructed me to handle her divorce and you needn't worry about your daughter seeing the files. I've told my secretary to mark them confidential for her and my eyes only.'

'Fine, I...'

'I need the name of your man.'

'Martin Davies.'

'A wise choice.' John instantly hated him for being patronising. 'Esme says you're prepared to admit adultery.'

'To speed things up, yes. There isn't...'

'I'll contact Martin today and fix a date for us to thrash out the details of the settlement. Tell him to pass on the evidence as soon as he has it.'

The line went dead. John stared at the receiver in his hand, scarcely daring to believe that it was going to be so simple.

'Congratulations.'

Joe, Emily and Robin studied Angela, looking for signs of sarcasm or insincerity, but there were none. Her smile was open, her eyes sparkling with warmth. Then Emily recalled Angie's performance in the sixth form production of *Macbeth* and remembered what a consummate actress she could be when she chose.

'Thank you,' Joe said, grateful Angela had taken the news so well after their last meeting.

'I've invited Joe and...'

'Lily,' Angie supplied, widening her smile.

'Lily, to your birthday bash, sis.'

'How marvellous. You will come?' Angela asked Joe.

'If it's all right with you.'

'I can't wait to meet her. It will be quite informal; Pops has hired this new skiffle group everyone is raving about. Well, Em and I must be off if we're going to make our life-drawing class. We're still looking for a male model to volunteer for a private showing,' she teased.

'I hope you find one.' Joe returned her smile.

'I'm sure I will.' She kissed his cheek as she left the table, 'And that's one I'm sure your Lily won't miss, seeing as how she got her man.'

'You tidied the salon quickly.' Joy noted the neatly folded towels and scrubbed sinks. 'Have you done the trolley?'

'Yes, and sterilised all the curlers, hairbrushes, combs and scissors, and washed as well as swept the floor.'

'You're going out with that boy again.'

'His name is Brian and yes, I am.'

'Do you have time for a cup of tea and a sandwich?'

Judy glanced at the clock. 'No. I've arranged to meet Brian at two and it's ten to now.'

'You get these half-days off to study, not to go out with boys.'

'I get them to make up for the hours I spend in night school,' Judy corrected.

'It's important I talk to you.'

'Brian's shift starts at eight, I'll be home before then.'

Joy watched her daughter walk out of the door. It had taken her weeks to decide that Judy had a right to know her father was alive. She only hoped she wouldn't lose the courage to tell her before Judy gave her a chance to talk, because if she and Roy were ever going to get together again, she knew it would only be when she could go to him with the news that she had finally laid all her lies – and ghosts – to rest. And it had taken the emptiness generated by Roy's absence for her to realise just how vitally important he was to her life and happiness.

'Come in, Miss Griffiths.'

Nerves stretched to breaking point, Helen

437

entered Richard Thomas's office. He rarely bothered with any of the office staff, leaving day-to-day administration to the senior secretaries and Philip Butler, but when she saw Mr Butler, wearing an uncharacteristically sombre expression, sitting alongside Mr Thomas she feared the worst.

'Miss Evans said you wanted to see me, sir.'

'Mr Thomas, not "sir", Miss Griffiths, you have been with us now for one month. It is time for your review. Come closer.'

'Yes, Mr Thomas.' As no chair had been placed for her, she continued to stand, feeling just as intimidated as she had done when she'd been sent to the headmistress's study for punishment in school.

Richard Thomas flicked through the papers on his desk. 'I see you managed to misplace several clients' files.'

'That was only in the first week...'

He glared at her above his half-moon reading glasses. 'I am not unaware of your misdemeanours, Miss Griffiths, no matter what the rest of my staff have led you to believe. I am also neither blind nor deaf, not even to the efficiency or otherwise of the office junior. And as this is a review of your performance in Thomas and Butler, procedure dictates that you will answer either yes or no to my questions, not one word more. You will be given an opportunity to speak when I have finished. Understood?'

'Yes, Mr Thomas.'

'To continue, you misplaced several clients' files?'

438

'Yes, Mr Thomas.' She wondered how he had found out. Isabel had assured her that no one would tell him, as everyone else in the office knew juniors needed time to settle in.

'You jammed the switchboard when you relieved the telephonist during her lunch hour?' He fell silent, evidently waiting for an answer. Mr Butler gave her a sympathetic smile but after four weeks in Thomas and Butler she knew Mr Butler carried no weight in the firm. She also realised that if Mr Thomas had been cataloguing her errors, that particular one could have been picked up by anyone trying to contact the office.

'Yes, Mr Thomas.'

'The senior secretary has had occasion to reprimand you several times about dirty teacups. I overheard her speaking to you,' he added, in case she should dare to try to contradict him.

'Yes, Mr Thomas.'

'There are other misdemeanours mentioned in your file, but the ones I have outlined are sufficient to give you a formal reprimand. We will review your situation in two weeks. If you have made no effort to improve your performance during the intervening time we will have no option but to let you go.'

'Yes, Mr Thomas but...'

'But?' He glared as he interrupted her.

'I have been making a real effort this last week, Mr Thomas.'

'Evidently not enough for us to notice, Miss Griffiths. Have you anything else to say in your defence?'

She racked her brains, but all she could come

up with was that her father would be dis-appointed if she lost the job and she could imagine the sneering comment Mr Thomas would make if she tried that one. 'Only that I will try harder, Mr Thomas.'

'Seeing is believing. Miss Griffiths. You may go.'

'Yes, Mr Thomas.' Helen closed the door behind her as she left the room.

'You didn't give her an opportunity to defend herself,' Philip Butler remonstrated, as he rose from his chair and carried it to its customary place against the wall.

'There is no defence against sloppy work, Philip.'

'It's her first job.'

'And you're a sentimentalist.'

'Perhaps I could ask Isabel to keep a closer eye on her, help her...'

'And waste Isabel's valuable time, that we pay dearly for, to supervise the lowest-paid member of staff in the organisation? I think not, Philip. If you are to succeed in this highly competitive profession it is not enough to merely know the law and win in court; you also have to think like a businessman. Now, if you'll excuse me I have a heavy workload.'

Leaving the stack of files unopened in his 'in tray' Richard continued to sit, staring into space, after Philip left. One of the first things he had discovered on becoming a solicitor was the pleasure to be gained by studying the office girls and, to use the colloquial term, young Helen Griffiths was a 'ripe little piece', much the same as her mother had been at that age. He had always been attracted to the type – blue-eyed, well-built blondes with a healthy outdoor look about them – and he'd enjoyed seeing her around the office. But a totally unexpected pang of conscience after calling in on Esme to discuss her divorce and finding Joseph visiting her had led him to reconsider the situation. Afterwards, he'd decided it would be better for everyone concerned if Helen Griffiths left Thomas and Butler, not least because she was his son's half-sister and her presence reminded him of his affair with Esme and – although he was loath to admit it even to himself – because it made him feel uneasy, as though he and the girl were related – he was even beginning to dream about seducing her.

John Griffiths would be disappointed but he would soften the blow by putting the word out and finding the girl a position in another office. And it wasn't as if he had fabricated the evidence against her. She was undeniably attractive, but she was also careless and slapdash. Another position would suit her better, preferably one where her slip-ups wouldn't matter quite so much, one of the estate agents on Walter Road, perhaps: less pressure all round and the girl would be happier.

Easing his conscience with that thought, he lifted the topmost file from the stack and opened it: Griffiths versus Griffiths – petition for divorce.

'You all right?' Isabel Evans asked, when Helen dropped a teacup on the floor of their small kitchen area.

441

'Yes.'

'Really?' Isabel pressed, as Helen took a dustpan and brush from the cleaner's cupboard and began sweeping up the fragments.

'I've just had my review. It wasn't good.'

'We've all been through it, Helen. Mr Thomas's bark is far worse than his bite.'

Helen recalled the look in his eye as he'd threatened to let her go and wasn't quite so convinced.

'You don't have to...'

'I don't mind, Mr Griffiths, really,' Katie insisted. 'If I help out with the booking in and tagging now, the Christmas toys can be on the shop floor tomorrow morning.'

'I thought you girls were going to a dance tonight. Helen's been talking about nothing else all week.'

'It's only in the youth club, Mr Griffiths, hardly a special occasion. Helen's probably only been talking about it because Jack's group are playing.'

'Well, it would be a help if you stayed on,' John agreed, not too reluctantly because the warehouse manager and half the shop-floor girls had been press-ganged into working late and there was little likelihood of him being left alone with Katie, unless he offered her a lift home. 'Hadn't you better telephone your young man to let him know you'll be late?' he suggested, reassured by the thought of Adam Jordan. Helen had told him that Adam was madly in love with Katie and if that were really the case, then it really was time he forgot all about the kiss Katie had given him.

'I'll telephone Lily, Mr Griffiths. She'll let the

442

others know.'

'And Adam Jordan?' He smiled.

'We're just friends.'

'Sorry,' John apologised as she sorted the relevant paperwork, 'but I thought...'

'There's nothing between us,' Katie protested more emphatically than he'd ever heard her speak before, 'nothing at all.'

'I wish I could go to the dance with you tonight.'

'So do I.' Judy curled next to Brian on his bed. She knew her mother would be furious if she suspected that she and Brian indulged in what the magazines called 'petting sessions' in Brian's bedroom when Martin and Jack were out, but it was comfortable – and safe – now she had firmly established her ground rules with him.

'You going with Lily and the others?'

'You don't expect me to sit in and mope just because you're on duty, do you?'

'No.'

'Yes, you do.' She looked up at him. 'I can see it in your face.'

'What time does it finish?'

'You only want me to tell you so you can turn up in your uniform and escort me home like some criminal.'

'The thought had crossed my mind. I could even escort you down to the station. We've always an empty cell or two. I could lock you up and...' Wrapping his arms round her, he nuzzled the nape of her neck.

'...Forget about me?'

'You are the least romantic girl I have ever met.'

'But a brilliant kisser.' Linking her arms round him, she kissed him long and satisfyingly.

'You ever think of the future?' he asked, sliding his hands under her sweater and into her unclipped brassiere, the one liberty she allowed him to take.

'All the time. I qualify in January.'

'And?'

'I've applied for a job with the BBC. I want to be a make-up and hair stylist.'

'In Alexandra Road.'

'Think about it, they don't need make-up artists and stylists for radio.'

'Cardiff?' he asked cautiously.

'London.'

'London!' Pushing her aside, he sat up.

'I haven't got it yet.'

'And if you do?'

'I'll move up there.'

'And us?'

'Us? Brian you're twenty-one, I'm eighteen.'

'The same age as Lily and Joe.'

'They're idiots. I have absolutely no intention of getting married until I'm thirty.'

'Thirty! You're mad.'

'What's mad about it? Women can manage very well without a man to run round after. I want a career that will bring in enough money for me to live comfortably so I can have a lot more fun than my mother who was housebound at eighteen with a child and widowed at twenty-eight.'

'That was because of the war.'

'Which was started by stupid men.'

'I thought...'

444

'That we'd get married?' Kneeling on the bed, she struggled to fasten her bra and tuck her blouse back into her skirt.

'Eventually, yes,' he admitted seriously.

'And how eventually is eventually?'

'Six months, maybe a year.'

'What is it with you boys? Girls are supposed to be the ones who want the wedding rings but from what I can see you lot can't wait. Joe with Lily, Jack with Helen and he hasn't even done his National Service.'

'Now I agree with you there. They are being stupid.'

'No more than you, expecting me to forget my training to walk up the aisle with you. I'm in no hurry to contract out the rest of my life to cleaning, cooking, scrubbing and having babies.'

'Marriage doesn't have to be like that these days. You could work if you want to.'

'Where, in my mother's salon?'

'It's where you work now.'

'It's where I train and I have no intention of staying there. I want a life.'

'You think I don't?'

'I don't want a policeman's wife's life in Swansea, Brian.'

He swallowed hard as her words hit painfully home. 'And London is going to be so much more exciting?' he mocked.

'I don't know, but I hope so and I think it's worth going there to find out.'

'So these past few weeks you've been marking time with me. Amusing yourself until you go to London.'

'And you haven't been amusing yourself with me?' she challenged furiously.

'Apparently not in the same way,' he answered coldly.

'Brian...'

He left the bed and opened the door. 'I think you'd better go, now, before one of us says something we'll both regret.'

She looked at him for a moment. 'This is it, we're over because I won't agree to marry you in the next six months?'

'You finished it, not me.'

She flounced off the bed. 'Go find yourself a nice little "yes" girl who can't wait to get a wedding ring on her finger,' she snapped as she walked past him, 'but if I were you I'd try the Arabian slave market first. You obviously haven't heard that women in Britain are emancipated now.'

'You don't have to keep coming to the youth club with me,' Lily said, as Joe escorted her from the dance floor to a trestle table laid out with orange juices, lemonade and crisps.

'I know and that's why I'm taking you to a party on Saturday. It's time you met my university friends. I want to show you off before our engagement. You haven't changed your mind about asking your Uncle Roy, have you?'

'No, he's on afternoons this week. I thought I'd tell him about us when I go back tonight.'

'Want me to come in with you?'

'I'd rather you didn't.'

'Because he might be difficult.'

'Because it might be a bit of a shock.'

'Surely not after all the time we've spent together the last few weeks.'

'Perhaps it won't come as much of a shock to him as it did to me on the day you asked me to marry you.'

'What do you think? Engagement next week-end and July wedding after my finals?'

'Sounds perfect.' She smiled.

Tossing a shilling on to the dish holding the money, he picked up two orange juices and led her to the back of the hall. 'We haven't talked about where you'd like to go for our honeymoon.'

'Anywhere would be perfect, it only matters that I'm with you.'

'London, Cornwall, Scotland, Ireland, France...'

'France!'

'Why not, and please don't mention the expense. We have enough money.'

'Surprise me.'

'I may do just that.' Taking her empty paper cup, he crunched it together with his own and threw them into a litter bin. 'Want to stay?'

'Not particularly.'

'My father's working late, Helen's here, how would you like to come back to my house for half an hour?'

'I'd like to.' She slipped her hand into his. 'Very much indeed.'

'I thought you weren't going to the dance,' Joy sniped as Judy ran downstairs in a new straight skirt and skin-tight black polo-neck sweater that she disapproved of, but had remained silent

447

about, on the premise that it was better keep her condemnation for larger transgressions – like Brian. 'I changed my mind.'

'Brian changed shifts?'

'No.'

'Judy, I really do need to talk to you.'

'Later, Mam. I want to get in the hall before they close it to latecomers.'

'Adam, I had no idea you were waiting out here.' John dumped the boxes he'd carried out to the cage where the warehouse paper rubbish was kept for collection by the refuse department. 'If you'd knocked you could have come in. But please, come in now.' He opened the door and ushered Adam inside.

'Lily said Katie was working late. I thought I'd meet her to see if she still wanted to go to the dance.'

'Katie.' John called her over from the rack where she was checking the last batch of teddy bears to go out on the floor. 'Adam's here, if you'd like to go with him...'

'No, it's all right, Mr Griffiths, I don't mind finishing up here.'

'There's barely half an hour's work left, thanks to you. The shop-floor girls, Mr Harris and I can do the rest. I insist you go.'

'The dance is on until ten thirty,' Adam interrupted. 'If we hurry we can be there by half past nine. I thought you'd like to hear Jack play.'

'I'll get my coat,' Katie agreed unenthusiastically.

John watched her as she left the warehouse and

448

climbed the stairs to the office. She suddenly seemed subdued, flat, totally unlike the girl he thought he had come to know so well and was at pains to keep his distance from.

'Lift at eight o'clock tomorrow?' he asked as she returned downstairs.

'Yes, please, Mr Griffiths.'

'And remind Helen she has to be home by eleven, whether your brother has packed up all his equipment or not.'

'I will, Mr Griffiths, goodnight.'

'You angry because I came to get you?' Adam asked as they walked away from the warehouse.

'There's a rush on to get the new Christmas stock on the shop floor; Mr Griffiths could do with all the help he can get.'

'He said you could go.'

'Only because he's too nice for his own good. My leaving now probably means he won't get away for another hour or two.'

'It is his business,' Adam reminded her.

'And my job, and I happen to like it.'

'It's obvious he thinks a lot of you, so he's hardly likely to sack you.'

'That's not the point. He gave me a chance to prove what I could do when no one else would. He deserves my loyalty.'

'Please, Katie, let's not quarrel. Look, there's a bus. If we hop on it we'll save ourselves a ten-minute walk uphill.'

'This sofa is the most uncomfortable I've ever sat on.'

'Most definitely.' Joe moved closer to Lily and kissed her again.

'On the other hand the sofa in Helen's room is comfortable. Why are you looking at me like that?'

'Just wondering how well acquainted you are with the sofa in the basement.'

'I've sat there often enough with Helen.'

'Sorry, yes, of course you have.' Cupping her face in his hands, he kissed her again. She moved even closer, slipping her hands beneath his sweater.

'Any more of that from you and we'll be having our wedding night nine months early.'

'We haven't talked about that.'

'Yes, we have. You agreed tonight that our honeymoon was to be my surprise to you.'

'I mean about how far we should go before our wedding night,' she said shyly. They had talked about just every other aspect of life –money, houses, furnishings, food, pets, even children, but never sex. Lily had discovered while she'd still been in school that Norah had been far more open with her than most mothers with their daughters, explaining not only the sexual act itself, but the emotions it generated and how important a slow courtship and a gradual awakening of the senses was to a satisfactory married life. But Joe had never done any more than kiss her. And although she was the first of her friends to get engaged, Helen's inability to keep a secret and Judy's frank admission that she often removed her blouse and brassiere for Brian had led her to believe that she and Katie lagged behind the rest of the group.

It wouldn't have worried her if Joe had discussed his reluctance to go any further. But even when they were alone, their lovemaking remained oddly chaste and Norah's lessons had made her wonder if he was expecting too much from her on their wedding night.

'You think we should make love before we're married?' He looked and sounded shocked at the suggestion.

'I think we should talk about it.'

'What's there to talk about, Lily? You're a decent girl and decent girls don't jump into bed before they're married, and if you're thinking of Helen and Jack, I've had severe words with her about her behaviour in that department.'

'I just...'

'What?' he asked sharply.

'Don't want to disappoint you when the time comes.'

'You couldn't.' He moved closer again to reassure her. 'There hasn't been anyone else, has there?'

'You know there hasn't,' she answered, concerned about his constant need for reassurance. 'What about you?'

He thought of Angela, the night of Robin's party when he had seen her breasts and afterwards – the night in the shrubbery when she had touched him.

'No, please, I didn't mean to ask that question.'

'You have every right to. I told you there had been other girls but I haven't been to bed with any of them, or been naked with them.'

'I didn't mean to pry.'

'Lily, you're going to be my wife and it's only right we tell one another everything.' Kissing her again, he moved his hand over her sweater to her breast, but his touch was so light that she could barely feel it. 'Don't you see, darling, any more than this will detract from our wedding night and I want that to be perfect.'

CHAPTER TWENTY-ONE

'No!' Katie pushed Adam away as he tried to kiss her. Running ahead, she walked on quickly down the street.

Following her, Adam grabbed her by the shoulders and pulled her towards him. 'I don't understand you.' He hadn't meant to be rough but his irritation – and temper – escalated as he sensed her recoiling from him. 'All I want is a goodnight kiss. Is that too much to ask? We've been going out together...'

'We are not going out together!' His anger, his height, even the way he was standing over her reminded her of her father and she instinctively drew closer to a house with lights burning in the front windows.

'What have we been doing, then?'

'I've been going out with Lily, Helen and Judy.'

'But you're walking home with me.'

'Only because Lily left early with Joe, and Helen and Judy stayed to help Jack.'

'So I'm only all right to go around with when your friends aren't available.'

'I didn't ask you to come to the warehouse tonight to pick me up.' His indignation spawned a resentment that welled into anger. 'And who are you, Adam Jordan, to tell me I should kiss you, just because you offered to walk me home?'

Taken aback by her uncharacteristic outburst, he reached out and touched her shoulder. 'Katie, let's not argue.'

'If you want me to be your friend, fine, but that's all I'll be.' She knocked his hand away. 'There'll be no kissing or mauling...'

'Mauling!'

'I can't stand you touching me.'

'Then there's something wrong with you.'

'Only where you're concerned.'

'And you wait until now to tell me. You've known all along that I wanted more than friendship from you.'

'I made it clear from the first time you asked me to dance that there couldn't be anything else between us.'

'You led me on...'

'If I did it was unintentional.' She looked at him, seeing hurt pride and a strange vulnerability she had never thought boys capable of possessing – except perhaps Jack. She searched her mind for something to say that would appease him. 'Adam, you'll find someone else...'

'Spare me the bloody patronising lecture. Thanks for nothing,' he shouted, too angry to care who was listening as he strode off ahead of her.

'I couldn't be more pleased for you, love, or sadder that Norah won't be here to see it.'

'You don't think it would be disrespectful to her memory for Joe and me to hold an engagement party so soon after Auntie Norah's funeral, Uncle Roy?'

'No, love, Joe's a fine boy, she would have approved. My only concern is you're both a bit young, but' – he smiled as an apprehensive look crossed her face – 'Norah did bring you up to be older than your years.'

'Thank you.' She kissed his cheek.

'We'll organise the party here for as soon as you want it. Can you girls do the food or do you want me to ask Mrs Lannon?'

'We can manage, Uncle Roy.' Something in her tone told Roy that things weren't getting any easier between her and the housekeeper he'd hired.

'Katie, come in,' Roy called as she opened the front door. 'I'm just going to open the sherry. Lily's getting engaged to Joe.'

'That's good news.' Katie tried to smile, but Lily saw her lip tremble.

'What's wrong?'

'Nothing.'

'Funny nothing that makes you cry,' Lily murmured as Roy went into the dining room to fetch the sherry.

'I'm not crying, just angry with Adam for making me lose my temper.'

'I knew you two weren't getting along all that well.'

'I wanted him to be a friend, like you, Judy and Helen...'

'But he wanted more.'

'Much more, all that kissing and pawing.' Katie shuddered. 'It was horrible. I should never have let him walk me home.' She smiled determinedly. 'But he won't ask again. It's fantastic news about you and Joe. You will be having a party?'

'We most certainly will,' Roy confirmed, carrying in a tray that held the sherry decanter and three glasses.

'And I'll need all the help you, Judy and Helen can give me.'

'Sausage rolls.'

'Sandwiches.'

'Fairy cakes,' Roy suggested as he filled the glasses.

'We're not three years old.' Lily laughed. 'This is going to be a grown-up party with grown-up food.'

'And grown-up drinks?' Roy enquired warily.

'Beer for the boys if they want it; we're over eighteen.' Lily took the sherry he handed her.

'I am a policeman, love.'

'I promise you, no one will get drunk.'

'I'll hold you to that.' He made a mental note to check that Brian received an invitation just in case.

'Lily?'

'Mm.' Lily turned sleepily towards Katie but didn't open her eyes.

'You don't think there's anything wrong with me, do you?'

'In what way?' Lily mumbled.

'Not wanting Adam to kiss or touch me.'

'I think you have to be in love to enjoy a boy's kisses.'

'He said I led him on.'

'Did you?'

'I walked home with him a couple of times when you weren't around but I never told him I liked him or agreed to go out with him – just the two of us, that is.'

'He's good-looking.'

'I think that's part of the problem. He's used to getting his own way with girls and that first time in the Pier after he came home I couldn't help feeling that he picked me out instead of Helen or Judy because he thought I'd be grateful that a catch like him should even notice me.'

'So you never liked him?'

'Not enough to want him to kiss me.'

Lily sighed sleepily as she turned over. 'There's nothing wrong with you that falling in love won't cure. You'll meet the right one, Katie, I'm sure of it. Now I have to get some sleep. Big day tomorrow, interview for a typist's job.'

As Lily snuggled down, Katie buried her face in her pillow. She suspected that she had already met the right one. He was old enough to be her father and married but that didn't prevent her from remembering – and dreaming. She touched her lips, recalling the kiss she had given him. Had it been her imagination or had he responded – just a little?

'You've nerve, Miss Sullivan, I'll give you that.

456

Most juniors are content to be just that – junior for at least eighteen months'

'But I can do the job of shorthand typist, Mr Hopkin Jones. I know I can,' Lily dared to interrupt, lowering her voice, not wanting to sound too desperate.

'I rather suspect you can.' He looked to the assistant manager and office supervisor who were sitting beside him. 'Miss Oliver? Mr Collins?'

'A month's trial?' Miss Oliver suggested.

'I agree.' Mr Collins smiled at Lily.

Trying to forget his high-handed, arrogant treatment of her, Lily returned his smile.

'You're the living embodiment of "ask and thou shalt receive", young lady. If you hadn't gone to Miss Oliver requesting an interview for this post you would have been overlooked. However, if you disappoint us at the end of four weeks you'll be back at everyone's beck and call for another year.'

'Yes, Mr Hopkin Jones.' Lily fought the urge to leave her chair and dance around the office, and tried to look suitably sombre as befitted a newly promoted shorthand typist.

'We'll advertise for a new junior – Miss Oliver?'

'I'll see to it, Mr Hopkin Jones.'

'It may take a week or two to find someone. I trust it won't be beneath your dignity to carry out some of your present duties until then, Miss Sullivan?'

'No, Mr Hopkin Jones.' Sensing she'd been dismissed, Lily rose from her seat. 'Thank you, Mr Hopkin Jones, Mr Collins, Miss Oliver.'

'Miss Sullivan?' Mr Hopkin Jones called her back from the door.

'Yes, Mr Hopkin Jones.'

'Congratulations.'

'Promise you won't leave me alone,' Lily pleaded as Joe parked his father's Rover next to Robin's sports car in the courtyard in front of the Watkin Morgan house.

'Don't tell me the audacious girl who shocked her colleagues by asking for – and getting – promotion is frightened of meeting new people.'

'These people, yes.' Lily glanced at the substantial turn-of-the-century villa that had taken on the proportions of a mansion to her inexperienced eye.

'Don't worry.' He tilted up her chin and kissed her. 'They're only human and by the end of the evening they'll all love you as much as I do.' Leaving the car, he walked round to the passenger side to open the door for her.

'Joseph, I'm so glad you could come.' Angela walked out to meet him with Emily in tow. They were both resplendent in evening frocks that even Joe recognised as haute couture. Angela's was a blue silk with a diamante-ornamented bodice; Emily's a red chiffon, embroidered with jet beading.

So much for informal, Joe thought, already regretting his lounge suit and his directive to Lily 'keep it simple.' Extending his hand to Lily he helped her out of the car. 'Lily, I'd like you to meet, Angela Watkin Morgan, and Emily...' He deliberately omitted the 'Murton Davies.'

Straightening the skirt of the simple white cotton shirtwaister, Katie had helped her pick out in Joe's father's warehouse, Lily felt like a dowdy country cousin, as first Angela, then Emily, kissed her cheek.

'Joseph, she's charming.' Angela surveyed Lily from the tip of her white stilettos, to the top of her dark hair brushed into a simple chignon at the nape of her neck, guessing the cost of Lily's outfit with more accuracy than Lily herself could have hazarded. 'You're a lucky man. And such a pretty dress, Lily. I think simplicity never goes entirely out of fashion no matter what Vogue says. Please, call me, Angie,' she directed, linking her arm into Lily's. 'I've heard all about you from Joseph and my brother Robin and I'm sure we're going to be great friends. Now, let me show you to my bedroom so we can indulge in some girl talk while you check your make-up.'

Joe shrugged his shoulders helplessly at the backward pleading look Lily gave him as Angela and Emily swept her inside the house and up the stairs.

'Game?' Robin was lounging in the doorway of the billiards room; cue in one hand, the inevitable glass of whisky in the other.

'I promised Lily I'd stay with her.'

'Stay with a girl! At a party!'

'She doesn't know anyone here,' Joe demurred.

'Em and Angie will take care of her. You have serious drinking to catch up on.'

'Later...'

'I'll not take no for an answer. Michael, George, Alan,' Robin called for reinforcements who had no compunction about pulling Joe into the room. 'We're playing for whisky. Loser has to drink as many inches as the winner dictates.'

'Seems to me, you've already lost a few,' Joe commented as Alan rather forcefully helped him off with his jacket and Michael passed him a cue.

'Quite spectacularly,' Robin slurred.

'I'll play you one game, no more. Then I'm going to look for Lily and investigate the food. And you've any sense, you'll come with me.'

'Borrow anything you want,' Angela offered generously as Lily stared at the array of perfume bottles and cosmetics on the white and gilt, French Empire style dressing table. Lily had always thought Helen had more things than she could possibly use in one lifetime. Angela's jars and bottles were not only more numerous, but marked with names she had only ever read in magazines. *Chanel, Dior, Balmain...*

'We're so envious of you catching the handsome Joseph,' Emily purred. 'He's such a dish and so polite and helpful, not at all like the rest of the boys. Do anything for anyone, won't he Angie?'

'He's a darling,' Angie concurred. 'Oh, but then perhaps you didn't know, Lily. Joseph and I were together.'

'He's told me all about his other girlfriends,' Lily murmured, not entirely truthfully.

'*All?*' Angela raised her eyebrows. 'I hope not *all*. But then, the magazine agony aunts do say honesty is the best policy before embarking on an engagement. What do you think, Emily, do you tell Robin *all?*'

Emily burst into peals of laughter. 'What a silly question.'

460

'I suppose it is when it's put to you.' Angela lifted Lily's stole from the stool where she'd left it, while she checked her hair. 'I'll lay this on the bed.'

Lily looked at the bed buried beneath a mound of handbags, hats, fur coats and stoles.

'I'll take it downstairs with me, if you don't mind. Just in case I get cold.' Lily's thoughts were already turning to the journey home. She didn't want to leave anything in Angela's bedroom that might delay her retreat.

'Joseph's fiancée, Lily–'

'Sullivan,' Lily offered quietly.

'So glad you could come, dear.' Mrs Watkin Morgan frowned slightly as Angela abandoned Lily to follow Emily into the sun lounge where the skiffle group were playing. Her husband and his friends had taken possession of his study, tactfully leaving the billiard room for the younger male element. Her female friends were ensconced with bottles of sherry and bridge tables in the drawing room. It had been tacitly understood that the hall, sitting rooms, sun lounge and den were the province of the young people, and the dining room where the buffet had been laid out, common territory open to all groups. The problem was, she couldn't see any young people free to offload Lily on to.

Sensing her hostess's dilemma, Lily murmured, 'If you'll excuse me, Mrs Watkin Morgan, I'll look for Joe.'

'He's in the billiard room with my son Robin, dear, and I wouldn't go in there if I were you.

Masculine preserve,' she hissed in a stage whisper. 'Richard,' she greeted Richard Thomas as he walked through the front door. 'How kind of you to bring Philip and Amelia.'

'None of us could bear to miss one of your events, darling, even Richard's wife and the poor love's at death's door. I practically had to tie her to her bed to keep her from coming with us.' Amelia Butler kissed Mrs Watkin Morgan's cheek.

'Neuralgia?'

'She sends her apologies,' Richard kissed his hostess. 'Where is the birthday girl?'

'Dancing. Philip, why don't you take, Miss...'

'Lily,' Lily broke in.

'Lily, to the buffet,' Mrs Watkin Morgan smiled. 'She must be famished and Mrs John will be so cross if there's anything left on the table at the end of the evening.'

'My pleasure.' Philip offered Lily his arm. 'You're a friend of Angie's?' he asked as he led her into the dining room.

'No.'

'I wondered why you looked slightly lost when we came in.'

'I'm here with my boyfriend, Joe – Joseph Griffiths, do you know him?'

'Only as a name on a client file, I work in Thomas and Butler...'

Richard watched through the doorway as Philip moved around the buffet, heaping delicacies on to his own and Lily's plate, more sociable than he ever was in the office.

'Who is the girl?' he asked Mrs Watkin Morgan.

'A Lily something or other. Joseph Griffiths is engaged to her – or will be in a week.'

'I sense disapproval.' He tried to sound disinterested, although he'd had the full story from Esme, plus copious details of how much and why she disapproved of her son's liaison.

'There's no denying she is pretty.' She gave a theatrical sigh. 'Such a shame, he's such a sweet boy and she ... well, for all that look of wide-eyed, fresh-faced, innocence, you can see there's no real education or breeding there. And not much in the way of conversation either, she hardly has two words to say for herself. I dread to think what she'll be like when she's twenty-five with nothing but her fading looks to fall back on. She'll become – well–'

'Common?' Unlike his hostess, Richard had no compunction about saying the word. 'When and where is the engagement party?'

'Next Saturday in her house, she lives next door to Joseph. Robin will go, he can hardly do otherwise as Joseph has asked him to be best man when they marry next July but I can't pretend I'm pleased about it. Would you believe Emily has volunteered to go as well, such a sweet girl. I'm sorry about the noise,' she said, apologetically as the door to the sun lounge opened. 'Angie insisted on hiring one of those ghastly, tinny skiffle groups. All wash boards and broom handles with strings. My husband caved in of course, he always does when it comes to Angie. But you know fathers and their daughters.'

'Fortunately for my peace of mind and wallet, I

463

don't.' Richard took a glass of champagne from one of the waiters. 'I see no sign of Joseph Griffiths, he can't think a great deal of his fiancée to leave her alone at a party where she knows no one.'

'Robin enticed him into the billiard room.'

Richard smiled. His son was in the next room. 'His son.' The phrase had an odd ring and a peculiar effect on his consciousness. Strange how Esme and her family had suddenly reappeared in his life. Although she had asked him to handle her divorce, she had taken care to let him know that she had no desire to renew their acquaintance on a more intimate level, but there was no denying their past – or the product of it. All he had to do was walk into the next room, start a conversation and he'd be talking to his son. But first he decided to take another look at the girl Joseph Griffiths had become mixed up with. A girl he had even sounder reasons than Esme to think unsuitable.

'Aren't you going to introduce me, Philip?'

Philip looked at Richard in surprise. 'Lily Sullivan, Mr Richard Thomas.'

'How do you do.' Richard held Lily's hand fractionally longer than necessary. Unlike Esme, he could see why a young man would be attracted to the girl. Pity. Given the right pedigree...

'Mr Thomas is the senior partner at Thomas and Butler, where I work, Lily.'

'What Philip is trying to tell you is that I'm his boss.' Richard took a couple of smoked salmon canapés from the buffet and dropped one on to her plate. 'You must try this. No one makes a canapé like the Watkin Morgans' cook.'

'Thank you.' Lily moved closer to Philip Butler. Helen had told Lily that Richard Thomas made her flesh creep; now she'd met him she understood why.

'So, Lily, are you a modern woman?'

'I'm not sure what you mean by that, Mr Thomas.'

'I was asking if you work.'

'Yes, in a bank.'

'Ah, a clerk.'

'Shorthand typist, Mr Thomas.'

'Don't know how you bright young things keep all those squiggles in your head or move your fingers around so quickly on your typewriters. Dexterity, eh, Philip?' He nudged Philip in the ribs. 'See you later.' He headed for the billiard room.

'You don't like smoked salmon?' Philip asked as Lily left it lying, untouched, at the side of her plate.

'No.'

'And I take it you haven't been in this house before?'

'No.'

Taking her plate together with his own, he laid them on a side table. 'I'll give you the grand tour. It's a pity it's so dark and dismal outside, the gardens are worth seeing, especially in spring and summer.'

'Cigars?' Richard pulled a handful of tubes from

his coat pocket and distributed them among the young men in the billiard room.

'Thank you, sir. Whisky?' Robin picked up the decanter.

'If it's your father's, yes, he knows how to buy a good malt. Please don't let me interrupt you. Only called in to escape the crush outside.' As George returned to the table he moved closer to Joe. 'How are your mother and grandmother?'

'Well, thank you, Mr Thomas.' Joe recalled Robin's warning about Richard Thomas's loose tongue and prepared himself for derogatory comments about Helen's slipshod work, or his parents' impending divorce.

'I heard you on the radio. You sounded so professional I couldn't believe it when your grandmother mentioned it was your debut.' Clamping a hand across Joe's shoulders, Richard led him to a couple of chairs at the window end of the room. 'Tell me, do you have aspirations to a career in broadcasting? Because if you do, I might be able to recommend you to a couple of fellows I know...'

'Do you mind if I show Lily the Minton-tiled sculleries, Mrs Watkin Morgan?'

'Not at all, dear.' Mrs Watkin Morgan's attention was fixed on the sun lounge. Angela was dancing with a perfectly presentable boy from a sociably acceptable if dull family, but she knew her daughter had set her heart on Joseph Griffiths. And the particular young man she was with had no trust fund – or at least not one substantial enough to be talked about. Turning back, she smiled at Lily, 'Philip is *the* expert on this house. His grandfather built it in 1898. Why don't you take advantage of his knowledge and get him to give you the full conducted tour?'

'I couldn't possibly...'

'Of course you could, dear, we're quite proud of this little pile of bricks and mortar although Philip's grandfather, not Mr Watkin Morgan, has to take credit for putting them together. And don't forget the old servants' quarters in the attic, Philip,' she called out, as he led Lily in the direction of the pantries and sculleries. 'Ignore the dust and neglect, and look out of the windows. The view from up there is said to be the best one of Mumbles Head in Swansea.'

Joe checked his watch as Robin rather unsteadily refilled his glass and Richard Thomas's. The old man's stories about the people he knew who worked at the BBC were fascinating, but he suddenly realised he'd left Lily alone for over two hours. 'Please, excuse me.' He placed his full whisky glass on one of the coasters the housekeeper had set out on the windowsill. 'It's been nice talking to you, Mr Thomas, but I've been neglecting my fiancée.'

'Small, dark, pretty – Lily something?' Richard Thomas removed three more cigars from his pocket and handed two to Robin and Joe.

'That's her.' Joe handed back the cigar. 'No, thank you, Mr Thomas.'

'Been introduced, last I saw Philip Butler was taking care of her.'

'See, sh ... she's fine.' Robin was so full of

whisky he could hardly stand.

'All the same, I'd better check.' Joe pushed past Robin.

'Schpoilsport, breaking up the fun. You'll be back?' Robin pleaded plaintively.

'You wouldn't notice whether I was here or not.'

'Joseph, angel pie, you promised me a dance.' Angela zoomed in on him from her station in the drawing room the moment he emerged into the hall.

'I have no memory of promising you any such thing.'

'It is my birthday.' She pouted.

He had the grace to blush. 'And I've forgotten to give you your card and present.' Patting his pockets, he extracted a creased and battered card from the inside of his jacket and a small box that held the gold earrings he'd picked out for her in his father's warehouse. Now his mother wasn't looking over his shoulder, he had no compunction about buying his friends' presents at family discount prices.

'Thank you, sweetie. Kiss for them.' To his embarrassment she linked her hands round his neck and planted a kiss on his lips. 'Come on, they're playing our song.'

'We never had a song.'

'We have now.' Dragging him backwards, she pulled him into the sun lounge. 'I'm here, Joseph,' she complained as he looked around the room while dancing rather perfunctorily with her.

'I can't see Lily.'

'It's bad form to look for one girl while you are

with another, but as you're engaged I'll forgive you. And you don't have to worry about Lily. Philip Butler is looking after her. The last I saw, he was taking her upstairs.'

'And this leads to the servants' attics.' Philip led Lily up a flight of stairs, less than half the width of the curved grand staircase that linked the ground and first floors.

'It's quite dark and eerie.' Lily looked down a long, windowless corridor interspersed with doors set opposite one another at six-foot intervals.

'Single low-wattage bulb, designed not to waste electricity on underlings,' Philip explained solemnly. 'You're not cold, are you?' he asked, seeing her shiver.

'A little. I'll wrap my stole round my shoulders.'

'Here, let me.' He pulled the woollen wrap round her neck before opening the first door on his right. 'When I was a boy this used to be my favourite room in the house.'

'You came here a lot?'

'I used to. My father and Robin's were great friends. It was practically my second home. Then my father died and I went away to university...' Leaving her to construe whatever she wanted, he left the sentence unfinished, walked to the far end of the cubicle and opened a dormer window.

'What a wonderful telescope; and all these maps, they look fascinating.' Lily peeled back a pile of astronomy charts.

'Robin had an interest in astronomy when he was twelve and the Watkin Morgans aren't people to do anything by halves. They bought him all the right equipment, including this telescope, which incidentally cost an absolute fortune, for his thirteenth birthday. Robin lost interest in the stars before he reached fourteen and if I remember correctly went on to horses. They in turn gave way to yachts, and I believe girls, in the shape of Emily Murton Davies, are his latest passion. Here.' He beckoned her forward. 'This is the view Mrs Watkin Morgan was talking about. Magnificent, isn't it?'

'Beautiful. I had no idea we were so close to the sea.' The night air was freezing, icy and clear, the lights of the cottages nestling in the land curve that culminated in Mumbles Head glistened like stars against the blackness of the cliff. And beyond was the deep blue velvet of the bay... She started as the door banged violently back on its hinges.

'Excuse us.' Grabbing Lily's hand, Joe yanked her into the corridor.

'Joe, this is Philip Butler...'

'I know who he is.'

She looked back at Philip who was staring after her in bewilderment. 'Joe, please, you're going to pull me over,' she protested as he dragged her down the stairs.

'Going too fast for you?' He released her hand and glared at her as they reached the top of the main staircase on the first floor.

'I don't understand...'

'I do and we're leaving.' Pushing her ahead of him, he watched her run down the main staircase.

'Joe, Lily...'

'We're leaving,' he repeated loudly to Angie, attracting the attention of most of the people in the hall. As they fell silent, he turned to Mrs Watkin Morgan. 'Sorry to have to rush off like this, but I have a headache.'

'Can I get you something, Joseph?' she enquired solicitously, 'an aspirin and a glass of water perhaps...'

'When the pain begins like this, the only thing I can do is lie in a darkened room.'

'We have plenty of spare rooms upstairs, Joseph.'

'I really would prefer to go home, but thank you. If you'll pass on my apologies to Robin. Lily?' Ignoring the stares, he hauled her through the front door.

'I see what you mean about lack of breeding,' Richard observed to Mrs Watkin Morgan as he left the dining room with a fresh plate of food.

'You wouldn't believe the detrimental effect that girl has had on him. Joseph used to be so thoughtful. I only wish I could do something to help. You've heard about his poor mother – sorry, that was tactless of me. For a moment, there, I forgot you're the family solicitor. I remember the dreadful fuss when Esme married that awful man but that's going to be nothing in comparison with the scandal of their divorce.'

'After meeting that girl, it wouldn't surprise if the son's marriage goes the way of his mother's.'

'Such a tragic waste of a talented young man.' Mrs Watkin Morgan shook her head. 'Angie's putting a brave face on it but she was devastated

471

when Joseph brought that girl tonight. She absolutely adores him.'

'If I were you I'd persuade her to attend Joseph's engagement party with Robin.'

'How can I, in the circumstances?' Mrs Watkin Morgan lowered her voice. 'We all hoped...'

Balancing his plate, Richard patted her hand. 'Tell Angie she will be very sorry if she doesn't. Because young Joseph will need her before the evening is out.'

'What do you...'

Richard tapped his nose. 'Not a word to a soul. If you speak I'll deny I said anything. Just get her there.' He beamed as Philip's mother walked past. 'Amelia...'

As Richard walked away, Mrs Watkin Morgan looked at Angie, still hiding behind her brave smile. Richard Thomas could be overbearing and arrogant, but she had never known him be wrong about anything.

'Mrs Watkin Morgan...'

'Excuse me, Emily, I'll be with you in a moment, but I have to have a word with Angie about something before I forget.'

'Get in the car.'

'Not until you apologise for making a spectacle of both of us.' Lily returned Joe's furious glare as she stood, shaking with anger, beside the Rover.

'Get in, we can't quarrel here.' He glanced nervously across to the front door as he suddenly realised the truth of what she'd said.

'Either you're drunk or mad, and whichever it is, I'd prefer to go back into the house and telephone for a taxi.'

'Lily, get in...'

'Not until you apologise.'

'Me? After I find you in a bedroom with another man when you're engaged to me!'

'I didn't see any bed, Joe. Did you?'

'The room was upstairs.'

'And I was looking out of the window, admiring the view of Mumbles Head. Mrs Watkin Morgan suggested Philip take me up there because she felt sorry for me. You'd disappeared for over two hours. I didn't know a soul...'

'Mrs Watkin Morgan suggested Philip take you upstairs?'

'Not "take me upstairs" as you put it. She suggested Philip show me the house. His grandfather built it...'

'I'm sorry.'

Relenting, Lily finally opened the car door and stepped inside.

'I really am sorry, Lily.' He climbed in beside her. 'I shouldn't have left you...'

'I'm more concerned with what happened just now than you leaving me. It's obvious you don't trust me further than you can see me.'

'I wasn't thinking straight.' Starting the engine, he reversed the car across the courtyard, then, putting his foot down, he drove out through the gate. 'Angie told me you'd gone upstairs with Philip Butler. I know what happens at these parties...'

'Angie! She would. It's obvious she's in love with you.'

'We're over.'

'Have you tried telling her that?'

'Yes.'

'But because Angie told you that I'd gone upstairs with Philip Butler you assumed I'd gone up to test one of the beds with him.'

'I was angry, I didn't know what to think.'

'We're engaged, Joe. We should trust one another absolutely.'

'I didn't know if you'd been drinking...'

'If you'd been with me you would have known that I'd had one glass of champagne and by the look of you, that's a lot less than you. And even if I had drunk more I wouldn't have forgotten that I'm as good as engaged to you, no matter what usually "happens at these parties". Don't tar me with the same brush as your friends, Joe. I am – or rather was – a one-man girl. Now I'm not so sure.'

'How many times can I say "I'm sorry"?'

She stared at the road ahead, not saying a word until he drove the car down the lane at the back of Carlton Terrace and into his father's garage.

'Damn and blast,' he cursed vehemently as he scraped the bumper on the garage wall. Shutting off the engine, he opened his door, banging it back against the wall and chipping the paint-work. 'I wish to God I'd never heard of Angela Watkin Morgan, or her bloody birthday party!'

'It wasn't a good evening.'

'Lily, I really am very, very sorry' He gazed at her, silently pleading for forgiveness.

'The food was good.'

Uncertain if she was making fun of him or not, a wary look stole into his eyes.

474

'It gave me some good ideas for our party next weekend.'

'Lily, Lily, Lily!' Gathering her into his arms, he hugged her as she left the car. 'What would I do without you?'

'Another evening like this one and you'll find out.'

'Come in for a coffee. We can try out Helen's sofa if she and Jack aren't using it.'

'They might have broken the springs.'

'I'm prepared to risk it if you are.'

'On one condition.'

'Name it.'

'Never leave me alone at a party again. Next time I really might be tempted to look for another man.'

CHAPTER TWENTY-TWO

Helen was alone with Jack in the front room of the basement. She was waiting for him, lying naked on the sofa, watching him undress. She looked into his eyes and as the slow, lazy smile she had come to love played across his mouth, he opened his arms, leaned over her and was instantly transformed into the wrinkled, grinning figure of Richard Thomas. A bell began to ring, a discordant warning bell that droned on and on and on... She screamed – but although she opened her mouth as wide as she could, she was suddenly struck dumb. Shaking, terrified, she was catapulted from sleep into a harsh, cold sweat. Sitting up, she reached for the alarm clock to silence it. The walls of the room wavered around her as the furniture began to blur. Turning her head, she almost fell out of bed as she vomited on to the floor.

'You look peaky, love,' John commented as Helen staggered into the kitchen in her dressing gown.

'I have a terrible sore throat,' she whispered, pitching her voice several octaves lower than usual.

'A Monday-morning sore throat?' Joe enquired cynically, as he arranged the bread he'd cut on the grill pan.

'A heading-for-tonsillitis sore throat,' she rasped back. Unfortunately for her, Joe had always been able to tell the difference between her real and feigned illnesses, and had never balked at telling their parents whenever he thought she was perfectly well, apart from wanting a day off school.

'Who can that be at this time of the morning?' John pushed the toast he was buttering aside, as the telephone began to ring.

'Someone who didn't go to bed last night,' Helen answered flippantly, suddenly losing her croakiness.

'Your throat seems to be better.' Joe gave her a sideways look as their father abandoned his breakfast and went to the phone.

'Look at it, if you don't believe me.' Sticking out her tongue, she opened her mouth.

'Please, I'm trying to eat.'

'Quiet!' John shouted from the hall.

'Bad news?' Joe asked, as John returned.

'Your mother is divorcing me. We have a meeting this afternoon with our solicitors to discuss terms. I don't know how much your mother has told you, but if you have any questions I'd rather you came to me, or talked to her, than listen to any gossip. Helen, Richard Thomas is your mother's solicitor. Is that going to cause problems for you in work?'

'I shouldn't think so, Dad.' She rose unsteadily from her chair. 'I think I'll go back to bed.'

'You're white as a sheet.' John frowned. 'I'll telephone the doctor.'

'No.' She shook her head violently, making the room swim. Gripping the door handle to steady herself, she repeated, 'No, thank you, if I'm no better tomorrow I'll call him myself.'

'I haven't a lecture until eleven. Do you want me to telephone Thomas and Butler and tell them you won't be in?' Joe offered, feeling slightly guilty as he realised she was suffering from more than a tactical sore throat.

'Please.' She lurched unsteadily down the passage into the hall.

'Mrs Jones will be in soon, I'll ask her to keep an eye on you.' Following her, John watched her climb the stairs as he slipped on his coat.

'I just want to sleep, Dad.' This time she didn't have to pretend that her voice was husky.

'I'll keep an eye on her until Mrs Jones comes and I can be back here by two.' Munching toast, Joe followed his father into the hall.

'There's no need, I'll call back lunchtime.'

'I'm sure it's nothing,' Joe reassured.

'Even if it is, what's the betting your mother will see it as evidence of my neglect.' John took his keys, opened the door and left.

Stripping off her dressing gown, Helen lay on top of her bed. She wanted to be cool – freezing, if possible. Closing her eyes, she tried to fight the waves of nausea that washed over her but it was hopeless. She rushed into the bathroom, made it to the toilet in time, but there was nothing left in her stomach to come up. Crawling back to her bed, she climbed into it, covering herself with the sheet and blankets. She'd wanted to be cold, but not that cold. She slid out her hand, opened the drawer in her bedside cabinet and extracted her diary. Taking the key from a chain around her neck, she unlocked it, flicking through the pages without lifting her head from the pillow. Whichever way she calculated it was always the same. Her period was two weeks and six days late. The magazines said that didn't prove anything one way or another. Young girls could be irregular, particularly if there was trouble at home, like parents divorcing. But she *knew*. She had never been late before and there was that first time – the night Jack's mother had died. Turning on to her stomach, she buried her face in her pillow, trying not to think of the awful night in the police station and the doctor's damning pronouncement: *One of the constables said you come from a respectable family. They won't be regarded as quite so respectable if they have to visit you in an unmarried mothers' home.*

She'd end up like Mary Davies from Hanover Street. Her parents had told the neighbours she'd gone to help out on her cousin's farm in North Wales, but everyone knew she'd been sent to an unmarried mothers' home in Cardiff. When she'd come back she'd said it was horrible. That they'd made her look after the baby for six weeks, feed it, nurse it day and night, make clothes for it and then hand it over for adoption.

A baby – she was having a baby! Her mother and grandmother would disown her – albeit from Langland – her father would put her in a home because no family could survive the disgrace of an unmarried pregnant daughter in the house. And then what? She'd be on her own with a load of strangers, most of them girls in the same situation.

Jack had talked of living together but he barely made enough money to keep himself and she'd have to give up work as soon as she started 'showing'. Perhaps she could get rid of it. That was it! She'd heard women talking in Norah Evans's house when she'd been there with Lily and Norah had been out of the room. Hot bath and gin – that's what they'd said. Someone one of the women knew, a cousin or a friend, had done it but it hadn't worked and she'd almost died. Baby or not she didn't want to die. Not now she'd found Jack. Turning restlessly in the bed, she closed her eyes and feigned sleep as a board creaked on the landing outside.

'Helen.' Joe tapped on the door. 'You all right?'

She heard him open it, listened as he tiptoed towards the bed but she kept her eyes firmly closed and her breathing steady. After a few moments the door closed and she turned over and reached for her diary again. If only there were someone she could talk to. Jack – it had to be Jack – but what if he left her, never wanted to see her again? Then she remembered. *After this I won't ever leave you, or let you leave me. You know that?* She only hoped he hadn't been lying. If he stood by her she felt as though she could face even her father's pain and disappointment.

'Let her have it.'

'John, I strongly protest.' Martin Davies held up a cautionary hand as Richard Thomas beamed triumphantly. 'If you agree to these demands, this will go down as one of the most unfair and overgenerous divorce settlements in Swansea history. Your shop in Mumbles is a prime piece of property and the allowance you give Mrs Griffiths is twice the average wage for this area...'

'And a reflection on the prosperity of Mr Griffiths's business, which Mrs Griffiths helped him expand.'

John looked across to where Esme was sitting, cool, composed and elegant in a Dior shantung silk costume that had been part of the warehouse's autumn range. He wasn't even aware she'd taken it. 'I had no idea you helped me in the business, Esme,' he said impassively.

'I recommended the warehouse to my friends...'

'Ah – recommendations, of course. How could I forget serving your friends?' He turned to

Martin. 'You'll forward me the appropriate papers when they're ready for signing.'

Richard Thomas pushed a file across the table towards Martin. 'We took the liberty of drawing them up.'

'Sure of yourself, weren't you.' Martin opened the file and began to study the papers, while Richard and Esme conversed in whispers and John left his chair and went to the window. 'If you're intent on giving away half your assets, John, they're in order.' Martin pushed the last sheet back into the file.

'Then, as both parties are agreed, it might be as well if we signed them now.' Taking his fountain pen from his top pocket, Richard unscrewed the top.

'My client will sign only after Mrs Griffiths produces a disclaimer renouncing all rights to renegotiate a future settlement, in favour of accepting this one.'

'Agreed?' Richard looked at Esme.

'If you recommend that it's in my interests to do so.'

'We agree. I'll send over the relevant paperwork as soon it's drawn up and signed.'

'Once we're in receipt of the document I'll forward this settlement contract.' Taking the file, Martin left the table.

'There's still the evidence of adultery. As your client is the guilty party, my client will have to sue for divorce as the injured party,' Richard reminded him.

'I also studied law, Richard, and you'll have the evidence, together with this contract on receipt of the disclaimer.'

'In that case I think I can safely predict that most of the paperwork will be completed by the end of next week and we can press ahead with a court date.' Richard offered Esme his arm and led her out of the room.

'John...'

'No more lectures, please, Martin.' John sat back at the table, slumping as though all his energy had been sapped.

'I wasn't going to give you one. It is clear to me that for whatever reason, you want to be a free agent as soon as possible. It would take a bit of time to set up the adultery evidence but we've a cancellation...'

'Someone wants to delay committing adultery.' John smiled at the thought. It all seemed highly ridiculous, like a plot from a Whitehall farce.

'I'm aware it sounds peculiar, but the couple in question have reconciled. There's no chance of you...'

'Absolutely none.'

Delving into his pocket, Martin produced a piece of paper and handed it to John. 'This is the address of the hotel, if you can call it that. The woman will be there at half past two this afternoon, the private detective and photographer at a quarter to three. The woman will expect fifty pounds in cash, the detective thirty, the photographer twenty and a further ten to secure the negatives. If you don't pay the extra the photographs could end up in the Sunday press. The papers that specialise in covering the more gruesome murders and salacious divorce cases have been known to pay well, especially for ones they have to paint black letterboxes on to cover private parts.'

John glanced at his watch. 'That's all right, I have time to go to the bank.'

'Drop the money for the photographer and detective off in my office, if someone sees you paying them it could lead to a charge of collusion and we need a nice clean case.'

'Clean...'

'The room will be twenty-five...'

'This is going to be the most expensive hotel stay on record.'

'That will also cover the cost of the chambermaid's and receptionist's statements. We need a witness, two are better, and three including the private detective better still. Don't forget to wait for the woman if you get to the hotel ahead of her. The receptionist has to see you booking in as Mr and Mrs. Use the name Smith. And John...' Martin paused, clearly embarrassed. 'It's all going to be – well – a bit seedy, if you know what I mean.'

'I expected it to be.'

'It will go through more quickly if you provide a good clear shot where both parties can be easily identified, but I don't have to explain. The photographer, the woman and the hotel staff know the drill.'

'Thank you, Martin.'

'If I pull a few strings and call in some favours I may be able to get this case into the next half-yearly Assizes and organise a decree nisi in a year, give or take a few months – that may not seem quick to you but take my word for it, it is.'

'It's not what you think, Martin. There isn't another woman.'

Martin gave him a sympathetic look as he opened his briefcase and placed the file Richard had given him inside. 'You don't have to explain anything to me, John. If I had a wife like Esme I'd want a quick divorce too.'

The hotel was everything Martin had hinted it would be: peeling paint on a rotting front door that opened without him having to ring the bell; cracked lino that housed thick furrows of dirt; greyish walls that might have been almost any colour once; and an overwhelming smell of greasy food, damp and decay.

'I'm Mr Smith...'

He didn't have to say another word. The middle-aged man behind the desk thrust a register at him and removed a key from a row of hooks on the wall behind him. 'Mrs Smith has already signed, sir.'

John turned and saw a heavily veiled woman sitting on a bench behind him. Nodding briefly, he signed *Mr Smith* below her *Mrs Smith*.

'Room four, sir.'

Allowing the woman to walk ahead, John climbed a flight of creaking, groaning stairs. She stopped outside a door that bore an inexpertly painted number four. Opening it, she stepped inside.

'Close the door but don't lock it.'

John did as she asked, walking in as she tossed her hat and veils on to a chair. He recognised the woman, almost any man who lived in Swansea would have. One of the oldest streetwalkers who plied their trade on the Museum steps, and the seedier pubs down the Strand and dockside end of the town.

'When you've finished gawping you can pay me. I like to get business over and done with at the outset. That way we can both relax.'

'How much?' John asked, recalling that Martin Davies had said fifty, but he doubted any professional who looked like her made that in three months.

'Fifty.' She saw him hesitate and added, 'if you know someone who'll do it cheaper in the next five minutes, go get them!'

Extracting his wallet, he counted out ten five-pound notes. She stuffed them into a tiny velvet bag attached to her wrist by a silver chain.

'Now we can get down to business.' She looked at her watch. 'We only have ten minutes.' Taking off her coat, she stubbed out the cigarette she was smoking on the rickety wooden bedside cabinet, adding to the rash of existing burns.

Although he'd had no lunch, John felt sick as she unbuttoned her lacy black cardigan to reveal a grubby, greyish slip and beneath it a black brassiere with thin, twisted straps. Tossing the cardigan on top of her hat, she unbuttoned her skirt. As it fell to the floor she pulled her slip over her head. He averted his eyes as she yanked down the straps on her brassiere and turned it round. Her breasts, wrinkled, flabby, flopped over the band as she unclipped it.

Left in red suspender belt and a pair of fishnet

stockings that had more holes than they should, and nothing else, she climbed into bed. 'Never wear panties,' she grinned, revealing gaps in her large yellow teeth, 'they get in the way in my line of work. And although that wasn't strictly necessary I like to give value for money.'

Repulsed and revolted, he nodded dumbly.

'Most of my regulars like me to keep on the suspenders and stockings but if you want me to take them off, or go for my special services it'll be another tenner...'

'No.' His voice was as hoarse as Helen's had been that morning.

She patted the bed beside her. 'Take off your shirt then, ducks. The others will be here any minute and that way there'll be no mistaking your intentions in the photos.'

Turning his back, Jack removed his coat and looked around for somewhere to hang it. The wardrobe gave the impression that it would fall apart if he opened the door. Seeing a hook on the back of the door, he left it there and removed his jacket.

'No need to take off more than your shirt,' she said as he kept his back turned to her. 'There'll be no way of telling if we're naked down below or not once the sheet is pulled to our waists. Course, if you want it afterwards, and I can see that a man who looks the way you do, would, I wouldn't mind. Tell you what, I'll drop down to a fiver, seeing as how you were so good at paying upfront.'

John went home before returning to the office.

Helen was in the dining room eating a late lunch Mrs Jones had made for her. After listening to her assurances that she felt much better and checking that her colour had returned, he went to the bathroom. Stripping off his clothes he bundled the whole lot, including his suit and overcoat into the linen bin. They could be sorted later. He couldn't wait to scrub himself raw. He had never felt so soiled in his life, but as the second change of scalding bath water washed over him he realised the tainted feeling went deeper than his skin.

According to the detective, the photographer had been quick, but the five minutes it had taken him to set up the required shots had seemed to last an eternity, an eternity when the prostitute – he hadn't even asked her name – had insisted on wrapping her arms around his chest and placing his hand on her naked breast.

Sickened and disgusted by a system that had forced him to degrade himself to break free from a loveless marriage; he left the house an hour later with his skin tingling, but feeling no cleaner, wearing a complete change of clothes and more aftershave than he had ever put on in his life before.

'Judy, I don't know what's got in to you,' Joy admonished as they took an unexpected break, courtesy of a mid-afternoon cancellation. 'You mixed Mrs Jordan's perm solution double strength. You turned up the heat on Mrs Harris's dryer instead of down, the poor woman was almost roasted...'

'Sorry.'

'Sorry isn't good enough, when you hand my customers excuses enough to sue me. Something gone wrong between you and Brian?'

'And wouldn't you love it, if it had?'

'No.'

'I don't believe you.' Turning her back on her mother, Judy went into the kitchen and set the kettle on the stove.

Joy stroked the hair away from her daughter's face. 'All I want is for you to be happy. I'm sorry I behaved the way I did, but your father made me very miserable when we were together. I saw similarities between him and Brian and was afraid that if you allowed Brian to get close, he might do the same to you.'

'Well, he won't be making me unhappy now.' Walking away, Judy spooned tea into the pot as the kettle began to boil.

'Want to tell me what went wrong?'

'Not particularly.' Judy poured boiling water into the teapot, and set out two cups.

'If it's anything I can help with...'

'Why did Dad make you unhappy?' Judy asked suddenly.

'Because he wouldn't leave other women alone.'

Judy poured the tea before looking at her mother, 'I had no idea.'

'I hoped you hadn't. I wanted you to have a happy childhood and it's not the sort of thing a child should be burdened with.'

'But it must have been humiliating for you.'

'It was, and,' Joy took a deep breath, 'it was why

he never came back at the end of the war. He's not dead, Judy. He moved in with another woman, in London.'

Judy sat down suddenly, slopping the tea she was holding over her skirt. 'Dad's alive.'

'He asked me to divorce him; I wouldn't, or let him see you, because I didn't want people to know he'd abandoned us – me,' she corrected quickly. 'I felt it reflected badly on me. You know how people talk – "there goes, Joy Hunt, she couldn't even hold on to her man." If we could have arranged it quietly I would have agreed, but we couldn't have finalised a divorce without a notice in the *Evening Post* and then everyone in Swansea would have known about it. Not only the neighbours and my customers but your school friends. But, please, don't think I was considering you, I wasn't. I did what I thought best at the time and it was mainly for my own benefit.'

'Did he want to keep in contact with me?'

'Yes.' Joy was taken aback by Judy's composure. After the arguments of the past few weeks, she'd expected her daughter to show her anger. But no matter what it cost in terms of their relationship, now she had started on the truth she felt it would be a betrayal to tell Judy anything less. 'I see now that I had no right to keep you apart by telling you he was dead.'

'Did he write?'

'To ask for a divorce, to tell me he had other children. You have two half brothers. The letters are in the house, you can read them for yourself.'

'Who else knows he isn't dead.'

'Roy Williams.'

'You told...'

'Not until the night Norah Evans was buried. Remember, he came round and we were quarrelling because you wanted to go out with Brian and I didn't want you to. He...' Joy brushed her hand over her cheek and was surprised to find it wet. Since Bill had left she'd prided herself on always keeping her emotions firmly under control. '...He was angry because I was trying to stop you seeing Brian. I tried to explain why. That part was easy, I didn't have to tell him about your father's other women, Roy worked with him before the war and if anything, he knew more than me. He understood that I was afraid for you because Brian is tall, dark, handsome, and a policeman like your father and it would be just as easy for him to be unfaithful, but he wouldn't leave it there. Roy's been asking me to marry him for years and he thought I felt the same about him, that being a policeman he was just as likely to stray. He gave me an ultimatum, so I finally explained I couldn't marry him because I was still married to your father.'

'What did he say?'

'That I thought more about what people would say and gossip, than I thought of you or him. That we could have married years ago and been a family... I've made a mess of all our lives. Yours – Roy's – your father's – and mine...' Unable to bear the bewilderment – and pain – in Judy's eyes, Joy went into the salon and opened her handbag. Rummaging for her cigarettes, she found them and lit one. Judy followed her.

490

Summoning her courage, Joy turned and looked her daughter in the eye. 'You have every right to be angry with me.'

'I know I do.'

'Are you?'

'Not now you've explained, and after what Brian put me through; I thought he knew me, what I wanted, that I loved him and...'

'He found someone else?'

'No, he wanted me to marry him and forget about the job in the BBC in London.'

'You haven't got it yet.'

'If I don't, there'll be others I can try for. And in the meantime I think you should apply for that divorce and marry Constable Williams before he finds someone else and marries on the rebound.'

'Judy...' As Joy hugged her daughter she realised Judy was crying as much as her. 'Thank you.'

'It was always us against the world, Mam, remember. And Brian – all you had to do was explain.'

'You still would have gone out with him.'

'Yes, but at least I would have realised why you were so set against him.'

The bell rang as the salon door opened. Releasing Judy, Joy reached for a towel and blotted the tears from her face.

'We'll talk more later.'

'After you've seen Constable Williams, and sorted everything out with him.' Judy reached along the shelves. 'You'll need perming solution.'

'The right strength this time,' Joy warned.

'Nice flowers, Katie,' John observed as he returned to the office.

'For Mam's grave. It's her birthday. I thought I'd go up there after work.'

'The cemetery closes at six in winter.'

'I didn't know.' Katie bit her bottom lip to stop it from trembling.

Confident that Katie was courting Adam Jordan, unsettled by the events of that afternoon and stung by compassion, he succumbed to impulse. 'I don't feel much like working, so why don't I drive you there now.'

'But, Mr Griffiths...'

'Don't tell me what needs doing, Katie, or I'll have a guilty conscience.' He fastened his raincoat. 'Come on, you could do with some fresh air by the look of you.'

Ten minutes later they were driving through the Hafod in the direction of Morriston. Hands clasped around her knees, Katie stared straight ahead out of the window, embarrassed by thoughts of her behaviour the last time she had been alone in the car with her boss. Whenever she glanced across at him, he seemed, stern, remote, and she wondered if he was deliberately being aloof, because he was wary of her making a fool of herself again.

John drove into the cemetery and parked close to the crematorium. Pulling a newspaper from his pocket, he switched on the interior light. 'Take as long as you like, but remember where the car is, it's going to be dark in another ten minutes or so. And,' he peered out at the drizzle

492

that was getting heavier by the minute, 'take my umbrella, it's bigger than yours.'

'Yes, Mr Griffiths, thank you.'

Sitting back, he watched her struggle to put up the man-sized umbrella. Seconds later, her slight figure bobbed along the path through the neat rows of headstones to the mounds of newer graves beyond. She looked thin, small and fragile, in total contrast to the cheerful bunch of yellow chrysanthemums she was carrying. His heart went out to her. For the first time in her life she should be free from fear, but given Ernie's treatment of his family over the years he wondered if it were possible for anyone to give her the safety and security she craved and had so far eluded her in life. Particularly when he considered the warning Roy had given him, that Ernie was due for release in the next few days. She must be concerned that her father would come looking for her and what guarantee could he, Roy, her brothers, or anyone else give, that he wouldn't.

He was half way through an article on an earthquake in Algeria when Katie returned. 'You weren't long.' He turned up the collar on his raincoat. It was thinner and not as warm as his overcoat.

'I remember you telling me that you go to your family graves to talk to your parents and grandparents, Mr Griffiths, and after Mam was buried and I first saw her grave I thought I'd feel the same way. But I don't. Mam isn't really there, she is with me all the time and I don't have to go to one special place to talk to her. It's not that I'm ungrateful,' she added quickly, lest he think her

493

unappreciative. 'And I really wanted to put the chrysanthemums on her grave to brighten it up.'

'I'm sure they will, Katie,' he turned on the windscreen wipers as hailstones began to hurtle earthwards.

'Not for long in this.'

'Your Mam will be grateful that you thought of her, Katie.'

'You understand everything don't you, Mr Griffiths?'

John was glad of the thickening darkness so she couldn't see the expression on his face.

'I saw a five in your window and as I'm never home until six, I thought it might mean you're missing me more than usual.' Still in his working clothes of plaster and paint spattered jeans and sweater that was more hole than wool, Jack fell on to the sofa alongside Helen.

'I didn't go to work today.'

'Lucky you, I wish I could skive off on full pay. But in my business no work no money,' and he viewed the empty table. 'No sandwiches.'

'Is that all you come here for,' she snapped. 'The sandwiches.'

'You know it isn't.'

'I don't know anything.'

'You trying to pick a fight?'

'No, to find out whether you love me or not.'

'You know I do.' He put a grubby hand around her shoulders and hugged her.

'You never say it.'

'But I show it,' he grinned, his teeth whiter than white against his grimy face.

494

'How much?'

'What?'

'How much do you love me?'

'This much.' Putting his thumb and forefinger about two inches apart he waved them in front of her eyes.

'Is that a lot?'

'Why you asking?'

'Because I'm having your baby.'

'You can't be.'

'I think it happened that first time, the day your mother died.'

'You're serious...'

'Of course, I'm serious. You think I'd joke about something like this! What are we going to do, Jack?' she asked in a small voice, terrified of his answer.

Releasing her, he sat forward on the edge of the sofa. 'We could go to Gretna Green; you don't need your parents' permission to get married there if you're under twenty-one. I have some money saved; it might be enough for petrol for my bike to get us there ... why are you looking at me like that?'

'I thought you'd leave me.'

'When you're having my baby. No way.' He pulled her close. 'You're my girl, Helen, I told you I'd never let you go and I meant it.'

'And you want it?'

'Our baby! It goes without saying that I want it, God, you didn't think, you didn't try to...'

Overcome by his reaction on top of days of worry, she burst into tears. 'I didn't know what to think...'

'You're my girl.' Holding her, he kissed away her tears. 'I'll look after you, Helen, just as I said I would, I promise. I just have to work a few things out. But what the hell, we could go tonight...'

'Tonight!'

'Tonight,' he repeated. Given what Martin would say when he found out what he'd done, the best time seemed the soonest. 'And we'll survive, Helen. I promise you, I'll take good care of you and my son.'

'It could be a daughter.'

He shook his head. 'It's going to be a boy, you'll see. Now, I'm going to wash, change and pack and write a note for my brother. It might be as well if you write one to your father so he doesn't worry. Don't forget to put on warm, waterproof clothes. It's going to be freezing in this weather on the back of the bike. I'll be back as soon as I can, and the minute we can sneak out without anyone noticing – we'll be off.'

'Are you in a hurry to get home, Katie?'

'No, Mr Williams is on afternoon shift and Lily is seeing Joe.'

'In that case, if you don't mind, I'll call in at the warehouse. I want to check it's secure and nothing urgent has cropped up.' He didn't tell her he was thinking more of messages from his solicitor than suppliers. He wouldn't be happy until all the negatives and prints taken that afternoon were in Martin Davies's hands, and he had a signed piece of paper to say no others were in existence. 'But I don't expect you to do anything – understand.'

'Yes, Mr Griffiths, and thank you for taking me to the cemetery.'

'You sure there's nothing wrong?' He gave her a sideways look, as he pulled into the loading bay.

'Can I come in with you, please? I could check the office while you check the warehouse.'

'Mr Williams told you that your father could be out any day?' he asked perceptively.

'Yes.'

'Come on then, I'll lock the door behind us.'

John switched on the warehouse lights as Katie charged up the stairs. Cold, wet, dark winter days weren't good for trade. It wasn't yet six thirty and the fact that everything had been put in its place and the warehouse securely locked, said it all. He doubted they'd had a customer in after five o'clock. After checking all the floors, he double locked the doors and went to the office. Katie was sitting at her desk, her head bent over an open file.

'What do you think you're doing?'

'Checking a delivery note against our original order. They've sent us too many cutlery sets, the expensive solid silver...'

'You can put it right in the morning and give them a telling off while you're at it.' He'd been amazed by Katie's business manner. Insecurity and diffidence vanished once she picked up the telephone or met a rep. Consistently polite and pleasant she never hesitated to tell a supplier exactly what she thought of them if she suspected they were trying to offload second-rate goods, or more stock than had been ordered.

'Sorry, Mr Griffiths...'

'And stop apologising.' He sank into the guest chair beside her. He had a sudden aversion to the prospect of an evening at home. He didn't doubt Helen would be well enough to have Jack around, Lily and Joe would be discussing their engagement party and after the day he'd just had, he didn't feel like coping with young love.

'You hungry?' he asked Katie.

'Not really.'

'I forgot, you'll want to be with your boyfriend. Come on, I'll take you home.'

'Adam Jordan is not my boyfriend,' she burst out emphatically. 'No matter what he says, he is not...'

'Katie...'

'Why does everyone think he's my boyfriend,' she shouted, 'when...' Her voice trailed as she looked at him.

He tried to smile sympathetically and reassuringly. One of the first things he'd discovered about Katie was that she had absolutely no confidence in her own looks or personality beyond her work capabilities and Adam Jordan was an exceptionally handsome young man, just the sort to make an insecure girlfriend jealous. Presuming that she and Adam had quarrelled, he murmured, 'I'm sorry, Katie. But if it's any consolation, all young people have spats when they start courting. You and Adam will make it up...'

'There's nothing to make up!' Paternal understanding from the man she loved was more than she could bear. No matter what it cost, she felt she simply had to tell him the truth. 'I hate Adam Jordan!'

'Katie, if he's done something to you...'

'He's done nothing to me because I wouldn't let him. But that didn't stop him from telling me there was something wrong with me just because I wouldn't let him follow me around and kiss and paw me every chance he got. And it didn't help that everyone thought he was my boyfriend or kept saying how lucky I was, just because Adam's good looking. As if I should be grateful that he decided to pay a plain little mouse like me some attention. I can't stand Adam Jordan. I can't stand him touching me, or even near me because...' She bit her lip so hard she drew blood.

'Those feelings are understandable after what happened to your mother but it doesn't have to be like that between a man and a woman. Lots of married couples are happy...'

'Please, Mr Griffiths.' She looked into his eyes, begging him to see the love etched in hers, so she wouldn't have to spell it out for him.

'Katie, if there's anything I can do to help I will. But I think you should talk about this to a woman. Mrs Hunt, or even one of the girls...'

'You don't understand,' she threw all caution to the wind, risking his respect and the job she loved. 'I love you. Only you. I go to sleep every night thinking about what I'm going to say to you the next day and when the next day comes I lose my nerve and say none of the things I imagined myself saying the night before. And all the time you are kind and caring, but only in the way you are with everyone who works here. I'm not a child, Mr Griffiths. I'm a woman and I love you. It doesn't matter that you're married or think I'm a child because I can't help the way I feel. I've tried to hide it because I didn't want to embarrass you again like I did that time on the cliff top but...'

'Katie...'

'Please, don't try to be kind,' she whispered, 'not now ... I'll go...'

As she turned, he stepped forward and opened his arms.

Afterwards, John had no idea how he and Katie got from her desk to the sofa in the alcove. Or how long he held her while she dried her tears, or how they came to kiss. He only knew that he hadn't been wrong about the way the first kiss she'd given him, had made him feel.

CHAPTER TWENTY-THREE

'That's the buffet menu sorted.' Lily closed the notebook she'd used to list the food. 'Mrs Jordan's offered to make the cake and Uncle Roy thinks we should let her. Her cakes are really good and ever since she did that evening class in icing they look as professional as any that come out of Eynon's the baker's.'

'Dad's ordered a barrel of beer, sherry and champagne for the toast.'

'Uncle Roy thinks the bride's family should provide everything.'

'And my father thinks that's an old-fashioned

idea, and we should share the cost.' Grabbing her hand as she tried to walk past, he pulled her down on to the sofa next to him. 'Somehow, all of a sudden, this seems to be more complicated than you and me getting together. Half the street appear to be involved, as well as our families.'

'Wait until we start organising the wedding.'

'That I leave to you.'

'Coward.'

'Does it matter what kind of wedding we have as long as we're together afterwards.' Pinning her against the sofa, he kissed her.

'Not to me,' she murmured, returning his kiss, 'but Uncle Roy will want to feel that he's doing everything right.' She shifted uncomfortably. 'This feels as if it's stuffed with bricks.'

'It probably is. Want to go downstairs.'

'Aren't Helen and Jack there.'

'Probably, there's always your house.'

'And Mrs Lannon.'

'Why did your uncle have to pick the most meddlesome woman in the street to be your housekeeper.'

'Because she's the only widow without ties.'

He kissed her again. 'Compromise, we'll stay up here for another half hour, then go down and throw little sis and Jack out. She should have an early night anyway, seeing as how she was too ill to go to work today.'

Jack looked at the case Helen had smuggled into the basement while Joe had been eating his tea and shook his head. 'There's absolutely no way I can strap anything that size on to the back of my bike. We'd end up toppling into a ditch.'

'I only packed essentials.'

'You'll have to make do with less of them. What the hell do you call essential anyway.' Dropping Helen's suitcase on to the sofa he flicked the catches and opened it. 'Five pairs of high-heeled shoes!'

'They're different colours. I couldn't make up my mind what dress to get married in.'

'So you need five pairs of shoes?'

'Yes,' she answered defiantly.

'How many dresses do you have in here – and no lying?'

'Twelve.'

Taking the half empty rucksack from his back he tipped it out on the floor. 'One set of clean underwear, two pairs of socks, two shirts and a pair of trousers. Given that women need more things, you can bring twice as much provided you can get it into this bag and you can carry it on your back. I'll pack my stuff in this.' He produced a tiny suitcase less than a quarter of the size of hers.

'But I need...'

'Are we eloping, or not?'

'Who's eloping?'

They turned to see Joe and Lily standing in the open doorway.

Immersed in a new, overwhelming and strangely humbling world of fulfilment, John kissed Katie's small, perfect breast. As his lips moved downwards over her soft, extraordinarily white skin, the fever that had consumed him began to ebb and the enormity of what he'd done, sink in.

'Katie ... I ... Oh God, what have I done! I didn't mean for this to happen.' Moving away from her, he sat up on the edge of the sofa and buried his face in his hands.

'Is it me, Mr Griffiths? Did I do anything wrong?'

'No, Katie, you didn't do anything wrong,' he mumbled wretchedly, 'apart from be born twenty years too late.'

'I'm sorry...'

'It's me who should be sorry. I took advantage of you.' Reaching for his clothes he separated his underpants from his trousers and pulled them on. 'You're a young innocent girl, a neighbour, a friend of my daughter's. I should have protected not seduced you. I should have exercised more control.' Stepping into his trousers, he fastened the fly. He turned back and looked at her, shame almost – but not quite – overshadowed by a breathtaking feeling of love.

'Why? I wanted it to happen, Mr Griffiths.'

'After what I've just done, don't you think you should call me, John. And nothing can alter the fact that you're eighteen years old, a child...'

'I am not a child and *we* did it, not just you.' Furious, she rose to her knees. Acutely disturbed by her slim, almost painfully thin, nakedness, he handed her the clothes he had helped remove such a short time before.

'I'm thirty-eight, Katie. You may not be a child, but the twenty years between us makes me think of you that way. Compared to you I'm an old man – and I'm not even free to ask you to marry me...'

'Marry you,' she whispered, as if marriage was some magical state.

'You'd marry me?' he whirled around and stared at her as if he were seeing her for the first time.

'I've imagined it, but I never thought it could happen.'

'That make sense? When you're a young woman of thirty I'll be fifty...'

'And when you're ninety, I'll be seventy,' she smiled defiantly.

'It's a wonderful, impossible dream.'

'Because you don't want to marry me?'

'Because I'd ruin your life.'

'Without you my life would be ruined anyway. I'll never love anyone else. Never. Until you I thought all men were like Dad. But you're kind, gentle, and...' Trusting and unembarrassed, she looked him in the eye. 'When Adam tried to kiss me I felt dirty and sick. I told Lily I never wanted to get married, but what we just did together was – I can't describe it – it's the most marvellous, fantastic thing that has ever happened to me. I never thought it could be like that not after Mam and Dad...'

'It was special for me too.' John looked down at the shirt he was holding, lest she see just how special, mirrored in his eyes. 'But marriage is much more than just sex, Katie. It's living with someone day and night, being with them, watching them grow old and ugly, and let's face it, I'm not very pretty now.'

'Yes, you are.' Kneeling on the sofa, she wrapped her arms around him and rested her face against his chest. 'You're beautiful where it counts, on the inside.'

'Have you considered what your brothers and Roy Williams will say if they find out about this – and that's without bringing the women of the street into it.'

'My brothers want me to be happy.'

He held her in his arms for a moment, naked she felt as light and fragile as a bird. 'But do you think you really could be happy with me?'

'I couldn't be happy with anyone else, John.'

'Then we'll have to find a way round our problems.'

'You want me?' she whispered incredulously.

'I think I've just proved how much I want you, Katie. My head tells me I should let you go and find a younger and better man, but my heart tells me to never let you go.'

'You really love me?' She lifted her head to be kissed and he gave her all the reassurance he could before holding her firmly at arm's length.

'But until my divorce is finalised you have to realise that we can't tell anyone about us, not if you are to keep your reputation. If my wife gets wind of this, she'll drag your name through the courts. As it is, she's going to think I only wanted a divorce so I could marry you. But,' he kissed the top of her head, 'If it does mean that we can eventually be together, it will be the best thing I've ever done. Time to dress, I have a lot of thinking to do, and that's best done when you're not around, especially in the state you are now.'

She sorted out her underwear and clipped on her suspender belt. 'I'm afraid you'll feel differently about me tomorrow,' she murmured as she began to roll on her stockings.

'I won't,' he smiled, 'but I may have difficulty in believing what's just happened.'

'I'll keep trying to convince you that I love you.'

He fell serious. 'Katie, you know about my divorce.'

She nodded.

'And you've probably gathered that my marriage wasn't a normal one.'

'I knew that you and Mrs Griffiths had separate bedrooms.'

'But for the moment we are still married. The solicitor warned it could take a year or more to finalise everything and I won't risk you being hurt by scandal or exposed as "the other woman" before I can marry you...'

'I wouldn't mind.'

'I would, Katie. It's going to be hard enough for us after we make it legal, without inviting gossip before.'

'But I can still work here. See you every day? Steal time like now...'

'And make plans.' He looked at her scarcely daring to believe that in only a year she could be his – if she didn't change her mind. But did he have the right to allow her to sacrifice her young life to his...

'A year seems forever,' she murmured disconsolately.

'I won't hold you to any promises, if you should change your mind.'

'Don't say that.' She hugged him with all the strength she could muster. 'Please, don't ever say that again.'

'I'll try not to, Katie, but it's not going to be easy to accept that someone like you can love a cripple like me.'

'I'll make you believe it,' she insisted fiercely. 'You'll see.'

He kissed her again. 'Yes, sweetheart, I'm beginning to believe that you will.'

'Think of Dad, Helen, you can't just walk out of the house like this.' Joe spoke to his sister but he was watching Jack.

'If Dad knew what I'd done he'd want me out of the house.'

'Jack, what have you got to say about this?'

Jack turned aside, unable to meet Joe's searching gaze.

'You're pregnant, Helen.'

'What if I am, Joe,' she retorted angrily. 'It's no one's business but ours.'

'All right, fine, it's your business. As I heard the word "elope" I take it you're going to Gretna Green.'

'I'm not the sort of boy who leaves a girl in the lurch,' Jack bit back belligerently.

'And after you've married my sister, what then? How will you support her and the baby when it comes?'

'I'll find rooms and a job that pays more...'

'And when you have to do your National Service?'

'I'll send her money.'

'In Scotland, away from her family and friends.' Jack fell silent.

'If you won't talk to Dad, Helen, at least let me.

507

Can't you see this needs more sorting than a quick-fix trip to Gretna Green?'

'I won't give up Jack.'

Lily sat next to Helen and held her hand as a tear fell from her eye.

'And I won't leave her.' Jack squared up to Joe.

'You're a pair of bloody idiots.'

'You're a fine one to talk.'

'What do you mean?' Joe stood protectively close to Lily, half expecting his sister to say something derogatory about her.

'You're not even Dad's son.'

'What!'

'It's true, Joe. I overheard Dad and Mam talking before she left. She only married Dad to give her bastard a name. And you're the bastard, Joe.'

'There's lot of noise coming from down here. I could hear you upstairs.' John stood in the passageway looking from the four of them to the suitcases. 'Are you all running away from home, or only some of you?'

'This is where I take you home, Lily.' Joe went to the door. 'See you tomorrow, Helen.' Lily followed him out.

'You heard her...'

'You know Helen. She was angry at being caught out; she wanted to hurt you.'

'You think so?'

'I think you have to talk to your father before you do anything else, Joe.'

'What if it's true, what if...'

'Talk to him, Joe.' She hugged him but for the

first time he didn't respond. 'It's half past ten. I have to go home. Do you want to come with me?'

He shook his head.

'Joe...'

'I need to be alone, Lily. I'll see you tomorrow.'

She looked at him for a moment, wishing she could help, then she walked away.

'Right, Jack.' John sat in the chair Joe had vacated. 'Are you man enough to tell me what's going on, or do I have to drag it out of Helen?'

For over twenty minutes the only sound in the room was Jack's voice. Helen knew, because she spent the whole time staring at the second hand on her wristwatch, watching it jerk slowly round and round.

At first Jack was blustering and defiant, almost as though he were trying to goad John into throwing him out. Then, as John remained silent and it became clear that he was prepared to listen to what Jack had to say, Jack's voice gradually grew softer and calmer. 'I love Helen, Mr Griffiths,' he said finally, 'and I'll do whatever I have to, to give her everything she has here.'

'You won't do that on a labourer's wage, Jack.'

'I won't always be a labourer.'

'I'd say the likelihood of you having the money or time to train for anything better when you've a wife and baby to support is negligible. Helen, you haven't said anything.'

'I love Jack and I'm going to marry him. If you try to stop me I'll go to court...'

'I never said anything about stopping you.'

'You'd give us your consent?' Jack asked in amazement.

'It appears to me you've given me little choice if Helen is to keep anything of her reputation.'

'I'm sorry...'

'I'm glad you have the grace to apologise,' John murmured, feeling like a hypocrite after what he'd just done with Katie. 'Although I think you'd both better be prepared for some wagging tongues once the old wives have dusted off their arithmetic.'

'I don't care.'

'It's time you began to care, Helen, if not for your own sake then for the sake of your child.'

'Sorry,' she muttered, shamefaced.

'I'll be honest with you, Helen. I realise I haven't done a first-class job of bringing you up. I thought your mother was too hard on you and I tried to compensate by being too lenient. As a result you had your own way far too often, particularly when it came to things like clothes and money. Frankly, I'm convinced you don't know the value of a pound but I also think that if you marry Jack you're about to find out. And you, Jack, everyone says you're wild... No, you've had your chance to talk,' he continued when Jack tried to interrupt, 'now it's my turn. Well, anyone who can sit down in front of me in my own house and say "I've made your daughter pregnant, Mr Griffiths" has courage. And I've always admired men who face up to their responsibilities, but I think it's naïve of you to believe that you can look after my daughter and her child without help. I have a proposal to make. It may not suit you but

I want you to think about it. First, you marry Helen.'

Jack smiled and reached for Helen's hand.

'You can set up home in this basement. I'll put in a proper kitchen and build a bathroom where the back porch is now. It will be a good investment. If you move out I'll be able to rent it when I'm too old to work and need a pension. And just so there's no mistake, you'll pay rent at the going rate. A pound a week all right?'

'I earn three most weeks on the site, Mr Griffiths, so we will be able to pay a pound.'

'I'd also like you to leave the site. You can have a job in my warehouse, starting on the lowest rung of the ladder. I know you're strong enough to do the donkeywork of shifting the goods, but if you're as bright as I think you might be and you manage to stay on the straight and narrow, I'll promote you. But a warning, and a serious one; I catch you thieving or up to any of the tricks that landed you in Borstal and I'll report you to the police. And don't think I won't because you're my son-in-law.'

'I've stayed on the straight and narrow since I came out.' He looked at Helen. 'And I've a lot to stay on the straight and narrow for now.'

'I hope you do.'

'The wages, Mr Griffiths, I'll have a wife and baby to support.'

'Three pounds ten shillings a week.'

'Thank you.'

'Make no mistake, you'll earn them. There'll be no favours because you're family. And one more thing. You two fight, throw pots and pans around,

511

it's your affair but you don't bring your quarrels upstairs. Once you marry and move down here, Helen, you stay down here. Your bedroom will be turned into a guest room and you will no longer be able to use it. You two got yourselves into this mess, you sort it out.'

'Yes, Dad.' Helen flung her arms round John's neck and hugged him tighter than she ever had before. 'There's one more thing Jack didn't tell you.'

'You gamble on the horses and have run up an enormous bookie's bill?' he asked, not entirely humorously.

'I ... I told Joe he's a bastard.'

'You what!'

'He was angry, I lost my temper and I wanted to hurt him.' She paled at the rage in her father's face. 'I overheard you and Mam...' She looked up and saw her father's back as he left the room and made his way as quickly up the stairs as his disability would allow.

'Is it true?' Joe asked John as he walked into the lounge.

John noted Joe's full glass as he reached for the whisky bottle. 'Whisky doesn't help when you've a problem.'

'I asked if it's true,' Joe repeated.

'Yes.'

'Who is my father?'

'I don't know. Your mother never told me.'

'You must have some idea.'

John hesitated for a moment. 'None and that's the truth. You were born six months after I married your mother. Even allowing for her insistence that you were premature, I knew you weren't my son because I didn't make love to her until our wedding night. But once you were born, it didn't seem to matter who your father was. I soon forgot it wasn't me...'

'You forgot!'

'Look at me, Joe. Look at my face and body. A beautiful woman like your mother doesn't marry a cripple without good reason. But before we were married I was too busy thanking my lucky stars to ask why she chose me and afterwards, when I found out that you were the reason, I was too besotted to care. Please don't be angry with me for wanting to bring you up as my son.'

'And Helen?' Joe asked coldly.

'She looks too much like my mother to be anyone else's child. Joe...'

'No, don't touch me! Don't come near me. Have you any idea what this feels like? I get up in the morning thinking everything's fine, apart from you and mum splitting up, but I decide she left because neither of you was happy. And as you seemed to be happier since she went, I sincerely hope she soon will be, too. My tutors tell me I'm on line to get a first. I have an excellent post waiting for me when I graduate from university, a beautiful girl who loves me enough to want to marry me. In short, a bright, shining future. Then my sister gets pregnant and when I try to tell her she's been a stupid brat for not heeding my warnings she informs me I'm a bastard. That my whole life has been built on a pack of lies.'

'Not lies, Joe. I love you. You couldn't be more

my child if I had fathered you and whatever you say I will always regard you as my son.'

'But I'm not. My mother is a whore...'

'Don't say that.'

'You defend her, after what she's done to me and you?'

'She did what she thought was best for herself – and you – at the time. You saw how frightened and worried Helen was tonight. Try to imagine what it's like for a girl to be alone, abandoned and pregnant.'

'I hope she rots in hell.'

Exhausted by the intensity of Joe's anger, John sat back and looked at the man he had regarded as his child since the day he'd been born. He could understand Joe lashing out, wanting to hurt someone – anyone. He had felt like it often enough himself after his parents' death. But understanding didn't bring him any closer to knowing how to cope with, or ease, Joe's pain.

'All those late nights, all that time spent away from the house, she was with other men, wasn't she?'

'I never asked her.'

'You're divorcing her for adultery.'

'She's divorcing me.'

'Now you're telling me you've got another woman,' Joe sneered.

'I wanted to be free, not to have to think about who your mother was with, or what she was doing. My solicitor arranged a set-up. I was photographed today in a hotel room with a stranger.'

'God, you disgust me.'

'Because I want to divorce your mother and put an empty marriage behind me?'

'Because you put up with her for so long; because you resorted to subterfuge rather than force her to face the truth about herself to get rid of her. You must have known. I was a kid, I had some excuse, but you, all those nights out, her coming home in the early hours...'

'I was afraid to question her because I thought that I, and you and Helen – no, that's not fair – just me, couldn't live without her. Then I suddenly discovered I could and I didn't want to carry on living a lie any more.'

'And all these years you never thought to tell me that I wasn't your son.'

'I hoped you'd never find out.'

'Hoped! Haven't you heard a word I've said? I'm another man's son. That makes me a bastard and you a stupid dupe. I can't even look at you.'

'Where are you going?' John called after him as he left the room.

'To see Lily. Perhaps she can help me sort out whether I'm Joseph, Joe, or someone who wants nothing to do with either of his so-called parents.'

'Joe, it's eleven o'clock. She'll be in bed.'

'Then I'll wake her.'

'You'll be back?'

'I don't bloody well know.'

'For Christ's sake say something, Lily. Don't just sit there looking at me as if I'm a worm you want to squash.'

Tightening the belt on her dressing gown, Lily

sat next to Joe. It hadn't been easy to persuade Mrs Lannon and her uncle to let her talk to him alone at that time of night. She only hoped her uncle was keeping his promise and watching the door to make sure Mrs Lannon didn't creep back downstairs and try to eavesdrop. 'What do you want me to say, Joe?'

'That you couldn't lower yourself to marry a bastard.'

'You're not and it wouldn't make any difference to me if you were. No one can hold a child responsible for his parents' actions.'

'Haven't you heard a word I've said? My father...'

'That's just it, isn't it. Your father! And he *is* your father. He brought you up, paid for your uniform when you went to grammar school, sent you to university, taught you to drive, and I remember that time Helen caught measles from me. When I went round after I recovered your father was sitting in the living room with both of you on his lap, reading you stories.'

'I don't understand what you're getting at.'

'I'm trying to say it's not who fathered you that's important, but who brought you up.'

'Rubbish.'

'Perhaps it is,' Lily murmured, 'but I happen to believe it and if you came here hoping I'd agree with you, you're going to be disappointed. You picked the wrong girl, Joe. I have no idea who my father – or mother – was. But I do know if they turned up on the doorstep tomorrow they could never take the place of Uncle Roy or Auntie Norah in my heart. Because my uncle and aunt

516

were always there when I needed someone to take care of me, like when I turned up on Swansea station as a three-year-old with a label on my coat. And again when I was six and terrified of the dark. Auntie Norah sat by my bed, holding my hand until I went to sleep every single night that I can remember for three years. They checked my schoolwork, met my teachers, advised me how to fight my battles, made tea for me and any friends I brought home, encouraged me at least to try whenever I thought I couldn't tackle something and loved me unconditionally when I made mistakes. just as your father did you. Now, if that's all, I think you should go.'

He rose to his feet.

'You'll think about what I said, Joe?'

'I'll think about it after I find out what kind of bastard fathered me and abandoned my mother.'

'Joseph, what a surprise, and so early.' Esme left the table to kiss him as the housekeeper ushered him into the breakfast room.

'Where's grandmother?'

'She has breakfast in bed these days. She says a lady of her advanced years shouldn't put in an appearance before eleven. Have you eaten? If you haven't I'll ask Mrs Brannigan to make you something.'

'I've eaten.' He closed the door. 'I've come for information, actually.' Looking her straight in the eye, he asked, 'Who is my father?'

Esme gripped the edge of the table, wrinkling the fine damask cloth. 'Who told you John wasn't?'

517

'Helen.'

'How...'

'She overheard you and Dad ... John Griffiths talking.'

'I see.' Esme reached for her cigarettes.

'I think I have a right to know who he is.'

'A right?' She looked him in the eye. 'A right to know a secret I've kept for over twenty years.'

'When it concerns me, yes. A child should know its parents.'

'Not if the parent isn't aware he has a child.'

'So you won't tell me.'

'I can't. And even if I did it wouldn't do you any good.'

'Why?'

'You're my son. I brought you up as best I could and you didn't want for anything. I think that's reason enough for you to accept the situation and be grateful I didn't have you adopted.'

'Be grateful that you brought me up, by deceiving an innocent man and forcing him to take me on as his child!'

'If I deceived John Griffiths I paid for it with twenty years of marriage and the daughter I bore him.'

'I talked to – Dad – last night.' Joe hesitated over the word but he was finding it almost impossible to think of John as anything other than his father. 'He told me he's prepared to admit adultery to be rid of you. Personally, I think it would simpler all round if he and I just had blood tests.'

'Blood tests can only prove that a child wasn't

fathered by a man.'

'Precisely.'

'Joe, you wouldn't – not after all these years. You can't. I won't let you turn my life into a mockery.'

'It seems to me that you've managed to do that very well yourself, Mother.' Turning on his heel, he opened the door, strode out of the room and the house.

'So what do you want to do, Joe?' John asked. Joe had turned up in the warehouse at midday, raging and upset, and John had done the most politic thing he could think of, taking him to Swansea's best and most expensive hotel for lunch in the hope that the privacy of their table would encourage Joe to do some real talking and the public setting discourage him from making a scene.

'I don't know. If she won't tell me who my father is ... I just can't bear the thought of not knowing.'

John took the bottle of white wine he'd ordered from the ice bucket and replenished both their glasses. 'Have you thought that he could be dead?'

'You suspect someone?'

'No. I met your mother for the first time a month before we married. She played the part of a love-struck young girl extremely well. Never mentioned anyone else. I admit I've occasionally wondered if it could be this or that one of her family friends, but it was only wondering. I never discovered any evidence and your grandmother was very fond of telling me I was Esme's first and only boyfriend.'

'You really don't know.' After confronting Esme, Joe knew she would never tell him the truth and he felt his last hope slipping from his grasp.

'I really don't know,' John echoed. 'What did Lily say when you told her about it last night?'

'That your birth parents don't matter as much as the people who brought you up.'

'Sensible girl, Lily. You've done well for yourself there.'

'Better than I deserve.'

'I wouldn't say that; a father always wants the best for his son and I was hoping you'd still think of me that way.'

'To be honest, I'm finding it difficult to think of you as anything else. Just don't ask me to forgive my mother.'

'As I said yesterday...'

'She did what she thought was best. But I'll never believe she was thinking of anyone other than herself. She certainly wasn't thinking of you – or how I'd feel when I discovered I was another man's son.'

'Your boyfriend's waiting for you,' Isabel muttered *sotto voce* to Helen as she passed her desk. 'Do you think you could ask him to stand somewhere less conspicuous in future. If Mr Thomas should see him...'

'I'll see to it.' Helen cut Isabel short as she closed her desk drawer and went to the coat-stand. She didn't need Isabel to elaborate. A labourer dressed in the filthy jeans and ripped sweater that was almost a uniform on the building sites in and around Swansea was not a sight Richard Thomas would want near Thomas and Butler. And neither was Jack. Even clean and tidy, dressed in his best suit, he was not the sort of young man Thomas and Butler would wish their office juniors to associate with.

'Hi, Jack.' Helen walked out of the front door and gave him an enormous hug and kiss in full view of the office window.

'Some greeting, I take it you've missed me.'

'I've been told to ask you to stand somewhere less conspicuous when you pick me up in future, as the sight of a labourer offends the sensibilities of the refined Thomas and Butler staff, but I've decided to hell with Thomas and Butler, and their job.'

'You're leaving?' he asked warily.

'I'm not going back there to be told where my boyfriend can and can't stand.'

'You've been sacked?'

'Threatened with it in two weeks if I don't change my ways. It's a foregone conclusion.'

'So what do you do now?'

'We're getting married...'

'Not for a week or two and you'll still work...'

'How can I? I'll have the flat to look after. What difference does it make if I stop work now or a couple of weeks from now?'

'I'd say at least twenty quid if you carry on until you start showing. And that will buy a lot of nappies.'

'My father has all the nappies we need in his warehouse.'

'I won't have you running to him for every little

thing after we're married, Helen.'

'*You* won't! And who are you to tell me what I can ask my own father for, Jack Clay?'

'Your soon to be husband.'

'Talk to me like that again and you won't be anything of the sort.'

'If we're going to make it on our own...'

'Why should we struggle when my father can help us?'

'Because you'll be my wife and that makes you my responsibility, not your father's. Didn't you hear what he said to us last night? We made the mess, it's up to us to sort it out.'

'And I thought you'd care enough about me to want me to stay home and rest until the baby's born.'

'Rest where, Helen? Your father wants to put a proper kitchen and bathroom into the basement. Even if everything goes to plan that's going to take weeks and you'd be better off spending your days in a clean office until it's finished.'

'You don't expect us to move in until it's ready, do you?'

'Where else?'

'When my father has all those rooms...'

'Your father's rooms, not ours.'

'And in the meantime, you expect me to work.'

'For pity's sake, you're pregnant, not incapacitated.'

'You want me to make an exhibition of myself...'

'What exhibition? You won't be showing for a couple of months, and in the meantime we can do with all the money we can lay our hands on to furnish the flat and buy the things we'll need for the baby.'

'My God, I can't believe I'm hearing this!'

'It's not as if I'm suggesting you go down a coal mine, Helen. And it is only for the next couple of months. I wouldn't expect you to carry on working when the baby's born.'

'That's big of you.' Turning, she stalked off up the hill.

'Helen ... Helen...' He ran after her. 'What's got into you?' he panted as he caught up with her.

'You, Jack Clay. Expecting me to work in my condition.'

'Your father was right, he has spoiled you.'

'How dare you'

'I dare because it's the truth. And if we're going to make a go of it...'

'Forget it, Jack. I wouldn't marry you now if you were the last man on earth.'

'So you're going to run back to Daddy, is that it?'

'It's none of your business where I go.'

'Go ahead, then,' he taunted as she began to walk away. 'But you can't ignore what's coming, and when you see sense I'll be waiting.'

'You'll wait a long time if you expect me to come back to you after what you've just said, Jack Clay,' she called over her shoulder.

'And what have I said that's so dreadful? That I expect you to pull your weight when we're married?'

'When I'm pregnant,' she corrected.

'For God's sake, Helen, you can't afford to be childish now we've a baby to consider.'

523

'I've just told you. You have nothing to consider, Jack Clay. And if you think I'll marry you or let you have anything to do with the baby after what you've just said you have another think coming.' Keeping her back firmly turned to him, she quickened her pace.

CHAPTER TWENTY-FOUR

'Helen, Joe, anyone in?' John walked from the deserted lounge through the dining room into the kitchen.

Helen was sitting alone on the window seat, apparently reading a novel. He might have been more convinced if it hadn't been upside down.

'You're late, Dad.'

'A few problems with deliveries,' he hedged evasively, making a note to watch his timekeeping until she married Jack. 'Joe not in?'

'Playing engagement parties with Lily.'

'Talking of which, have you and Jack fixed a date for your wedding? I think it will have to be Register Office...'

'I'm not marrying Jack.'

'Oh?' He lifted the lid on a pot of stew that Mrs Jones had left on the stove. It didn't look as though it had been touched. Setting a match to the gas beneath it, he opened the cupboard and lifted down two soup bowls. 'I take it you haven't eaten.'

'No.'

'Shall we sit in here or the dining room?'

'Wherever you like,' she snapped in a brittle tone.

'In that case let's make it here.' Laying the bowls on the table, he opened the cutlery drawer.

'Aren't you going to ask what happened?'

'No.'

'Don't you care?'

'Of course I care, Helen, I just assumed you had made other plans for yourself and the baby.'

'No.'

'I see.' He stirred the stew with a wooden spoon before reaching for the bread bin.

'Jack expects me to work until the baby is born.'

'Until the day before it's born?'

'Until I begin to show.'

'He's probably thinking of the money. You could do with all you can get.'

'That's what he said.'

'He's right.'

'You won't help us?'

'I'm helping you by employing Jack and converting the basement.'

'I see.' Tight-lipped, she left the seat.

'You can't run away from this one, Helen.'

'So I have to marry Jack no matter what. Is that what you're saying?'

'No. You have other choices.'

'An unmarried mothers' home and adoption,' she scoffed.

'That's one.'

'You'd see your own grandchild put up for adoption?'

'He or she might get a more mature mother that way.'

He was aware that she'd been about to slam the door. He'd even braced himself for the bang.

But instead she continued to stand and look at him. 'I'm behaving like a spoiled brat, aren't I?'

'You said it, not me, love. Think about what you want. If you're not sure marrying Jack is the right thing to do, then don't. There's nothing quite so heartbreaking or messy as divorce, especially when there's a baby involved.'

Joy Hunt walked past Roy's front door twice, before plucking up enough courage to ring the bell.

'Mrs Hunt, how nice of you to call. Please come in.' Lily ushered her through the hall into the parlour where she and Joe were sitting.

'I came to see if I could help with the buffet on Saturday night,' Joy prevaricated.

'Thank you, but I think we have everything under control.'

'Mrs Hunt, I thought I heard your voice.' Roy stood in the doorway in his uniform.

'Constable Williams.' Joy knotted and un-knotted the handkerchief she was holding.

'I was just off to the station. Can I walk you home?'

'Yes, thank you,' she stammered.

Joe winked at Lily as Joy left the room. 'There's something going on there.'

'Sh.' Lily waited until the front door closed behind them. 'It's been going on for years. Auntie Norah said she'd given up waiting for an announcement. But perhaps now we're getting married and Judy's going off to London they'll finally get together.'

'Must be catching.'

'What?' she asked, snuggling closer to him.

'Love.' He smiled, kissing her.

'Is Jack in?'

'Yes.' Brian eyed Helen suspiciously as she stepped into their basement kitchen.

'I'm sorry, I didn't mean to interrupt your tea,' she apologised as she saw Martin and Jack sitting at the table.

'We've reached the Battenburg cake stage, so why don't you join us?' Brian pulled the chair alongside his, out from under the table.

'No I ... only came to apologise to Jack.'

'Sit down, Helen.'

To Martin's amazement she obeyed Jack's command.

'Apologise for what?' Martin asked, watching his brother.

'Jack and I had a stupid row earlier,' Helen divulged recklessly.

'Over what?'

'Wedding plans.' Leaning back on his chair, Jack picked up a couple of clean side plates from the dresser. 'Pass the cake, Brian.'

'Wedding ... Jack, you bloody idiot. I warned you not to get mixed up with this one...'

'That's your future sister-in-law you're talking about.' Cutting two slices of cake, Jack eased them on to plates and handed Helen one.

'You're pregnant?' Martin asked Helen bluntly.

'Yes.'

'I have things to do in my bedroom.'

'There's no need to go on our account, Brian. Tea everyone?' Jack left the table, and cleared his and Brian's sandwich plates into the sink.

'Where are you going to live and, more to the point, what are you going to live on?' Martin demanded.

'We're going to live in our basement. My father's doing it up for us and he's given Jack a job in his warehouse.'

'Your father knows.'

Helen nodded. 'Jack told him last night.'

'You told Mr Griffiths that you'd...'

'Made Helen pregnant. Yes.'

Brian glanced from Martin to Jack and Helen in the silence that followed. 'In that case, all that's left to be said, is congratulations.' Brian shook Jack's hand, then kissed Helen's cheek. 'I hope you'll both be very happy.'

'Martin?' Jack looked to his brother.

'You'll have your work cut out keeping this one in order.' Following Brian's example, he kissed Helen's cheek.

'I think it's more likely to be the other way round,' she said seriously, giving Jack a small smile.

'I telephoned Bill last night. He's happy to furnish all the evidence of adultery I'll need for a divorce and as we've been living apart for so long there shouldn't be any problems. Of course it will take time.'

'Of course.'

528

'But if you want to get rid of Mrs Lannon I could move in as your housekeeper...'

'No, Joy. Let's do this thing properly. We'll start living together when you've my ring on your finger and not before. But' – he glanced up and down Verandah Street – 'if you've got your keys on you, we could finalise the details in the shop bedroom.'

'You're due at the station.'

He checked his watch. 'Not for another two hours, I'm not.'

'What a lovely old Edwardian house, Lily.' Angela looked around the hall as she handed Helen her coat.

'Thank you, it's been in my guardian's family for three generations. Helen, this is Angela Watkin Morgan. Angela, this is Joe's sister Helen.'

'How do you do.' Angela kissed Helen's cheek. 'My friend and my brother Robin's, Emily.'

'That's the car parked.' Robin strode through the door. 'Hello, beautiful.' Following Angela's example, he kissed Lily's cheek. 'And – remember you.' He had the grace to remain silent as he looked at Helen and remembered exactly where he'd seen her last and the state she'd been in.

'My fiancé, Jack Clay.'

Robin pumped Jack's hand up and down. 'Joe told me his sister was getting married, you lucky fellow.'

'There's food and drink in the dining room.' Lily indicated the way.

'Thank you, where's the second lucky man?'

Robin asked.

'Pouring beer last time I saw him.' Lily stepped forward to greet Adam as he walked in. After what had happened between him and Katie she hadn't been certain that he'd turn up.

'Judging by the noise, or lack of it, they seem an orderly bunch,' John commented as Roy took the tops off two bottles of beer and handed one over.

'Let's hope they remain that way. Lily only agreed I could stay until Joe gives her the ring on condition I keep the door between this room and the dining room closed.'

'Roy.' Joy knocked on the door. 'I brought the fruit punch and pasties Judy volunteered to make.'

'And didn't,' Roy suggested, as he let her in.

'I think she was a bit over ambitious offering. Between work and her final examinations she didn't have time.'

'I hear she did very well.'

'Top of her year in college.' Joy made a conscious effort not to sound as though she was boasting.

'That's what I always say about the children in this street,' Doris Jordan sang out from the sink where she was already washing glasses, 'they all seem to be going as high as they can go.'

'They seem to be doing well,' Mrs Lannon concurred.

'Yes, well, Roy.' Joy glanced at the others and hesitated awkwardly. 'Just thought I'd show my face and pass my good wishes on to the happy couple.'

'Joe will be giving Lily the ring in a half hour or so. Why don't you have a sherry and stay and watch? After that, John and I are going down the pub to hide.'

'And the girls will have banished me and Mrs Lannon to my house,' Doris chipped in. 'You can join us if you like.'

'Thank you but...' Joy tried to think of an excuse.

'They insist they can cope, but I'm not so sure,' Mrs Lannon pronounced, tight-lipped and evidently disapproving. 'You know what girls are these days, too flighty by half to keep an eye on where the forks, plates and spoons go after people have finished eating.'

'They can't be too flighty. Lily and Helen will be married women before too long.' John topped up his beer glass.

'I only wish one of them was marrying my Adam. I thought him and that little Katie...' Doris turned round as someone hammered on the front door.

'Who can that be, banging on the door like that? They'll have the glass out of it,' Mrs Lannon said tactlessly. Embarrassed lest she'd inadvertently stirred up traumatic memories of Ernie breaking down the door, she began to heap the glasses she'd dried on to a tray.

'Don't worry.' Roy lined up the sherries he'd poured on the wooden draining board. 'One of the boys will see to it and give them a good ticking off.'

Brian heard the knocking as he walked from the

dining room into the parlour. Dumping his plate of food on Adam who was hovering close to Katie, he walked down the passage into the hall and opened the door.

'Roy Williams live here?'

He stared in disbelief at the woman in front of him. He had patrolled Swansea long enough to recognise one of the prostitutes.

'Gawped enough?' Flicking back her tightly permed, improbably dyed red hair, she stepped towards him, widening a split in her tight skirt that revealed fist-sized holes in her fishnet stockings and a puckered expanse of grubby thigh.

'Constable Williams is busy.' Brian blocked her path.

'Not too busy to see an old friend.' She tried to push past him.

'This is his niece's engagement party.' Brian half closed the door on her.

'That's why I've come, to congratulate the happy couple.' Grabbing the lapel of Brian's suit, she breathed gin and pep fumes into his face.

'This is not the time...'

'I'm a close friend of the family; very close.' She stamped her foot against the doorpost, preventing him from closing the door. 'He'll be glad to see me.'

'And I think he'd prefer to see you later,' Brian persisted, aware of whispering and movement behind him.

'If you want "later" boy, we can work something out.' She grinned, exposing a row of crooked yellow teeth.

'Please...'

'You want a taste now, I can give it.' She lurched forward, making a grab for his crotch. He retreated, just as she'd expected him to, giving her the opening she'd been waiting for.

'Can't you come back tomorrow?' he appealed as she finally succeeded in pushing past him.

'No, I can't. I warned Roy and that sister of his that I wanted my daughter back the minute she started earning and he wouldn't listen. Norah was different, God rest her soul. She saw sense because she realised what a mother's entitled to. I'm here to make sure I get my rights.'

'Look...'

'Out of my way.' She thrust him aside with a surprisingly strong hand. 'I've stood here freezing my fanny long enough. Roy?' she shouted. 'Roy, where the hell are you?'

Roy's face darkened as he stepped out of the kitchen into the passage. 'What are you doing here, Mary?'

Brian had never seen Roy so angry, or heard his voice quite so cold.

'What do you think? Looking after number one because no other bugger will.'

'Whatever it is, it can wait until tomorrow. I'll meet you wherever you want.'

'Don't want me dirtying up your nice, clean, respectable house, is that it? Well, tough, I'm here and I'm staying until you agree to pay me what I'm owed.'

'I don't owe you anything.'

'Me and Norah had an agreement, thirty bob a week on the nail to cover my rent until my girl got married, then a hundred pounds pay-off. It's no more than I'm entitled to, seeing as how you and her robbed me of my only child.'

'Norah paid you!' Roy stared at the woman in horror.

'Like I said, thirty bob a week on the nail.' Her voice rose to a screech and Brian realised she'd not only been drinking but was drunk. 'I'm not daft, Roy, I know what my girl's been earning in that bank. That was my money by right, not yours. But I'm not greedy, just want my rights. The hundred pay-off Norah promised.'

'Uncle Roy.'

Lily was standing in the dining-room doorway next to Joe and half a dozen curious guests.

'This is her, isn't it?'

Roy stared helplessly, apparently rooted to the spot.

Taking Roy's silence as assent, Mary approached Lily. 'You haven't half grown up nice. I haven't seen you in years, not to talk to. Snotty Roy and Norah thought you'd be better off not knowing your old mam. But I'm here now. Well, come on, ducks, give us a kiss.'

The silence that closed in on the hall buzzed, red-tinged, ringing hollowly in Lily's ears.

John Griffiths was the first to react. Taking Mary by the shoulder, he muttered, 'If it's money you want you'd better come with me.'

'It's you again. Small world, innit...'

'You want paying – out.' As John frogmarched the woman through the door, Lily looked at Joe. He met her gaze, hesitated, then, clearly embarrassed, averted his eyes. Even as he did so he sensed he was making the worst mistake of his life but he simply couldn't help himself.

'Joseph, we have to leave...'

'Go with your friends, Joe.'

'Lily...' Steeling himself to meet the hurt in Lily's eyes, Joe finally stepped towards her.

'Joseph, this is no place for the girls...'

'Shut up, Robin,' Joe broke in savagely, taking his anger out on his friend.

'Robin is right, Joe.' Lily was astonishingly cool and composed. 'This is no place for decent girls – or boys with ambition.' Turning, she ran up the stairs, Roy following in her wake.

The telephone began to ring. Everyone ignored it. Joe looked towards Lily as though he couldn't make up his mind whether to go after her or not. Sensing her brother's dilemma, Helen tried to fight her way through the crowd in the dining room.

But before she could reach him Robin laid his arm on Joe's shoulder. 'I'll take Em and Angie home but I'll be back.'

'You don't have to.'

'I want to.'

Angela slipped her hand into Joe's, as he followed Robin to the door to see them out.

'Lily.' Roy knocked on her bedroom door. 'Please, Lily, love, let me in. I need to explain.'

'I'd leave her for a while, Roy.' Joy lit two cigarettes and passed him one as she sat on the first step of the stairs that led up to the attic.

'We should have told her about her mother years ago.' He took the cigarette and sat beside her.

'You did what you thought was best at the time, like me with Bill and Judy. And just like me with Bill, if you'd looked for the right time to tell Lily about her mother I'd take bets on you not finding one – until now, when you've been forced into it.'

'I had no idea Norah was paying Mary. If Norah had only told me I would have carried on paying the woman after she died. Oh, God! Did you see the look on Lily's face?'

'Yes.'

The telephone began to ring again.

'I'll get that and clear up downstairs. If Lily hears us talking she may not come out. Try again, Roy in ten minutes or so. That girl needs you, now more than ever.'

'And ten makes one hundred.' John Griffiths handed over the final ten pounds. 'And that's it, there'll be no more, so don't try coming back.'

'I won't.' Mary folded the notes into her bra.

'But in case you forget, it might be as well if you sign something.'

'Something legal? Don't make me laugh. It was a bloody lawyer who sent me here in the first place.'

'What lawyer?'

'Norah always said if anything ever happened to her she'd see me all right in her will. I never got a bloody penny. When I went to see about it the toffee-nosed berk said there was something wrong with the papers and I wasn't going to get what was mine by right. He gave me a fiver. A bloody fiver – and what's that? Hardly enough to get pissed on. It was him who suggested I call in person...'

'What lawyer?' he repeated.

'Richard Thomas. Thinks he's so bloody hoity-toity. I know his sort and what they're like once they've got their knickers down around their ankles.'

'Did he tell you when to call?' John's blood ran cold as he recalled Esme's reaction to the news about Joe and Lily. Richard was her lawyer ... surely she wouldn't have...

'You think I would have walked up here on spec? My room's the other side of town; it's a long haul...'

'Quite.' John cut her short. 'You've got what you came here for, Mary. We don't want to see you around here again.'

'You'll come calling when you want your next divorce, ducks,' she cackled.

'I need to see her, Mr Williams.'

'You're welcome to try, boy. I only hope you have better luck than me.' Roy rose to his feet and moved to Lily's door. Knocking on it, he murmured. 'Joe's here, love.'

'Tell him to go away.'

Roy looked at Joe. 'That's the first time she's spoken since she locked herself in there.'

'I won't go, Lily.'

'Yes, you will.' Lily wrenched open the door. Her face was white, her eyes puffy from shock and tears but she looked him in the eye. 'Go away, Joe. I don't want to see you again.'

'Lily...'

'Just consider the reaction of your fine university friends. They couldn't get out of the house quick enough. It wasn't good when they looked down their noses at me last Saturday night. Then I was only a nobody, now they know I'm the daughter of a common prostitute think what that will do to your ambition and the fine career you've mapped out for yourself.'

'You said it didn't matter who your real parents are,' he murmured, conscious of Roy Williams standing behind him.

'I was wrong. Do you think you'll have any friends left if you get engaged to me now? Do you think you'll still be able to take that job with the BBC? And don't say it doesn't matter to you, because I know it does. You've talked about nothing else for weeks. We're over, Joe. It's finished between us.' Looking past him, she murmured, 'Uncle Roy, I need to talk to you.' She held the door open. Roy glanced at Joe, then stepped inside and closed it.

By the time Joe returned downstairs most of the guests had left. Helen, Judy, Katie and Joy were clearing the food and dishes while Brian, Martin and Jack were moving the furniture back into place. He gave them a hand.

They had just restored the dining room to order, when Robin returned. 'Sorry sounds pretty inadequate,' he muttered as he followed Joe into the hall.

'Lily told me to go. Said I should think about my friends and career at the BBC. She won't even talk to me, Robin, and I haven't a clue how to make her.'

'Seems to me there's nothing you can do around here for now. Why don't we go for a drink? You never know, talking it out might help.'

Too miserable and wretched to think straight, Joe followed him out of the house.

John walked in and looked around the parlour and dining room before going into the kitchen where Helen was drying dishes. 'Where's Joe?'

'His friend Robin Watkin Morgan came back and took him out for a drink. Lily wouldn't talk to him...'

'So he thought getting drunk would help.' John didn't bother to conceal his disgust. Furious, he returned to the hall. He found the telephone directory in the top drawer of the Georgian chest Norah and Roy used as a telephone table. Flicking through the pages, he found Dr Watkin Morgan's number, but before he could dial the telephone rang.

'Roy Williams's house,' he answered tersely.

'Swansea police station here, tell him to ring in as soon as possible.'

'He's busy at the moment.' Cutting the line, John dialled out. It was picked up on the third ring.

'Watkin Morgan residence.'

'I need to speak to Joe Griffiths. It's urgent.' He could barely conceal his irritation or impatience.

'There is no one of that name here, sir.'

'He is a friend of Robin...'

'Mr Robin is not at home. If you'd leave a message and a number, sir...' John slammed the receiver down, before the woman he assumed was the housekeeper finished speaking.

'Who was that, Angie?' Robin called from the den where he was sitting with Joe and Emily.

'Someone for Pops. I gave them the number of his surgery.' She walked in with the whisky bottle. 'Top up, Joseph?'

'Getting drunk isn't going to help.'

'I couldn't agree more, but neither will you going back to Carlton Terrace when Lily doesn't want to see you.'

'I need to see her.' He left his chair.

'Think about it from her point of view, Joe,' Angie coaxed persuasively. 'She's had the most terrible shock. She's ashamed, embarrassed. She made it clear to you that she doesn't want to face anyone just yet.'

'I'm her fiancé.'

Robin flicked his head towards the door.

Taking the hint, Angie pushed the ice bucket at Emily. 'Give me a hand in the kitchen.'

'Love to.'

After the girls left, Robin sat forward in his chair and confronted Joe. 'The house was packed. Half Swansea saw that woman claim Lily as her daughter, Joe. You have to think of yourself. Once word gets out that Lily's mother is a streetwalker, Lily will be finished socially and so will you, if you insist on getting engaged to her.'

'It's not important who her mother is...'

'That's rubbish and you know it. Why do you think I got the girls out of there as fast as I could? No decent man will allow his wife or daughters to associate with the daughter of a woman who can be bought for a few bob down the Strand.'

'That's Lily's mother, not Lily!'

'Of course it is, but Lily's mother has just made a scene at *your* engagement party. If she can do that without a qualm of conscience, think what she'll do at your wedding or any dinner or cocktail party you organise to entertain your boss when you have one. Joe, Lily no longer has a reputation worth speaking of. Stay with her and you'll be tainted too. Especially at the BBC. You'll lose that job before you even get it and that means kissing everything you've worked for goodbye.'

'That's what Lily said but do you really think it will happen?'

Joe pleaded, wanting to hear otherwise as he turned an anguished face to Robin's.

'I know so. There's no way you can marry Lily and have the life you dreamed of. It's Lily and obscurity, and I mean obscurity – no Swansea school will take the husband of a girl with Lily's parentage on to their staff. Or a degree and a high-flying career in broadcasting.'

'That look on her face...'

'She realised the score before you, Joe. Here.' He handed his friend another whisky. 'I'll have a word with Mums and Pops; ask them if you can stay here for a couple of days, out of it. Then, when it's blown over...'

'I can't stay here.'

'You can't go back. Not yet.'

'Lily...'

'As you said, she won't even talk to you, so what's the point of going home and trying, and upsetting yourself even more? You're in shock and not thinking straight. At least wait until Pops comes home and takes a look at you. He'll help you decide how to deal with this but it's obvious to anyone in their right mind that you have to put yourself first on this one, Joe. Come on, sit back, finish your drink and try to put it behind you until tomorrow. Believe me, there's nothing you can do about it until then.'

Joe found it surprisingly comforting to do as Robin suggested. It almost felt like regressing to childhood when his father had made all his decisions for him. Sit back, drink, and try to forget the look on Lily's face just before he had looked away until such time as she allowed him to apologise to her.

Robin nodded to Angie as she walked through the door.

'Ice.' She dropped two cubes into Joseph's glass before sitting beside him on the sofa.

'It's not all lies, Lily. You did come into Swansea on an evacuee train.' Roy handed her a cup of tea as she sat, hunched in Norah's favourite easy chair in the kitchen. 'Norah saw you arrive with your mother. Mary may have been younger then, but it was still obvious what she was. Arrangements were made to billet the both of you in a room in Dyfatty Street. Norah was concerned enough to draw the attention of the senior WVS helpers to your situation and she also mentioned it to me. My beat covered Dyfatty in those days. It didn't take long. Two nights after you arrived there was ice on the roads, it was freezing and I

542

found you wandering the streets in the blackout with only a vest on. I picked you up, wrapped you in my coat and took you down the station. You weren't just cold, you were starving. We fed you and at the end of the shift I took you home. I cleared it with the duty sergeant. There were so many evacuees in the town no one cared where they were, as long as they were reasonably well looked after.'

'My...' Lily couldn't bring herself to say the word. '...that woman. Did she come looking for me?'

'We went looking for her to charge her with abandoning and neglecting a child but we couldn't find her. Six months after Norah and I took you in she reported you missing in Cardiff. By then, Norah wasn't the only one who loved you. We'd had a chance to get to know you and see how you'd been treated. When I brought you home you were filthy dirty, but that didn't bother Norah, a lot of kids who came in from London were filthy, it was to be expected given the times the water was cut off there due to bomb damage. Only when Norah washed off the dirt, we saw the bruises. Norah took you to the hospital. The doctor said you'd been beaten. They X-rayed you and found several fractures that hadn't been attended to. You hadn't been fed properly either and Norah always worried that was why you remained short, although I kept telling her you were just perfect.' He fought to control his emotion. 'It was another three years before you stopped falling to the floor and crying every time someone raised their hands above their head. It was obviously something you associated with the beatings.'

'I have a lot to be grateful to you for.'

'No you don't, love, you brought Norah and me far more happiness than we ever gave you. I only wish I could have spared you this. I'd like to say Mary reported you missing because she was worried about you, but it wasn't that. She'd been arrested for soliciting, knew she faced a gaol sentence and pleaded she had a child to look after. The Cardiff police checked the address she gave them and found it was the room you'd been billeted in. When Mary was told you were with us she demanded you back and refused to give you up for adoption. Norah went to see her the day she came out of prison. On her return she told me she'd sorted it out and we were going to keep you. I was so pleased I didn't ask any questions. I had no idea Norah had paid Mary or agreed to keep paying her.'

'You would have stopped Auntie Norah if you'd known?'

'I might have tried, but I never would have given you up. I've been thinking about it and it's my guess Norah did it to protect you. You saw Mary; saw what she's capable of. I think Norah hoped to keep her away from you. And she succeeded for a few years. I'm only sorry...'

'It's not your fault, Uncle Roy.' Lily left the chair and hugged him. 'I told Joe only a few days ago that it's not who your parents are that's important but who brings you up. Now, I can't believe I was so stupid.'

'Love...'

'Didn't you see the way everyone looked at me

when she said she was my mother? How fast Joe's friends left the house? They despise me and I can't blame them. To be related to that ... that woman ... to know she's my mother!'

Roy watched her crumple back on the chair. Not knowing how to help, he sat and watched her, wishing he could turn the clock back to a wartime afternoon in Swansea police station so he could lie to a cockney prostitute who'd been sent down from Cardiff and tell her that the child she had abandoned had frozen to death in the street four hours after she had left her.

The telephone began to ring again and he ignored it. John had given him the message but whatever was going on at the station, he wanted no part of it. Swansea could collapse as far as he was concerned. Just like his and Lily's world.

'Scrambled eggs, à la Powell, with fried tomatoes, beans and toast?' Brian asked, turning to Jack, Katie and Martin who were sitting round the kitchen table in the basement as if there'd been a third funeral in the house.

'I'm not hungry,' Katie answered as he looked at her.

'That's because you have no idea just how delicious my cooking is. Come on,' he cajoled, 'you have to eat something.'

'There's a mountain of sandwiches left upstairs.'

'I want something more substantial before my shift and so do you.'

'Just some toast, then,' Katie capitulated.

'It's worth saying yes so you'll keep that pinny

on,' Jack mocked. 'It looks good with the uniform.'

'Like it?' Brian turned to show off the floral apron he'd cadged off Lily the week before. 'The duty sergeant will have my guts for garters if I turn up with grease spots on my trousers.'

'So you turn up in drag instead.'

'Damn that bloody telephone,' Martin cursed. 'Doesn't it ever stop ringing?'

'I think Roy is in the kitchen with Lily.'

'How can they ignore it?' Picking up his coat from the back of his chair, he rose to his feet. 'I'm going down the pub.'

'Peace,' Jack smiled, as the ringing finally stopped.

'You spoke too early.' It started again before Martin could open the front door.

'I'll answer it.' Brian set aside the eggs he'd been beating. Taking the narrow basement stairs two at a time, he reached the telephone the second it stopped ringing. Cursing, he waited a moment. He could hear voices in the kitchen. It was something that Roy had managed to get Lily to talk; earlier he'd wondered how anyone could recover from a shattering experience like the one Lily's mother had put her through.

The telephone began to ring again as he was halfway back down the stairs. Almost falling over himself, he returned and grabbed it.

'Roy Williams's house.'

'Who is this?' barked a familiar voice.

'Constable Brian Powell, Sergeant.'

'What the hell's going on there? I've left six messages for Roy...'

'There's been a bit of crisis, Sergeant.'

'I'll say there has. Ernie Clay's been released.'

'Released from prison?' Brian couldn't believe what he was hearing.

'That's what I said. You'd better let Roy and the Clay children know immediately.'

'Yes, Sergeant.'

'And don't use that as an excuse to be late for your shift.'

'No, Sergeant.' Replacing the telephone on the chest of drawers, Brian walked to the kitchen; he could hear Roy and Lily talking. Hating having to disturb them, he tapped on the door.

'That's Helen,' Katie left the table at a knock on the door. 'She said she was going to call in later.'

'Talk to her for a minute, sis, I want to comb my hair.'

'You won't be able to do that when you're married.' She smiled, opening the door. The smile froze on her lips as her father stepped down into the room. Dumping a brown-paper bag on the table, he swayed as he turned to look at her.

'Making tea for me?' He peered at the eggs Brian had been beating. 'They told you I'd be out this morning, then.'

'No.' Too terrified to speak, Katie mouthed the word as she shrank away from him.

'Well, here I am. I'll have my tea, then I'll be off out. You got money?'

Katie shook her head.

'Yes, you have. Come on, a couple of quid for your old dad.'

'No!' Walking backwards, she slammed into a

chair, knocking it over.

'Don't you dare defy me like your stupid bitch of a mother.' He jabbed a finger into her chest, sending her reeling against the door. 'I knew her tricks, keeping money from me just so she could have a big bloody do of a funeral, leaving me without two halfpennies to rub together to toast her passing. A word of warning, missy, don't even think about it...' Grabbing her by the shoulders, he shook her like a rat.

'Touch her again and I'll kill you.' Jack pushed Katie behind him and closed his hands into fists.

'You bastard. Raise your hand to me like your brother...'

Ernie dealt Jack a blow that sent him hurtling across the kitchen into the bath. Katie screamed and Ernie turned on her.

'Always whining, just like your bloody mother.' Lifting his hand, he stood over her before lashing out with all his strength.

CHAPTER TWENTY-FIVE

Brian, Roy and Lily all heard the screams coming from the basement, but although Brian was nearest, Roy was first down the stairs. Someone was already hammering on the outside door but Roy stood transfixed in the passage, trying to take in the horrific scene in the kitchen. 'Just a minute,' he shouted, as the banging grew more frenetic.

'Roy!'

Roy took command as he sprang to life. 'Go upstairs, John. Lily will let you in through our front door. Lily, call an ambulance, let Mr Griffiths in and stay upstairs.' Blocking the door and Lily's view of the kitchen, Roy turned first to Jack who was lying next to the bath, his head covered in blood, his arm bent high, at an unnatural angle behind his back. 'Don't try to move, boy.'

Ignoring the directive, Jack struggled to sit up. 'Katie...'

Roy looked at the girl who was standing with her back pressed against the wall, too traumatised to move or speak. Seeing no obvious wounds, he finally studied Ernie. He was lying on his back on the floor between his son and daughter, the knife Brian had been using to cut bread sticking out of his chest.

'Is he dead?' Sickened, Brian averted his head.

'Keep back,' Roy ordered sternly, stepping into the room.

'I killed him,' Jack shouted hysterically. 'I took the knife and killed him, he was trying to hit me ... I killed him ... I...'

'Quiet, Jack!' Kneeling beside Ernie, Roy checked the pulse in his neck. Quite certain he was dead, he pulled a tea towel from the back of a chair, covered his hand with it, and slowly and deliberately wiped the knife from the tip of the handle down to where the blade protruded from Ernie's chest. Then he lifted Ernie's hand and folded it round the handle, pressing the dead man's fingers tight against the black plastic. 'It's obvious what happened here, Jack. I can smell the drink on your father. He must have spent all day since his release in the pub. Then he came here, attacked you and your sister, and when you tried to protect Katie, he picked up the knife. Too drunk to stand, he fell on it when Katie stepped away from him. I was here in time to see him fall on it.'

'You saw...'

'I saw it happen, Brian,' Roy repeated. Straightening up, he kicked Ernie over with the toe of his boot until he was lying face down on the floor. 'That's not an indication of what I feel for him. I can't touch a body with my hands for fear of contaminating evidence. Brian?' He stuffed the tea towel into his pocket as he looked at the young man. 'Did you see what I saw too?'

'No...'

'Of course not, how could you.' He looked Brian in the eye. 'You were behind me. But you do agree that's what happened here.'

Brian glanced at Jack, battered, bruised and broken on the floor, Katie paralysed, staring blankly with round, unblinking eyes.

'Do you agree, Brian?' Roy pressed sternly.

'That...'

'Do you agree?'

Brian gazed at Katie and saw the blood on her right hand.

'*Do you agree?*' Roy repeated heatedly.

'I agree,' Brian whispered. He couldn't argue against the justice of what Roy was doing, but it went against everything he believed in and had been taught in training school. What price fair dealing for all, irrespective of who they were and what they'd done, if a solitary constable could act as judge and jury, settling a case before it even reached court?

'Take Katie to the sink; wash her hands, then the sink thoroughly. Don't leave any traces. Dry her hands in her skirt. She shouldn't have tried to help her father, but it's an instinctive reaction even when casualties are beyond assistance. Then take her upstairs and telephone the station. Tell them there has been an incident and an accidental death...'

'I'll take care of Katie.'

He looked up to see John standing in the doorway. 'How long have you been there?'

'John...' Screaming and sobbing, Katie flung herself into John Griffiths's arms. 'I killed...'

'I just heard Mr Williams explain how your father fell on the knife he was holding when you stepped away from him; that's not killing him, Katie.'

'I...'

'She needs to be sedated, John.'

'I'll phone my own doctor.'

'Tell him Katie is traumatised and needs heavy sedation...'

'I know what to do.'

'Don't leave Katie alone for a moment before he gets here, or allow her to talk to anyone else.'

Avoiding touching her hands, John laid his arm round her shoulders. 'Come with me, sweetheart,' he murmured gently, taking her to the sink. Washing and drying her fingers, just as he would a child's, he led her out of the kitchen and up the stairs.

Roy turned his attention to Jack. 'I told you to lie still. Move again and you could do that arm a lot of damage.'

'Katie and Mr Griffiths...'

'He'll look after her.'

'And my father?' Jack stared at the body humped over the knife, the blood oozing thickly on to the tiled-floor.

'You heard what I said to Constable Powell. First thing I learned as a young copper was the least said, the sooner the case file will be closed. The last thing we need is any false heroics or confessions from you. Right?'

'Right,' Jack murmured as he passed out.

Realising he had little choice but to trust John, Roy stayed in the basement kitchen. He sent the first constable on the scene down to the pub to fetch Martin, and asked Brian to accompany Jack to the hospital and wait until he came round, so he could caution him again against saying anything more than he had outlined about the events leading up to his father's death. Just as he'd closed the ambulance doors on Jack, Martin and Brian, the sergeant arrived.

He answered his superior's questions clearly and concisely, persuading him that neither Katie nor Jack had anything of value to add to his and Brian's version of events and as both needed medical attention before they could make a statement it would be as well to leave their questioning until the morning. John's doctor came down to the basement, confirming that he'd no choice but to sedate Katie and she was unfit for questioning.

After the forensic team arrived, the sergeant returned to the station. Roy waited, watching the team work and supervising the removal of Ernie's corpse when they gave the go-ahead to remove his body. Finally, after the last of the team left, Roy cleaned the basement, washing the blood from the floor with hot water and bleach, but even after he'd changed the water half a dozen times and scrubbed until his arms ached, he felt the place would never be clean again. The last thing he did was remove the tea towel from his pocket and flush it down the outside toilet with the bleach water he'd used to clean the kitchen floor.

It was three in the morning before he finally returned upstairs. Lily was sitting in his kitchen and Brian was making tea.

'Katie with Martin and Jack?' he asked.

'They kept Jack in hospital,' Brian revealed flatly.

'You saw him?'

'I saw him and the sergeant back at the station. He said as you and I were first on the scene it would be appropriate for us to take Jack's and Katie's statements.' Unable to look Roy in the eye, Brian lifted three cups and saucers on to the tray.

'Is John Griffiths still with her?'

'And Martin, Uncle Roy. The doctor gave her something to make her sleep but she woke up about an hour ago.'

'Has she said anything?' Roy looked at Brian.

'No, but she can't stop crying. I thought tea might help.'

'I'll take it in, boy. Why don't you two get to bed? You look done in and there's nothing left for either of you to do.'

Lily left the chair without argument and walked to the stairs.

'Is it all right for me to go downstairs?' Brian asked.

Roy nodded. 'Forensic have finished with the place. I cleaned it up as best I could but it could probably do with another going over tomorrow. Brian?' he called after him softly as he went to the door. 'Thank you for your help tonight. I couldn't have managed without you.'

Brian remained silent.

'You disapprove?'

Brian hesitated, looked down the passage, then closed the door. 'What about the law?'

'What about an eighteen-year-old girl who's been terrorised all her life by a drunken father who battered her mother's life away inch by painful inch? You think the law would be best served by hanging her?'

'There were mitigating circumstances. She could have pleaded manslaughter...'

'And ended up serving ten years or more in jail. Have you been inside a women's prison? Seen the whores, thieves and criminals she would have had to live with?'

'No, but then it's all hypothetical, isn't it. The sergeant told me it's an open-and-shut case.'

'You won't talk to anyone?'

'What could I possibly tell them when I was

554

behind you and didn't see what happened? Goodnight, Constable Williams.'

The room was warm and luxurious, the bed comfortable but Joe couldn't sleep. Every time he closed his eyes the whisky he'd downed earlier rose sourly within him and he saw Lily's mother, hag-like, cackling, hovering before him, and behind him, Lily, pale, beautiful, an almost unbearable anguish dimming the tawny light in her eyes. Why hadn't he ignored Robin's advice and gone back and tried to see her? What did it matter that his friends wouldn't speak to him if he had Lily? His job – that was it, his job, he had to work. Could he cope with ostracism, with moving away – would Lily even want to move away and if they did, could they ever escape that dreadful woman...?

'Joseph?'

Acutely aware that his chest was bare, he pulled the sheet to his chin. The pyjamas he'd borrowed from Robin had been several sizes too small and he'd settled for the half-mast trousers. 'Angie, you shouldn't be here.'

'I couldn't sleep.'

She switched on the bedside light and slipped the straps of the nightdress she was wearing from her shoulders. 'No one will know.' She smiled, as it settled around her feet in a silken whisper. 'They're all asleep. Besides, Mums and Pops are used to turning a blind eye. Em sleeps in Robin's bed whenever she stays over.' Turning back the sheet, she stepped out of the puddle of silk and lace, and slid in beside him.

'For God's sake, Angie...' Rolling over, he fell out of bed in his haste to get away from her.

'Sh, you'll wake everyone.'

Grabbing his clothes, he went to the door.

'Where are you going?'

'To the bathroom to dress.'

'It's three in the morning. You can't go home...'

'Watch me.'

'How will you get there?'

'Walk.'

'Darling Joseph, so moral and so bourgeois. Robin warned me you might be.' Leaving the bed, she went to him and wrapped her arms round his waist, inching them lower. 'Just a bit of fun...'

'No!' Furious he pushed her away. It didn't matter that she was naked, or offering herself to him – nothing mattered except Lily and that he get back to her. Jerking open the bedroom door, he ran down to the bathroom, turning the key in the lock as soon as he closed the door behind him.

'Tea.' Roy carried the tray into the parlour and set it on the table. He glanced from John, who was sitting on the sofa cradling Katie's head in his lap, to Martin.

'Thanks,' Martin replied tersely, glaring at John.

'Katie?' Roy murmured gently, looking at the girl.

She burst into tears. Roy crouched before her. 'Look, love, it wasn't your fault...'

'I killed him...'

'No you didn't. I know you stepped back, but if you hadn't he would have fallen on you and the knife he was holding would have gone into him anyway. It was inevitable the way he was holding it...'

'I...' She stared blankly as her mind groped for the truth but she was too drugged and exhausted to know what it was any more.

'It was an accident, love. An accident caused by drink. You and Jack may have to make statements in a few days but after I made my statement tonight the sergeant agreed it's an open-and-shut case. Accidental death of a drunk.'

'I didn't...'

'You didn't do anything, love. Believe me. I'll take you to see Jack tomorrow. If anyone can convince you he will. He was there too, remember. Now, how about getting some sleep? I'll take you up to Lily.'

'I really didn't kill him?'

'No, love, you didn't.'

'John... Martin...'

'Get some sleep, Katie. I'll see you tomorrow.' John opened the door as Roy helped her out of the room. He closed it and turned to Martin after Roy had left. 'I'm sorry; I didn't want you to find out about Katie and me until I was in a position to offer her a wedding ring.'

'Are you insane? You're old enough to be her father!'

'I love her, she loves me, I hoped you'd understand...'

'Understand! I understand all right. That a man your age – with your problems – would want to take advantage of a young, innocent girl Katie's age! God, when I think of it I could strangle you. Jack and I thought you were being kind – giving her a job with decent money, taking her back and for to work in your car, arranging Mam's funeral – and all the time you were planning to seduce her.'

'It wasn't like that.'

'Then what was it like, Mr Griffiths?'

'Please, not so loud, she'll hear you.'

'I hope she does. Perhaps then she'll come to her senses...'

As Martin railed, John tried to find words to describe what he felt for Katie and what he thought she felt for him, but every phrase that sprang to mind sounded hackneyed or, even worse, sordid, as though he were some corrupt, ageing Lothario and Katie an ingenuous child. When the sound of a step on the stairs finally silenced Martin, John said the one thing he felt needed to be explained above all else: 'Katie had nothing to do with the divorce proceedings against my wife. I honestly never thought of Katie that way until...'

'When?' Martin snapped.

'A couple of days ago. I drove Katie to the cemetery to put flowers on your mother's grave; she would never have got there before it closed otherwise. Afterwards ... she told me she loved me.'

'And you believed her! She's a child. Our mother's just died; our father was in prison. Her idea of love is someone who'll hold her, cuddle her, look after her. She didn't understand what she was saying.'

'I'm not a child, Martin.' Katie was standing in the open doorway.

'You should be asleep,' Martin admonished.

'I could hear you arguing when I went to the bathroom.'

'Please, Katie, Martin's right, you should be in bed. This can wait until morning.'

'No, it can't, John. Please, Martin,' she begged, 'John's telling you the truth. I love him and when his divorce is finalised we're going to be married.'

'Katie...'

'I've heard all the arguments you've just brought up from John but they made no difference. John's good and kind, not like Dad...'

'I should never have gone down the pub tonight. I should never have left you and Jack. I knew he was coming out...'

'It wouldn't have made any difference if you'd been there, Martin.' As tears began to roll down her cheeks, she clung to John, burying her head in his neck.

'Katie's right. You had no way of knowing your father was out of gaol. None of us did.'

'Mr Williams warned me.'

'And I could have insisted the sergeant tell me why he wanted to speak to Roy when I took the telephone call earlier. But I didn't. If you persist in thinking of all the "what ifs" in life, you'll drive yourself mad. It happened; he's dead.'

'And I can't say I'm sorry. Perhaps we'll finally be able to sleep at night knowing that he can't come after us and wreck our lives any more.' Looking anywhere except at John and Katie,

Martin left his chair and paced restlessly to the fireplace. Crouching on his haunches, he stirred the coals with the poker.

'Martin, please, can't you be happy for me?'

Martin continued to study the flames. 'Are you serious about marrying Katie, Mr Griffiths?'

'My name is John and yes, I'm serious if she'll still have me when I'm free.'

'Is that why you gave Jack a job?'

'Katie and I are nothing to do with Jack and Helen.'

'No? Jack will be both your son-in-law and brother-in-law.'

'Don't you think that has occurred to me?'

'And Jack has a far more vicious temper than I have.'

'Which I hope he'll learn to curb. There's been enough anger in our lives, Martin.'

'You're right about that, Katie.' Rising to his feet, Martin turned and faced them. 'I won't pretend I like the thought of you with my sister, Mr Griffiths, but if you're serious about marrying Katie I'll try to understand how she feels about you.'

'You'll give us your blessing?'

'Ask me again before you get married, Katie.'

'I promise you one thing, Martin,' John said as he held her in his arms. 'I will never hurt her.'

'And when the gossip starts?'

'Unless you tell anyone, it won't until after we are married.'

'I wish I had your faith in people. From where I'm standing it's obvious what's going on between you.'

Roy was on the doorstep looking up at the sky when John finally left the house. 'I owe you an explanation, Roy.'

Roy shook his head. 'Not at this time in the morning, you don't.'

'It really will be all right?'

'Fine, if Katie gets over it.'

'She's calm now. She went to bed half an hour ago.'

'You and Martin sorted things out?'

'As much as we can for now.' John opened a packet of cigarettes and offered Roy one. 'I wasn't looking for it, it just happened and when it did I wasn't strong enough to turn my back on her.'

'You know what people will say.'

'They can say what they like.'

'It might hit business.'

'If it does I'll ride it out.'

'You're a braver man than your son.'

'I'll have a word with him.'

'No, don't.' Roy lit both their cigarettes. 'I spoke to Lily earlier. She needs time to come to terms with who her real mother is and frankly I think that's all she'll be able to deal with for now. Joe, his problems and hers with him, will have to wait.'

'You don't think Joe can help her?'

'It's not what I think, or want, that's important. It's what Lily wants and she doesn't want to see him.'

'If Joe has any sense he'll be round in the morning.'

'Give her a few days. Lily doesn't say things she

561

doesn't mean.'

'Monday, then.'

'She'll be in work.'

'After everything that's happened?'

'Especially after everything's that's happened, John.'

Esme checked her reflection in the hall mirror. Freshly bathed, made-up, with her favourite perfume dabbed on her wrists, she looked good, knew it and intended to make John realise just what he was losing in her. He was standing on the front porch looking out at the view of the bay. Head high, she walked briskly towards him. 'The housekeeper said you wanted to see...'

'You had to have your way, didn't you, Esme,' he interrupted brusquely.

'Aren't you coming in?' Struggling to keep her equanimity, she opened the door wider. Her mother's house had a long drive but John hadn't bothered to lower his voice and several neighbours were in the habit of walking their dogs before breakfast.

'No.'

'If this is about the settlement...'

'I couldn't give a damn about the settlement. I just wanted you to know that I intend to inform Joe exactly who was responsible for sabotaging his engagement party and leave what action to take entirely up to him.'

'I have absolutely no idea what you're talking about.'

'No? You went to Richard Thomas; he sent that woman...'

'What woman?'

'Very good, Esme, I take my hat off to you. All those hours of practice and years in the Little Theatre have paid off. I've seen you turn in some good performances but none quite so consummate as this one.'

'I really don't know what you're talking about.' Leaving the porch, she stepped down into the drive.

'The prostitute Richard Thomas sent to Joe's party yesterday. Lily's mother...'

'Lily's mother is a prostitute?'

He found himself almost believing her surprise. 'Richard Thomas sent her to Roy Williams's house in the middle of Joe's and Lily's party. He couldn't have timed her appearance better. Even gave her money to get drunk first to heighten the "surprise".'

'Are you sure it was Richard?'

'The woman was.'

'He had no right!'

'Right! What have rights to do with this?' As he stared at her he suddenly understood why she hadn't married Joe's father when she'd become pregnant and why she'd been furious when Richard had offered Helen a position in his office. 'My God!' He stepped away from her in disgust. 'Richard Thomas is Joe's father, isn't he?'

'I...' Unable to lie, she turned away from him.

'Dear God, Esme, he was your godfather – almost family ... you called him uncle. Christ! You even asked him to give you away at our wedding.'

'He had no right...' She repeated dully.

'No, he didn't.'

'Please, don't tell Joseph,' she pleaded. 'Richard manages his trust fund. It's grown, because... Joseph might think Richard had put more money into it and Joseph needs the security of that fund if he is to make anything of himself... You and I both know that Joseph would take this the same way you are now. Please, John. I'll waive the right to a settlement, agree adultery, anything you want, but don't let Joseph find out or think any the less of me than he already does.'

'Keep the settlement, Esme, and your precious secret. But don't think I'm doing it for you. For once we agree. It may be best if Joe never finds out who his father is, or the depths he can sink to in order to destroy other people's lives, and all in the name of decency.'

'Miss Sullivan?' Miss Oliver waylaid Lily as soon as she walked into the bank on Monday morning. 'Mr Hopkin Jones wants to see you immediately. In his office.'

Lily's heart started thundering as she looked at Miss Oliver.

'Immediately, Miss Sullivan.' Miss Oliver gave Lily a smile, but Lily didn't even see it as she hung her coat on to her hanger and left the cloakroom. She'd expected the scandal to spread throughout the town but not this quickly. Steeling herself for dismissal, she knocked on the manager's door.

'Miss Sullivan, it's good of you to come so promptly.' The manager indicated a chair. 'Please sit down. I think we've finished, Mr Collins.'

Mr Collins gathered a pile of forms from the desk.

Mr Hopkin Jones waited until Mr Collins had closed the door and he'd watched his silhouette bob away across the general office. 'Miss Sullivan, we have appointed a junior and it is time for you to take your new position. Mr Collins, Miss Oliver and I did some reshuffling this morning and it has been decided that you should take Miss Drew's position.'

'But she's Mr Collins's secretary,' Lily murmured in bewilderment.

'You don't think you're up to the work?'

'Yes – yes of course, but Miss Drew...'

'Has been transferred to our Wind Street branch. The manager's secretary left suddenly last week. Her husband is in the Civil Service and was offered promotion in Cardiff. She had little choice but to go with him, but it was rather unfortunate from the bank's point of view. In my opinion, just one more reason not to employ married women. They are so unreliable.'

'Mr Hopkin Jones. I have to tell you...'

'I know what happened at your engagement party, Lily. I should think most of Swansea has heard the story by now.'

'Is that why...?'

'As you know, Miss Drew had a small office next to Mr Collins's. You would be out of the public eye most of the time. It seems the circumspect thing to do right now,' he added kindly. 'A week or two and everyone will be talking about something else, but for the moment I thought you might rather not be pointed out and stared at. However, the work load will be heavy.'

'I'll cope.'

'I'm sure you will. I'd appreciate it if you move desks right away. I don't doubt Mr Collins will have some dictation for you.'

'Yes, Mr Hopkin Jones, and thank you.'

'Nothing to thank me for, Miss Sullivan. We're getting a bargain. You'll be paid shorthand typist rates for a secretarial post.' He glanced at her over his horn-rimmed spectacles. 'But come and see me after your month's trial. I don't doubt Mr Collins will have let me know exactly what he thinks of your competence by then and if you think you warrant a rise, we'll discuss it.'

'Joe wants to see you, Lily.' Roy hovered in the doorway of her bedroom.

'I'll be down in a minute, Uncle Roy.'

'Don't do anything hasty, will you, love?'

'Like get engaged? Sorry, Uncle Roy, bad joke.'

'It took courage for him to knock on the door after the way you sent him packing on Saturday. The least you can do is listen to what he has to say.'

'Where's Mrs Lannon?'

'In the kitchen, don't worry I'll keep her there.'

Lily took her time. Brushing out her hair, she twisted it into a neat knot at the nape of her neck. She cleaned off every trace of make-up with lotion and cotton wool, and reapplied it, working slowly, mechanically, not thinking about what she was doing but about the changes that a single weekend had wrought in her life. She had expected to be ridiculed or ostracised. Instead, she had been pleasantly surprised by her colleagues' attitude both to the gossip and her sudden and rapid promotion. They had been sympathetic and quietly supportive, asked her if she felt like talking and, when she'd said 'no' had offered commiserations on having to work for Mr Collins, trotting out all the well-worn jokes about his obsessive behaviour.

Helen and Judy had done their best, rallying round her and Katie yesterday, organising visits to the cinema and gossipy girl evenings for the coming week, but they all knew it wasn't the same as it had been before she had gone out with Joe. Judy's main topic of conversation was London and the job she'd been offered at the BBC. Helen's conversation, much to her and Judy's amusement, revolved around curtains, linens, cake tins, recipes – and Jack's opinions on every topic under the sun. And Katie had been unusually quiet and withdrawn, which was only to be expected after seeing her father die.

Applying a final coat of lipstick, she looked at herself in the glass. It was no more than a perfunctory check. Neither her pallor nor the strained look in her eyes registered. Finally she left her room and walked down the stairs. Joe wasn't in the parlour; he was in the hall, waiting for her. She looked at him for a moment, then went to meet him.

'Lily, I'm sorry...'

'Please, let's talk in the parlour.' She led the way. As he followed her in, she closed the door and turned to face him. 'There's no need to apologise, Joe. Given the circumstances you have nothing to be sorry for.'

'I behaved badly...'

'You behaved as any up-and-coming young man with a career to look forward to would have.'

'Try telling that to my father. I was a fool, Lily, and a bigger one than you know. I should never have gone home with Robin ... I should have stayed...'

'Angie?'

'Nothing happened between us.'

'Not for want of her trying, I know.' She gave him a small smile as she sat in an easy chair.

'I know I don't deserve you, but...' He held out a box. She recognised it as the one that contained the engagement ring he had bought for her. 'I'd be honoured if you'd take it.'

She shook her head.

'Because I let you down?'

'Because, as Uncle Roy hinted, we're too young. Auntie Norah used to say that you're not really grown up until you learn to ignore what other people say. I think our engagement party proved we're both a long way off that.'

'So what are you going to do now?'

'Same as I did before, go to work – the new junior began today and instead of starting as a shorthand typist I've been made secretary to the assistant manager. I even have my own office.'

'Congratulations.'

Coming from him, the word rang oddly hollow.

'I had hoped we could at least go out together again...'

'No, Joe.'

'Please, Lily, give me a chance to make it up to

you. Please...'

'You've got enough to do with your finals coming up and then there'll be your job at the BBC.'

'Will you at least allow me to try to change your mind?'

'Perhaps, when we've both had time to forget Saturday night.' She suddenly realised she meant it. She was talking to him face to face. It hurt, but it was bearable. She hadn't thought it would be when her uncle had told her he was in the house.

'It will be a long time before I do that.' He walked to the fireplace. 'You'll be at Helen's and Jack's wedding.'

'I'm bridesmaid.'

'My father's arranged a small reception in the Mackworth. Save me a dance.'

'I will.'

'Then I've something to look forward to.' Taking her hand, he drew her gently towards him and kissed her cheek.

'Goodbye, Joe.'

'Not goodbye, Lily. We'll see one another and I won't stop trying.'

'I'd rather you didn't start for a while.'

'I'll try to understand.' He opened the door. She stood watching his tall, dark figure, vault the low wall that separated their two houses. She felt very alone but oddly free. She was eighteen years of age; she had a good job, friends prepared to stick by her, an uncle who loved her. The whole of life was waiting. Who knew what it might bring if she let it?

CHAPTER TWENTY-SIX

'You sure you have everything, Judy?' Without waiting for her to reply, Roy began to list the most vital things he could think of. 'Money, ticket, handbag...'

'Kitchen sink, bath?' she teased.

'Be careful crossing the road and look after yourself. London is a...'

'Big, vicious city.' Judy stepped into the carriage. 'Don't worry – I'll be fine.' She smiled at Roy and her mother. 'What do I call you? Constable Williams sounds as though you're going to arrest me and Uncle Roy sounds as though you're Mam's brother.'

'You could try just plain Roy.'

'That sounds disrespectful. How about Dad when we're not quarrelling and Stepdad when we are?'

'Judy...'

'Just joking, Mam. I won't quarrel with him after you're married – much.'

'Who says we're getting married?' Joy demanded indignantly.

'That smile on your face when he stands next to you. Don't they look sweet, Lily?'

'Wait for us.' Helen charged down the station platform, ahead of Jack, her coat flapping in the breeze, scarf flying round her neck. 'You promise you'll be back for the wedding?'

'A date with Dirk Bogarde wouldn't keep me away,' Judy assured her.

'That I don't believe.'

'You take care of yourself.' Lily kissed Judy through the window.

'Telephone as soon as you get to the hostel.' Roy and Joy shouted in unison as the guard blew the whistle.

'I will,' Judy cried above the noise of the engine.

Joy fought back her tears as the train began to move out. 'Give your father my best wishes when you see him.'

'Really?' Judy shouted sceptically.

'Take care and don't forget to have a good time every chance you get. And having a good time means not doing anything you wouldn't want me to see.'

'Or me,' Roy added.

Judy leaned out of the window and waved. She was still waving as the train pulled round the corner and there were only rails and the backs of buildings at the top end of High Street to be seen. Blowing her nose in an effort to control the tears pricking at the back of her eyes, she took a seat opposite the only other occupant of the carriage, a middle-aged woman with an expression that suggested the lemon sherbets she was shovelling into her mouth at regular intervals were too strong. Feeling apprehensive and very alone, she pulled the *Woman's Weekly* she'd bought from her bag, opened it and pretended to read.

The prospect of going off to London all on her own had seemed exciting until this moment.

What if she didn't like living there? Made no friends? Discovered she couldn't do the job she'd been given...?

She turned to the window, staring at her ghostlike reflection superimposed over the dull grey winter landscape. To quote Mrs Jordan, she'd felt like 'the bees knees' when she'd left the house, in her grey costume with its pencil-slim skirt, the small black hat and clutch bag, but what was the use of feeling like the bees knees when she'd lost the only man she might ever love and, more important, who loved her.

'Judy?'

Brian was standing in the corridor.

'Is there room for one more in this carriage?'

'What are you doing here?' She pinched herself, wondering if she were dreaming as he lifted his case on to the rack, before sitting beside her.

'They need coppers in the Met. Rumour has it there's better promotion prospects, so I got a transfer.'

'Better promotion prospects?' Judy echoed uncomprehendingly.

'Prettier girls, too, or so I've heard. Constable Williams happened to mention that you're staying in the YWCA.'

'Only until I can get a room somewhere.'

'He gave me the address. It's quite a coincidence. I'll be billeted round the corner from you, about ten minutes' walk away. We could' – he looked into her green eyes – 'see if it's worth picking up where we left off,' he suggested quietly.

'I'm still only just eighteen and not at all sure what I want.'

'I know what I want.' He bent his head to hers. 'But I'm prepared to wait for it.' Turning his back on the disapproving lemon-sherbet-sucking woman, he kissed her.

'Lily,' Martin ran breathlessly towards her.

'You go on ahead, Uncle Roy, Mrs Hunt.'

Roy offered Joy his arm. 'Something tells me our Lily is not going to miss us for the next hour or so.'

'Just as well I've aired the bed in the shop, then, isn't it.'

'You've been seeing Judy off?' Martin blurted, gasping for air as he caught up with Lily.

'Yes.'

'I've been seeing Brian off.'

'Brian's going to London?'

'He got a transfer to the Met. Didn't your uncle tell you?'

'No. But we've hardly seen Brian since...' She fell silent. Something had happened between her uncle and Brian the night Ernie Clay had died in their basement. She was sure of it. But whatever it was, given her uncle's tight-lipped attitude to the whole affair she doubted she'd find out. 'If Judy sees him she'll be pleased. She was putting a brave face on it, but I think she was beginning to wonder if she was doing the right thing in moving so far away from her mother and friends.'

'Hopefully it will work out for them.' He fell into step beside her and they walked along in silence for a few minutes.

'Lily, about what happened last Saturday, I'm sorry.'

'Thank you.'

'I was wondering ... well, seeing as how you and Joe aren't getting engaged now, if you'd consider going out with me some time. If you'd prefer a foursome I could ask Jack and Helen...'

'No, Martin.'

'I understand. Sorry'

'I wouldn't prefer a foursome.' She linked her arm in his. 'I remember you telling me that you have night school on Tuesday and Friday. Well, as today's Saturday and there's a good film on at the Castle, how about we go and see it?'

The publishers hope that this book has given you enjoyable reading. Large Print Books are especially designed to be as easy to see and hold as possible. If you wish a complete list of our books please ask at your local library or write directly to:

Magna Large Print Books
Magna House, Long Preston,
Skipton, North Yorkshire.
BD23 4ND

This Large Print Book for the partially sighted, who cannot read normal print, is published under the auspices of

THE ULVERSCROFT FOUNDATION